W9-BIJ-969

a novel by

Jimmy Chesire

NAL BOOKS

NEW AMERICAN LIBRARY

A DIVISION OF PENGUIN BOOKS USA INC., NEW YORK

PUBLISHED IN CANADA BY

PENGUIN BOOKS CANADA LIMITED, MARKHAM, ONTARIO

PUBLISHER'S NOTE

This book is a work of fiction. Names, characters, places, and incidents either are the product of the author's imagination or are used fictitiously, and any resemblance to actual persons, living or dead, events, or locales is entirely coincidental.

Published simultaneously in Canada by Penguin Books Canada Limited.

NAL BOOKS TRADEMARK REG. U.S. PAT. OFF. AND FOREIGN COUNTRIES
REGISTERED TRADEMARK—MARCA REGISTRADA
HECHO EN BRATTLEBORO, VT., U.S.A.

SIGNET, SIGNET CLASSIC, MENTOR, ONYX, PLUME, MERIDIAN and NAL BOOKS are published *in the United States* by New American Library, a division of Penguin Books USA Inc., 1633 Broadway, New York, New York 10019, *in Canada* by Penguin Books Canada Limited, 2801 John Street, Markham, Ontario L3R 1B4

Library of Congress Cataloging-in-Publication Data

Chesire, Jimmy.
Home boy / by Jimmy Chesire.
p. cm.
ISBN 0-453-00664-7
I. Title.
PS3553.H384H66 1989
813'.54—dc19 88-35323
CIP

First Printing, July, 1989

1 2 3 4 5 6 7 8 9

PRINTED IN THE UNITED STATES OF AMERICA

This book is dedicated to
Robin Suits,
whose love and kindness made it possible

1

THE MAN IS FAST. THE FASTEST FUCKER IN TOWN, NO lie. I have been to mass all over the Miami Valley—Dayton, Xenia, Fairborn, Kettering, Centerville—you name it, I've been to mass there and ain't nobody faster than the Monsignor.

Monsignor stands between us, bent slightly at the waist. My friend Whiteworm and I kneel on the marble floor.

Monsignor is racing through the confiteor:

". . . mea culpa, mea culpa, mea maxima culpa," he chants, striking his breast with each "mea culpa"—three rapid little taps to the heart.

He inhales sharply, deeply, and races on.

I dip to look beneath the Monsignor's chin and take a peek at my friend.

Through my fault. Through my fault.

Whiteworm senses me looking his way.

He turns his head to me.

I catch his eye.

My temperature rises.

Through my fault. Through my fault. Through my most grievous fault.

Monsignor comes to a screeching halt: our turn.

Whiteworm and I immediately bend double, whipping our foreheads to within an inch of the icy marble step. We ask Almighty God to have mercy on the Monsignor, to forgive him his sins, and to bring him to everlasting life.

"Amen," the Monsignor concurs.

Whiteworm and I do the confiteor now, at light speed.

It is too thrilling. The Monsignor's so fast, so impatient.

Move, boys. *Move.*

You do not serve for the Monsignor if you cannot keep up.

He just ain't got the time.

Whiteworm and I keep up.

We are good, Whiteworm and I. Among the best. Our Latin is clear, articulate, spilling from our lips effortlessly. We could be Romans, how easily it trips off our tongues.

We *are* good.

We finish the Prayers at the Foot of the Altar. Monsignor straightens up:

''Dominus vobiscum,'' he says. That's ''The Lord be with you.''

And with your spirit, Whiteworm and I say back—in Latin, of course.

Monsignor climbs the steps to the altar.

Whiteworm and I lift ourselves and then immediately lower ourselves to the foam-filled pads on the first step. We touch as softly as leaves settling to earth on a warm and windless autumn afternoon.

We are perfect harmony.

I steal another look at my friend. I have a physical sensation like none I have ever had. It is as if a joyous terror has risen from the very marrow of my bones.

This is much too dangerous. I immediately whip my head back around and face front. I force myself to focus on the task at hand. I dare not let myself think about this thing that is happening to me. We have been friends these past seven years—and now *this.*

I manage to remain pure and thoughtless all the way through to communion time.

The priest takes communion first. Then the altar boys. Then the regular folks.

Whiteworm gets up the moment Monsignor takes communion. I watch him lift himself in that airy way of his. I watch him as he glides across the altar to the cruet table, moving through the air as a dolphin in the sea. A boy of great silence, a mystery unto himself. My friend.

He removes a pair of gold-plated patens from their velvet sheaths and spins about ever so gracefully on the balls of his feet, his cassock ballooning gently as he swirls. He returns to the center of the altar, genuflects, and hands me one of the patens in mid-genuflection.

Nice move.

I accept the paten from his hand. There is extra moisture in my mouth. I feel the slightest wind come off his gliding, genuflecting self.

Monsignor is munching his host. I fix my eyes on him.

Monsignor swallows his host, all done.

Time.

Whiteworm and I rise in unison, meet at center altar, genuflect as one. We go out to the communion rail to flip the cloth. It is a linen skirt that hangs down on the inside of the communion rail. We lift it and toss it backward, up and over the rail. The communicants will come, kneel at the railing, and insert their worshipful hands up under the cloth. This ensures that nothing but their tongues shall ever touch the consecrated host.

We move in perfect sync, Whiteworm and I. We are quick, precise. I thrill to it. I am proud of both of us. I am proud of how crisply and correctly we march, how sharply we go about our business.

We march toward each other. We will meet in the center, our work finished, arriving dead center simultaneously if we do it right, each keeping an eye on the other—it doesn't happen by accident, this precision.

We do arrive dead center simultaneously.

Timing. Yes.

We spin in to face the altar, our shoulders softly grazing. You don't see it, the grazing, we move so swift, so neat.

We march back to the altar, our spines erect. We take our places.

Monsignor has the tabernacle open. He lifts out his ciborium, its bejeweled lid gleaming and flashing in the high altar light. Father Flat appears in the doorway of the priest's sacristy. He will help this morning. When we have a full house like we do today, a Mandatory Day—Sundays for all, Tuesdays and Thursdays for the high school boys, Mondays and Wednesdays for the grade school boys—it takes awhile to give communion to everyone. You always need a second priest to help out.

Monsignor spins around to face the congregation. He hoists the ciborium on high, holding a single host above it.

I stand and take two steps up to the top step. When you receive as an altar boy, this is where you position yourself. I am going to receive. I am in a state of grace. I expect Whiteworm to step up with me. He does not.

I look back at him, alarmed. You're not receiving?

He doesn't look at me.

Shame.

Monsignor lays a host on my outstretched tongue. He immediately bolts down the steps and races out to the gathering mob of communicants.

I swallow the Lord Jesus Christ my Savior and bolt down the steps right behind him.

Father Flat dashes out onto the altar. I can feel him at my back as I exit the altar in hot pursuit of the fleeing Monsignor.

Flat gets his ciborium out. Each priest has his own ciborium. It is usually a gift upon ordination—if the priest is lucky enough to have family that can afford to make such a gift. All they are is fancy, bejeweled chalices fitted with lids, made especially for carrying consecrated hosts for distribution at communion time.

He whips his ciborium out, genuflects, and races down the steps, bolting out to the communion rail. Whiteworm is hot on his heels.

We are swift, Whiteworm and I. We are swift.

A wave of communicants come, kneel at the communion rail before us, stick out their tongues one by one, receive the Lord God Jesus Christ, cross themselves quickly, and peel reverently away—only to be followed by another wave. Each wave descends, waits on the Lord, receives at the hands of the priest, and peels away. Each wave is handled easily by the sprinting Monsignor and the fleet-footed, easily weeping, big-toothed Bambi Gambi—that's me, thank you very much. My real name's Fred Gamble, Frederick J. Gamble to be precise, but most people just know me as Bambi.

Monsignor sails along. The communicants, originally three deep, thin out. I am crisp, proud, backpedaling briskly, never losing my balance, just a backstep and a prayer ahead of the Monsignor at each communicant.

I can hear Flat behind me trying to match the Monsignor's pace. It ain't even a contest. You serve with the Monsignor, you get to handle twice as many communicants as with any other priest, period.

Ezra drops to his knees at the rail. He's one of my original friends, too, from our Building One days and the terror of Lyman Hall, head counselor. Four years of that madness—me, Ezra, Whiteworm, dodging the flying hands.

We reach Ezra. I pop him one up under the chin. I get him right in the old Adam's apple. He's cool, though. He doesn't bat an eye until the Monsignor and I move on to the next poor soul. Then he opens his eyes and gives me a great toothy smile. He immediately begins to chew up his host.

It kills me. And he knows it. I personally disapprove of that, chewing the host. There's no rule against it, exactly. It's just not right, that's all. The asshole. He's doing it on purpose.

I give him a lowered-eyelid warning.

He only smiles more.

He lifts himself away from the communion rail, making only the faintest popping, farting sound. His peg leg. He strides away with a barely distinguishable limp—you need to be really watching to notice that it is a limp. He's still chomping away on that host.

After Peg Leg Bates came to perform—they are all the time bringing performers out to entertain the boys—we'd play Peg Leg. We'd strap our legs back, bent double at the knee, using our belts, trying life with one foot. It was great fun pretending. Ezra had both his legs then.

Flat's finished behind us. I hear him and Whiteworm hoofing it back to the altar. Monsignor and I finish off the remaining communicants. The Big Dick's one of the last. Dick's my counselor, former inside guard with the Ohio State Buckeyes, Class of '57. He's been my counselor these last two years. He's such a complete and total asshole that last year we all started calling him The Big Dick. Which is exactly what he is.

He kneels before us, his thick, frosty tongue jutting out of his bloated face. I grit my teeth as despair engulfs my very soul: the fucker will never recommend me.

Monsignor lays a host on his fat tongue. Even as I fill with this sickening rage I know this is why. You gotta get along if you want to be chosen as a commissioner. You can't be hating your counselor and then expect him to turn around and nominate you for a position of responsibility and privilege.

I am lost to it, have no control over it: I just want to slice his fucking throat with this paten.

I will not be lost to it.

I get a grip on myself. I resist this loathing that makes me loathsome as well.

Dr. Janovich and his two daughters come next.

This helps.

The younger one's a sophomore. Cute, I think. I yearn to graze her chin with the paten. I resist. I do not touch. I want to touch.

That's it.

Monsignor pauses, holding a single host in his fingertips. He looks about, surveying the scene. I smile to myself as I imagine a cloud of dust lifting, then settling about us as finally we come to rest.

Yep.

None left.

Monsignor whirls, whipping me with the edge of his stiff, beetle-back chasuble. He speeds back to the altar, Bambi hot on his tail.

Everyone stands for the Last Gospel. The Gospel according to John.

When I am not serving I pride myself on being able to read it in English as fast as the Monsignor can recite it in Latin:

In the beginning was the Word and the Word was with God; and the Word was God. He was in the beginning with God. All things were made through Him and without Him was made nothing that has been made. In Him was life, and the life was the light of men. And the light shines in the darkness; and the darkness grasped it not.

Monsignor races, fever-pitched, to the end:

"*. . . plenun gratiae et veritatis.*"

He leans forward and kisses the book.

That's our cue, our final line:

"*Deo Gratias,*" Whiteworm and I conclude. That's "Thanks be to God."

The mass is ended.

Go in peace.

2

I SNUFF OUT THE CANDLES AFTER MASS. WHITEWORM takes in the used cruets and finger towel. It's our little ritual: I take the candles, he takes the cruets. He likes the cruets. When we were seventh graders he would trot the cruets back into the sacristy, check about to see if he was alone, and then he would down the last of the wine.

That is, if the priest left any.

Most do. A few, though, they'll polish off the whole cruet. Which is about two full glasses of wine. Flat told us that. We were teasing him once—he's real touchy, he says he doesn't like the wine at all. Sure, sure, sure, we say. He says it is really tough drinking wine at seven-thirty in the morning. Sure, sure, sure, we say. Only I think he means it. He does leave most of it in the cruet.

Father Bolan, though, he really likes the wine. He taught us religion last year when we were juniors. We're seniors now, as of this month—the Class of '62 has just graduated and been sent off into the real world. That's how it is here at the Home, Father McFlaherty's Home for Boys. You can only stay until you graduate from high school and then out you go. Like it or no, ready or not, out you go. Out on your own, bye-yeee. And then the juniors, that's us, we move up. We're the Hotshits now. The senior class. The Class of '63.

Anyway, Bolan, he likes the wine. He drinks it all. He'll stand there and make you shake out every last drop. He's breathing heavy from all the extra weight he carries, holding that chalice low, bumping the lip of his chalice up against the lip of the cruet:

More. More. All of it.

You pour. All of it.

That's it.

Bolan's one of those guys who said he knew my mom. We're in religion class, it's right at the bell and he says to me:

"You don't remember me, do you?"

Kids are gathering up their books, trotting out.

I look at him. You talking to me?

He is. He's looking right at me, smiling at me.

He's not a regular priest out here. He's not a dean of anything. He's just an extra priest they brought in to teach religion this year, this big fat guy with the red nose.

Well? he presses.

"No," I tell him, "I don't remember you."

"I knew your mother," he says. He says it in a way that means he now has the inside track.

"Yeah?" I say, Mister Noncommittal.

I do not want to hear anymore of this. Most of these assholes tell you they knew your mother when they're about to twist your arm:

"Your mother wouldn't like that, now, would she?"

Real dumbshit stuff like that. No lie. You wouldn't believe how many assholes will use this shit. Even the assholes who are honestly trying to do you good. It is always a serious mistake. Always. Don't go bringing up no kid's mom unless he does it first. Period. And he won't. So don't.

My choir-section friend, Rasco — hold your tongue and say his name and it rhymes with ass-ho: Rwass-hoe— he thinks Bolan's an alkie.

"Check it out," he says when I catch up to him after class.

"He says he knew my mom," I say.

Rasco and I went to the same grade school together in Dayton, Sts. Peter and Paul. We were in the first grade together. He says I am meant to haunt him. He told me he liked this girl in the first grade, Emily Petrouka, and he'd walk her home nearly every day after school, trying to get her to tell him she liked him and she'll never say squat until one day he tells her he has decided to marry her and does she like that idea?

"You know what she says?" he asks me. It's as if he's ready to clobber me one.

"No," I say, backing off a hair, ready to duck for cover. "What?"

"She says, 'No. I like Frederick Gamble.' "

We go to different schools after his dad dies, and then both of us show up here at the Home.

"You gonna haunt me, Gamble?" he asks.

Guess so, I say.

I want to, ever since his dad's funeral. It was our first grade year. The whole class went, all of us in Sister Mary Mercer's class. God, you should have seen him. Break your heart. This tiny little fart up there in his shiny suit. He's sitting right on the aisle. He's the man of the family now.

Which is bullshit, of course.

But it ain't, because he was after that. Forever after, Rasco's the little man. Really.

His funeral did something to me. I mean, his dad's funeral did something to me. Seeing him being the little man made me jealous. I had this idea during mass watching him sit up there in the first row without shedding a tear that it could have been my dad. I would've liked that. Then people would feel sorry for me, pat me on the head, give me fresh-squeezed orange juice, and crush me into their bodies with great bosomy bear hugs.

"You think so?" I ask Rasco, not wanting it to be true. We're still talking about Bolan being an alkie. I am at my locker now. I work my combination. He waits on me.

"I think so," Rasco says evenly. No skin off his nose.

"I don't know," I say. It ain't a whole lot of fun for me to be thinking on whether yet another adult is a drunk. I don't like to think about it too much on account of all the trouble Dad used to have. That and how just thinking about it can make me feel real sick and helpless and like I got the flu or beriberi or something. No lie.

I come in off the altar. I hang the candle snuffer on its hook right next to the full-length mirror. I stand before the mirror for a moment and stare at my reflection. I hoist my surplice up over my head. I hang it on a hanger and hook it on the rack that's right next to the mirror.

I ain't so skinny, I don't think. People say I'm skinny. Lyman Hall was always saying that. He was all the time telling me how much I needed fattening up. That and fucking with my hair. The sonuvabitch just couldn't not fuck with my hair.

I lean in close to check out my Ivy League. I smooth it down with my right hand. The part ain't straight. I reach for my comb, forgetting that I'm still wearing my floor-length cassock. I jam my hand into the cassock, damn near breaking the first three fingers on my right hand. I stop, look down at my hip—there's a slit down there where you can get through to your pocket. I find it, reach in and around to my hip pocket, and get my comb out. There.

I comb my part out. I can feel the butch wax. Same shit I used when I was just an eighth grader and wore my Hollywood—that's a flattop on top with the sides long and combed back into a DA. DAs were forbidden, of course. Just like the Twist, now. Too dirty. No shit. The Twist is too dirty, so we are not allowed to do it.

I hear Whiteworm coming around back. I give myself one last look. I like looking at myself, I do. I am always surprised, too. I always look different than I think I am going to look. I have this idea inside of me, this idea about me, which is, to tell you the truth, a very nice idea. Then I see myself: Huh? Who's that?

Whiteworm's here. He whips off his surplice and hangs it up. He's standing right behind me. He is going to tear open his cassock in one fell swoop. I watch him in the mirror as he clutches his cassock at the top, making a pair of fists—he's got snaps, not buttons. You can't do what he is about to do with buttons. I know, Ezra tried it once. Buttons fucking flying everywhere.

"Ready?" he asks.

I half step to my left. We both stare at his long, lovely self in the mirror.

"Yup," I say.

Boom! He yanks her, his fists exploding apart, both of them shooting out across his shoulders: *errrrr-rrrrippp.*

It makes us both smile. Big, happy smiles.

Dumbshit stuff, I know, but it thrills us both.

He does a dancer's, Dracula-cape swirl across the room, spinning over to the cassock locker. He's a graceful kid.

"Hi, Bambi."

It's Ronnie. Right behind him is his best friend Turtle. They're a couple of sixth graders. They will serve for the grade school mass. Flat will say it.

Turtle walks right up to me, his back to the mirror.

"Got a zit?" he asks, pointing to the pimple on my chin.

Thanks, asshole.

I ignore him, say hi to Ronnie.

I was their den chief when they were just fourth graders. Miss Thicket asked me. She was my sixth-grade teacher. I would do anything for her. Absolutely fucking anything. And I mean it.

When me and Whiteworm—and Ezra and Rasco, too—had her, she showed us slides from her summer vacation first thing. Here she is in this tiny little boat with this tiny little outboard motor, and she's all bundled up in one of those fat, orange life jackets that come all the way up into your face so you look like a huge fat orange goose. And the look on her face: the poor woman is absolutely terrified.

Well, we all crack up. She looks so silly, so tiny, so frightened. We always laugh at someone who looks tiny and frightened.

She says it is okay, go ahead and laugh at her. She says it gives her an opportunity to tell us that she is afraid of the water, that she has always been. That it is a terribly crippling thing. That she hopes and fervently prays that none of us ever lets this happen to us. That we should learn to swim now.

She is standing there with the slide clicker in her hand looking loving and forlorn. It is a terrible thing to go through life with such a fear.

I could have just died. Me, I am terrified of the water. Since I don't know when. None of us understand it either. Franklin, my little brother, he's a star on the grade school swim team. This year will be his fourth year competing in dual meets. Matthew, my older brother the marine, never had any trouble like this either. He would go out water skiing up to Lake St. Mary. He even did the slalom—that's where you put both feet into one specially designed ski. He just loved all water sports.

''Lyman still the total asshole?'' I ask Ronnie and Turtle.

Ronnie turns around. ''Do big bears shit in the woods?'' he asks.

Turtle's turn: ''Do chickens eat popcorn?'' he asks.

I get in the groove: ''Is the pope Catholic?''

We all laugh.

They're good kids, both of them. Feisty fucks, too—which is important. You gonna survive around here, you gotta be a feisty fuck.

Whiteworm goes to the stools by the door. He sits and puts on his street shoes. They're four low stools, each with a four-fingered hole right in the middle of the seat. You can lift them and carry them about just like a lunch pail—very handy. It is just a coincidence those holes are lined up so perfectly with your bunghole.

Whiteworm sits squarely on one now, that tiny, dumbbell-shaped, four-fingered hole directly beneath his you-know-what.

He's up. He skeddadles. I watch him go. I yearn so.

I wonder. Is he going through the same weird shit I am?

"Guess who's gonna be our commissioner this year?" Ronnie asks.

I know the moment he asks: Franklin.

"Yeah," Turtle jumps in, "We're going to be in Franklin's apartment this year."

The grade school buildings are divided up into apartments, two on the first floor, two on the second. Each apartment has a coat and shoe room—which we call the Tin Room in Building One even though they are now made out of wood—a study hall, a little living room—and that is what it is called, a "little living room"—a can with three shower stalls, a urinal, three commodes with the doors removed (we got to see what you are up to, son), seven sinks under a long mirror, and a twenty-five-bed dorm with wooden lockers built right into the wall. There is also a Prefect Room, which used to be a private room, just eight-by-ten, for a high school boy who would serve as super commissioner. A prefect. But they stopped that long ago. The prefect rooms, at least in Building One, my old building, are just storage rooms now where they keep all the confiscated paraphernalia like knives, comic books, marbles, flashlights, good shit like that.

"You guys get along with him?" I ask.

"He's okay," they both sort of mumble.

Right.

"Listen, you guys," I say, noticing their sudden discomfort, "You don't have to like my little brother."

They both look up, startled, the shame receding from their mugs. Ronnie gives me a big smile.

"I mean it," I say.

"Okay," Turtle says.

"I better get a move on," I say. I want to touch them. I give Ronnie a little love tap on the shoulder.

"Adios, punk," I say. He whirls, throws up his dukes. "You wanna die, son?" he challenges, smiling big and wide.

"See ya, Turtle," I say. Turtle's totally engrossed in

buttoning up his cassock. He mumbles adios without looking up.

I head out.

I am glad they told me about Franklin's new job, about him being picked as a commissioner. It's a big honor on the grade school side, too. Same as being picked as a commissioner when you're a senior; shitfire, how I want to be picked.

I'm glad I know about Franklin's being picked today especially. Today is Pass Day. We'll be together with Dad. He'll be here around 9:30 A.M., so I can say something to him about it. I can brag on my little brother in front of his dad. Yeah.

I march down the side aisle. Grade school kids are pouring into the chapel now. On Sundays like this the high school boys have mass first. The grade school kids have mass right after we do. God, they sure as hell are noisy.

I step out the front door into the brilliant morning sun. I can see the main highway a thousand feet below, the Home's Great Lawn running gently down and out. A great place to practice your driving. I've lost many a Spalding out here.

Mobs of little kids are marching down toward me, toward the main chapel here. I decide to wait out here until Franklin comes down.

3

I SIT ON ONE OF THE FRONT LEDGES. THEY ARE MASONRY ledges, one on either side of the broad apron of steps leading up to the main chapel doors. I see Franklin coming down the Private Drive, which runs down to a little cul-de-sac right at the Monsignor's garage. There's a sign right at the beginning of the drive that says that: ''PRIVATE Dead End DRIVE.''

Franklin spies me, waves, and breaks into a trot. He's upon me in no time. The boy is quick. He'll be able to outrun me in no time.

''Dad's coming today!'' he proclaims from fifteen feet out.

I wait until he is close.

''Right,'' I say then. ''I hear you got promoted,'' I add.

This startles him. His mouth drops open.

''How'd you find out?''

I throw my head back a hair. ''Oh, I have my ways,'' I say, trying to be wise and mysterious. It's no use, though. Not around Franklin.

''Ronnie told you, didn't he?''

They post the list of servers on the bulletin board in Building One's front hallway. They did when I was there. They do now.

''Yeah,'' I admit.

''Can we go to a show?'' he asks suddenly. He's come right up to the ledge. He's about to come up. I watch him as he grabs on with both hands, springs off his toes, and lifts himself in a forward chin-up motion. He spins his body around in midair, aims his butt for the smooth masonry ledge top, and slides home free. Nice move.

"Sure," I say, about the movie. We do that a lot. Go to a show on pass. He's got it picked out, too. Says he wants to see *Come September* with Rock Hudson and Gina Lollobrigida. He rocks on his bum, getting comfortable. The boy has that Gamble butt. You know how people will talk about colored kids having those high, rounded bums? Which some kids have and some don't. Most don't, in fact. Well, that's the kind of bum the Gamble boys carry. Brother Thaddeus told me once when I was in the clinic. I was real sick with a case of the Asian flu. It laid me up for ten days. They had to take me to the clinic, which was full because there was this epidemic. I was delerious, Brother Thad told me. I do remember dreaming about Mom and flying and being married to her, being all tender loving with her and on the wing.

Anyway, I was really out of it. Every day Brother Thad came around to give me my alcohol rub, which is one of the things they did to break my fever. I had to take three aspirin four times a day and drink a full glass of water each time. Plus all the juice I could get down.

Brother Thad's working his way down, reaches my bum, sprinkles that icy-cold rubbing alcohol on my derriere, pats it, pats me. The chills race all up and down my body.

"You can tell a Gamble," he says, pat pat.

"Huh?" I say. I am feeling better. It's been a week now and my temperature is finally down to a hundred.

"You got that Gamble butt," he says with a twinkle in his eye. Then he tells me my bottom is just like Matthew's—"Franklin's, too, for that matter," he adds, remembering something. Probably the time Franklin was in here for poison ivy. He had it all over his body, had taken a dump out in the woods, on a bus hike. He either sat in it or wiped with it.

I roll over. That's enough down there, huh? I look at

him. He is gazing out the clinic window, daydreaming, smiling to himself, off in some lovely reverie. Suddenly he turns to me.

"You could spot Matthew at a hundred yards," he announces.

I get fidgety-fuck, Yeah, sure thing. Can I go down to the library now? I've finished my book. I wanna get another one, 'kay? Huh?

I asked Dad about it on pass once. If you live close you can get passes into town once a month. Like if you live in Dayton or Xenia or Fairborn. Anything close qualifies. If you have family, that is. There has to be someone who wants to come get you. And who will.

We're from Dayton. Dad comes out once a month, pretty much. The time I asked him about what Brother Thaddeus said was an Easter Sunday, the Easter right after Brother Thaddeus said this thing to me. It'd been January when I was sick. I'd been worrying about it, about having this big butt, all that time.

We are walking up the sidewalk in front of Dad's house, on Kenilworth. Dad is ahead of me. Franklin is still down at the street, getting his shit out of the car.

"How come the Gambles have such big asses?" I say to his back.

Dad is cool. He doesn't look back, nor does he miss a beat. He simply says,

"You can't drive a spike with a tack hammer."

Right.

I spent the rest of the day on that one. Trying to be sure, ya know, I knew what he meant. And that he really meant that after I was sure that was what he meant.

"Eight twenty-nine," Juan Carlos says as he scoots past us. He taps the face of his wristwatch as he heads up the steps.

Franklin leans into me, shoves me affectionately, mashing my shoulder with his. I mash back.

He leaps off the ledge, throwing himself out and down.

Boy has great spring. He spins and flies up the steps, beating Juan Carlos to the door.

"See ya," I call.

"Yep!" he says with a toss of his head. Could be a colt how he does that.

I let myself down slow and easy and head on over to chow.

4

I AM HAVING A SMOKE IN THE STUDY HALL, THE ONLY place you are allowed to smoke. I hear The Big Dick yell it out:

''Pintner! Tell Gamble his old man's here!''

I hear the brass fitting on Dick's office door click shut, *schlick.*

I mash out my Winston. Pintner comes in as I am leaving.

''Dick says your—''

I interrupt him, start to shout it back, the asshole:

''Tell Dick I—''

Then I catch myself. He'll come out here, kill me or forbid me my pass.

''I know,'' I say to Pintner. ''I did hear him.''

I get my shoes quick. I'm afraid now. Get out quick before he decides to do something. Pintner's shaking his head.

When I step outside I don't see Dad anywhere. And he's right there in front of me.

''Wanna ride, son?'' Franklin says. He's riding shotgun, has his window rolled down, his elbow jutting out. Mr. Cool.

I bound down the steps.

''Where'd you get this?''

It's a brand-new 1962 Ford Falcon, four door, baby blue.

''Garage sale,'' Dad says. He grips the wheel, releases it with both fists simultaneously. He's real proud.

''She's a beauty,'' I say and reach for the back door. It's locked. ''But you gotta let me in.''

''Oh!'' Dad says, starting to reach.

''I got it,'' Franklin says. He whirls around in his seat. He pops the button for me.

I hop in.

''I take driver's ed this year,'' I say as Dad pulls away from the house—that's what we call our cottages, our houses. My cottage is my house. ''Maybe you can let me drive her sometime, huh? After I take driver's ed, get my license? Huh?

I see Dad smiling in the mirror.

''Sure,'' he says.

We go out the back way and get on Tarbox Cemetery Road. We always go this way. It takes us right past Massies Creek Cemetery, one of my favorite spots—really. We like cemeteries.

From Tarbox we get on State Route 42 which will take us all the way through Wilburforce and right on into Xenia. Route 42 is high and elevated right here at Tarbox. Then she starts dipping and climbing, suddenly full of *S* curves so you have to slow down to twenty-five and then twenty, and there are trees and woods all about. In the summer the entire road is hooded, one great green canopy. It's just terrific.

''How 'bout some music?'' Franklin asks.

Fine, Dad says.

Franklin turns her on, tunes her to WING. The Highwaymen are trying to get Michael ashore:

Mike—ull row ohhhhh
the boat A shore
Ah—lay loooooo ya.

Franklin and I are a couple of gorps. We reach the Devil's Backbone, this high spot where there's this precarious ninety-five foot sheer drop to Massies Creek. We're swaying back and forth with each and every twist and turn in the road while trying to keep time with the music, too:

Ah—lay
LOOOOOOO ooooo

Ya.

Dad's handling her very nicely.

''How's she feel?'' I ask as we zoom over the top of the Devil's Backbone. It's a long, downward-sloping run from here into thick, heavy woods.

''Very nice,'' he says, giving her an appreciative nod.

He's a good driver. We Gambles pride ourselves on our good driving.

''Can we visit the grave?'' I ask suddenly.

Franklin registers surprise.

Me, too. I don't know where this is coming from. We haven't done this in years.

Franklin twists around in his seat and just stares at me. You'd think I just said I'd like a shit burger sandwich.

''Yeah?'' Dad asks.

Yeah.

''Okay by me,'' he says.

Franklin is still gawking.

''Don't stare, shit-for-brains,'' I tell him.

''Yeah?'' he challenges, leaning a way forward, really gawking now. You tell a Gamble what to do and he'll do just the opposite.

''Thanks,'' I say to him. '' I appreciate your consideration.''

He stops being a total asshole and asks, ''Why you want to go out there?''

I don't really know why. I remember when the urge hit me, in church this morning, after seeing Ronnie and Turtle.

''I'm just proud of you,'' I say. I turn to Dad now. ''Did you know Franklin has been picked to be commissioner this year, Dad?''

Franklin turns around now. He's blushing.

''He's been picked to be one of the commissioners in Building One,'' I say.

Dad looks over to his youngest son.

''That true?'' he asks.

''Uh huh,'' Franklin admits, nodding, still blushing.

''Good work,'' Dad says.

Franklin sneaks a look at me, makes a face, the kind of face you make when you are about to stick your tongue out. He doesn't stick his tongue out. I do.

Mom's grave is just below the fourteenth station: Jesus is laid in the tomb. Dad parks the car at the curb. We get out. There are no aboveground tombstones here. It's why Dad picked Calvary, he says. Matthew says Dad didn't do any picking—other than picking himself up off the floor. Dad was in pretty rough shape when Mom died.

Franklin runs on ahead. It's fifty yards or so to her grave. I avoid stepping directly on anyone's grave. It's as if I am standing on someone's belly. Franklin thinks I'm an ass and just laughs at me. He's stepping on one now. Just to get me, I know.

"Franklin! Don't!"

He laughs, acts as if he is about to start stomping on her, balling his fists up, crouching down into a half squat.

"Don't!" I order. I mean it.

He shrieks with joy, runs off to Mom's grave, yelling over his shoulder as he goes: "They're all *dead,* you know."

No shit, Sherlock.

I kneel beside her grave. I say a Hail Mary. I'm still not sure why, exactly, I wanted to do this.

Dad kneels next me. Franklin's climbing about the 14th station—they're huge altarlike jobbies, each station big enough to climb on, sit on, take pictures in front of. They have little lips or porches in front so you can sit right down. We've got pictures of us from the first year after she died. We came a lot that first year. An awful lot.

I remember her. She was funny. I'd bring my little friends over—me, I'm just this no-butt, my forehead barely reaching the knobs on the stove.

"Make Michael laugh," I say to her.

I am absolutely certain—as in Absolutely Certain—she can make anyone laugh anytime.

She turns from the stove to look at us.

"Be funny," I say.

I must be five.

She turns from the stove and tells us in this lisping, Daffy Duck voice what a sillikens I am to be-weave such nonsense about a mudder making her siwwee foow chiwd waugh.

The next thing I remember is standing on the back porch with Michael, both of us chuckling.

"See?" I say proudly.

The sun is lovely and powerful upon my face. Its warmth gives me deep, body-shivering chills as I stand there with my little friend.

I kneel here now and feel that sun again upon my face. I am five again. I surprise myself when I hear myself say it aloud, be-weaving it again:

"See?"

"What?" Dad asks.

"I didn't say anything," I say, meaning it.

Okay, he says, crosses himself and gets up.

I'm gonna stay a sec, 'kay?

Dad and Franklin head back to the car.

I know why I came. Ridiculous, perhaps, but what the hay: Mom, help me, okay?

I look behind me. Dad and Franklin are at the curb, out of earshot. I say it aloud, "See if you can't get one of them to pick me, okay?"

I get embarrassed and stop.

I do want that commissioner's job. I really do.

I hear the car door behind me. I say another quick Hail Mary, say adios, cross myself, and scat.

Dad drives us to Kalt's, the drugstore. It's just down the street from where he lives. He'll have coffee. Franklin and I will order cheeseburgers, french fries, and cokes.

"Make mine a cherry coke," Franklin says to Judy, the skinny old lady with her top front teeth missing. She just loves Jack's boys. That's Dad. We let her. It doesn't hurt anything.

"Slow down, boys," Judy says.

Me and Franklin, we wolf our food down. Some say it's because of the Home, where we have fifteen minutes to eat and we eat by bells. I don't know. I think I'd probably eat this fast anyway. I know Franklin would. You can't keep a piece of food safe when he's around.

I finish my burger, slop up some catsup with the last few fries.

"You still want to go to a show?" I ask Franklin. Dad's on his second cup of coffee, black. There are three butts in his ashtray, Camels. I light up a Winston.

"Yeahhhh," Franklin says.

I tell Dad. He says fine. We finish up and stop by Dad's apartment for a minute before he takes us to the Loew's Ames, where *Come September*'s playing.

Dad uses the restroom. Franklin uses it next.

"You gotta go?" Franklin asks as he comes out, still zipping up.

May as well, I say, and go in to take a turn.

Then we go to the Loew's Ames. Dad hands me the money, drops us off.

"Four-thirty," I tell him. That's what time it lets out.

"Okay," he says. He'll go home and take a nap. He always takes naps on our pass days.

Dad picks us up after the movie and we go downtown to Nixon's Smörgasbord. It's one of our favorite places. We eat here a lot.

Downstairs they have booths along the walls. Upstairs, on the mezzanine, there are larger tables for families like ours. We always go upstairs and take one of the round tables. I especially like it when one of the round tables next to the railing, looking down on the first floor, is free. From here you have a clear shot on the double swinging doors that lead into the kitchen. You can see the front door and all the booths from here, too. Whenever a waitress enters or exits through those double swinging doors, there's this blast of light from the brilliant fluorescents they have inside the kitchen. You have this momentary explosion of harsh, bright light followed immediately by a dim softness and dining room quiet. I just love it.

"Look!" I say, spying the round table next to the railing free. We'll take this one, please, I say to the hostess.

Our waitress comes up immediately after the hostess seats us. She's this real nice old lady named Millie. Dad says she's about thirty, thirty-five. She wears her hair up, sprayed, in a beehive. That's what Dad calls it. I thought he was being mean at first. But that's a real name for how you can fix your hair if you're a girl and want to fix it like that.

Millie knows us because we come here a lot. Dad comes here even more on his own. He never fixes any food at his apartment. He always eats out, when he eats.

"Good evening," Millie says, smiling sweetly. She smells real good.

Dad orders the antipasto, which is this plate full of things like radishes, carrots, celery, black and green and pimento olives, those baby finger onions, shit like that. Franklin and I both order a half of a spring chicken, Southern fried.

The name kills me. I always picture this young, smiling cheery little chicken ready to be murdered for someone's din-din, right?

Millie zooms away. I watch her dash down the steps. She blasts open the right side of those double-swinging kitchen doors. A great explosion of light and kitchen noise booms out into the dining room.

"Ready?" Franklin asks. We play word games. It's a lot of fun. Dad's real good at it. Sure, we both nod.

"Okay, I'll start," Franklin says.

Okay.

He turns to me, I'm on his left.

"Can you spell 'hors d'oeuvre'?" he asks, his eyes shining.

He ain't fucking around.

I spell it: H O R S D apostrophe U E—"No, no. Wait," I say. I start over. I always need to start over if I fuck up.

I can't just pick up right in the middle like Dad can. "H O R S D apostrophe O E U V R E. Right?"

"Right," Dad says.

We go right, ask left. So Dad's next.

"Can you spell 'smörgasbord'?" he asks Franklin.

Franklin spells it okay, but he forgets to mention the umlaut over the first O. You gotta do that. Just like I said the apostrophe in hors d'oeuvre.

"You forgot the umlaut," I point out.

"Big deal," Franklin says.

"You lose a point," I say.

"Your turn," Dad says.

"How do you pronounce S C H E D U L E?" I ask, spelling it out.

Trick question. In Dad's dictionary there are two pronunciations, a preferred, the English usage, and the other, the boob American usage.

"Let me! Let me!" Franklin pleads.

Dad looks at me, lifts his eyebrows in query. Yes?

Yes, I nod.

Franklin beams.

"The preferred pronunciation," he starts, clears his throat, the little shit. He's so proud. Makes me proud. "The preferred pronunciation," he repeats, his throat clear, "is shed' yool. The common usage is, however, skej' ool."

Dad and I applaud.

"Everything okay here?" Millie asks as she brings the dinners. She sets the tray down and then serves us one by one. It is very nice being waited on. I like it.

She's back the moment we finish up. She got ESP or something?

"How we doing?" she wants to know. She smiles real pretty. I get warm and goofy inside when she comes up like this. She's standing right next to me here. Her hip's right at my shoulder. Her perfume floats about her and remains a moment after she's gone.

"We're just fine, Mill," Dad says. He calls her 'Mill.'

"Dessert for these growing boys?"

I can almost feel her hip against my shoulder. Her perfume is making my eyes water, not from pain either. It's funny. She says corny shit like this all the time: ''these growing boys.'' We hear a lot of cornporn like that. Most of the time it drives me straight up the fucking wall. But when Millie says it I feel okay. I'm not exactly sure how she's different, only I do think she likes me and Franklin. And thinks of each of us as two distinct kids. Does that make any sense? Can you like someone just because she thinks you are distinct?

''Chocolate cake,'' I say immediately.

''Lemon merengue pie,'' Franklin says.

''And you, Mr. Gamble?'' she asks Dad. There is great respect in her voice. My heart melts. I appreciate her more for that, for calling Dad Mr. Gamble—and saying it with pleasure. It's as if she's making a little gift to all of us here with that Mr. Gamble bit. I don't know. I just like it a lot. And like her a lot for it.

''Just coffee, Mill,'' Dad says, smiling. He likes it, too, I can tell.

Millie zooms away, her perfume lingering here a moment behind her. Then it is sucked up in the whirling vortex of air that races behind her.

Dad gets us back to the Home a little before seven. The movie starts at seven so that's what time you have to be back.

We park in front of the auditorium. The Building One kids haven't come down from the building yet. I can see the two kids who are watching the doors. They are still sitting out on the bank in front of the main chapel. A great job, that, to watch the doors. The moment the doors open they will leap up, shout it back to someone on the front porch, and then be free to race lickety split on to the auditorium, the first ones there. A tremendous thrill, that, to be the first one. I don't know why. It seems sort of odd now. But then I'm an old one now. I walk more than I run now.

''There's the bus,'' Franklin says. I look up to the post house, this little bus-stop-like place right out by the main entrance. Kids coming back from passes whose families don't drive.

"There's Rasco," Franklin announces next.

"Who elected you secretary?" I ask.

"Drop dead," he says.

"Rasco's mom lives in town. She doesn't drive, so he takes the bus.

I hear the shrill, soprano scream: "The doors are open! The doors are open!"

I look back toward the chapel. I can see the two boys leaping, screaming. The next instant they bolt down the hill, heading this way, running as fast and as hard as they can.

The kid on the doors, a choir section kid, has them propped open with the little brass eyehooks latched at the base.

"I'm going to go, Dad," I say. I stick my hand over the seat. We shake. I jump out, start across toward the mob milling around the pair of open doors, and then stop.

"Nice car, Dad," I say. He smiles, waves.

Franklin leans over and kisses him on the cheek. "See ya, Dad. Thanks for everything."

I run across the street and get lost in the milling, shoving mob of boys.

5

I MASH RIGHT INTO THE MOB. IT CARRIES ME, FUNNELS me, right into the middle set of thrown-open double doors. They never open all three sets of double doors. I don't know why. It's the same thing up to the chapel, up to the high school dining hall. They only open the middle set of double doors.

Once inside, the crush of boys fans out. I go to the right. I head down the outside aisle to Cottage Fourteen's two rows of seats. I'm in luck: an aisle seat.

I leap into it.

"Move it, bub."

Huh?

It's The Big Dick.

"I got the aisle seat," I explain stupidly.

"Not anymore, you don't," he retorts, shooshing me away.

I go around to the other end of the aisle. I cannot sit near him. I will not sit near him.

Rasco's best choir section friend—my friend, too—Destern, sticks his foot out into the aisle to trip me.

I see it, fake it, and fall all over myself.

"Have a nice trip?" he asks. "Come again next fall."

"Har, har," I say. "Where's Rasco?" They usually sit next to each other.

Destern tosses his head. I follow the line of it and spy Rasco at the other end of the row Destern's in now. He's sitting right next to the madman himself, Felix. No one ever chooses to sit next to Felix.

"He in trouble?" I ask, concerned.

Destern starts to answer me—

"Sit, Gamble!"

The Big Dick has half hoisted his huge self up out of his seat. He is swinging on his arms. He has himself propped up on either armrest. His face is red from the exertion.

I stand here just staring at him. I do nothing.

"You hear me, bub?" he barks.

I sit.

The movie's *Twelve Angry Men* with Henry Fonda. It's great. Fonda has to convince the other eleven jurors that maybe they went and voted to convict this young kid a bit too hastily. It's touch and go until this sweet old gimp discovers and points out that the lady who testifies to the boy's presence at the scene of the crime wears glasses—only she ain't wearing them on the stand. But our sweet old gimp sees the little near-to-permanent indentations at the top of her nose where the glasses sit.

So then he starts to annoy the hell out of the others with this tiny but critical detail.

At first it drives them crazy. Then they act it out. A juror walks to one of the windows, lifts his glasses to his face as he goes. It takes time. Too much time. She could not have identified the murderer in the few seconds *she's* testified he, the murderer, was there at the scene.

Whew.

Get the details, son. You gotta get the details.

I intend to.

I follow Destern out after the show.

"Rasco in trouble?" I ask again.

"Nope," Destern says over his shoulder. We worm our way out through the mash of boys. We get jammed up in the foyer. It's wall-to-wall flesh out here. Destern and I break free on the auditorium porch. I grab him by the elbow: "Well?"

"You'll never guess," he says all sly and mysterious. Rasco pops out onto the porch right at this minute.

He's been picked to be a commissioner. That's it. I just know it.

"Hey!" I exclaim joyously. "Destern says you've been picked!?" I am terrifically excited for him. It's a great honor to be offered one of these jobs. I'm the Fonda juror, putting two and two together. Only Rasco is very strange.

"Thou sayest it," he says low. He's murmuring, hardly moving his lips at all. Thou sayest it? Thou sayest it? Ain't that what Christ says to Pilate? Right before they hang his ass?

I look at my friend real hard. He's lugging a nearly full IGA grocery bag. It's overflowing with loot brought from pass. He's been into town today, too. Felix is right there at his elbow, like a barnacle, his fingers pinching Rasco's elbows. It's like Felix is attached. As if he'll blow away if he ain't connected directly to my friend's skin.

Felix steers Rasco off the porch.

"Congratulations," I say to Rasco's back.

Rasco says nothing.

Felix nods down to me. "Kid," he says in greeting.

I shiver. It's friendly. I can thank Matthew for that. Felix is a Former Boy, too—that means you were a kid here once and now you're a Former Boy; I look forward to the day when I become a Former Boy. Felix was here when Matthew was here. He thought Matthew was cute. And Matthew had a lot of colored friends. His best friend, Jordan, he was almost as black as Felix here.

Destern jabs me in the ribs.

"Gotta go," he says and beats it off the porch.

I hop up onto the concrete railing that outlines this end of the auditorium's porch. Another railing matches this one on the other side of the porch. The sun-warmed concrete is lovely against my bottom. I settle down to watch the kids come out of the auditorium and head back to their cottages—or buildings if they're still grade schoolers.

The Home's Great Lawn spreads out in front of the auditorium. It's nearly twenty acres of Kentucky bluegrass trucked in direct from Lexington. There's bluegrass pretty much all over the Miami Valley. I didn't always know that. I used to think it was just the Monsignor being such a first-class hotshit—you know, nothing but the best for the Monsignor.

The main chapel looms massively above the Great Lawn. It's situated on the Home's highest ground. Nice move that, the house of God watching over it all. The Monsignor's residence is attached directly to the chapel. It's obscured from here by the pines and the row of elm trees that run the length of the PRIVATE Dead End DRIVE. You should see these guys, these lovely vase-shaped elm trees, after a heavy rain. The water will run down the long twenty-, thirty-foot trunks, on only one side so half the trunk looks juicy jet black—a liquid-velvet look that is simply stunning.

The whole place, the entire Home, in fact, is simply stunning. "Landscaped to the teeth," Matthew used to say.

The Admin Building and Visitors' Center are to my right. The high school building and the high school dining hall run up the street to my left. The Home's main thoroughfare bends right at the dining hall, shoots straight up past the trade school, zooms past the Founder's statue and takes you right on into the grade school side.

The Founder's statue is this huge mother stone statue. It stands on a six-foot base with a life-sized founder surrounded by five life-sized boys: one black boy, one white boy, one Asian boy, one Jewish boy, and one Indian boy. The Founder has on one of those godawful silly priest's caps—the biretta carved in stone right there atop his head. It cracks me up every time I see a priest put on one of those silly things.

Someone smashes me fast and furious right in the shoulder.

I whirl to catch a glimpse of Ronnie's flying self leaping out and down. He's shrieking with joy and abandon: "Gotcha!"

He's a golden boy, no lie. The kid's Hawaiian. He's—now get this—Spanish, Filipino, Japanese, and Chinese. A gorgeous kid. And you should see him toast up come summer. Amazing. Just amazing.

Franklin comes out with Juan Carlos, a counselor from Building One. Juan Carlos is okay, I think. He's tough but okay. He got my ass once. I'd just fired the bird at this kid who'd tried to kill me at third base. This kid had come slamming into me with his arms folded up across his chest. He's a battering ram, coming at me as fast and as hard as he can. He knocks me on my ass but good. I'm sitting in the dust. ''Asshole,'' I yell and give him the bird.

Juan Carlos has me into the office afterward. He has me in and says to me: ''I see you do that again and I'll have that finger cut off.''

Scared the fuck out of me. I thought he could do it. And that he would. Wooo.

Neither Franklin nor Juan Carlos see me. They are engrossed in conversation. Fucking Franklin. I don't know how he does it. He talks to these guys. He gets along with these guys.

It is totally beyond me.

I watch my little brother cross the street with Juan Carlos. I pull my knees up to my chest. I hug myself. Everyone's out. No more children inside. A choir-section kid appears. He bends down to unlatch the brass eyehooks at the base of the double doors. He steps back inside and lets the doors swing shut behind him.

The choir section has charge of the auditorium. At Christmas time they do a job. We celebrate the twelve days of Christmas. They turn the place into what the Monsignor calls the Boar's Head Inn. They get a real boar's head, too. No lie. They mount that mother out front, right over the middle set of double doors. A real live boar's head. Only it's dead, of course. And it looks human, it does. In its face. Eerie.

We do something special every day for the entire twelve days of Christmas. Like the St. Stephen's Day stoning. This is the day after Christmas. St. Stephen is supposed to be the first person martyred for being a Christian, so we celebrate his feast day the day after Christmas. He was stoned to death. So on December 26 anyone whose name is Stephen gets stoned right out in front of the auditorium. Right after the afternoon matinee—which is another thing we do for the twelve days of Christmas: have a movie every day. And after the movie on December 26, anyone who wants to is given a handful of raw eggs and all the Stephens are rounded up—or Stevens, it doesn't matter how you spell it—they're all rounded up, and at the signal the boys plaster the holy hell out of them. It is hellacious. No shit. I just thank God every year my name ain't Stephen. Or Steven.

I watch as the last of the grade school kids disappear into the coming night. The Building One kids head out across the sidewalk that cuts across the Great Lawn. Every other grade school kid takes the Home's main thoroughfare up and around.

We always keep the little ones separate. They were mildly frantic about it when I was one of those little kids. Don't want none of those older boys getting at you, now, do we? You know what those older boys want, now, don't you?

God, it was crazy. And it scares the fuck out of you. It sure did me. And now I'm one of those older boys.

I am all alone now. I have the entire place to myself. There's not a living soul in sight.

I like it. I like being alone, being the last one out.

I take a deep breath. I release my knees, letting my feet drop back over the edge of the still warm stone railing. I lean forward, setting my hands on either side of my bum and rock. The air is perfectly still.

God. It's a lonely place.

The streetlights come on.

Oh.

I push off and head back to the cottage.

6

DICK ANNOUNCES AT NIGHT PRAYERS THAT HE HAS picked Pintner as his commissioner. Everyone applauds, hurray. Pintner beams. He's a swimmer. He's been here a hundred years, too, just like me.

Pintner leads night prayers. You can hear the joy in his voice.

We finish.

"Good night, boys," Dick says. Pintner hangs back. We file out. They will be talking in The Big Dick's office after we go on to bed. Talking. Watching TV. Maybe even making and eating some popcorn. The Big Dick can't ever get enough of his popcorn.

I pad upstairs behind Ezra. He's got a sock over his peg. Keeps it from showing. The peg sort of grosses people out.

He's gotten real good with it. When he first had it, it was rough. It didn't fit. His stump would swell. It would hurt all the time. And then there was the smell. That was the roughest part. We had to tell him, me and Whiteworm. No counselor would.

The phantom pains are tricky, too. The doctor told him about that when he was still laying up in the hospital bed with this empty space up under the sheet.

They told him his foot would hurt, that his toes would hurt, and they're gone, see? They took it off two inches below the knee. He's got this knee joint and a couple of inches of meat and bone below the knee. That's all.

"Lights out, you guys," Pintner says. He's standing in

the doorway. Ezra's sitting on the edge of his bed, undoing his leg. It straps up over his knee. The leg itself, a beige color, it's an odd-looking thing. The foot is arched. Permanently arched so his shoe is curled this real unnatural way. Pointy-toed and arched.

"It itches," he says, wincing.

It's been two years now and it still itches. He ain't got no foot and it's itching. My skin crawls when he tells me. Every time.

Pintner leaves on that one. Big help. He goes down the hall. We hear him saying good night to the guys down in bedroom five.

"Here, scratch mine," I say, offering my foot.

Both of us tear into my foot. A couple of gorps. Shit, you gotta laugh.

Pintner's back, flicks the lights.

"Good night," he says.

Ezra swings his stump up into bed with him. His peg sits at the foot of his bed, airing out. The first year he had it guys used to hide it so when he got up in the morning he had to hop all over the house, trying to chase the assholes who stole his leg. Har har.

As soon as we hear Pintner's footsteps on the hollow wooden staircase we know it's safe to talk.

"Guess what?" Ezra whispers.

"What?"

"Kuhns got picked today."

I am immediately interested. Kuhns is one of my best friends. He's been here since 1954. He got here about the same time Whiteworm got here, about nine months before I did. He's one of the Home's outstanding athletes. He's a real natural, honest. He is just terrific at anything athletic or physical, he really is. He's our star quarterback. Started as a sophomore. He's also a first-string guard for the varsity basketball team and a great pitcher on the baseball team—a great pitcher who bats .350 every year.

"Who picked him?" I ask.

Morton, Ezra tells me. Lovely Lester Morton. He's

Matthew's old counselor. Kuhns and his football pals just started calling him that this year: Lovely Lester Morton. He's the head counselor over in section two—me, Whiteworm and Ezra, we're in section one. Rasco's in the choir section. Then there are two other high school sections, three and four.

Morton's been around for a thousand years. He's famous for his birthday swat routine, his elephantiasis, and his love of jocks—he's always got a bevy of jocks in his house. His elephantiasis is where his nuts swell up every year to the size of volleyballs. I've never seen it, but I asked him about it once when we were just sophomores. He'd been off for a couple of weeks recuperating. The first time I saw him after he got back I just asked—I didn't know. No big deal, right.

"Kuhns says your elephantiasis has been acting up? You OK now?"

He's standing in the doorway to his office. Me, Kuhns, and this other hotshit football player and good friend of ours, Foster, we're talking and listening to Gary U.S. Bonds on Morton's stereo in Morton's office. I ask and Foster chokes.

Morton hitches his pants and says, "I'm fine."

His birthday routine is something else. On your birthday he has the other boys capture you and bring you to him. He sets up in the study hall and they set you across his lap, holding you down while he administers the swats. He will smack you with his bare hand as hard as he can full on the buttocks and then clasp your butt real firm-like and give you a whale of a shake. He does this same thing with each swat: smack, clasp, shake. If you're seventeen it is seventeen times he smacks you, seventeen times he clasps onto your ass, seventeen times he shakes your bum. Foster says this just proves the guy's a fruit.

"Foster got picked, too," Ezra whispers.

This hurts.

"No shit?" I say, amazed and hurt. See, Foster's only been here for two years now. He only came as a sophomore.

He hasn't been here for a hundred years like the rest of us—like me and Ezra and Whiteworm and Kuhns. Even Pintner, my new commissioner here in fourteen. We've all put in six, seven, eight years.

"Who picked him?" I ask.

"Marrone," Ezra says.

He's another fucking madman. Down in Cottage Nineteen. God, why do I even want one of these jobs? Most of these counselors are weird or mad or mean or stupid or queer. Like Marrone. He used to work in the cage up to the grade school gym, handing out rolls, helping the gym class. No mental heavyweight either. Then we all move over to the high school side, and suddenly Marrone's a counselor with a cottage of his own.

Shit, we all thought it would be neat, having Marrone as your counselor. Just this yo-yo, har-har hardy har-har type of guy, see? A guy who loves sports. Loves to laugh and fool around all the time. It'd be sweet having him.

Wrong.

It turns out he's a real madman. Tony Mondino told me, this friend I had as a freshman. We wrestled together. But he's gone now. Largely because of Marrone, too. It seems Marrone's this Jekyll-and-Hyde kind of character. All laughs and yuk yuk in the daytime and a fucking madman with a bongo bat after dark. Coming around after lights out all hysterical and out of his mind about shit you're supposed to have done during the day—stuff that makes him look bad, Tony said. And Tony had the bruises to prove it.

God, I don't understand how they pick people around here. I really don't.

"Unnnh."

Take Lester. Lovely Lester Morton. Everyone acts as if he's this terrific person and sensational counselor who is just great with the boys.

"Unnnh."

"What's the matter?" Ezra asks, concern in his voice.

"Nothing, why?" I'm okay.

"You're moaning," he says.

"I am?"

"Yeah."

God.

I get out of bed and go into the can. I try to take a leak. I dribble some, not much, give it up, and return to bed.

I remember that time in Lester's basement. Jesus, it gives me the willies. They got me to go out for the wrestling team. Lester, Matthew, and Jordan. I didn't want to do it. I was really scared. I figured someone would get me in a headlock and choke me to death. I am terrified of being choked to death or drowned or smothered.

But they were persistent. I only weighed a hundred pounds. Which is why they wanted me to go out. They wanted me to wrestle at ninety-five. Jordan and Matthew had been on the team together for three years now. Matthew had started out at ninety-five when he was just a freshman. They thought I'd be perfect. And they wouldn't leave me alone until I said okay, I'll try it.

Then all of a sudden they tell me I have to work out on the weights. It is absolutely essential that I work out. I'm too skinny. Too weak. I need to build up my strength. I need to build myself up.

Well, I ain't no Charles Atlas. Ain't never been. Nor ever will be.

Ain't too terribly interested in being one either.

But I am skinny.

So I agree.

Lester has a weight room in the basement of his house. Weights, mats, bench, mirror—"The whole nine yards," Lester says, smiling proudly.

The asshole. He got me over there alone.

I squirm here in bed remembering it. It makes me feel ashamed of myself.

Stop, I order myself. Stop.

I can hear Ezra's breathing. It is regular and deep. The boy is gone. The house is still.

It pops into my head.

Don't think about it, I order myself.

I roll over and see Ezra's leg. It's in silhouette there by the foot of his bed. He lost it about the same time Daly, my counselor my freshman year, fired me and had me moved out of his house. He had me moved over to Father Leaver's house. Leaver was our dean. I was so bad I had to be put in the dean's cottage.

Oh, God.

I roll over again, my back to Ezra and his leg now.

Daly. That motherfucker.

He seduced half the kids in the cottage.

We were just brand-new freshmen. Our first summer over to the high school side. Everyone was happy. It was wonderful having a cottage, having only one counselor and living with only twenty other boys. And then something happened.

Kids got funny. Daly started calling boys into his office at night after night prayers. One by one. Keeping them in there for all hours. And O'Toole goes mute.

He's one of our friends from Building One, too. We'd been in the same classes together for three years. Moved over to Daly's house together. He'd let me use his calligraphy set, the one his mom sent him for graduation. Then he has his turn with Daly and goes mute. He just stops talking. Every day he just goes into the study hall, sits down at a table all by himself, and speaks to no one.

I tried to talk to him. He just ignored me. Looking furious and ignoring everyone.

I ask Kuhns. He's one of the boys called in.

"What's going on?"

"We all got caught doing it together over on Leaver's porch."

I am dumbfounded.

Doing it together?

Yeah. And so everyone has to talk to Daly, he says.

I go back to O'Toole.

I know what's going on, I say. I just talked to Kuhns. He told me, I say.

O'Toole looks at me. There's such loathing in his look I think I'm a fucking cockroach.

God, O'Toole, talk to me. What's the matter. You're not being yourself.

He turns to me and levels me: "He made me do it with him."

Who? Daly? Made you do it with him?

I am horrified and totally and completely disgusted with my friend.

How could you do something like that? Why didn't you go to Father Leaver?

O'Toole looks at me with complete and utter disdain.

"I told him I'd go to Father Leaver and he said to me, 'Who's he going to believe? A thirteen-year-old boy or a counselor he's had for seven years?' "

I have nothing to say. I think he's so gross. So disgusting.

"So I did it with him."

We're all so bad. I feel so bad. How come we'll do things like this?

I say a Hail Mary.

I am going to get this shit out of my head.

I say the Hail Mary and Daly's there right along with my prayer.

I try again. This time I think about the words, I think about Mary full of grace, the mother of God.

Someone's up.

I stop my prayer. I listen. He's coming down the hall. Coming from bedroom five, going to the can. I hear the door open and shut.

Daly's in my face. I was his assistant commissioner. This great honor. "You've disappointed me," he says.

Hail Mary, full of grace, the Lord is with thee.

The can door opens. He's out, coming back down the hall. Who is it? I try to figure it out from the sound of his footsteps. You can tell a person by the sound of their walk. You really can. Just like you can tell a person from a great distance, before you can see them clear enough to make out who they are, just by noticing the way they walk, the way they carry themselves, how they move.

I listen intently.

Got it: Janson.

Ah.

I fill with blood.

Janson.

Soft, silent Janson. He has a dick just like mine. No lie. It really amazed me. I was washing my jeans in the shower. Quincy, my commissioner when I was a sophomore—he liked me—he taught me how to wash your jeans in the shower, using regular Maxine bar soap. You wear your pants in the shower. You just shower with your pants on, get 'em wet, lather 'em up good with the bar of Maxine, rinse 'em, lather 'em up again, rinse 'em, and that's it. This way, Quincy says, "You don't have to take the crap shoot of the laundry," where you turn in your dirty clothes and never know whose or what you will get back.

It is a Friday night. I am washing my jeans in the shower. Friday nights are different. The usual routine is off. You can stay up late so you can shower anytime you want after eight, watch TV, smoke in the study hall, whatever.

Janson comes in. I am in the stall by the wall. The other stall's empty.

He gets into the empty stall. I am hot. He makes me hot. We've done it before, he and I, furtively, without a word to each other, before the TV set, one reaching and stroking, the other being reached and stroked.

I flip a bar of Maxine over the top of the stall.

I wait.

The bar of soap comes flying back over.

My pulse quickens.

I get hard.

I flip it back over again.

I wait.

It comes flipping back over again.

I take a deep breath. One more time. To be sure.

I flip it a third time, up and over.

I can hardly breathe. The light goes funny. I shiver.

I wait.

He flips it back immediately.

It hits me on the shoulder and drops to the floor of the stall. I leave it lay. I step out of the shower with one foot and reach around to the curtain on his stall. I tug it back. He's standing there looking like a bird in a blizzard, his stiff pecker tucked down between his legs. He's trying to hide it.

I look at him.

He looks at me.

I look down at it. I ain't breathing.

I reach for it, for him. He shakes, shivers, and spreads his knees apart. His cock springs free. I catch it up and take it softly, carefully into my hand. Holding onto it like a handle, I step into the shower with him. I let the curtain fall shut behind me. It is a moment of supreme terror: someone will walk in.

I step around behind him, unzipping myself as I move. The zipper catches so I have to release him for a moment. I get it unstuck, zip it down, open my jeans, and let myself spring free. I step into his rear, pressing myself flush to his crack, pressing, pressing, pressing. I reach around to the front and clasp him in my hand as I press into him from the rear. He is big and hard and soft. The water is hot and wonderful on my back, on my shoulders, splashing so I have to close my eyes some. I ride his ass. Suddenly, surprising me, he lifts up onto his toes, his dick gliding in my fingers, his ass addressing my pressed cock. Holy shit: he wants it, he is lifting to it, he wants it, oh, mother of God, he wants it.

I roll onto my stomach remembering, no longer tortured by memories I do not want to remember. It is Janson I remember, our night in the shower, and I do myself, scooting, scooting, scooting.

I finish quickly, lay perfectly still, and let sleep overtake me.

7

"TIME," PINTNER SAYS, WIGGLING MY FOOT. "Morning prayers." He moves over to Ezra's bed.

"Time to get up," he calls down to Ezra. He doesn't touch Ezra. He won't touch Ezra. That missing foot really spooks people.

Ezra moans in his sleep and rolls over to face the wall. Pintner looks horrified for an instant. He's not sure what to do. He will not touch him.

He gives it up and goes around to the other side of our bedroom to wake up the two guys over there. Ezra snores away.

"He still ain't awake," I say to Pintner as he comes back around. I'm sitting up with my feet on the floor. I face my friend's back.

Pintner stops. I got him: it's your job, asshole, so wake him.

I don't know what it is. I am feeling this same desperation I felt all those years as a kid in Building One, the same great irritation and discombobulation I'd feel when Lyman Hall would come around for wake up.

He'd come slamming into the dorm, banging away on the metal door that covered the eight light switches for the raft of overheads.

Bang bang bang

"Rise and shine! Rise and shine, boys!"

Bang bang bang

"Up and at 'em. Rise and shine!"

Then he'd commence with the loudest, most obnoxious hand clapping ever have you heard while marching briskly down the center aisle hunting for sleepyheads—finding scores, of course—and when he found you, sleepyhead, he'd grab you fiercely about the ankle and shake! And I mean shake! He'd damn near snap your head off. You're the whip and he's playing crack the whip—and your head, right? It's the end of that whip. Talk about early morning headache. I got so I could sense him coming, honest to God, this is the truth. I would awaken a split second before he got his fist going on that metal door covering the eight light switches. I'd awaken and bolt upright in bed.

How he loved to get to you before you were fully awake. He thought it was just great fun. He really did.

So Pintner's being an asshole here, now, afraid to touch our friend because he's a freak with only one leg. Well, it's your fucking job, asshole, so do it. They pick me, I'd be able to do it.

Pintner stands and stares. He's coming to a decision, swallowing hard, gulp.

"You wake him," he snaps at me and walks out of the room as quickly as he can.

Right.

I lean over to Ezra's bed. I shake him.

"Hmmn?"

"Time to get up, shithead," I say softly.

He pulls the covers up over his shoulder, snuggling in.

I shake him harder and give his shoulder a little pinch. He's a strong kid. Real well built, naturally. If he'd been willing to work like a slave and put up with the Old Man's abusive ways, he'd probably still have his leg and be a starter to boot. Only Ezra, he don't take to abuse too much.

That's my opinion, anyway.

"You awake?" I ask, my hand still squeezing his shoulder.

"Yeah," he says, peeking out from under his snuggled-up covers, his azure blue eyes stunning. Seminoles have those eyes, he says, which I say is bullshit, though he is half Seminole. His mom, she's full-blooded Seminole. Still lives down there in the original Seminole country, in Florida.

"Morning prayers," I remind him.

Okay, he says. He still hasn't made move one toward getting his ass up.

He played midget football with us. He was great. Fierce, too. He was big enough to play high school ball, too. I wasn't, thank God.

He sits up, both of his legs shoot out from under the covers. His stump startles me. It always does. What a fucking basket case I am. It's been two full years now and I am still freaking out at the sight of his footless pjs.

He did try out for the team. As a freshman. And quit immediately. He said he'd rather take the job Juan Carlos offered him as staff with the Home's summer camp. That's where the team starts its season, up to the Home's summer camp on Lake St. Mary. We have this mansion up there, it was donated, right on the lakefront. Every kid in the Home gets to spend a week up there each summer. Swimming, rowboating, motorboating, water skiing, fishing, archery, shit like that. Movies every day and roller skating over to Playland on your last day—roller skating out in public where there are real people, *girls,* shit like that.

So every summer, in August, anyone interested in trying out for the varsity football team signs up for a week at Lake St. Mary. Where you practice three times a day and have a chalk talk every night.

And Ezra, who could have made the team as a freshman, quits. I couldn't feature it so I ask him about it.

"Which would you choose, Bambi?" he says. "Having your brains beat out every day, having your face smashed in the sand three times a day or working with Juan Carlos on the lake crew? Huh? You tell me, asshole? Which would you choose?"

Well, if you put it that way.

So he quit and stayed on as a staff member on Juan Carlos's lake crew. And of course he has to go and do something crazy and dangerous like sitting down on the hood of one of the Home's red riding mowers, sitting right down there in front, his feet dangling, holding onto I don't know what.

People say they hit a rock. Or a stump. No one knows for sure. All we do know is they hit something that stopped that mower dead in its tracks and Ezra goes flying forward face first into the sandy grass dragging his feet behind him, *scranch.*

It cut right through the bone and everything. It was just hanging on by a bit of skin. His leg was twisted back most unnatural, his eyes glazed, his face pasty white, he's lying in the grass.

Poor fuck.

We get down to morning prayers all right. Ezra hops down. He'll put his leg on afterward. He's pretty agile, too. He can hop down those hollow wooden stairs as softly as you and I with two feet, no lie.

The Big Dick comes out of his office, scowling. It's how he is in the morning—you just try to steer clear.

Dick stands, not bothering to kneel, as we say our morning prayers. Afterward I give Ezra a hand getting up.

"He's a big boy, bub," Dick says.

I'm surprised.

"You talking to me?" I ask. I am being sincere.

"I ain't talking to your mother," he snarls.

I release my friend and lift my hands up to either side of my face, my palms facing out: peace.

He glares at me.

I honestly do not understand this guy.

I step away from Ezra and make a wide circle around Dick with my hands still splayed. I know he never put me on the list. I just know it. That's how you get picked to be commissioner. Your current counselor recommends you, puts your name on the list. Then all the counselors caucus and choose who they want from the list. You ain't on the list, you ain't got a prayer.

I am sure I ain't on Dick's list.

I hoof it back upstairs to get dressed. Ezra's right behind me.

"It's no big deal," he says. He hops to the mirror and starts to wash up.

I say nothing. Fucking assholes. The world is full of fucking assholes.

I dress quickly, quietly. I cannot trust myself to speak. The assholes. They treat you like shit and then punish your ass when you react to the shit they dish out. Me, I "act out," they say. I don't know what the fuck that means. Act out, huh. You wanna see act out. I'll show you act out.

"Forget it," Ezra says. He's strapping on his peg now.

I look at him. I'm fuming. Just fucking fuming. They always get me fuming.

"Really," he says, lifting his peg up the way you'd lift a boot. He pulls it over his stump. I see the thick, stitched scarring that crisscrosses down there. "Just forget it. Forget him."

He's reading me like a book. Ain't that the shits? And here's my friend, Ezra. He's lost a goddamned leg to these fucking idiots and he's being cool.

What a shit I am. There is something definitely wrong with me.

I slam my locker door. I slam it hard.

Ezra stops strapping his peg, holds it on high for a second and just watches me.

"You'll be all right," he says.

"I ain't mad at you," I say.

"I know."

Which helps. Which helps a lot. Then Pintner shows up in the doorway. He heard the locker slamming.

"What's all the racket in here?" he asks, acting the boss.

"None of your fucking business," I say.

He flinches. He didn't expect that.

I storm out, brushing past him as I go: out of the way, fuckface.

He collects himself and says to my back:

''You better cool it, son.''

This stops me. I turn to stare at him. Son? Son?

He's shaking his head.

The Big Dick says that shit: son. Putting you down, thumping you on the head: Got a problem, son? Wanna take this outside, son?

''You asshole,'' I say and beat it the fuck out of here.

8

I GET OUTSIDE AND I AM SIMPLY SHAKING WITH IT—trembling and shivering uncontrollably.

"Goddamn," I say aloud. I walk as fast as I can without breaking into a run. It is all so familiar. So very, very familiar.

"It's your attitude," Lyman used to say to me all the time. I got the bad attitude. He's got me on work crew, me and Ezra, breaking records for the most hours on work crew. At least that's what Juan Carlos used to say, "A couple of record breakers," he'd say, "you're on work crew more than you're off, hmmm?"

He's probably right. I was an eighth-grader then. I had wanted to be picked back then. As commissioner then. And I ain't picked, which pisses me off, it ain't fair, I should have been picked.

"It's your attitude, Freddy-me-boy," Lyman explains to me. I'm on work crew, buffing up the floor, and he's here trying to explain to me why someone has to be the disciplinarian and why I can't be a commissioner because of my attitude. "You have to learn to change your attitude, Freddy boy. You have to give up being so bitter, Freddy boy. I'm sorry, but there it is."

I stop my buffing and glare at the asshole: My *name* is Fred.

Then Daly, I'm a freshman, and he gives me the job—I mean, I had it in my hand. I had it and still fucked it up. Shit. I can't win for losing.

The dining hall doors open. I march right in. Still fuming. Only the dining hall, this beautiful, cathedral-ceilinged monstrosity with its humongous floor-to-ceiling fireplace up against the back wall, its rock-hard, easy-to-clean quarry tiles, shit, it's simply gorgeous. It softens me. Every time, no matter what's what, this place, just walking into this place, it softens me.

I go to my place, stand next to my chair without speaking to anyone. I look up. I stand here next to my chair and look up at the corkboarded—soundproofed—ceiling.

There are hundreds and hundreds of stainless steel table knives stuck in that corkboarding, soundproofing stuff up there. It's amazing. I discovered it once by accident. I was giving a church group a tour of the Home. I brought them in here and decided to get on a chair so everyone could hear me, and as I climbed up I happened to look up and there they were. Literally hundreds and hundreds of table knives flung up into the soundproofing. Hundreds of them stuck in the ceiling. Kids have been doing it for I don't know how long. Twang.

Whiteworm comes in. I watch him move to his place. I struggle to hang onto my anger. It ain't easy with Whiteworm around.

Lovely Lester's on the bell: *Brrrrriiiinnnnnnnggggg!*

He leads us in grace.

Brrrriiiinnnnnggggg!

We sit to eat.

I eat in silence. I want to hang onto this feeling, but I can't. Breakfast is just too wonderful. I just love breakfast. Honest. There's cold cereal—K E double L O double G, Kellogg's good for you—toast, sweet rolls, baked right here in the Home's own bakery, baked by the boys learning a trade, baking bread and rolls every day as they prepare for life on the Outside. There's fresh fruit every morning, too—oranges, bananas, grapefruit. And all the milk you can drink. Produced right here, too, on the Home's dairy farm, where more boys learn a trade, learning how to be farmers.

We have elephant ears this morning. They're great, wafer thin, crackly and crumbly and covered with this glazy hard-rock sugar. Make me happy. Make me very happy.

"Pass the milk, please," I say.

"Oh, it talks," Pintner says. He and The Big Dick, peas in a pod.

Ezra passes the pitcher down to me.

I am going to be okay. I pour myself an icy glass of frothing, bubbling milk—Mom used to say it meant you'd be rich if you got a lot of bubbles in your milk. I got a lot of bubbles. This makes me happy, too.

We're done in no time.

Brrrriiiinnnnngggg!

Everyone shuts up at the bell. We stack our dishes and pass them down to the end. Dick comes out from the counselor's dining hall in back. Half the counselors stay back there all through chow. The other half patrol the aisles as we eat. Most of them come out at the bell to supervise the silence before the final grace.

Waiters cart away the dishes and the uneaten food, what little there is of it.

Brrrrriiiiiinnnnnnggg!

We all stand at our places, shove our chairs in, and face the crucifix. Lovely Lester leads us in the grace after meals:

We give Thee thanks. . . .

The dining hall explodes immediately upon completion of the grace after meals. Four hundred kids bolt for the middle set of thrown-open double doors.

Chow's over.

You're free to go.

9

SOMEONE PINCHES MY ELBOW. I AM RIGHT AT THE doorway.

"Bambi?" he says.

I turn toward the voice, but the mob pulls me along.

"Look out, punk!" someone next to me snarls. I look. This tiny fart, a freshman—he's a sophomore now—flies flung forward. Someone's just given him one terrific shove. He smashes into the post separating the double doors and ricochets off. Ouch. His eyes bulge. Froth forms at the corners of his mouth.

I spy Rasco just beyond the panic-stricken kid.

"Rasco!" I call out. "Hey, Rasco!"

He does not hear me for the roar.

The little fart freshman-now-he's-a-sophomore is going down. I see him sink, see his head drop out of sight. You go down, you're dead.

"Bambi?" That voice again. I turn. Charles, the counselor in cottage twelve.

"Outside," I shout to him. Now where's that little fart? I mash to my right, toward the spot where he went down. I find him. He's curled up, has his hands up over his head, is immobile, about to die, you ask me. I lean down to grab him under his arms. I am bent at the waist. The crowd of boys is tipping me over. This won't do.

The kid's bawling. Scared.

I straighten up and do a quick squat, latch him under the arms, and shoot right back up with the kid in tow. He squirms, manages to spin around, and latches onto me, a barnacle on my chest. Squeezing the life out of me.

We're trapped. The mob has frozen in front of us. Behind us kids keep jamming into this tiny foyer that separates the inner screen doors from the outer oak doors. I rubberneck. The kid's eyes are bulging out of his head. We got nowhere to go. I feel the kid crawling into me.

Jesus, don't panic. You panic and I'll panic.

As suddenly as we are trapped we are set free. We pop out onto the flagstone porch. The morning sun is brilliant and blinding. My little barnacle peels himself free of me and skitters away, melting into the crowd.

I stand in the brilliant light, collect myself, let my eyes adjust to the light. I feel much better now. I just saved that little fucker's life. Makes me feel just fine.

''Bambi,'' he calls to me again. Charles is touching my elbow. I pull away. I see Rasco walking off the other side of the porch. He's a big kid. He played center on the reserves last year. I was quarterback. I bet he starts varsity this year.

''You got a minute?'' Charles asks.

Boys swirl around us, past us, hopping, leaping, running off the porch, all of us heading back to our cottages. Charles and I are like a pair of stones in the middle of a fast-moving creek.

''Got a minute?'' he repeats. Rasco disappears around behind the dining hall.

''Yeah,'' I say.

We walk off the porch together. We go in the opposite direction that Rasco just went. We walk around the dining hall to the cottage area. I don't feel too weird walking with this guy. That's important to me.

Charles's house, Cottage Twelve, is the second house in. It is right at the crest of the hill. You can see most of the other cottages from his front porch. He stops at the steps leading up to his house. He turns to me, lifts his hands waist high, fingers aimed at me: I think he's going to touch me. He doesn't.

"I would like you to by my commissioner," he says.

I cannot believe my own ears.

"That's right," he says, smiling wide.

I can find no words. This is too good to be true. I want it so bad.

He looks past me at boys traveling past. He waits for me to say something. I am simply dumb. He smiles again.

"I have just informed Langley that I would like you to serve as my commissioner," he says.

Langley is the head counselor in our section. Every section has one.

"Well," he says finally, "do you have anything to say?"

"Sure, sure," I start, hop around on my toes a bit, "sure, sure."

He laughs. His teeth seem too long. I am scared. I have wanted this for so long. This is just a joke. No, it ain't. He means it.

"I—" I start. I don't know what to do, what to say. I'm about to explode. I am so happy. I can't, though. Not in front of him. Shit. Oh, shit.

"Perhaps," he says, "if you have time now . . . ?" He extends his hand in invitation. "We could talk now?"

"Okay," I say.

He turns, heads up the steps to his cottage. I check him out. He's pretty old. Thirty-five, I'd say. Wears thick-lensed glasses, black plastic frames. Sort of pear-shaped. I chuckle to myself: he looks a little like a bowling pin. His shoulders are soft, sloping. No athlete he.

I am watching him and wishing he were better looking.

Actually, it is better he's not.

I cannot believe this. After all these years.

Oh, holy shit. After all these years. Here it is. Can you handle it?

I can handle it. Yes, I can.

I follow him up the steps, oh, holy shit.

He's at the door. He is being terribly gracious. He's holding the door for me.

I am going to explode. I'm too happy. I am about to burst out laughing.

"Thank you," I say, step up and in.

I am the little lost puppy done been found. My entire body is a tail wagging, yes, yes, yes.

10

WE GO INTO HIS OFFICE.

"Here," he says, offering me a seat.

I sit on the loveseat. I scrunch up against the armrest. I pack myself in tight. The plastic cushion pops and farts beneath me. It embarrasses me.

Sorry.

We have these suckers in every building on the grade school side and in every cottage on the high school side. They're brilliant, blinding Day-Glo colors. And noisy! God. The plastic catches on your clothes and body the way a balloon will catch on your hand if you drag your hand across it. *Berr-opp.*

He takes a seat across from me. The window over his shoulder looks out onto the circle drive that runs through the cottages.

His office is just like every other high school counselor's office. The room we sit in is a ten-by-twelve box that doubles as his office and living room. There's a short hallway right here at my shoulder that connects the office with his bedroom in back. He has his own can back there. A can with his own shower. A single-stall shower. Nice having your own private shower.

Charles leans to one hip. His cushion pops and farts under him. He digs out his Zippo. Plink. He opens it with one hand, lights his Camel.

"Smoke?" he offers.

"No thanks," I say. I left my Winstons back at the house.

He wants to talk basics first. Which means talking about how soon before I can move in.

"Right away," I say. "If that's okay with you," I add. I am going to try to get along. I really am.

"Good," he says. "Right away would be fine."

Terrific. The sooner the better, I say.

I thank him for offering me the job. I didn't think I was on the list.

"There really isn't any list," he says. "Counselors recommend boys, but you can hire anyone you want. Unless the kid's a complete screwup," he says.

We both think about that for a minute. It sounds real serious, you know, like terminal. Then he smiles, looking right across this tiny room at me, giving me that smile. "But you're not a *complete* screwup."

I know even as he says it that he is trying to make me feel comfortable. Sorta teasing on me, see? But I take it real personal. I mean, I am a complete screwup.

I see Kuhns and Foster walk past. I see them out the window just over Charles's shoulder. I want to run out to tell them the great news:

Hey, you guys! I've been picked, too. I've just been picked. You guys!

Charles is talking about us working together. We're going to be a team.

Kuhns and Foster pass out of sight. Now I'm like them. Commissioners. We're all three commissioners. And Rasco, too. I like that. I like that a lot.

"You with me?" Charles asks.

"Huh? Oh! Yeah. I'm just all excited," I say, which is true. "Sorry."

He smiles and says it's okay. He says he understands.

"This is a big deal," he says.

I like that.

"Yeah," I agree, "it is." It really is, too.

I look at him. It's odd. I think maybe this guy does understand.

The idea sort of makes me nervous. I don't talk to

counselors or sit in their offices. This ain't exactly my cup of tea, and I'm ready to bolt. In fact, I just want to run out the door and tell someone the good news.

"Listen," he says, "why don't you run along?"

I panic: have I fucked this up already?

No.

He's smiling. He's telling me he can see that I need to get going, that maybe I should just get moved in ASAP, huh?

ASAP?

As soon as possible, he explains.

Right, I say.

I look at him. He *is* a funny-looking guy. Ain't nobody gonna mistake him for handsome, that's for sure.

"All I ask," he says "is that you be open and honest with me. You do that," he concludes, "and we'll get along just fine."

Right.

"Think you can handle that?" he asks.

Sure, I say. Sure.

Okay, he says and leans back in his seat.

We sit here a second, neither of us saying anything. I am about to shit my pants, ya know. It has been seven years. Seven years I've been wanting this. Seven years I've been yearning for this, for exactly this. And here it is. Oh, holy shit. Oh, holy shit.

"Well," he says, lacing his fingers together and lifting them back up over his head, stretching, "let's give her a whirl, eh?"

You bet.

11

SO WE GIVE IT A WHIRL.

I move in right away. Same day, in fact. I throw all my shit in a box, haul ass right on over—The Big Dick's out, up to the field house, so I get away clean, thank you.

And then Charles and I start the process of getting to know you, getting to know all about you—Charles sorta sings it, smiling, making me laugh.

Right.

I feel so comfortable with this guy. It's strange. Not weird strange. Just different strange. I've never known an adult who really wanted to listen to me.

Yeah.

That's it.

Charles really wants to listen to me.

And me, I'm a yakker. Ask Whiteworm. He'll tell you. Yak, yak, yak, Whiteworm says. "Shouldn't call you Bambi," he says, "we should call you Yak."

It's true. I don't know why, don't care to know either. It's just such fun, yakking away. And here's this funny-looking guy just soaking it up, shit. It does stuff to you, someone soaking up your words, it really does.

Like making you feel good. Real good.

Even when it ain't all such wonderful shit you're yakking about. See, I got to telling him about my friend, Kelly Kuhns, how we've been friends now pretty much the whole seven years I've been holed up here. It's that first night, right after night prayers. All the other boys are in bed. It's just me and Charles alone in his office. I tell him about us hibernating, a way back in the olden days, we're just sixth and seventh graders.

Hibernating?

Yeah, in the leaves that blow up against the snow fences?

Yes, he says, he can picture that, too.

Every fall they put up these raggedy, splintery, rust-colored picket fences, snow fences they call them, to catch the drifting snow, I guess. I ain't sure why, exactly. But in the fall, before it snows, it is the leaves, zillions and zillions of fallen, crinkly, crunchy, sweet-smelling leaves that get caught. And Kuhns and I will pile right into them after school, just diving right in, those leaves swallowing you whole and the whole world ceases to exist. It is just you and your own breathing completely engulfed in this wonderful scent, this spine-tingling sound and this funny yellow-orange-burnt umber light softly sifting all about, Oh.

Hibernating, huh?

Yeah. Silly, huh?

I'm all mushy, soft and lovey-dovey here. Kuhns and I, ya know, were best friends. You go and put your arm around each other and just beam you be best friends. Kids do. We did. No sex in it either. Not then.

Later. Our freshman year Kuhns gets all sexed, wants some, no thank you.

Not back then, though.

Later, yes, but not back then.

Our freshman year, it all changes. We all change. That's the year my brother, Matthew, and his best friend, Jordan, and Matthew's counselor, Morton, Lovely Lester Morton, talked me into going out for the wrestling team.

I'm the ninety-nine pound weakling who gets sand kicked in his face at the beach. Only I'd *never* go to the beach. I ain't about to be appearing nowhere in no swim-suit, thank you.

"He got me to, though," I say.

Who, Charles asks.

Morton, I say. Lovely fucking Lester Morton.

* * *

Now, this is important. I'm real surprised here in my being open and honest, you know? I know it is okay to be open and honest about something sweet and wonderful, where everyone is okay. I know most regular adults around here would allow that. But when I start remembering fucking Lovely Lester and his swimsuit shit. . . .

I mean, I hate the fucker.

He got me to work out down there, in his basement, over to my brother's cottage—they had a whole weight room set up down there with weights, benches, mirrors, mats, the whole nine yards. He got me over there alone once. Morton did. Matthew and Jordan weren't with us. Just me and Lester.

What happened? Charles wants to know.

I am fucking fuming here. Can I say this? Dare I say this? Dare I be it?

I am so fucking pissed.

He made me work out in this goddamned skintight swimsuit.

I say it. I tell Charles about the goddamned skintight swimsuit.

Hmmm, Charles goes.

My skin crawls now as I remember. He had me do sit-ups, he wanted to sit on my legs, ya know?

Charles doesn't. He ain't no jock. Doesn't know shit from shinola about working out. I have to explain.

''He's got a bench in his basement,'' I say, ''like they do up to the field house, you know? For bench presses and sit-ups?''

Yeah, Charles says. He knows that bench.

''So I am up to ten pounds, behind my head, see? You hold a weight up behind your head,'' I say and act it out here, acting as if I have a ten-pounder in my hands, lifting my hands up behind my head the way an arrested person or prisoner of war has to do.

Right, Charles goes.

"You sit on the edge of the bench and bend way over backward. You try to touch the back of your head to the floor behind you and then come back up again. It's terrific for your stomach muscles. And you need a strap or a person across your ankles to keep you from flipping over backward, see?"

He does.

I let go here. Somehow I know it is okay to go all the way here. I am so fucking pissed. And it is okay. I sense that.

"All he really fucking wants to do," I say—the sonuvabitch, I see it again, relive it again—I come up, pull myself up, and he's got his grubby hands a way up over my knees. You don't have to be a way up there. Down on the ankles is fine, really. I come up and here he is staring at my fucking nuts, ya know?

I tell Charles.

"All he really wanted was to get into my pants."

I am totally fucked up now. That's what girls say. I am girl. He's trying to get into my pants. Trying to trick me. Boys trick girls.

It is terrifically confusing. The sonuvabitch. A head counselor. Morton. Everyone says all the time what a terrific counselor he is, how he nurtures the great athletes, is an all-around wonderful fellow. And I feel the whore beneath him.

It is pitch black outside Charles's window. Far below I can make out a yellow light from another counselor's office. I'm vibrating here, I'm fucking furious and happy, too. Oh, holy shit. I better get out of here. It's too much. I ain't never let loose like this before. You ain't allowed to dump on no counselor. That is rule number 1A.

I am embarrassed.

I think I'll get on to bed.

Fine, Charles says.

It okay I talk all this stuff? I ask. I am very nervous

about this. Happy, yes, furious, yes, but mixed up some, too.

Charles reassures me it is okay.

I thank him for that.

I scat, get my little ass into bed.

Good night, Mr. Commissioner.

12

CHARLES NEVER MENTIONS MORTON TO ME. I DREAM funny. Morton's in it, but he's my mother, too, and I'm the hot one, hot for him/her: I don't understand it. I wake up worried. Charles will say something. He'll use it on me. You can't go and be that fucking pissed and have nothing come of it. I just know it.

He doesn't. It's as if it never happened.

What he does do is expect me to work with him. In the yard.

I think I will curl up and die.

Yard work.

But I made this decision—I am going to try to get along. I am really going to try.

So when everyone's off to summer school, which is nearly every single boy on the high school side, Charles and I go out to the front yard. It's odd, this summer-school business. The whole place is like a ghost town, not a soul in sight. It is like that a lot around here, this huge expanse of Home and not a soul in sight. Eerie.

Black Jack told me about the summer-school thing once. Black Jack is our dean. Father John's his real name. Everyone calls him Black Jack because he boxed when he was a boy here some nine million years ago. He's got the lethal hands. A pair of black jacks, they say. Put your lights out he put his mind to it.

He *is* tough. He has this terrific scar that runs the entire length of his nose, from his eyebrow all the way down to his left nostril. It looks like a ravine eroded by the rains. It ain't. Old boxing wounds.

He told me they have all the freshmen go to summer school, I had to go when I was a freshman, to help the kids adjust to life on the high school side. That doesn't explain why almost every other kid also has to go.

"Looks pretty bad, doesn't it?" Charles says.

We're at the street surveying our yard.

Yeah, I agree.

It does, too. One, we need rain. Where there is grass it is pretty dry. But then there's this patch of bare earth right under the living room windows. Looks like hell.

Charles walks up the slope, he's going to get a closer look.

"Maybe we could dig it up, replant some?" he says with his back to me.

I hear a cottage door open and shut behind me. I look.

It's Whiteworm. He's alone, has a bat and glove.

I watch my friend for a moment, forgetting Charles. He was my first best friend in Building One. We were just fifth-graders. He taught me how to do fractions that summer, the summer before we started fifth grade. I was so scared. I am every year. Afraid I will fail. Afraid I will not understand and not be able to learn. A fear that makes me sick to my stomach. And he knew it, he noticed it, noticed me and taught me how to add and subtract fractions.

He sent me a used Christmas card in August, just before we started back to school. They save all the cards that come in and then give 'em back to you when you ask for a card to send to your family or friends. They open and read all your mail. Before I got here in '55 they even used to red-line stuff so sometimes you wouldn't know what your dad or mom or sister actually said in the letter because the counselor reading it thought it was bad for some reason. So Whiteworm got a used card from Lyman and sent it to me: "Remember me," he wrote, "I'm the one who taught you fractions." I still have it. I was in bed 66. He was in bed 72.

"Wanna play Home Run Derby?" Whiteworm asks as he reaches me.

"Yes, I do," I say immediately. I turn, look at Charles. He's pretty set on me being out here with him. All morning, I'd say. I turn back to my friend. I feel it again. I've been feeling it for him these past few weeks. God, I want to, oh, how I want to.

"I can't," I say. "Not right now . . ." I finish, nodding up toward Charles.

Whiteworm understands.

"Maybe later," he says.

"Yeah," I say.

He turns around, heads back toward his house. I watch his back. I am fucking faint with desire. Oh, Jesus.

"He's got no one to play with," I say aloud.

Charles stops his fidgeting with the naked spot in our lawn. He looks up to me, then over to Whiteworm, who's already walking up the steps to his house. Charles says nothing. He's got our yard on his brain.

"Flowers?" he asks.

"Huh?" I say. I have to tear my eyes away from my friend. "Flowers?" I look at the spot. "Naw," I say. "Sod. I'd say it needs sod."

I remember the sod truck we saw, I was just a sixth-grader. Sebastian and Mack, my eighth-grade friends, were walking me from church to chow. This open-bed sod truck roars down the highway. It is loaded with thousands and thousands of rectangles of freshly cut sod piled atop one another.

"Pussy lips," Mack sings out, nodding to the truck roaring down the hill.

Sebastian whips his head around, sees the truck, cracks up.

They know.

"What a great idea!" Charles exclaims. "Sod! That's exactly right. But where do we find sod around here."

"I thought you might buy it," I say.

Charles shakes his head. Uh-uh. No money for that.

"There's always the varsity football field," I say just to be saying something. I ain't serious. That's sacred turf. The Old Man's turf. He's the athletic director out here, and next to the Monsignor he's the most powerful person in the place. You don't fuck with the Old Man. Or anything of the Old Man's.

"You're right again," Charles exclaims. "The finest turf in the state," he quotes. It's in our literature, up at the Visitor's Center. I've read it, too. Been on it as well. We sneak out on it sometimes. It's a dream, it's so thick, so rich, so very, very green. We climb over the cyclone fence, run out on it, roll around in it, wrestling, just laying on it, gazing up at the sky—beat it the fuck out of there, the paddy wagon come cruising by. They catch you on it, there is hell to pay.

"You can't be serious," I say to Charles. He's really ruminating on it here.

"It would be fun," he says.

"C'mon," I protest. "They'd kill us."

Which is true. You do not fuck with the Old Man. But Charles is oblivious. He's calculating away.

"We aren't talking about much," he says, pacing it off.

"I'm telling you, they'd *kill* us," I repeat.

"If they knew who to kill," Charles says, smiling wickedly.

"You are serious, aren't you?" I finally realize.

Yup, he says, rubbing his hands together like an excited housefly.

So we plot it. Charles and I. I get our spade out. We can't do it during the day. We decide to wait until dusk. The gloaming, Sebastian calls it. It's one of the reasons I liked Sebastian so much, how he trotted out all these interesting words on me.

I need help.

Charles and I put our heads together: who can we trust? This is a delicate mission.

We have four seniors in the house beside me, five each who are juniors, sophomores, and freshmen—the eighth-graders came over two days after Charles got me in as his commissioner.

I think all the seniors are assholes. Naw. None of them.

Both Charles and I are hot on this new kid, Winston. He's a sophomore, just came from Chicago. He's a beautiful kid. He turns my ass on, you want to know the truth. It's tough. You can't be making any moves on a kid who is in your charge, a kid who is under you. Not fair, that. Besides, I should be over this shit by now. Here I am, a senior, and still walking around with a hard-on for half the kids here. Whiteworm especially. And now this new kid, Winston.

Thank God he's the only one in my house. It is hard enough keeping myself in check with him. He's walking around the house in his bright red, stiff cotton basketball shorts. He wears them all the time. His legs are so lovely. And he hasn't the foggiest. New kids, kids who come to the Home late, like as sophomores or later, they come from out there, from the real world. There are boys *and* girls in the real world. They would never believe you if you were to tell them what really goes on around here. Like Jimmy Sears. He fucking sells it. He will make out with you, no lie, if you pay enough. Rasco told me and Rasco doesn't lie.

Shit. I'd never make out with anyone.

We agree on Winston. He's cool, see? A big-city boy. We figure he will be game. Besides, he doesn't know about the Old Man and his power.

It is almost dark when we set out. Just me and Winston. I am in my second week as commissioner. My second week as commissioner and here I am, slinking through the near dark, my spade and wheelbarrow and new friend, about to vandalize the Old Man's beautiful football field.

It is a lot more difficult that I thought it would be.

We swing a way out around the intramural fields. We come up on the varsity field from behind the wooden scoreboard. The cornfield's at our back. We park the wheelbarrow up next to the cyclone fence, wheeling it in under the trees the Founder himself planted some eighteen years ago.

You cannot see us or our wheelbarrow. We scurry up over the fence and get in under the scoreboard.

"Here." I say.

"Fine," Winston says.

At least we have enough sense not to go digging out in the middle of the goddamn field. I thought about it. The grass is thickest out there. Can you see our asses out on the fifty-yard line?

No one is out. Not even the paddy wagon. No one sees us.

It takes forever. Forty minutes of digging, prying, peeling, lifting, lugging, trying not to drop it—you drop it, it breaks apart, ain't worth shit. We hoist the first chunk up and over: now what?

"Drop it," Winston whispers.

"It'll bust," I whisper back.

I try it anyway. I'm right. It shatters into twelve pieces.

"I'll get over," Winston whispers. "You hand it to me."

"Right."

When we get it loaded up, the wheelbarrow weighs a ton. No lie. We didn't count on this. So it takes us another forty minutes to wheel that mother back around the intramural fields—we are still trying to avoid the road, trying to stay back out of sight. But it is killing us so we finally say fuck it and wheel her right down between Cottage Twelve and Thirteen. The darkness covers us. We make it back to the house, roll up onto the concrete slab that's our back porch, and no one's spotted us.

Winston runs inside and gets Charles. Charles dashes out, spies our load. He's terrifically excited. He says he thought we got caught, we'd been gone so long.

"No shit," I say. I'm dying.

He punches both of us on the arm, nice going, guys. We are all three giddy with triumph and panic—we got to unload this gold and quick!

We roll her around to the front and hurriedly drop the turf in.

Oh, shit.

"It doesn't fit."

It is sticking up. It is so fucking obvious.

We frantically unpack it, shove it aside, careful not to break the chunks apart. Winston and I start digging furiously, trying to quickly deepen our little plot.

"Where do I fling it?" Winston asks. He's got a shovel full of fresh dirt.

"Up here," Charles directs. He's up in the corner, where the outside wall dips back from the living room to Charles's office.

I can't see shit. It is pitch black out now.

"How we doing?" I ask. We've got her dug deeper, got the turf plopped back in.

Winston goes down the slope, lays down in the grass near the circle drive. He surveys the scene.

"It's okay," he announces. "We did good. It looks pretty even now."

Charles and I give it a couple of quick pats with the backs of our spades. I can see Winston's shape in the dark, his bottom lifting up, a nice little melon curve there: think I'll just take a little laydown myself, see for myself, right?

"You can't tell," Winston says. He is lying on his belly. He says it looks even. No one will be able to tell, he says.

"Let me see," I say and saunter down the slope, acting as if I am only interested in this little project. I lie down next to him. My hip barely grazes his. I fill with It. I cannot see for a moment. I do not breathe.

"You're right," I finally force myself to say. As I do, I turn to this beautiful boy and look him right in the eye: he has no idea, none whatsoever.

Damn.

"He's right," I say, tearing my eyes away as I call out to Charles.

I push myself up.

"Looks good," I say, rubbing my hands together.

"Nice work," I say to my new friend, who is still lying in the grass—and oh, I wish he weren't.

"Yep," he says proudly.

This kid. Oh, God. He is good. He is innocent. He has no idea. He would never guess in a million years that we are all queer around here. He does not know that you cannot resist it. Not around here. It is too strong. It is a fragrance upon the air, not to be resisted.

I resist. I tear myself away.

"Better get in," I say.

Winston gets up. We put our stuff away and go inside.

We have done our deed. We three. We have done our deed.

13

THERE IS A SHORT, DISTANT, FURIOUS STORM OVER THE hole dug in the Old Man's perfect football field. By dinnertime someone has found the scar under the scoreboard. The counselors are all talking about it in the counselor's dining hall. The Old Man is stark raving mad about it. Charles tells me about it all tongue in cheek. We are coconspirators.

''Someone's dug up the football field,'' he says to me. It's after chow. We're in his office. I'm in my spot on the loveseat. He's in his up in the corner. We are both still a bit giddy about it all.

I was panicky at first. I heard people speaking of it. People who were aghast. But Charles ain't sweating it. He's just beaming away as he relates the awe and wonder of the other counselors. Everyone is overwhelmed with disbelief. It is a great and violent sacrilege. Someone has desecrated holy ground.

Shit, if I'd had any idea it was this big a deal, you wouldn't have gotten me within a hundred miles of that fucking field.

''We're dead, aren't we?'' I ask. I can't help it. The Old Man. He has his ways. He will find out.

''They will never know,'' Charles says. He is absolutely certain. ''Not in a million years,'' he says with a wink.

This is our little secret.

Winston comes to the door of the office.

''Someone's gonna pay,'' he says. He's one of our

waiters and he's still wearing his waiter's jacket. It's a starched white cotton affair, waist length with a little Nehru collar. Very sexy.

"What's that you say, young man?" Charles asks, feigning total innocence. I admire his theatrics.

Winston smiles his Chicago smile. He shifts his weight from his right hip to his left. The boy is very cool. Has the nice ass, too.

"Everyone's talking about the grass thieves," he says. I tear my eyes off his bum. "Atlas and everyone. His whole crew, they're just buzzing away," he says, his eyes shining, his face lit up with pride and excitement.

Atlas runs the high school dining hall. He's an Indian from Peru. He loves boys, is a great chef, prays all the time and hates communists. He and the Monsignor: "For Gawd and Cunt-tree," the Monsignor muletones it, every month up to the auditorium—he has us in, has the boys in for his monthly chat.

Charles clicks his tongue: ain't it awful?

I look at my new, sexy friend, my friend who has no idea, none whatsoever. Then I look at Charles, my new adult friend. Can this be real? I am so happy. I think this guy Charles is going to be all right.

There is this bond between us now. We have done this thing, this outrageous thing, together. He can be trusted. He is an adult I can trust. It stuns me. He stuns me. He never chastises me. He only encourages me.

Oh, I have to work in the yard every morning, which I hate. Not so much because the work itself is so terrible. I am surprised, in fact, to discover that it is sort of fun. Getting down in the dirt, digging with your fingers, the smell of it right up into your nose—I don't know, it is good. And making the yard look better makes me feel better. Like our stolen sod. That spot does look a thousand percent better. I am proud of that. It is as if I have done something that will last beyond me. You know, the grass will be here next year when I'm gone—and the year after that and the year after that, too.

What I hate is how I can't be with my friends. Kuhns ain't working with Morton every morning. Neither is Foster—he ain't working with his counselor, Marrone. I see them on their way up to the field house every day. Every day inviting me to join them. At first anyway.

"Wanna shoot some baskets with us, Bambi?" Kuhns asks.

Charles looks up from where he's working on the flowers along the edge of the house. Impatiens. We're putting in a bunch of impatiens, pink impatiens, right up along the side of the house. They grow in the shade. They prefer the shade, in fact.

"Sorry," I say to Kuhns. "I can't this morning."

Off they go, no big deal. But by the end of the second week of this gardening routine it is clear that Charles and I are into something different than they are into with their counselors. And they think what Charles and I are into is hilarious. Now they invite me only as a joke, hardly able to contain themselves.

"Can you tear yourself away from your petunias, dear?" Foster asks.

They don't even stop now. They just motor past. I watch them throwing their heads back, having a good laugh.

I'm sorry. I just can't get away. I have this job here. I have my responsibilities.

It ain't easy, though.

I can't get together with Whiteworm either. He's still looking for someone to play Home Run Derby with him. Actually, he is still looking for me to play Home Run Derby with him. And I can't. I have this job, these responsibilities.

God, sometimes I just hate it.

But then at night everything is cool.

We put everyone to bed. Then we go into Charles's office to talk. Or we go into Charles's office to listen to me talk.

It is amazing. I trust this guy. I trust this guy like I

never trusted anyone before. I think he is a real counselor, a good one, too. You know, like he really wants to listen, really wants to understand, really wants to help. It simply amazes me.

He calls it unloading. All these stories about jerkoff counselor after jerkoff counselor, asshole after asshole. Like Lyman Hall, who will nail you for the least indiscretion, his hands flying down and through your face. You even look sideways and his right hand comes flying down and through your cheek. He is quick, lightning fast. He prides himself on his quickness, too. His agility. You fuck up and he fore-hands you, snapping that right hand through your cheek. He catches his swing about shoulder high and brings it back through your other cheek with a blistering backhand. You stand there bleary-eyed, trying to focus through all the stars and stellar dust—and you do see stars when someone clob-bers you like that. Your own spit is flying off your face in a straight line and he is repeating his forehand-backhand combo one more time.

Wham bam.

Wham bam.

I don't know why. He always does it twice.

Up and back.

Up and back.

It makes you want to kill. It doesn't matter, either, whether it is you or one of your friends or some kid you don't even give a shit about. It is just infuriating whenever it happens.

Wyckoff is another one. He was this real skinny guy with the terribly pockmarked face. Rasco used to say Wyck-off got into a pickax fight and he was the only one without a pickax. George Wyckoff and his two-and-a-half inch, silver-star-studded, black leather cowboy belt. George's specialty, when he wasn't working you over with his cowboy belt, was the double splat. He would lurk around the build-ing hoping to catch you goofing around. The moment he does he is all smiles, a-ha! His lips would spread back in a smile that is in perfect sync with his hands lifting up to the tops of his ears. He is going to get you with both hands simultaneously. He is so pleased. His timing is perfect: he lets fly, both hands colliding with opposite cheeks simultaneously. It is murder.

"He got Ezra once," I say to Charles.

Yes?

It was during siesta. Building One kids were called the "Babies" by the other boys. Lyman made us take a nap on Sundays during the school year and every day during the summer. A one-hour siesta. One hour of quiet, in bed. No talking. No fooling around. No getting out of your bed.

Ezra's out of bed, of course. Fooling around.

He's chinning himself along the floor. You lie down on your back on the floor and pull yourself along from bed to bed. It's a great game. See, the beds in the buildings are about two and a half feet apart. Two rows of beds. Thirteen in one row, twelve in the other. Each bed has this bar that runs on either side, a couple of inches below the flat stretch of springs. These two bars connect the foot of the bed to the head of the bed. If you get down on your back on the floor, they're just like chinning bars. You can pull yourself right along—especially if someone's in the bed to anchor it. With a little practice you can learn to traverse the entire length of the dorm in a matter of minutes. It's great fun.

So this is what Ezra's doing one day during siesta. We are in Second Left, which makes us the youngest kids in the building. The babies of the Babies. Ezra's on his back chinning himself along when Wyckoff enters the dorm.

Wyckoff stands in the entryway, sniffing the air. His bug eyes bulge. His huge nostrils flare. The man yearns for trouble.

He spies the beds shimmying to his left.

It's Ezra bopping along, shaking those beds as he comes.

Wyckoff smiles and steps back a foot. This will give Ezra room to shoot out right at his feet when he reaches the last bed at the entryway.

We all hold our breath. We see it coming and can do nothing to stop it.

Wyckoff cocks his hands, his smile widening. He's gleeful as he lifts his fingertips to his ears. The dorm grows uncommonly still.

Ezra's at the last bed. He shoots out. He's oblivious. He has no idea that Wyckoff is waiting. His head shoots out. He's upside down to Wyckoff, who stands over him grinning from ear to ear. Wyckoff leans down into Ezra's face.

"We having some problem today?" he asks just to be asking. He does not wait for an answer. What he does is let fly with both hands. Both those hands he's had cocked up at his ears come flying down and catch Ezra's face between them. The famous double splat. Both hands coming at Ezra's face from either side, those hands tracing a short, quick arc through the air, a tiny parenthesis in the air—and boom! both hands smash into Ezra's face simultaneously, one on either cheek.

All twenty-four of us gasp and leap in our skins. Ouch.

He made Ezra cry.

No one makes Ezra cry.

"He had a headache," I tell Charles, "the whole rest of the day, too." I can still see Ezra's startled look, his blood-red cheeks. And the power of the double-handed pop slammed his head against the floor—that solid, sickening sound of human head against tile-covered concrete haunts me. Jesus.

I tell Charles about St. Martin, too. I'm in my pjs now. Charles suggests to me one night, "Why don't you shower with the rest of the guys and get into your pajamas before we have our talks? Hmmm?"

Huh?

He explains. He's real good at explaining things to me.

"It's pretty late when we finish up in here, right?"

Right, I say.

"So, it will save you time and you won't need to make all that noise after everyone's in bed."

I don't see how it's going to save time, really. But it is terrifically, uproariously noisy when I'm showering at eleven or so.

So I agree. No sweat.

I'm in my pjs now—I wear my underwear underneath, thank you. I'm in my flimsy, six-thousand-year-old pjs, simply full of St. Martin.

"Who?" Charles asks, smiling. Saint?

I tell him. St. Martin. That's what we called him because he was so holy. All the time praying, clicking his beads. All the time telling us how unworthy he was, what a wretched sinner he was.

"I couldn't take it," I say. "I told him once that he was wrong. That he was really a holy guy. You know what he said to that?"

No, what? Charles asks.

"He said, 'If I am a holy man, then the streets of hell are lined with angels.' "

Charles gives a little laugh. Ain't no great shakes to him, I guess. It sure struck me.

"He's the one who made us give him swats," I go on.

Tell me, Charles says.

I like that. Charles wants to know.

"He made us punish him," I say.

Charles nods.

I go on. Me and Ezra and this other kid who is long gone now, we were fooling around in the Tin Room. The Tin Room's really just a coatroom, this tiny railroad car of a room with two rows of open wooden lockers facing each other. Originally the wooden lockers were made out of metal—they still are over to Building Two. That's why they're called tin rooms. You share a locker with another kid, hanging your coat or whatever on the hooks above, shoving your shoes in below. Each kid has a drawer for his shit, like marbles before Lyman outlawed them, pens, pencils, prayer books, rocks, gopher collars, and shit like that.

The lockers only stand six foot tall and they're completely open on top. So you can walk around on top if you want—only we are not allowed, of course. But that's what we were doing, messing around on top. Ezra's acting the monkey for real, ooh-ooh-ooh-ing around, scratching himself up under his arms, slapping down at us, snapping us with his fingertips, then leaping away when we try to retaliate. We're making a whale of a ruckus.

Martin was on duty. He'd come in two or three times already telling us to cool it. We didn't.

He comes in again and tells us, "This is it."

This is when he has us give him swats.

I say it and see Martin's naked back. His skin was so white, white like the underbelly of a bullhead down to the lake. There was this solitary black mole up near his shoulder blade. It had two unusually long black hairs jutting out of it.

"You had to give him swats?" Charles asks incredulously.

"Yeah," I say, "he came in for the fourth time and told us, 'This is it, boys, I have given you fair warning,' and we're getting ready to go on work crew or get swats or something when he launches into his unworthiness bit, telling us again how unworthy he was, what a wretched soul he was, what a miserable sinner he was and that our disobedience, our disrespect, is proof of his unworthiness in the eyes of God. It was amazing. He stood there and lectured us, telling us that should we so easily disregard him, that should we so quickly disobey him was proof, absolute proof, that he was this wretched sinner in need of mortification. So we had to mortify him."

God. It was pretty sickening. It is.

"Can you believe it?" I ask. I am incredulous. It was awful.

Charles surprises me, nodding. "Yes, Fred, I can believe it."

For a split second here I think Charles is going to go off on some "oh-how-unworthy-I-am" crap. In his eyes. Woeful. In his eyes. Baleful. In his eyes, something swimming, liquid, lost.

Whoa. All of a sudden I feel dizzy, like when you shoot up out of your chair all of a sudden and it takes a second to get over the lightheadedness. Whoa.

I do not look at him. He's saying something. I cannot listen. This speck of dust on the coffee table here is suddenly damned interesting. See it? I study it, fleeing my own panic. See it? In this light, the dim, yellowed light coming off Charles's lamp, I can make out three dimensions in this mote of dust. I like that. It soothes me to be able to see its angles.

Then I remember Kaufman. Kaufman was this weird kid who was in Building One with us. He used to pick dust motes out of the air. We saw it in a movie about a crazy kid who'd sit in a shaft of sunlight picking the dust motes out of the air. Kaufman started doing that. Picking dust motes out of the air and putting them on his tongue just like the crazy kid in the movie. Kaufman. He's the kid that Wyckoff really did in.

Charles is repeating himself, huh?

"How did he have you mortify him?"

I get a chill at the base of my spine. It leaps and races to my skull.

"On his back," I say. "On his bare back with his own belt."

I remember it.

"It was this little skinny, imitation-leather belt. A plastic belt that sort of stuck to his skin with each swat. Five swats from each of us. Three of us. Right up across his shoulder blades."

I can see Martin's single black mole. It stood out so. His skin so sickly white. His ribs sticking out in back. He was a very skinny guy.

I shiver. It starts at the tips of my elbows. It shakes me and ripples into my belly.

Booga booga.

I don't feel too good.

I shiver again. This one begins at my belly and shakes its way out to my elbows.

I have nothing more to say.

"I'm sorry," Charles starts. He's leaning forward in his seat. I think he is about to be all understanding and shit.

Not now. Please.

He opens his mouth to speak. I bolt from my seat. It startles both of us.

"Sorry," I say. I don't mean to startle you.

I stand before the loveseat a moment. My head hangs down. I am ashamed. I need to get out of here.

"No, no, no, no," Charles sings softly. Trying to be sweet. I can feel it.

I am no good. I know that.

I gotta get out of here.

I do.

I hustle my little ass right on into bed.

I feel odd. I feel naked, weepy, antsy. It is as if I need to shake something off. It is how I feel after I wrestle in the grass and get all itchy. That's how I am now, all itchy.

I yank the covers up to my chin.

Ain't enough.

I yank them up over my head.

I pray. I say the guardian angel prayer Brother Francis made up. He's up to the clinic. Matthew told me he was okay.

Dear angel sent me from above
Please guide me through the day;
Hold tight my hand
And help me love
My Savior as I pray.
My thoughts and words so purify
My actions make so kind;

And lead me so that when I die
My Savior I will find.

I finish my prayer. Then I jack off and fall asleep.

14

JACKING OFF IS A MORTAL SIN.

Pounding the pud. Flogging the log. Beating the meat.

A grievous offense against God.

Who's fucking unworthy?

I do not go to mass. I am blackened with sin. All my goddamned life, no shit, since I am too young to know, I am scooting on my sheets. It's the only way I know to put myself to sleep.

Lies. Lies. Lies.

It is not the only way. You're just weak.

I am weak. Weak and spineless. I am no good.

Bless me, Father, for I have sinned. It has been one week since my last confession. I have had impure touch with myself sixteen million times and with others twice.

Say four Hail Marys and make an act of contrition.

Oh my God I am heartily sorry for having offended Thee.

Do you want to know the truth? Do you?

I did it with Ezra after he lost his leg. Right out in front of the house, The Big Dick's house, one night right after confessions. No lie.

I've been delirious for Maya, too. Been out of my mind hot for him since at least the sixth grade—he's the kid who was monkeying around on top of the Tin Room lockers with me and Ezra that time we had to mortify St. Martin.

Kuhns tells me my freshman year, "He's been plenty hot for you, too."

Maya? You shitting me?

"No shit," he says. "You remember that night they woke you up?"

Yeah, I remember. We were eighth-graders. It was March. Freezing black blowing March.

"Yeah, I remember," I say. "So?"

"They didn't want to wake you, Ezra told me. They were doing you. They'd done you before, too, only this time you woke up."

Sonuvabitch.

I remember Maya's hand sliding across my mattress. I thought it was a tarantula. Damn near had a heart attack.

"That's the night we went and took everyone's covers off and threw open all the windows," I say.

"Yeah, I remember," Kuhns says with a big grin. "Dumbshits. You took everyone's covers but your own. Geez. I wonder who did this?"

Yeah, I laugh. And Swift had us into the office afterward, got all flapdoodle, and asks us: "You weren't doing it, were you?" Good old dumbshit Bambi: "Oh, no, of course not," I say.

Maya's gone now. He was the first one I ever did it with. Finally. Everyone else had been at it for years. Or so it seemed. I was hot for him right up to the very end, when he went AWOL. Too much queering, he said. I'd tried it with him when we were just beginning our junior years, almost a year ago. No more, he told me. We're too old, he said. So he ran away to escape it. Ran away and never came back. Not like most kids who take off—they usually get caught and brought back within twenty-four hours. Then they make you wear cutoffs and stand at meals.

God, I wish Maya hadn't gone.

Maya. Ezra. Kuhns. Rasco.

Everyone's doing it. Everyone, I tell you.

Bless me, Father.

Fuck.

Shoot me, Father.

If everyone is doing it, then everyone is confessing it, yes?

So what are all these priests doing with all this overwhelming evidence?

Shoot me.

''Wanna play Home Run Derby?''

I check with Charles. We've pretty well got the yard licked. The stolen turf is sunk in now. It's not so obvious anymore. No one even put two and two together all this time—I thought it was pretty obvious. For two or three fucking weeks it is sitting up above the rest of the turf—even after we deepened the hole—looking like a newly dug grave.

''You can go ahead,'' Charles permits.

So we do. We play Home Run Derby. Roger Maris and Mickey Mantle. I pitch. He hits. He stays at bat as long as he's hitting the ball, a hard ball, over the fence, a softball field fence. Anything but a home run is an out.

Just the two of us.

Out here all alone, just we two and the summer wind, the corn coming up behind us:

''Stay out of the cornfields, boys-a,'' the Monsignor says once a month.

No one ever does it in the cornfields, Monsignor.

Just the two of us. No talking. Just pitching, hitting, shagging.

He ain't even beautiful. Has a funny build actually.

No ass. None to speak of.

Long legs. Long arms. Long fingers.

Long white worm.

Pale boy.

Long face. Long, skinny body.

I could eat you, boy.

I pitch.

He hits.

I pitch.

He hits.

I pitch.

He hits.

Two grounders and a short fly ball.

My turn.

He pitches.

I hit.

Charles leaves the house at noon. Chow is at twelve-thirty.

We see him leave. We return to the house. Just we two.

We do not talk.

I quiver, quake.

"Wanna watch Dick Van Dyke?" I ask, walking to the TV set.

I see Charles walk up the back steps of the dining hall. He steps inside. Just we two.

"Yeah," he says, hardly able to speak.

Long, pale boy.

I flip on the set and return to the couch. I sit next to him. I sit at one end of the three seater, plastic-cushioned, Day-Glo blue couch. He sits in the single-seater, plastic-cushioned, Day-Glo orange easy chair.

Who needs to breathe?

He is large. In his jeans which are not Levi's. Our seats touch. There are a pair of armrests between us, his and mine.

He is large.

We do not speak.

I reach. I reach over, cover one fourth of the distance between us, my fingers aimed at his large. I stop just at his armrest and wait. Gimme a sign. A rejection. A go-ahead.

Nothing.

He is large. A large white worm. It is filling his jeans, lifting his zipper.

I am all blood.

I reach to him and let my fingers dangle just above his pants. I do not touch. I wait.

Whiteworm stares dead ahead. Dick Van Dyke, Mary Tyler Moore, Carl Reiner.

I move. That hand of mine is moving. There is deep agony in my shoulder as I move my hand while trying to not move anything else as if nothing else is going on. I am above him now. My fingers touch him through his soft cotton jeans which are not Levi's.

It is good. I am wet.

He sucks his belly in. My hand is atop his zipper. His belly is sucked in, the skin there dropping away from his belt. There's a space there. It is thick enough for a hand, for my hand. There is a darkness there, his belly is sucked, inviting, inviting, come in son some in come.

I suck my breath, slide my hand back, I'm reaching back, going for the darkness, trying to reach that space he's opened without moving my shoulder, trying only to move my hand from my wrist only, I can't, I can't, oh, can't make it, I must move my elbow, there, yes, yes, back, back, oh, yes, and reach, there. I slide and his hand is moving. It is disembodied, alive, on its own, coming directly to me, on me. I am sucking wind now, sucking belly muscles, room, room! Make room. His long fingers slide down, in, under, the elastic stopping him, his fingernails are long, I have none, I have him in my hand oh jesus fucking christ he is magic, his long long fingers to me, holding, squeezing, sliding, I want to lick, my mouth waters, we do not speak.

15

It is the last day of July when I play Home Run Derby with Whiteworm. We play again and again the first three weeks in August. Each time it is more difficult to stay on the diamond until noon when Charles leaves for lunch. Never do we speak of this thing we do. I feel like whipping him.

I watch him in the dining hall. I watch him when he is not looking my way. I watch him and wonder. Sometimes he will look at me and catch me staring, catch me wondering. I look away and fill with shame.

I am shame.

Maya was right. We're too old for this shit. He's probably out there right now, out there somewhere in the Windy City, another Chicago boy humping some girl, being normal.

I don't know.

I fear Charles knows what we are up to. I am terribly ashamed and too hot to stop. He will leave for chow and Whiteworm and I are already in front of the tube. *The Dick Van Dyke Show* hasn't even started yet.

Charles comes out of his office, walks past the entryway into the living room, where Whiteworm and I sit side by side. We are sitting too close. He suspects. He knows. I can tell.

''See you later,'' he says to us.

I grunt um— I dare not speak. I cannot speak. My tongue is thick. I dare not look at him either. He will read my mind, I know.

I wonder how this thing with Whiteworm starts. Is it because of Beaudene?

Charles exits. The door sucks wind as it shuts behind him.

I look at Whiteworm. He stares straight ahead. Staring straight ahead and waiting. Waiting on me. All I have to do is reach.

So I do.

I reach.

I reach and do him once. Do him twice.

And I wonder. How did this thing start? Is it Beaudene?

Beaudene was this kid we both liked as sophomores. Beaudene was a sophomore, too, only he was a year and a half older than Whiteworm, two years older than me. Whiteworm's exactly six months older than me. My birthday's June 3. His is December 3.

Beaudene was a real muscle boy, a weight lifter. And he was lightning fast. So fast he started as a halfback on the varsity his sophomore year. He could run like the wind.

He made a ring for Whiteworm that year, our sophomore year. This was the first year I really understood that everyone was doing it. He made a ring out of a dime he hammered out in sheet metal class.

Then he went for me.

It was the same kind of feeling I had for Sebastian when I was just a fifth-grader and Sebastian was an eighth-grader. It was my first year here. Me and Sebastian. Holding hands in the movies.

Sebastian was in Building Four. I was in Building One. His building sat right behind my building in the movies. So I'd race over to the auditorium and get a seat right in the middle of our last row. Building One, we had the youngest kids, we're the Babies, so we had the first nine rows in the middle section, right down front. Sebastian would already be sitting right in the middle of his building's first row. So I'd sit down right in front of him. When the movie'd start he would lay his hand over the back of my seat. His beautiful, piano-player fingers are sitting right there by my cheek.

The lights are low, the film's flashing on the screen, and I take his hand in mine. Sometimes I even put it to my cheek.

I loved Sebastian. Sebastian loved me.

It ain't queer.

I ain't queer.

Right.

Tell us another one, Fred.

Fred the Fairy.

In the movies I am holding Sebastian's hand close to my cheek. I fill with love. Chills traverse my entire body. It is wonderful.

God. Sebastian and Mack. What a pair.

The way I met them, made friends with them, was during a half-court game up to the gym. A bunch of us Babies of Building One were playing with Lyman. Lyman is fast-breaking us to death. Lyman Hall, the fucking tarantula, no lie. The hairiest bastard I'd ever seen. It's on his arms, his legs, his chest—he's just matted with this furry black wire, hustling our asses up and down that court: Hustle! Hustle! Hustle!

I am open in the corner. Lyman's out front with the ball, just above the key. He fakes to me, feints toward Maya over in the far corner, whirls back around my way, and fires that CYO all-leather game ball straight at me.

It is the famous Lyman Hall double-handed push pass.

Bambi's first encounter.

I am not prepared. I thought he was going to Maya.

"Freddy boy!" he whoops gleefully.

I eat leather. The ball smashes me full fucking force straightaway in the chops. It smashes my bottom lip through my teeth. I am an explosion of snot. There are stars and stellar dust everywhere. My nose is flattened. I taste salt.

Lyman Hall's electric lightning doubled-handed push pass.

I have seen him deliver it to other boys since.

I flee the court weeping. I find myself in the locker room slamming locker door after locker door. I am humiliated, enraged, and unable to stem my tears. My face is full of it—I cannot see for all the fucking tears. Visions of murder dance in my head. I am smashing his fucking nuts in a giant garlic press Atlas has over to the dining hall.

I sit down on the bolted-to-the-floor wooden locker-room bench. I put my face in my hands and weep.

Buh-wooop.

The bench dips beneath me: *buh-wooop.*

I take my hands from my face. My hands are wet and soggy. My face snotty, weepy. Baby Bambi.

I jam my tears. Pull myself together.

It's Sebastian. He's sitting right here next to me. Sebastian, CYO star. First-string guard. High scorer. And the most beautiful boy on the grade school side.

I clear my throat.

His best friend, Jimmy Mack, he's here, too. Giant, gorgeous, six-foot-one-inch Jimmy Mack, his jet black self glistening in his own perspiration, stands in the doorway. He is filling it. He is naked save for his white gym shorts with the purple BH on his thigh—BH: Boy's Home. He's got his arms lifted. He is a giant ebony cross barricading the door. A boy with a perfect, natural build. Ain't never had to work out.

He's a CYO star, too. Starts at center. Has the greatest smile.

"Guy's a fucking asshole, ain't he, Bambi?" he says to me.

"A gen-u-wine prick," Sebastian adds.

It startles me. Two stars paying me mind. I don't know what to say. Mack's the one who named me Bambi. I'd run past them when they are standing in formation before chow. Zoom zoom zoom. I'd run past them coming out of the auditorium. Zoom Zoom. I'd run past them on the way to church. Zoom.

"Hey, Bambi!" Mack would call out as I zoom by. Calling me Bambi and laughing. Laughing at me. Just making fun of me. Right? Right? Don't call me that. Bambi's a deer with big buck teeth.

"No, no, no," Sebastian would tell me. "Mack's calling you Bambi because every time we see you, you're running like a deer."

"Right," Mack says, still laughing.

"What're ya laughing at now?" I challenge.

"Come on, little deer," Sebastian says sweetly.

"I ain't no dear," I say.

"Running, leaping," Mack says.

"Dashing, darting," Sebastian says.

"Just like a deer, Bambi," Mack says with that great smile of his.

Yeah? Honest? You guys aren't just making fun of me? Honest?

Honest, Sebastian says, crossing his heart.

We *like* you, you little shit, Mack says.

Oh.

Okay, then.

And it sticks.

Bambi. Bambi Gambi. Gambi Bambi.

Sebastian sits silently, patiently next to me here on the bench. I look at him. He is a perfect beauty. I am falling in love. He's got the perfect, flawless complexion, his skin like caramel satin. His cheekbones lift, have this sculpted look. And his eyes. His beautiful amber-whiskey colored eyes. Luminous eyes. A great doe's eyes bathing me here, right this minute, soothing me here, this very minute. There is love in those eyes. Love for me in those beautiful eyes.

He reaches toward me with his lovely piano player fingers. He reaches toward me but does not touch. He is careful. Tender.

"You okay?" he asks after a long silent moment.

I snort my own goobers and wipe my nose on my arm. Great move. Now I've got goobers on my arm *and* on my face.

"Here," Mack says, tossing me a roll of toilet paper. It is as if they have come prepared.

Sebastian snatches it out of the air. He catches it right in front of my face. He rolls off a half-dozen squares and hands them to me.

I take them and dry my face. I wipe my nose and arm, too.

''I hate him,'' I say suddenly.

Neither of them says a word.

I panic. Lyman would kill me if he heard.

I look up, filling with fear.

''It's okay, Bambi,'' Mack says. ''He ain't nowhere near us,'' he finishes, reading my mind, I think. ''You're safe with us,'' he says.

My body fills with this buzzing that ain't so great at first. I seem to expand under my skin. I look from Mack to Sebastian. Mack's smiling. Sebastian watches my face. He is so intent. Shit. Two stars taking care of me. I get brave.

''Cocksucking motherfucking sonuvabitch,'' I spit out.

''How you talk, Bambi,'' Mack says, throwing his head back, laughing.

Sebastian relieves me of the wad of messy tissue I'm still holding. He offers me another batch. It makes me think of my mom.

''Ready?'' Mack asks.

What?

I look at Sebastian, then at Mack. Ready for what? You guys gonna make me?

Mack gives Sebastian a nod. They have worked something out here beforehand.

I gulp.

Sebastian speaks. Softly, tenderly, the way you'd talk to an infant: ''We thought,'' he starts, articulating each word carefully, ''you might like to play a game of twenty-one with us.''

I am relieved. Flattered. Excited.

''With you guys?''

Mack laughs. ''Told you,'' he says to Sebastian.

''Okay,'' Sebastian says, starting to get up.

''Lookit Bambi,'' Mack says, pointing, smiling plenty.

The heat has filled my face. I've been so dumb here about acting like a fan, fawning over the stars. I am a beet. These guys are stars.

"C'mon," Sebastian says, tapping the bench next to me. He's up. I get up and follow them back up onto the court. Lyman is still out here, fast breaking all over the court, still trying to dominate the boys, which he does—all except for Maya. Maya's too swift, too agile, too fleet-footed, here again, gone again. With his pretty little jumper, his toes pointed, he's six inches off the floor, which is a bunch, flicking the ball off of his fingertips. It's in the wrist. *Swish.*

We are invisible to Lyman, me and my two new friends. Which is fine by me. Just fucking fine.

Sebastian never got funny. Neither he nor Mack ever tried anything. I never worried about it either, even though I was really and truly in love with Sebastian. Matthew never batted an eye. Here's Fred and his new love, Sebastian, going everywhere together. We'd walk to mass together. We'd walk back to chow together, back from the movies together—talking, talking, talking. Walking along bumping into one another, shoulders ka-boom, oops, ha ha. For that whole year, Sebastian's eighth-grade year, we had a love, oh, we had a love. Then he and Mack moved over to the high school side and they split, went AWOL, I don't know why, never to return.

It is something like this, how I felt for Beaudene. He gave me the ring he had hammered out of a dime for Whiteworm. He even made a point of telling me he had made it for Whiteworm but that now he wanted me to have it. Which made me a bit nervous. I didn't think it was such a nice thing for him to be announcing the transfer, ya know? He'd plead with me to tell him I was his best friend and that nobody else was. Which I did. Which wasn't too hard.

I let him give me all my haircuts that year. He was in barbering then and had his own tools. He'd bring them back to the cottage for the weekend, come over on a Saturday afternoon, and do me. We'd set up a chair in the study hall, The Big Dick's study hall. He'd wrap that barber's cape around my neck and lean in real close, so close I am getting chills, so close he's grazing my cheek with his. I am letting him do it. I am wanting it, too. Scared, yeah, but letting it happen too—I'm safe here in The Big Dick's study hall.

We never spoke a word of this touching. If you don't talk about it, you can pretend it isn't happening, that it isn't real, that you aren't the fucking fairy you know you are.

He got caught queering with this kid named Em, an Indian boy from Building One with me and Ezra and Kuhns and Whiteworm. They kicked Em out. They do that if they catch you queering: kick you out. Only they didn't kick Beaudene out. Just Em, who everyone either hated or feared—he was ugly, pock-marked, and mean most of the time. I could never feature it, Beau doing it with him.

Beau got funny after this. As he should, we both agreed. Clearly this was an unfair thing that had happened to Em. I was glad, though. I was really afraid of Em. He's the kind of guy I thought wouldn't have any problem forcing you to do it if he felt like it and had the right opportunity.

Beau invited me for a walk after Em got the boot. We went for a long walk, we went all the way down to the *V* between the two tiny creeks that run into the southernmost diamond point of the Home's property—the Home is one square mile that is set like a diamond if you view us from the air on a regular north-south map. We do this a lot, walking, talking, bumping shoulders, being together. But this time he gets funny. He is fumble-mumble with his tongue and words. I know something's up—and it hits me like a ton of bricks: he's been doing it with Whiteworm. They're in the same cottage. They've been best friends. This ring. This fucking ring.

We are standing on the edge of the water.

"I brung you down here to ask you . . ." he starts, stumbling, fumbling, mumbling the words.

I know what's coming.

Oh, don't. Please, don't.

He's studying the grasses, weeds, and shit at his feet. I watch him carefully. He looks up. He is looking right at me now.

He's got the Charles Atlas body. He's a heavy-duty weight lifter. He's really muscle-bound, blown up all over just a bit too much.

He's got this Charles Atlas body and he's looking at me the way the skinny wimp in the ad looks. He is tiny, mousy, frail, fragile, afraid.

He's working on it. It is very difficult for him to get the words out. I know what he is about to say. I am not helping him one bit. No, I am not.

"I brung you down here to ask you . . . to ask you to do it with me," he finally manages to say. He drops his eyes to the grass. Then he lifts his eyes to me: he's got the wimpy puppy-dog eyes.

I am terrified.

He is stronger than me. He is bigger than me. He is faster and quicker than me. He is hornier than me.

Is he going to force me? Can I get the fuck out of here?

I take a step backward. I find my voice.

"I'm sorry, Beau. I don't feel that way toward you, I'm sorry. I just don't."

Kuhns did this to me, too. It was our freshman year. The asshole asks straight out. I do not understand. People are so brazen.

It is after one of Father Leaver's movies. He was our dean our freshman year. Every high school section has a dean. He was this real short guy, hardly five foot. And mean and mad most of the time. I lived in his house at the end of the year on account of Daly firing me and having me moved out.

He had two little nasty Pekinese. They were fierce little fucks. In the morning when we'd get up, we had to be perfectly quiet because Father liked to sleep in. So we had to be perfectly quiet so as not to waken his two little nasty Pekinese. If you woke them they'd go hysterical at the crack under his door, screaming and yapping and yiping away and wake Father up. And then he'd come out and raise holy hell with everybody, his two little nasty Pekinese loose and bit-ing on everyone, no lie. They'd go for your ankles and just sink their little fucked-up teeth right into you—and you can't kick their asses away, right? or Leaver'd kill you. Amazing.

Anyway, Leaver wanted his boys to love him. So he would rent full-length movies and show them on the wall of his study hall. He'd have all the freshmen over. All one hundred and sixteen of us packed into his study hall. Here we are, asshole to elbow: that study hall ain't nothing but wall-to-wall bodies.

It's *The Jolson Story.* I'm lying under one of those monstrous wooden study-hall tables—the kind you'd find in a library somewhere, big enough for eight people to sit around. I'm under there with Maya. Maya who I have been delirious for for two years now. Two mouth-watering maniacal, frothing-at-the-mouth years. And here we are, side by side.

Tonight. Tonight. Tonight won't be just any night.

Kuhns, the asshole, he's lying on top of this table. He drops his goony head over the edge. He's upside down. There's a vein bulging and about to burst that runs from his eyeball to his crown.

''Wha'choo guys up to? Hmmm?'' he asks with such filth in his mouth I almost lose my golden opportunity.

Forget you, shit-for-brains, I say.

Then the lights go down.

The lights go down and we become spoons. Me to his back. Me rolling softly, slowly into him, inching in, can I? May I? Oh, please.

When the lights go back up, it's time to change reels, boys rub their eyes all around the room and you can almost taste the jism, its scent is so strong upon the air.

Maya. My, my Maya.

Not two days later Kuhns is asking straight out.

I don't know shit. People just up and ask. Period.

Kuhns does.

We are walking back from chow. I'm still stunned about doing it with Maya. Maya, pretty little jump-shot Maya. After all these years. I've been hounding that guy, chasing him around the apartment up to the building, jumping on him, pounding, wrestling, never actually having the nerve, ya know . . . Wow. Me and Maya. Kuhns is walking next to me. The sun is on our faces. Sunny summer afternoon. We're freshmen now. Hotshits. He stuns me. He just asks.

"Will you do it with me, Bambi?"

Huh? How can this be? I do not understand. I don't feel that way toward you. How can you feel that way toward me? I have done something wrong, haven't I? I just know I have.

So I am apologizing.

"Sorry, Kelly, sorry. I just don't feel that way about you."

I have done something wrong. It is my fault he feels this way toward me. I know. My tiny little ninety-eight-pound soul is all jacked up here—it is just like it was with Beau down to the creek.

I miss a step, check out my friend Kelly Kuhns. I am ready to fight. I am ready to be had, want it or no. He's bigger, quicker, tougher. Oh. I am getting sick here, sick with fear and dread, he's gonna—

Then Kuhns surprises me.

"Okay," he says, shrugging. "No big deal. Just thought I would ask."

So now it's a year later and it's my friend Beau who is doing this to me. Only this time we're a way out here in the boonies, in the southernmost corner of the Home.

"I'm sorry," I say again, lame, terrified still.

"I'm heading back to the house," I say. I back away trying to empty my mind of the word—it—fearing my best friend, he's gonna take me, I just know it.

The sun is funny now. The light is too high. My forehead is moving on its own here. I back away. I apologize. I am all the fucking time apologizing: sorry. I just don't feel that way toward you.

Sebastian never did this to me.

I am furious with Beaudene.

It was physical with Sebastian. He never did this to me.

Beau stands before me, immobile, his toe messing with the shallow water. He is not looking at me. I am dying for fear. I will not turn my back: I back away, back away.

"Sorry, Beau. Really, I am. Beau?"

He studies his toe in the shallow water. His shoe's getting soaked. Mr. Charles Atlas is really just a skinny kid getting sand kicked in his face.

When I'm fifteen feet back I turn and run. Up the hill to the water tower next to the grade school ball diamonds. I am safe. I look back. He's not there. He's gone. Where? Where is he? I scan the cornfield just behind the creek and spy him racing lickety-split out on Conley Road, the Home's boundary. I watch him run. Relieved and brokenhearted—that powerful boy, all those muscles, and for what?

The third time Whiteworm and I play Home Run Derby we go over to the field house. We are not talking about it. We are having trouble concentrating on the game. It's only eleven-thirty, the chimes, count 'em: *dong dong dong; dong* dong dong *dong*.

"Wanna wrestle?" I ask.

He nods his head, swallows.

Up we go to the mat. We kneel, me riding, on his right. I always ride from the right. He is putty. It amazes me. Do with me as you wish. Do me. Trembly weak, both of us. I tug, how you do when the ref blows the whistle, Ready? Wrestle! I tug. He collapses into me. My riding hand slides down, finds him, I ride up behind him. I hold him in front, ride up his crack behind, it is ten milliseconds, I am done.

Shame.

I scoot away from him quickly. I rush to the drinking fountain. He ain't had his yet. He follows me to the fountain, he's leaning out, leaning a way out, to me, wanting, wanting, not understanding, we done? I am disgusted. He disgusts me. His neediness. My own goo, my own desire spent, *finie:* leave me be you fucking queer. I flee from him. I charge to the steps leading down to the intramural courts.

Charles is standing there, at the visitor's door that looks in on where the boys play intramurals. He sees me, looks at me, looks past me, above me. Whiteworm is there, above me, frustrated, leaning out, leaning a way out toward me, perplexed, lost, wanting his. I am cruel. Cruel, caught, found out. Cannot stop.

Beaudene ran away after our time at the creek. He came to my house that evening acting all nervous Nellie. He is terribly preoccupied with the pebbles on the porch. He is not looking at me. He tells me he is taking off.

"AWOL?" I ask.

He's working a pebble around the porch, two, three, kicking them.

"You're going AWOL? Not coming back?"

I am wicked. I am relieved.

"Yeah," he says. He looks at me now for the first time since he called me out—you are not allowed in anyone else's cottage. You come to the door, call them out.

"Yeah," he says, "and I was wondering, uh, you know, wondering if . . ."

"Yeah? What? Go on, ask."

I really want him to ask. Whatever it is. He is still that little lost boy, all his muscles for naught. He's a deflated child who can't have what he wants. He's been hurt—by me, by his counselor who caught him doing it with Em, who kicked Em out and not Beau. The counselor is oblivious. He worships Beau and doesn't know it is eating Beau up.

"You've got two letter jackets," he starts.

"You can have one," I say quickly, "honest. Sure. I'd love to give you one." I have two. I lettered as a freshman. I wrestled varsity at ninety-five pounds.

"Really? I was afraid to ask, after this afternoon," he says. He looks up at me, fills with shame immediately, and looks back to the porch, searching for those pebbles. He can't find 'em.

"I can't stay here anymore," he says with finality. "I'll take your old one, okay?"

I like the old one best. The new ones have a crummy style. The new ones have the shoulders sewn on like tubes attached to a sleeveless vest. I look awful in it. It makes me look real puny. The old ones, though, they have a different style. The shoulders start up at the neck, up at the collar. There are three seams running out and down from the neck. It gives you, even a tiny little fuck like me, that bruiser look.

"No. Take my new one."

"I can't—"

"Sure you can," I say. I explain to him how silly and puny I look in the new one. You know, with this wimpy build and all, right? He laughs. He knows about my wimpy build all right. Okay, he says, still smiling. I go get it.

"Here," I say when I bring it out. "It's still in its cellophane. I've never worn it." I meant it when I said I didn't like the new style.

"You mean it, don't you?" he says, reaching for it. "You don't like it, do you?"

Nope, I say. I take it out of its cellophane wrapper. They're wrappers just like the clear plastic wrappers you have on your dry cleaning when you get it back. I hold it for him to step into. I stumble some, miss his right hand a couple times before we get it on him. It even looks a little funny on him. His shoulders do fill it out better than mine do, though. I was right about that. My wrestling insignia is clipped on my letter. He's trying to get it off, can't.

"Naw, leave it," I say. "I got one on my old jacket. You can put your football insignia on, too."

He whirls. He looks good in it. Likes it, too, that's clear.

"You mean it?" he asks in the middle of a little whirl. "I can take this one?"

"Yep."

We stare at each other. What a couple of gorps we are. A couple of fool-child assholes who don't know shit from shinola about the real world. He's about to run off into it, back to his dad, who doesn't give two rats' asses about him nohow. At least my dad comes out for passes, writes now and then. But then Dad lives right in Dayton, close enough to visit. Beaudene's from Minnesota. That's too far for visits.

I know this is all wrong, me talking about Beau so much. What I am trying to do is figure out this thing between me and Whiteworm. We never had the hots for each other all these years—we've been friends for seven years now. And our freshman year, when everyone was doing it, no lie, we didn't have the hots for each other then.

And everyone was doing it, I know. Maya and I had done a tally. It was the week after we'd been spoons under that monstrous wooden study hall table. We'd counted off those kids he had done it with, and we'd counted off those kids the kids he had done it with told him they had done it with. We'd been sitting out in front of the dining hall watching the kids come up for chow.

Him? I had asked.

Uh-huh, he'd said.

With whom?

Bing bing bing.

We worked our way through one hundred ten of the one hundred sixteen boys in our class alone.

He told me about my brothers, too, both of whom have been very busy since grade school.

No shit!

Don't go telling them, now, he'd said, they'd kill me.

I swore secrecy and he told me it ain't from shitting in the woods up to Lake St. Mary that Franklin got all that poison ivy up his ying yang and all over his body.

Beau's dead. The mayor announces it at lunch. Just that he died. No details. No nothing. Just that he passed away at age seventeen. Hardly six months after he goes AWOL with my new letter jacket.

I think this is when it starts with Whiteworm.

No one makes a big deal of it, of Beau's dying. There

is no funeral, no memorial service. Not like we did for Winny when he died. He drowned. Of course, he was still here—we were freshmen—when he died.

I look over at Whiteworm. I don't know why exactly.

Yes I do.

McNamara, the mayor, announces it and I automatically look over to my friend, Beau's friend, Whiteworm. How will you handle this?

Whiteworm faces the crucifix. His face is immobile. Is he paler?

He loved Beau, too. He loved him first. And kept on loving him. Whiteworm was still Beau's friend after Beau took back that hammered-out dime ring. Even after Beau hands that ring over to me and asks me to wear it—it's Whiteworm's ring. Even after Beau asks me to be his best friend, Whiteworm still loves him. Still hangs around with him, still walks with him when I am not.

I don't know. I really don't. I don't understand this shit at all. Here I am, I've just had my seventeenth birthday and I am still queering around, still pounding the piss out of it damn near every night, as hot for Whiteworm as I have ever been for anyone, hot for Winston, too—oh, Jesus. I swear, though, I will never make a move on him and not just because he's so innocent of our queering ways.

I gotta tell it true or I am totally and completely fucked up.

The truth is, I am convinced that he wouldn't want it, that he would think it absolutely gross and demented, to say nothing of it being totally queer, and that he wouldn't like me anymore.

That's it.

I want him to like me.

I want to be liked.

I am damn near starved to death to be liked.

Ain't that the shits?

I gotta give it up. I really do. Not because I want to. Jesus fucking Christ, I don't *want* to.

I want it. Like the time up to the field house. Not on

the mat but after a volleyball game. Intramurals. The Home is ga-ga over intramurals. We are playing something all year round: baseball, softball, touch football, basketball, volleyball, water polo, badminton, track and field, shuffleboard—and then having field days up to our summer camp at Lake St. Mary's—that's a day of races, egg tosses, Frisbee contests, archery shoot-offs, and the greased watermelon contest in the lake with two teams facing off in the deep water, each team trying to motor that greased green mother into the other team's goal.

So it's volleyball time.

I gotta give it up. Gotta stop talking about it. Stop getting myself all worked up.

I slip into the can after the game. Everyone's gone. I have dawdled on purpose, of course. I am showered and dressed. No one's here except for me and Whiteworm, both of us hanging back, taking our dear old sweet time, letting everyone else get his nosy ass out of here.

I slip into the can. Whiteworm slips in behind me.

I am dying. I am faint, my mouth is dry, my soul drooling.

I face him. He is simply standing here cow-eyed, open, vulnerable, waiting on me, his face so open. He's offering me whatever I want, It's yours, take it.

I step into him, we do not speak. We ain't said boo to each other all summer, all fall. No lie. We have just been coming together whenever we have seen an opportunity. Like right now. We have the locker room to ourselves. Everyone's gone.

I step right up to him, face-to-face, I am just fucking dying. I can't breathe. I see him filling his pants. He is standing erect in there for me, he's bulging his zipper out, just for me, just for me. I reach to it, to him. I zip him down, zip me down, and step into him. Only our underwear separates us. He comes to me like a magnet, as if another power moves him, moves us. We bump, we touch—what do I do with my hands?

I reach around behind him and slip my fingers into his

underwear, under the elastic, slide my hands down his buttocks. Holy Jesus, his ass is so terribly soft. I ain't felt nothing like it. I am going to faint, my knees ain't nowhere to be found, I am floating as I pull him to me, our cocks press into each other, our cheeks, oh holy shit, our cheeks touching, grazing, the electricity is wet and everywhere about and in me, my lips but a millimeter from his long, lovely neck. We are wet, he and I. I feel it, feel him wet, feel me wet, it is okay, cock to cock, oh good God alive, I cannot take it—

The door booms open behind us.

We bolt apart. He bolts to a john and drops to the stool lightning fast. I bolt straight through where he just this instant stood. I don't know where I am going. I arrive at the sink trembling, shivering, lost: I don't know who I am.

I wash my hands, splash water up into my face, look at my face in the mirror: who's that? Oh, holy shit.

"Boys," Marrone says in greeting. He's Foster's counselor in Nineteen.

I frantically wash myself.

HeknowsheknowsheknowsOh.

"Up, John," I say and panic anew: what's that? Child can't talk. Child done checked out.

Marrone nods.

I concentrate something fierce on my hands. I hear Whiteworm in the stall ten feet away. I finish my hands, look at myself in the mirror: I still do not recognize myself. Oh, holy shit. I hoof it out, steal a glance at Whiteworm sitting on the pot. He is spread-eagled, his cock long, white, stiff, leaning to the left, his right.

Cover fucking up!

Boom. Out I go.

I gotta give it up.

Ain't no two ways about it.

I just gotta give it up. Or die trying.

16

CHARLES IS STANDING NEXT TO MY BED STAND WHEN I walk in. I surprise him.

''Oh,'' he goes and blushes. He's holding my tiny little blue novena booklet.

''What are you doing?'' I say with irritation. That's private. Hard enough admitting to myself, geez.

I panic when I realize how I sound. Can't go getting irritated with the boss. De boss ain't always right, but de boss is always de boss. Flaming asshole Lyman had that saying over his desk. On the wall in the main office in Building One, no lie. A picture of this toothless, idiotic, skinny old man fucking grinning out at you: ''De boss . . .''

''I'm sorry,'' Charles says quickly. ''You all right?'' he asks. He's still got my novena booklet in his hand.

He knows. I just know he knows.

I take a half step backward. I am on automatic pilot. There is a space between my skin and the rest of my body.

''Bambi?'' he asks.

I can't talk. He knows. I just know it.

He reaches up to my face with his left hand. I jump back, startled.

''Whoa,'' he says, ''I'm not going to hurt you. I just wanted to feel your forehead. You look peak-ed.''

''I'm okay,'' I lie, backing away some more. I can't find my knees again.

Sometimes I don't know who I am. My Aunt Margaret Mary said to me once, ''You have to think whose feelings you are feeling.''

"What's this?" Charles asks as he lifts up my novena.

"A novena," I say so softly I ain't sure I said it out loud. Don't ask. I am so ashamed. I am trying to quit. I am.

Charles looks at it, reads the cover: OUR LADY OF PERPETUAL HELP ROSARY NOVENA.

Margaret Mary gave it to me. She's my dad's sister. She's a paranoid schizophrenic. She got sick and thought the Russians were coming to get her. She's the most wonderful human being in the world.

"It's seen better days," Charles says with a big smile. He's trying to be sweet again. I know. Trying to help. But sometimes you can't help. Sometimes you just have to leave well enough alone. Okay?

"I know," I say. The edges are ragged. I've had it since I was just a sixth-grader. That is when I first started trying to be pure. Our Lady of Perpetual Help. Right. Some of us need perpetual help. She's up to the main chapel. Our Lady of Perpetual Help, a mosaic the Monsignor had brought in from Italy. He had an Italian artist come over with the crates of chips, this little old guy with his bushy mustache making me think of Einstein. He worked on it for three months, no lie. He had a couple of those sheet-metal spotlights shining brilliant over his shoulder the whole time. He made one helluva mess up there in the sacristy. There was something outrageous about the emergency-room lighting in the main chapel.

"I didn't mean to pry," Charles says as he hands over my novena booklet.

It's okay, I say.

It ain't, of course.

I am mortified.

Then he mortifies me all the more. It ain't no big deal. It is just that he's innocent and I am just full of shame and suspicion and ansty-wansty idiocy. I don't know which end is up.

"Later," he says, taps me softly on the shoulder, and scoots out of the room, leaving me be.

He's just trying to be one of the boys. Just trying to be my friend. He ain't into no big private-eye investigation of me and my perverse ways.

Sometimes I could just die.

17

THIS IS A REAL CONFUSING TIME FOR ME.

I am trying to be good. To be pure.

I am pretty excited about actually having an adult friend, someone I can really trust while all my friends are being totally different. Take football. Kuhns and those guys are razzing my ass something fierce in the locker room after practice. The very first week of practice and here's Kuhns—star, team captain, all-around hero, and popular guy—he's shoving his cock and balls down between his legs. He's got a pussy now. He comes waddling up to me, hardly able to contain himself, it is so hilarious he thinks:

"You want some of the real thing, Bambi?"

"C'mon," I protest. He's being pretty gross.

He's all over me, laughing wickedly—there's something else going on here. Everyone's laughing hysterically, really cracking up. There's some great joke here, see? Everyone's in on it. Everyone but me.

In fact, I appear to *be* the joke.

I don't understand. But I don't regret going out for the team. I don't care if all the starters are going to be total assholes about me. It's the trips I want, anyway. That's why I came out for the team in the first place.

See, we don't play in the city league. We were thrown out in 1955 when crazy fucking Felix was still a kid here. He was twenty then. He played end. Matthew was here then, too. He says there was a riot after the Alter game. Alter's this hotshit Catholic school in Kettering. They are supposed to be the best at everything. Matthew says Felix threw the first punch. He punched this white kid who called him a jungle bunny. Apparently Felix broke the guy's jaw and all hell broke loose.

I guess Felix was always nuts.

So now we play a road schedule. We go down to Kentucky and play in Lexington and Beria. We go north to Michigan to play in Hamtramck and in East Lansing. We even went to Chicago once—Kuhns went, he told me—and played on Soldier's Field. We travel by train, stay in hotels, and eat in restaurants. It's really great. The Lions were at the Sheraton-Cadillac with the team last year when we played Hamtramck. Kuhns says those guys were fucking behemoths. They made crazy fucking Felix look like Gambi Bambi, third-string quarterback, Hamburger Squad.

Halstead, our physics teacher, told us about hamburger squads. They are the ones who run the opponents' plays each week in practice. We pretend we are the other team. We run the other team's plays all week and let the first-string defense kick our asses. Then we turn around and pretend to be the other team's defense and let our first-string offense beat the piss out of us, too. Great job, huh? You spend all week getting the piss beat out of you.

I don't care. I get to suit up, get to make the trips, and get to be part of the team, which, until this year, was a pretty nice thing.

All that is changing now.

Kuhns and Foster have just gone crazy hating their counselors. Here I am making friends with mine. And they are coming at me every day, every day in the locker room, naked, their dicks shoved a way up between their legs, asking me if I've ever had the real thing? Want some, Bambi? Hmm? Do ya, huh?

I don't like it. My friends are being so different.

I am working in the yard and they are off drinking wine. I have no idea how they get their hands on it, but they do. They sneak into town. They have girlfriends. To hear them talk, they have girlfriends who put out all the time—whenever, wherever.

I have to put this queer stuff behind me. I really do.

It is a confusing time, which makes me really grateful to Charles. I'm sorry if Kuhns and Foster hate their counselors. Charles is really being good to me. Good for me. Honest. He is really helping me. He is.

See, the first week of school, the same week we go to Cincinnati to play Moeller, I make a decision: I am going to be pure. Gamble is going to give up being queer, he is going to give up this magic thing with Whiteworm.

Oh, God.

Just the scent of his skin sends me into delirium.

But I am going to give it up.

I do not tell anyone.

Charles, though, he's curious about me. And about this novena thing. He's just wondering, pressing—importuning, as Sebastian would say.

"There some problem? You want to talk about it? You know you can trust me, don't you? You do understand that, don't you?"

He amazes me. Here I am making this monumental decision. It is very private. I have decided to be pure again. To be in a state of grace again. I am a senior, after all. God, I remember Maya and how disgusted he got with me. It was the end of my sophomore year. I am still after his ass.

"You're almost a junior now," he told me.

I was so ashamed. I am standing there drooling and he's saying No, you are too old. No more, boy. Time to be with girls.

Right.

And where the fuck are they?

And he's right. Maya's right.

I must quit. I am too queer.

So I decide. I am dead serious.

I am still out of control, I know. I am still all aflame, I know. That is *why* I start this novena, which is a rosary a day for forty-five days. You have this little set of prayers you say at both the beginning and the end of the rosary. It's a little set of prayers you say to Our Lady of Perpetual Help.

And right at the end of the final prayers there is this little red parenthesis: (YOUR PETITION HERE).

Purity.

Oh, God.

Make me pure.

I am three days into it. Today is my fourth day. The Moeller game is tomorrow night.

"I'll miss you," Charles says.

We won't have one of our chats. I'll be in Cincinnati. We take the bus down and back.

Thanks, I tell Charles. I'm glad someone will. Miss me, that is.

"Well, I like you," he says.

Boing.

Straight to the heart.

Yeah?

"You're a sharp kid," he says. "Got your head screwed on straight," he says.

Wrong.

I ain't nothing but a seventeen-year-old who's having trouble not pounding his pud. Hardly what you'd call having your head screwed on straight.

I look at him. He's always trying to be so sweet. Shit.

So I tell him.

I mean he's been pressing, wondering, importuning, right?

He wants to know, right?

So I tell him.

"You're trying to be pure?" he asks, this real quizzical look on his face.

Yep, I say.

I am so ashamed. I look down at the coffee table. Ain't no dust mote tonight. I wouldn't be able to see it if it was there. I am confessing.

"I have done it. With myself and with others."

The room is so silent. It is thick, palpable, clutching at me.

I can feel the heat in my face. My face burns.

So say something already.

He says nothing. I do not look at him. I hold my head down. My face is scalding hot. There is moisture just under my epidermis. It is frantic to be loose, the moisture leaping. The light coming off Charles's dimly lit lamp is going Buh-wah, buh-wah.

Suddenly he speaks.

"Who?" he asks.

Huh?

I look up. Who? Who? You want to know who? Who what? Who I did it with? That it? That what you want to know?

Oh, God, I knew I shouldn't have said anything. I will pretend he didn't say that:

"So," I go on, taking a deep breath—Jesus, this is tough—"I'm doing Margaret Mary's novena again."

"Margaret Mary?" he asks, completely puzzled now.

I don't talk about Margaret Mary. She's nobody's business. Some things are just better kept private, that's all.

"Never mind," I say, "I'm just trying to be pure."

There.

I take a deep breath.

"I am going to be good," I say, enunciating each syllable. I am determined. Charles has been my friend. He'll appreciate that. He'll appreciate my determination.

Only he doesn't say anything.

We sit in silence together.

Which ain't so bad. The silence.

I thought he'd say something. I'm embarrassed as I realize I am disappointed: I thought he'd praise me. You know, right away with some praise. Is that why I do all this talking? Just to get his praise?

He breaks the silence. He speaks so softly I need to lean forward in my seat just to get it. "You want to tell me about it?" he says.

I strain to hear him.

Well, no. I don't.

"You want to tell me who you did it with? You can talk about that, you know."

He is talking very softly, very slowly.

I don't want to talk about who.

"You can talk about what you did, hmmm?" he encourages. Still very softly, very slowly, how you'd talk to a babe in a manger.

I look at him. I'm puzzled. What I did? I don't get it.

He looks directly at me. He presses me. He wants to know what I did.

"Do you mean you were aroused with others or that you touched others, actually ejaculating, or what?"

I don't like this.

He leans back in his chair. His movements are very slow and deliberate.

"It's okay," he goes on in that soothing, coaxing way. "It might help. And it would help me to understand . . . you . . . better . . ." he says, giving me this odd little nod at the end.

Yes, yes, yes, he says with his nodding head.

No, no, no, my heart says.

I'm sorry. It just ain't right. I can't.

I'm sorry.

He's being so soothing. His voice is so soothing. He's a tenor. I know because he sang to me once. It was, to tell you the truth, pretty embarrassing. It wasn't ten days ago. I was all wet-willied about how Kuhns and Foster and those guys had been treating me—they'd been really ragging my ass something fierce. They act like they think I am really a queer.

I was really down in the chops. Charles was being real quiet. It made me nervous and fidgety. See, I am usually yammering away, but when I got into those guys and what they were doing and I couldn't tell him, not about them jamming their cocks down between their legs and that shit, so I ain't talking much and so the room is all empty and silent. I am fidgeting about, noticing my underwear showing through my pjs, they're so old. When he breaks into song. Stun my ass. No lie. He's singing Too La Roo La Roo luh, Too Lah Roo La Roo, Too-laRooooola roo la, it's an Irish lullaby.

His voice is beautiful like on a record or something. It freaks me out. I get all weirded-out inside. I loved it. His voice, no lie, it is really beautiful. He really sings good. I really know now what a tenor is, after hearing him, it is just the two of us and he's going off all acapulca on me and it is really, honestly excellent. Except it simply freaks my ass out.

I mean, his voice was beautiful and I love that song and it made me sick.

"Yoo-hooo," he teases. "Anyone home?"

Huh? Oh. Sorry.

"It's okay," he says, smiling sweetly. He is still very interested. He asks a bunch of questions about who and how and what and where and when and how often and I don't know what all.

"I got to get to bed," I say. "I got to say my novena," I tell him. "I haven't done it today yet."

He says okay and lets me go.

I do my novena kneeling next to my bed, my brand-new $17.99 "buddy light," a beacon beaming down on my powder-blue booklet. I forget Charles. I forget Kuhns and those guys and their new way toward me—it's not mean, exactly, I don't think. I beseech and importune My Lady of Perpetual Help to rid me of my sin.

18

MOELLAR CLEANS OUR CLOCK, 19–7. THE OLD MAN plays only his starters, but it ain't too cold so I'm OK. Sitting on the bench, I mean. At the end of the season last year we were in Pittsburgh, playing South Catholic on their ain't-a-blade-of-grass-nowhere-to-be-found field in a freezing fucking rain. Talk about miserable.

I go over to Fountain Square after the game with Rasco. We hang around downtown Cincinnati. I am gaping at the humongous buildings. It's terrific. Gonna put a crick in my neck, bu-duh. We hoof it back to Riverfront—that's the Reds stadium—where our bus is waiting. It's the athletic bus. The varsity always uses the athletic bus. It's really nice. It's just like a real Greyhound with the soft, high-backed seats, an AM-FM radio, aisle lights. It's not one of those regular buses with the metal seats and cardboard cushions. It's a privilege to ride the athletic bus.

Just as we are about to pull out, The Big Dick steps on board. He steps into the doorwell. He's got this real lurid smile on his face. He hates the starters. The starters hate him. He was one of the counselors who went up to summer camp with us. The varsity always starts its season up to Lake St. Mary, where we have our summer camp. It's this great ritual, varsity football starts up to the lake, three practices per day, a chalk talk every night after supper, just like the pros.

Kuhns and those guys really razzed Dick's fat ass. Really hateful stuff. I don't understand it too well. What's going on with Kuhns and those guys, I mean. There's Kuhns,

Foster, this kid named Brower, who's a sensational tight end, a kid named McNamara, who's our mayor and who, I thought anyway, was just a great kid—he's real good-looking, a good student, is never in trouble, shit like that. And then there's Fogarty, the tackle who *loves* to hit. All five of them are captains. Acting very tough. Acting ever so cool. Better than everyone else, too cool to talk to us peons—which is okay. They are the returning lettermen. They are good. They are popular and good-looking and all that. But the part that really throws me for a loop is how they are being totally and completely hostile to almost every counselor in the place. Real smart-mouthed, see? Challenging everyone. The only adult I see them behaving around is the Old Man.

Part of it, I think, is that they have girlfriends. Kuhns and Foster do. Mac does, too. I don't know about Fogarty, but he's so cool, if he doesn't, it won't be long. Brower's girl is a boy here at the Home. Which is pretty amazing, too. You know how they've been coming at me with their dicks shoved between their legs, right? I'm the number-one queer, right? Well, Brower's best buddy—and I have to tell you that at the Home you never use the word "buddy" because a buddy is someone you sleep with—well, Brower's best buddy is this fine little creature named Smolinski. Smolinski is a natural bleached blonde. He's five-foot-four, has this real soft, baby-fat face, and his eyes are the clearest azure blue—I mean, the kid is a real beauty. Honest.

It is really hard to actually say it.

I will.

Smolinski and Brower are lovebirds. They go everywhere together. You see them strolling about the Home side by side, the love light shining all around them and not a soul says boo about it.

You do and Brower will kill you.

It is one of those situations where everyone knows and no one says.

I see them walking together, mooning at each other, bumping each other as they walk, laughing their giggly laughs, soft whisperings passing between them. The intensity of their togetherness is so great that you can't watch too carefully. You never look directly into the sun, you know. Same with these two. You look too close and it is just damned embarrassing. I mean, it looks like love.

And here are our hero-starters acting totally oblivious, right? They ain't saying shit about it. They're trotting around the locker room with their dicks shoved between their legs, glad-flashing all over me, right? And then they'll turn right around to Brower—someone has just stuck his head in the locker room door: "Smo's waiting for ya, Bro"—and act all fake-grown-up adult:

"So, how was your day at the office, Bro?"

Not those words.

It is just the swift shift from wicked, merciless harassment to sober, serious, make-believe maturity.

What a crock.

It is amazing.

The two biggest queers of them all.

The emperor wears no clothes.

But don't you fucking dare notice it. I know. I did once. And Kuhns nearly killed me. It was after practice, before our first game. We were back from the lake. We are down to one practice a day. Practice is over. I am one of the last ones out of the shower. I like that, taking my time, being the last one out. It makes me feel grown somehow. I act as if I am all together, Mr. Calm Cool and Collected takes his time, see? I am studied.

Kuhns, whose locker is right next to mine, comes up to me and grabs my ass.

Hey, asshole, I say, jumping back.

He thinks it is hilarious. His eyes are shining. He snatches at me again.

I jump away again and tell him to fuck off.

"Bambi getting touchy, eh?" he says and pops me one in the arm. No love tap either.

I don't know what comes over me. It has been three months of this shit now. Two of my best friends, Kuhns and

Foster, have gone through this weird transformation. Here's Kuhns, the same fuckface who asked me to do it with him not two summers back, the same Kuhns who had been doing it with Maya—Maya told me so himself, see?—the same Kuhns who is *this close,* right? to the most obvious love-queer thing I have ever laid eyes upon in all of my seven-and-one-quarter years here. So now I'm so strange?

"You should talk, *hero.*"

He freezes and gives me the most malevolent look: Yeah?

I am in it. I ain't gonna stop now. Couldn't if I wanted to.

"Tell me about your good buddy, the Bro."

The Bro. The Smo. That's what they are calling them. So cool.

I have crossed the line now.

Kuhns closes on me. I am back to my locker, facing in. I have shirt in my hand.

"Yeah?" he threatens. "Yeah?"

I know what's next. I go ahead anyway. I just do.

I turn to face him. I look him straight in the eye, bracing my skinny little self, spreading my feet apart, there. "Yeah," I say, "Yeah. You tell me, the Bro blow the Smo or the Smo blow the Bro?"

He flinches when I say it, those sacrilegious words. He jerks backward bodily and lets fly with his left at the same time. He blams me straight in my chest and knocks me back through my open locker into the next one, crash. He's on me like stink on shit, grabs me by the throat, and slams me into the locker.

I see McNamara just over Kuhns's shoulder. Mac's all wide-eyed and concerned. I think he wants to intervene and doesn't know how. He is a good boy, Mac is, really.

Kuhns rattles me by the throat.

I am gagging. My eyeballs, I just know it, they're bulging out sixteen times normal size. He's got me slightly hoisted up. It hits me: I could ruin the boy for life. Just lift my knee, ka-boom.

Of course, he'd slay me for sure then.

"You value your life, fucker?" he says. I can feel his breath on the word "fucker."

He shakes me, chokes me, rattles me some more, banging me against the metal locker a couple of times. There is complete hatred in his eyes.

Suddenly I am overwhelmed by a serene calm. I can hardly breathe, of course, but something strikes me. He is out of control. I'm not. This is a storm that will pass, just let it.

I let myself completely relax. I slouch against the cool of the locker. I drop my eyes and wait.

Mac is with me.

"C'mon, Kelly," Mac says.

It ain't as much fun if your victim's not squirming.

Kuhns grunts and rattles my throat one final time. He slams me into the locker, bang, and lets me go.

"Fucking queer," he says, and that's that.

The Big Dick just stands in the entry well of the bus. He has his right foot on the top step and lays his meaty paw atop the bar that runs across and in front of the first seat. He's still got this mysterious smile on his face. He looks mean, like he's got the goods on someone. He simply stares into the bus as the heroes in back shout out their abuse. Kuhns and Foster lead the bray.

"Hey, Fatman," Foster yells.

"Wanna sandwich, Lardass?" Kuhns chimes in.

"Hungry, Tubby?" Brower, I think.

This is all accompanied by loud guffaws, great hardy-har-hars, raucous, side-splitting laughter. And The Big Dick is very cool, maintaining. He is simply standing there, that smile on his face, his head bobbing. "Keep it up, boys. Just keep it up."

"At least we can get it up," Fogarty calls out to more wild laughter.

Suddenly he steps off the bus. He doesn't say anything more. He leaves with the smile he got on with.

* * *

Monday morning five starters lose their jobs. Kuhns is fired as commissioner in Morton's house. Foster is fired as Marrone's commissioner. Mac, who is mayor and commissioner, loses both jobs. Brower and Fogarty, they aren't commissioners, lose all their senior passes. All five of them lose all their senior passes. Twice a month, once you're a senior, you get passes into town. Noon to eight on your own. It's a wonderful thing to be free in the outside world for a day. Absolutely wonderful.

They were going to kick them off the team. The Old Man put a stop to that. He wouldn't have shit for a team without these guys.

The word is they had been drinking beer. And someone ratted on them. Someone turned their asses in.

Guess who?

Right.

Yours truly.

Frederick Joseph Gamble. The one and only Gambi Bambi. Pussy number one done ratted on his old friends.

Why'd he do that?

Revenge. Revenge, see, for how they have been treating me. Right? Revenge. Bambi got his revenge.

Only I don't know jack squat about it until Monday afternoon at practice. Huff, the head line coach, calls for his lineman. Time for tackling practice. You pair off and line up in two parallel rows facing each other. Then you take turns smashing each other into the ground. You and your partner.

The backs do the same. Kuhns, steaming, full of wickedness and venom, goes out of his way to pick me as his partner. Then he damn near kills me for the next twenty minutes. He flings every single fucking ounce of his one hundred seventy-eight pounds into me. He's grunting something fierce and just *blasts* me. Fucking snot is flying from my nostrils, oof. Hey, what's going on here? And he *blasts* me again, oof. I catch on, brace myself, trying to be ready. I crouch for each successive hit, trying to go with it, trying to throw myself into the force of his power, trying to take some of the punch out of it—only he is maniacal, smashing at me as hard and as furiously as he can and then driving me into the earth after I'm down. I think he's about to kick me when the Old Man tells him to just hit and git. Then I try to tackle him, right? My turn. And he's accidentally got his forearms up at the last second, damn near knocking my teeth out, thank you very much. Christ. This is gonna be one glorious afternoon.

After practice is worse.

Kuhns's locker is on one side of me and Fogarty, our tackle who loves to hit, he's on the other side. The two of them talk right through me. I am invisible. They are talking through me, over me, *into* me, wondering: "You have any idea who the fucking rat is?"

"No, but I sure would like to know—I'd kill the fucker."

"Me, too," Kuhns says as he flings his locker open as fast and as hard as he can, smashing my fingers with his flying door.

"Oh," he says, acting all bullshit contrite, "I'm so-oh sorry." As soon as he says it he walks right into me, smashing me backward with his bull's chest. I ricochet back into Fogarty, who is immediately horrified to be touched by such a contaminating force as the Bambi. He shrieks and shoves me hard back into Kuhns.

I jump out from between them, preferring the shower to a game of human Ping-Pong. I hoof it into the shower. Brower's in here lathering up. Rasco's in here, too. At least he's still my friend. I think. He hasn't been turned in. He hasn't lost his commissioner's job. He was with me Friday night. We were down at Fountain Square together. I take a shower next to Rasco.

Brower rinses the soap from his bod, opens his eyes, and discovers me. His whole face changes. He simply sneers: I am clearly the plague. He comes at me. He has a bar of Maxine soap in his hand. He's naked and very hairy. He offers me his bar of soap.

"Need some soap, Bambi?"

I turn my back and try to ignore him.

He grabs me by the shoulder and starts shoving the soap into my face. He's trying to shove it into my mouth.

I ain't no match for these guys. They all got me by fifty pounds easy.

I am quick, though.

I slip away. He only got a few shards into my face. It's bitter, acidic shit. Lyman made us chew it once. I don't remember what for. We were seventh-graders. We'd fucked up somehow. He marched a whole gang of us into the can and had us line up. We all had to take a chunk of soap.

"Take a bite, gentlemen," he directed.

We bite. We gag. No lie, that shit will make you upchuck. Your throat starts leaping back up into your mouth.

"Chew it, boys. I don't want any of you just holding it in your chops," Lyman says as he surveys the line of us gagging, tearing up—it'll make your mouth water, too, no lie.

"Chew it."

Two or three boys do throw up. On the floor. Into the sink.

"You can clean it up afterward. Now back in line and chew."

Your mouth burns for days, honest.

Teaching us lessons

That's Lyman's position.

He's teaching us lessons.

"Fuck off," I say to Brower as I slip away. I bump into Rasco. He gives me a helpless look and a tiny shrug. I understand. It ain't his trouble.

Brower ain't quitting. He is after me.

"C'mon. I didn't do nothing. What's *with* you guys?"

I cannot escape.

Brower traps me in the corner of the shower. He is blocking the only way out. He's still got his bar of soap. He waves it ominously and tells me: "Rats need to have their mouths cleaned out." He closes on me.

I back away, looking behind me as I do. I am a goddamned cornered rat. There is nowhere to run, nowhere to hide.

"Don't," I protest.

He has his arms up in a windmill. I am all the way back into the corner.

Oh shit.

He slams into me, naked and large. He's one-eighty to my one-twenty-five. I bolt but he blocks me with one thick arm and jams that soap into my teeth with the other.

"Eat it, rat," he says, baring his teeth.

He grinds the bar of soap into my teeth.

I squirm, wiggle, and lose my balance. I slip and bang my head on the wall as I go down. My bare butt slams hard on the gravelly shower floor. I start to cry.

"That's enough," Rasco says.

Brower turns around to look at Rasco. Huh? Who asked you? Then he shrugs and flips the bar of soap hard into my face. He hits me under the left eye. Then he walks out.

19

RASCO WALKS ME TO CHOW. I AIN'T TALKING. IT'S NO fun being the rat when it ain't true you're the rat.

"Don't sweat it," Rasco says as we turn the corner around the trade school. The dining hall is dead ahead. Four hundred fifty boys mill around. The porch is packed. A mob masses before the doors with more spread out on the sidewalk and grass in front.

"That's easy for you to say," I whine. I feel like a nine-year-old.

"You're right," Rasco says, surprising me. "It is easy for me to say."

I look at him. We pass beneath the windows of the tailor shop. Those windows stare dumbly down upon us. Beaudene. He tried that, too. Tailor shop. Barber shop. Sheet-metal shop. The boy could never make up his mind.

"You're right," Rasco repeats. "It ain't me they're after."

I appreciate that. At least he's noticing this nonsense. I look at him again and wonder. Last year we did a play. Rasco had a big part. He was one of the stars, in fact. Foster, too. One night after rehearsal they were wrestling around, Foster and Rasco, and Foster dumped him, dumped Rasco on the grass behind the auditorium. Rasco's a big kid. "Fat," Fucking Felix says. So here's Rasco on his back. Foster's got him acting like a turtle who's been flipped over onto his shell. The two of them are laughing till the tears come.

Foster stops the rest of us.

"Wait! Wait!" he calls, making us watch. He holds Rasco down with one hand, telling the rest of us to "check it out."

It *was* funny, too. *They* were funny. Rasco's on his back and he's too big, too fat, see? to roll over. Fat old jolly Rasco, right? And Rasco's laughing as hard as anyone. Harder.

It amazes me. Rasco amazes me. How can he do that? How can he laugh at himself, huh? Or let others laugh at him? You laugh at me and I want to kill you. I mean, like take your throat out, ya know?

"Nothing bothers you, does it?" I say. It is more an observation than a question. He has a way—how does he put it?—"I am what I am, Bambi. Ain't nothing gonna change that," he said to me once as he laid his hands on his jolly old St. Nick belly.

We are to the edge of the crowd. The doors are still shut.

Rasco stops and turns to me.

"Shit," he says surprising me again, "it all bothers me."

Suddenly he stiffens. He's a cat whose hair has just stood up all down his back.

What's up? I look around. It's Felix. Giant, ebony Felix.

He towers head and shoulders above the mass of boys. Boys spread at his approach. We *make way* for Felix. I watch the boys part: he is Moses and we are the Red Sea.

Just as he moves into the crowd, the dining hall doors open. It appears to be magic: Felix moves into the mob, the mob splits apart, a corridor appears, and the doors swing open. All of a magic piece.

It ain't magic, of course. Just an accident.

Two waiters in their stiff white cotton jackets are just doing their job: opening the doors. I watch them as they push out from inside. They mash a half-dozen boys as they shove the doors out. They stiff-arm another half dozen and hold them at bay as they latch the doors open with the tiny brass hooks that are at the base of each door. They appear to bow at Felix's approach as they bend to loop the brass hooks into the matching brass eyehooks embedded in the flagstone porch.

They bow, hook the doors open, and straighten up.

Just as they finish their bow, Felix strides past them straight into the dining hall, a great Watusi warrior.

Only the Watusi aren't so black. They're more caramel colored. We had a short film on them at the movies once. Most of the men are seven foot tall or taller, with their hair puffed up and out like a great wad of cotton candy. And handsome. It seemed like the whole tribe was handsome. Except for their hair. That was really odd, I thought, how puffed it was. Not natural either. You could tell they'd worked on those buggers.

Felix disappears inside.

A shiver runs through the mob. The corridor that magically opened at his coming closes immediately behind him.

I look at Rasco.

He is mute. He hasn't said much, either, about being Felix's commissioner. One thing's clear: he's going through something entirely different than I am.

The mob lurches forward. The push to the narrow double-door opening is on. I watch, hanging back. I prefer to wait until the mashing smashing shoving crush is over. Something smells funny.

I sniff.

"Smell that?" I ask Rasco, sniffing again.

Rasco shivers.

"Terror," he says and barrels into the still mashing smashing shoving crush of boys. Bye-yee.

I follow shortly, after things ease up a bit. Whiteworm's hanging around in the foyer—it's pretty huge with a serving line and the row of steam tables straight in from the doors. The kitchen crew, all the fat ladies in their stiff white dresses, are shoveling out the chow. We see each other, Whiteworm and I. We look into each other's eyes. I have been avoiding him for a week now. Ever since I started my novena.

There is pain in his face. In his eyes there is a plea. He is coming at me.

"Stay away from me," I say, spitting it at him. I reach to him and shove him. I shove him hard. I turn my back to him and leave him to eat my dust.

"Asshole," I say as I stride into the main hall. I stride past the electric watercooler, cut around the humonguous open-topped, twenty-gallon milk barrel, and head for my seat. I am full of righteousness. I am righteous and hateful: the fucking wimpy faggot.

I do it again, too.

It's no one-time lapse. No siree.

I am wicked and shameful to the core.

It is outside, after chow. He's waiting for me at the edge of the porch. He's got those fucked-up wimpy do-with-me-whatever-you-want puppy's eyes. I see him. He moons at me, mooning at me with those awful, needful cow eyes.

"Bambi," he says, reaching for me with his right hand. It is a question. It is a plea.

He deserves it all, every fucking last wicked bit of it.

I barrel through him and shove him hard. He stumbles back into the brick railing. He almost topples over backward.

"Just fucking stay away from me, ya hear?" I snarl.

He doesn't know what the fuck's going on. He regains his balance. He ain't finished yet.

"What did I do?" he whines.

He follows me off the porch. He's at my heels. He's leaning into me, leaning into me hard, yearning, yearning, hoping and I am all a rage.

I cannot control myself. I whirl on him. He is his soft, pliable, wounded self. He stands before me, his eyes wide open, begging me.

Those eyes. I cannot stand those eyes. I hit him.

I hit him straight away right in the breadbasket. I am

tiny and sickening. I drive my puny fist into his soft, pliable belly.

Ooof, he goes, doubling instantly.

"Asshole," I pronounce. I whirl back around and stride off with the old corncob rammed up my ass, harrumph.

20

WINSTON'S ON THE FRONT PORCH WHEN I REACH the house. He's beaming away and looking simply beautiful. He has a basketball in his hands. Chubby Checker booms from the house behind him. He dribbles while twisting to the beat—suddenly he freezes, snatches the ball up and holds it just under his chin. He's a rock 'n' roll picture.

"Take the world by the hand," he sings,

"and go like this:

"Round-and round-and round-and round-and

"Round."

He fires that terrific Chicago smile down upon me.

Manna from heaven.

"Shoot some baskets, Bambi?" he asks, still twisting away.

I think I am going to die. He's got on his stiff red cotton basketball shorts. He's the happy boy with the perfect arse. Inviting me to play.

"Huh? What d' ya say?" he offers brightly, still dribbling the ball in perfect time to the beat: one-two onetwothreefour one-two onetwothreefour one-two. He's bent at the waist. He's over that ball. His red cotton shorts are stretched tight across his perfect arse. He's barefoot to boot.

I could marry him.

Or kill him.

Come on, baby.

He has no fucking idea.

Let's do the Twist.

None whatsoever.

Take the world by the hand and go like this.

I swallow it. I swallow that fact fucking whole.

Round-and round-and round-and round.

"Naw," I say to him as I dash up the steps and breeeze right past him. I can't handle this now. I go in the front door of the house and straight through to the back door and out again.

I am charged. I am over-energized. I gotta move.

I run up the hill behind the house. I run to the road that wraps around the cottages in back. I book it on down the road past the football field to Conley Road. I hang a right on Conley, take it half a block to Tarbox-Cemetery Road, and hang a left onto Tarbox-Cemetery. I am clipping along.

I am charged.

I break into a trot and jog past the first farmhouse. I jog on up over the first hill. I can no longer contain myself. I explode into a total, all-out wind sprint. I run as hard and as fast as I can, full out, until I reach the hilltop entrance to the cemetery.

Massies Creek Cemetery.

I am out of breath. Gasping for air, I walk the last seventy yards to the main entrance. It feels good to bust a gut. I gulp the air and admire Massies Creek shining in the fading light. It's getting dark sooner now.

I stop at the main gate. I am still panting pretty heavy.

Massies Creek Cemetery. Organized 1814. Incorporated 1889.

I walk in through the stacked stone entryway. I hang a right at the first opportunity. Twenty, thirty feet in and I am at the Tarbox family cluster. I stand stupidly before the eight of them. A whole goddamned family right here at my feet.

Come on, baby.

You go another forty feet and there are more. More Tarboxes.

"I'm the fucking faggot," I say aloud.

The sound of my voice scares me. It is so very quiet out here. There aren't even any birds chirping. There are no cars on the road. Massies Creek a hundred yards out and down is oily black in this fading light. Sparks and diamonds leap from her shiny face.

"Oh, God," I moan.

What I have just done to my friend Whiteworm weighs me down. There's a whirlpool inside of me. It sucks all of me down and around this dark spiral that goes zooming through my bowels.

Round-and round-and round-and round-and.

Round.

Suddenly I hear this soft, distant roar of applause. It's an audience delirious with joy and abandon.

I jump at its suddenness.

What! What's that?

I am about to shit my pants.

The wind shifts and pushes the maples that stand all about me back again. I see. That's it. The wind.

These maples lean in the wind. They sway with it, I see that now. Their leaves, their millions and millions of leaves rustle one against another—this is my audience delirious with joy and abandon.

I gotta git outta here.

I do.

I book it back to the house as quickly as I can.

I strain to outrun the darkness that is swiftly falling all about.

I cannot stand it, to be alone in this darkness tonight.

I cannot stand it and in my terror I race the falling light.

21

EVERYONE'S IN STUDY HALL WHEN I GET BACK. Charles's office door is shut up. He's in there. I can see the light under the door.

I go to my desk. Commissioners get their own individual desks with drawers and everything. Everyone else, except for my assistant commissioner who has a desk identical to mine, sits at one of the four- or six-seater study hall tables. Everyone's busy with their homework. No talking. Winston looks up as I come in, his face expressionless. Just looking. I sit, open my physics book, and stare at the page.

Charles is still shut up in there when study hall's over. Time for charges.

"Charges," I announce. Books bop and pop shut. Chairs scream and screech. Everyone's up, flinging their books into their bins along the wall, heading for the equipment room.

"Someone with Charles?" I ask Winston. His charge is the study hall. He's pushing a dustmop around the room.

"Yup" is all he says. He's working a corner with that dustmop. You gotta really dig to get into those corners.

"Know who?" I ask. I am puzzled at my own curiosity. It is as if something of mine is being used without my permission.

"Uh-huh," Winston says as he moves up along the wall. He's still got on his red cotton basketball shorts. I cannot look at him below the neck. It is hard enough looking into his face, he's so beautiful and I'm so sick, yearning how I do, this thing in me, it's pulling me from way down deep inside so I'm leading here with my chin.

"Well, who is it?" I ask impatiently. I am leaning out. I will lean that way forever.

Winston's off in some reverie, oblivious to me. I have to know.

"Winston!"

"Huh? Oh," he says, coming back to the real world. "That kid you play ball with sometimes, what's his name? Wormwood?"

"Whiteworm?" I correct, asking.

"He the long, skinny kid?" Winston asks. "A senior, hmm?"

"Yeah," I say, noticing how nonchalant he is. I notice because I ain't.

"Where'd you go in such a hurry?" he asks suddenly. He stops dust-mopping, leans on the handle with one palm over the end, his chin sitting on the back of his hand.

"Nowhere," I say.

"Okay," he says and resumes his dust-mopping. He finishes, rounds up his three piles of dirt, dust, paper clips, and wads of crumpled paper, and pushes the new single pile out the room ahead of him. He crosses the front hall, heading for the equipment room. There are dustpans in there. I watch his tail as he exits.

Tollens, my assistant commissioner, comes into the room.

"Inspection, Bambi," Tollens says.

'Kay.

We have a half hour free time before night prayers. Charles is still in his office, his door is still shut.

"We watch TV now, Gamble?" Dannon asks. A junior. Zits everywhere. He spends hours and hours at the sink, scrubbing, scrubbing, scrubbing, plastering Clearasil, pHisoHex, and some chalky-brown shit he got from the clinic all over his cratered face. I pick at a zit on my chin looking at his wretched face.

"Sure."

Winston comes in. I'm at my desk, got my galaxies book out. Margaret Mary gave it to me for my birthday. A hundred billion galaxies with a hundred billion stars each.

"Smoke?" Winston offers. He smokes Winstons. Me, too. Dad smokes Camels just like Charles.

"Nope," I say. Winston lights up, blows a perfect oval smoke ring, that sucker holding firm all the way down to the study hall table in front of him, traveling two-and-a-half feet before it splatters softly apart on the table top. That's what goes on in outer space, giant galaxies smashing into one another. Sometimes, Halstead says. It's why I like him so much, Halstead, how he orgasms when he gets going on the stars and shit. We work it, work him, try to get him off, try to get him to forget the day's work, get him going on and on about the size of it all, the tremendous mystery of it all.

"You OK?"

"Huh?

"You're so quiet," Winston says.

"I'm all right," I lie. Just fucking fine. What's he got Whiteworm in there for?

"Miss Charles?" Winston asks innocently.

Charles usually sits out here with us, smokes one with us this last half hour before night prayers. He will sit at a regular study hall table like one of the boys. We shoot the shit. School. Football. Chow. The future. Chummy. Really. Easy, soft, like someone's real home somewhere in a real city.

"Naw," I say, shaking my head. I've been on this same page for zillions of years. M-31 in Andromeda. I can't ever find the fucker.

"You get off the bench?" Winston asks.

Martinez comes in. He's our other waiter. Each cottage has two. Primo job. You get to eat first, go in early, come out late, get to get up and move around during chow, get to wear those sexy waiter's jackets.

Martinez sits down at a table across from Winston, where Charles usually sits, lights up a Pall Mall.

"Bambi never plays," Martinez teases. "He just collects splinters."

Har har, I say, turn to Winston. "No, no action for the star," I tell him.

"What's Cincinnati like?" Winston wonders.

I tell him it's very cool, very big, the buildings amaze me, the streets seem so narrow, it is like being in a canyon.

Sounds like Chicago, he says. Butts his cigarette.

"Where'd you go after chow?" Martinez wonders.

"You writing a book?" I ask.

"Yeah," he sneers back playfully.

"Leave that chapter out," I say. I light up now.

We three chuckle. I am okay. Feel fine now. These guys like me. Don't know how queer I am. Never will neither. Not if I can help it. I'm okay with Martinez here, too; he's Winston's friend and does nothing for me, which cools me down. I can act like a normal kid, whatever that is, the three of us together.

"I know!" Winston says suddenly. "You went out to the cemetery, didn't you?"

I stare incredulously.

"I knew it," he says, banging his hand flat on the table top.

I eat it up. They spend so much time wondering about me, as if I'm important or something.

"Wrong," I lie.

Winston sits up, leans both forearms on the table top: "Now, why you wanna go and lie like that? Hmmm . . . ?"

It seems like everyone can read minds but me. I like it, though. Him knowing. Him being so sure about me. Fuck. Him just being interested.

Martinez says across to Winston, his eyes half shut, sly: "Something weird about a guy likes cemeteries so much. . . ."

Winston agrees one thousand percent.

It makes me think of Dad. On passes, once a month,

we go to cemeteries. We used to visit Mom's grave that first year, the first year after she died. Every month a visit to her grave. Dad's real proud of the plot next to hers, empty, paid for, his. We kneel to say a prayer over her grave.

We stopped going about the time the earth had settled and was all level. But we had found other cemeteries by then, lots of them. Little ones like Massie Creek. Old ones like the one in Yellow Springs. Lots of dead babies in those old ones. Dad says they died young back then. They put the exact lifetime on there, too, right on the tombstone.

1 YR., 2 MOS., 3 DYS.

I wonder about them. Never had a chance. I even think sometimes there ain't no heaven and that is all they got. 1 yr., 2 mos., 3 dys.

1 yr., 2 mos., 3 dys. of mindless baby life. What do you remember then? Rasco says maybe there's something to this reincarnation shit. Where your soul gets to live in a bunch of bodies until you finally work out all the things your soul has to work out. Until you know the answer. Like everything is love.

It ain't, of course.

"Showers, you guys," I say. Nine o'clock. Charles is still in there.

22

I KNOW WHAT IT IS.

I lead night prayers. Everyone goes to bed. I walk the house, check everyone, flip the lights.

"Turn it off, Johnson."

He moans, turns it off. No radios after lights out.

I know what it is.

When you're a shit, you're a shit all the way from your first cigarette to your last dying day when you're a shit.

It's in my head. I'm singing it silently to myself.

I shower.

They are still in there. Whiteworm and Charles.

When you're a shit, you're a shit all the way.

I hurry my shower, don't know why, yes I do. I come out, look, smell, sniff the silent air. What's that? I hear it, a radio, Johnson's at it again, it is very soft. I walk right into his bedroom next to mine—we're downstairs—I hear it just a hair better when I reach the double sink and mirror in the middle of the room. I see nothing. Never mind, I say to myself. I'd do it, too. I did it, in fact, hiding my radio under my covers when I was just a sophomore. Quincy was my commissioner. He called me Banana. He let on like he didn't know and let me.

I exit, go to my room.

When you're a shit—Please, Officer Krupke, just give us a break.

I hurt him. I did. I know that's it. Charles *knows.* Charles gonna heal this child, too.

I put my pjs on over my underwear and take one last cruise around the house. Everyone tucked in.

" 'Night, Bambi," Martinez says. Upstairs, bedroom three.

"Go to sleep," I say.

"Right," Johnson says.

Suddenly I fill with love, all wonderful Big Daddy powerful. These guys are just like me, OK—fucked up, sure, but OK. All the quiet, dark boy bodies tucked in. I'm checking 'em once, checking 'em twice, I just say it, don't know why, I am feeling so full of this thing, I wanna cry or something.

"You're OK, you guys, you really are."

I check bedrooms four and five. Winston's in five. It's dark, not a sound. I slip in, I slip out. OK. It ain't so bad being homeless.

I tiptoe down the stairs, the creaky wooden stairs roaring underfoot. The light is still shining under Charles's door. In for the night, boss, in for the night.

I turn out all the lights, all except the one lamp in the living room. I stand barefoot in the front hall under the clock. Ten P.M.

I remember my novena. I head back to my bedroom. I stop at the doorway, stand quietly listening: nothing. Kids, we fall asleep pretty fast. Most of us. Except Martinez. He always has a helluva go. Doesn't want anyone to know either. Doesn't know I know. I just check. Want everyone to be happy.

Satisfied that everyone's asleep, I go into my room, find my tiny Tensor lamp by feeling around in the dark. I click it on: it's a fucking beacon. I see my novena booklet gleaming in its light, where's my rosary? Where's my fucking rosary?

Fucking rosary? I am a lost soul for sure. I can't even *think* clean thoughts.

I don't see it anywhere.

I beam my tiny Tensor lamp toward my locker. It's closed, of course. I set the tiny lamp down and it immediately falls over on my bed. Fuck it. I open my locker and can't see shit at first. There, next to my toothbrush, okay.

I kneel by my bed, on the far side away from little dumbshit Cruise. No sense blinding him. He's this little ignorant shit freshman who is all the time wanting to hang around me and Winston and Martinez. We shoved his head in the toilet once because he never combs his hair. He wouldn't shower, only we have to and even then he never gets his hair wet. He gets up in the morning, puts his clothes on, never bothering to wash up, his hair sticking up every which a way how it does you just get up. We done gave the fool four hundred combs. "Comb your hair, that's all, will ya, huh?" I beg. He never will, never does. So we just hoisted his ass up one Saturday morning, me and Winston grabbing him by the ankles, Martinez holding the can door for us, and we stuck him in there, headfirst like a plunger. "You'll comb it now, won't you, Cruise? Say yes, Cruise," dunk dunk dunk and we're all laughing and Cruise is shrieking—only the little shit thinks it is the best thing since popcorn, all this attention, see, the little bugger is just eating it up. Still didn't fucking comb his hair either.

Was I that small then?

I pray my novena, whipping through it. I've got it down. I can do it in ten minutes if I want to. I want to tonight. I rush it, pushing that song out of my head as it refuses to go: When you're a shit, you're a shit all the way from your first cigarette to your last dying day when you're a shit.

I turn out my Tensor lamp. Whiteworm's still in. "It's okay," I try on myself. "It's okay. Charles is just gonna help him, too, that's all." He needs it, too, you shit, and I won't let myself remember it, what I did to him, it comes to me, this clear picture of him standing there all wounded begging pleading needing a-wanting lost and what do I do, Mr. Nice Guy the Rat.

Mom is in my dream. She is standing back, distant, indifferently caring. She is touching me, touching my toe. She's wiggling my toe.

"It's time. It's time."

It's Charles. He is wiggling my toe. He is touching the back of my right knee now, whispering softly, gently.

"It's time. It's time."

He lays his fingers, three of them, on my shoulder. He is nudging me awake. He leans in so close I can feel the warmth of his breath. Reminds me of Beaudene.

"Unnh?" I go.

"Time for mass," he says, straightening up.

I lift my head and see the first pale gray morning light.

"Okay," I say and curl up into a fetal position. I stretch my arms out straight from this position. I want him to leave. I don't want to get out of bed until he is out of the room.

He is lingering. He is staring down at me. I cringe and turn my head to the wall.

"I'm awake. Okay?" I say.

"Something wrong?" he asks tenderly.

"No. I am just not awake yet. That's all."

Geez.

He says okay and moves to Cruise. He wiggles him good, so I can hear the bedsprings rattling.

"Time to get up for mass, Cruisey-Bruisey," he croons lovingly.

I think this guy Charles really loves his boys. He's awful sweet this morning.

Cruise rolls in his bed. I roll over to look. Little Cruise swings his feet out, throws his covers back, and his little pecker is standing stiff. He doesn't wear skivvies under his pjs. Kid is oblivious.

I get up. It is my job to get everyone out for morning prayers. Charles wakes me, I wake the rest. I go to my locker and stand between the doors. Cruise is still sitting in front of his hard-on. I grab my jeans, step into them, and get a move on, tugging and buttoning as I go.

Tuesday mornings are high school mass days. We all have to go. The main chapel is packed. The Monsignor is saying mass this morning. Good. He is fast. He can get through a thirty-minute mass in twelve point five minutes.

I see Franklin, my little brother, in a pew on the side altar.

The mosaic of Our Lady of Perpetual Help gleams luminously just at the sanctuary. It is supposed to be a portrait painted by St. Luke. I read that on one of the little cards Juan Carlos passed out to us kids in the Legion of Mary at about the same time Monsigneur had her put in.

She's got these huge eyes. Juan Carlos says this is meaningful.

I don't know.

She just looks dumb to me. These huge, empty eyes. I mean, when I read that St. Luke is supposed to have painted her, the real Mary, mother of Jesus, God, was I depressed. See, she's a real homely dame. The dame in this picture anyway. And the baby Jesus ain't no great shakes either. He looks like a forty-year-old, no lie. Just like a midget with a grown-up face and baby's body.

And Juan Carlos is telling us: "The entire painting is rife with meaning—Jesus' down-turned palms, his dangling sandal, Mary's eyes. . . ."

I don't know.

What I do like is how brilliant and shining it is. The whole thing is painted on this gleaming golden background that simply beams out at you. It seems to jump out at you. I like that.

I see Whiteworm after mass and feel ashamed. I duck my head. Don't look at me. I know I have to do something. I have to say something to him. Not right now, though, okay?

"Freddy!"

That's Franklin. No one but Franklin calls me Freddy. No way.

He catches up to me halfway up the PRIVATE Dead End DRIVE that runs down in front of the main chapel.

"This Sunday," he says, starting right in the middle of a sentence. "Right?"

"I don't know," I say. I know what he's talking about. Our monthly pass.

"Well, it is," he insists. "Lyman told Juan Carlos to tell me."

"Must be true, then," I say.

"I wanna go to the Loew's Ames again," he says. He's already planning our day. We reach the black-and-white sign at the end of the private drive. Monsignor's residence is at the end of it, connected to and right next to the main chapel. There's a cul-de-sac at the end of the drive that whirls around in front of the Monsignor's garage. His plain black Chrysler sits in there.

PRIVATE Dead End DRIVE.

"We went to the Loew's Ames last month," I say. I give the sign a whack as we pass it.

"I know," he says. "I still wanna go. Will you go with me, huh?"

"Yeah, sure. Why not?" I say, which makes him happy. Me, too. "I like the movies as much as you do," I tell him so he doesn't get the idea that I am just doing it for him. It's true, too. I do like the movies as much as he does. Dad doesn't, though. He never goes with us. It gives him a chance to take his nap.

"We'll see what Dad has up his sleeve first, okay?" I say.

"He never has anything up his sleeve. You know that," Franklin says matter-of-factly.

He's right. Dad who is all the time saying nothing. Wha'-choo want to do today, boys?

We're at the flag circle that is in front of the grade school dining hall. We part company here. A bunch of Franklin's friends come up and herd him away.

"See ya," he calls out.

Yeah. See ya.

Boom!

What the fuh—

Someone has just slammed me hard. I go flying forward. I almost go down. I don't. I catch myself. I shoot my right hand out and push up. My knee comes within an inch of the pavement.

"Fucking rats everywhere," Kuhns says.

Kuhns, Foster, and Fogarty stride through, mowing me down.

I leap away and get off the pavement entirely. I let them pass. I can see this is going to be one wonderful autumn.

I watch them go. Droves of boys stride past as I let the morons get out of reach. This is when I see Rasco's eye.

Holy shit!

Rasco's walking with three other colored kids. It's a private thing. Off limits to white kids. It's not hostile shit, I don't mean that. I remember Sebastian and Mack had it, too, when they were hanging around colored kids only.

I don't know.

It is just a feeling. There is something invisible in the air that gets all over your skin if you try to barge in—if you are dumb enough not to notice you are not welcome and try stupidly to be a part of it. Lots of white kids do, too. And you can't. Not unless you are colored. I can't explain it, obviously, but I do know it is something good. Something good they have because they are colored. Something good they have that I cannot have, ever.

They pass me—Rasco, McNamara, Wright, Jackson—embedded in boy packs. Twosomes, trios, quartets. Kids sticking together like magnets. Kids yakking away shoulder to shoulder. Kids being kids together.

Suddenly it dawns on me. I see it as I stand here reviewing the passing horde: it is in moments like these, as we march from one activity to another, that we are truly free to be ourselves. Free from adult intrusion. Here, tucked up inside this moving mass of boys, kids are finally free to be themselves.

Rasco and those guys pass within three feet of me. I am up on the rolling, softly sculpted curb. I am rocking gently as I watch the parade of boys passing by. I see Rasco's eye *big as life*. It is the biggest, most Technicolor shiner I have ever seen. It shakes me physically. I lose my balance.

I have never seen a shiner this bad—except once in a newspaper photograph when I was a seventh-grader. Juan Carlos had cut it out of the morning paper and pinned it up on the prefect room door in First Left, the apartment I lived in that year. It was a shot of Carmen Basilio's face after his title bout against Gene Fullmer. Basilio's eye looked obscene. The caption under the picture read: THIS IS FUN?

Rasco's eye is that bad. Or worse. It's swelled shut and puffed out from his face something awful. Almost as big as a golf ball standing out from his face, no lie. It'll shake you up you see something like that.

I think I got trouble and my friend is probably going to be blind.

I am one of the last ones to the dining hall. I reach my place just as we say grace.

"Bless us, O Lord, and these Thy gifts which we are about to receive from Thy bounty through Christ our Lord Amen."

BRRRRRIIIIIIIINNNNNNNnnnnnnngggggg!

Four hundred eighty-eight boys drag their metal-tipped chairs across the quarry tile. It is the roar of a million horny elephants trumpeting to the wind.

We attack our breakfast fare.

I see Whiteworm. He seems so serene this morning. Charles done healed the boy overnight.

There is a hand on my shoulder. It startles me. I leap in my skin. My seat leaps with me.

"It's just me," Charles says, laughing at my silliness.

"A bit touchy today," Winston says. That surprises me, too. What? You got radar, son? I catch Winston's eye for a second. We look at each other. Someone asks for more milk. Winston grabs the pitcher. "Okay," he says and gets up to get it.

Charles's hand is still on my shoulder. He leans into me, brings his mouth close to my ear. I get chills as I feel his breath in my ear. My body gives a little shake all by itself.

"Your dad's coming Sunday," Charles says right in my ear.

I nod my head. I hold my body stiff. He's too close. I don't like it when people get too close. I lean my head away. He straightens up.

Thank you.

His hand's still in place.

On my shoulder.

I don't want to be touched.

Please.

I reach for a box of Sugar Pops. I slip out from under his grasp as I do.

After chow Whiteworm walks with Charles. Whiteworm goes up to him. They meet in front of the entrance to the counselor's dining hall. I motor past them. The temperature inside my face rises to 451 degrees Fahrenheit. I burn holes in the earth-colored quarry tiles with my eyes. They sure have become chummy. What fucking gives?

I remember Rasco's eye the moment I reach the flagstone porch. I stop and whirl back around to face the dining hall doors. Kids pour past me. The onslaught of exiting boys pushes me back. I let it and drift back to the low, knee-high brick wall. Kuhns comes out with Foster and Brower. I see them and pretend I don't. I look past them. I crane my neck. I look over their heads. I am acting very intent, see? Now where is he? Hmm? Rasco? Where is he?

If I pretend hard enough, you know. Maybe they won't notice me.

It's no use, though.

"Smell a rat?" Kuhns says as he comes right at me. All three of them alter their course slightly, aiming my way.

Ignore them, son. Ignore them.

I try.

"What makes a kid rat on his friends?" Brower says as they reach me. He reaches for my face. I flinch.

''C'mon!'' I protest. I back away.

''You know what rats get,'' Foster says.

The three of them keep coming at me even as I back away.

I back into the low brick wall. I am trapped.

''They get killed,'' Kuhns says. He lunges for me.

I leap up and back. I spring over the low brick wall. I land half on top of a couple of kids from the choir section.

''Sorry,'' I say hurriedly. I stumble and twist away from them. I am in a real panic. I bolt out across the pavement and run out onto the grass. I don't stop running until I reach the main road that runs in front of the dining hall. I stop all out of breath and look back. They are just yukking up a storm. Laughing their fool heads off. Smolinski's joined them now. They ain't about to be chasing me, though. I see that and breathe a sigh of relief.

I watch them walk off the dining hall porch and head back to their cottages. I forget all about Rasco's eye.

23

I REMEMBER IT AGAIN IN HALSTEAD'S PHYSICS CLASS. I am already in my seat when Rasco comes strolling in. His shiner's beaming away, all puffy and Technicolor. No lie, there's blues, blacks, even purples in there. It's shut up pretty tight, too. It hurts just looking at it.

I don't go up to him. I leave him be. I'm in a seat way up against the wall by the windows, away from the door. Safe from the Jock-O set. Or so I think.

Halstead, all six feet, four inches of him, comes striding into the room.

Foster and Kuhns come in right behind him. Kuhns spies me, stops in his tracks, giving me the dirty looks. He taps his friend on the shoulder and they part company. Kuhns is coming the long way around to his seat. He's coming my way. Terrific.

He passes in front of me and bumps my books. They spin sideways, but don't fly off the desk.

"Oh, I'm so-o sorry," he says and pretends to help me as I straighten them again. I'm like that. I like my books to be neat. I arrange them so their edges match the edges of the table top here.

He gives them a good little shove and flips them onto the floor. My papers go every which a way.

He's oh-so sorry, he says again and stoops to help me as I retrieve them. He lowers his voice so only I can hear: "Your ass is grass, fruit."

I scoop up my books and papers and scurry back to my seat.

"Okay, gentlemen," Halstead says at the bell. Then he notices Rasco's eye.

"My goodness," he says in shock. "What happened to you? You okay?" His voice is brimming with compassion and concern.

I whirl around in my seat. I am delighted. Yes, yes, yes.

Only it is all wrong, of course.

Rasco blushes.

"Nothing," he says. He drops his head and lifts his left hand to his face. He rests his fingertips on his forehead. His eye is obscured.

His color changes. He's purplish black now. It amazes me to watch a colored kid blush.

I turn back around. Don't look. Don't ask. Just leave him be.

Halstead is cool, no lie.

"Sorry," he says softly. Halstead gets the message. He leaves Rasco be.

The entire class is still.

Brower comes tooling in. He's late. He slithers past Halstead and takes a seat behind me. The moment he's landed, he farts into his wooden seat, *brr-rowww.*

It is stupendously noisy in this silence.

The whole class cracks up.

Halstead picks up his pointer and comes out from behind his desk. He walks right up to Brower, tapping his pointer against his open palm.

We all hold our breath.

Halstead is good. He doesn't go all haywire like our eighth-grade shop teacher, Mallone, did on me that time.

We had been talking about Miss Pritchard, this stunning beauty who taught remedial English. Maya had her.

She loved his ass.

And he's coming back to the building every day announcing what color her underwear is.

We're just chewing the fat, see, before the bell. We're in shop. We're hotshit eighth-graders. We're getting all fired up about this raving beauty who wears different colored underwear every day. And how does Maya manage it? Dropping pencils, right?

And we're imagining it, imitating it, dropping to the floor, looking up . . .

Suddenly Mallone jumps in. He's been at his desk in the front of the shop. We didn't think he could hear us. We didn't think he was paying any attention.

He is tut-tutting at his silly little juvenile eighth-graders. He holds his head tilted back so his words seem to come down out of his nostrils.

"You wouldn't be raving so much about her being shop teacher if she came in here wearing a pair of coveralls," he says. He's got this terrifically self-satisfied smile on his face.

Mr. Motor Mouth Gamble inserts one foot: "Not if they were skintight," I say.

My mind is brimming with Miss Pritchard's Coke-bottle form, her lovely lips rouged red, now salmon, now pink, now cerise, her sweet scent upon the air, her warmth for the boys real and soul deep, ah.

Mallone jerks from his seat. He comes around his desk and strolls down my aisle with his dowel in his right hand. He is smacking that dowel into his left hand. He bears down on me. I know I am dead.

"This punk here," he says as he nods down at me while not looking at me, closing on me the whole while, "this punk is still wet behind the ears."

He's on me now. He's standing right over me.

He is quietly enraged.

He snaps his dowel down upon my head, crack. He shifts quickly from my head to my shoulder, snap snap, and back to my head again, crack. He speaks softly to the class as he blazes away: "He thinks he knows it all, thinks he's all grown, doesn't he?"

I am ducking, flinching, trying vainly to protect my head with my hands and forearms.

He bops away, stinging me with his dowel, stinging my arms, my noggin, my shoulder. I'm taking most of it on my arms and forearms so he shifts his attack. He snaps that dowel against my shin. I reach down to protect myself and he cracks me solidly upon my scalp. I shoot my arm up and he goes again for my leg, setting my shin afire.

He drones on and on to the class the whole while I am under attack. I am a boy who hasn't yet learned how to talk about his betters.

He's cool. It is all in his wrist. He's snapping me with that dowel, going from my shin to my forearm to my scalp to my shin to my scalp to my forearm to my shin to my scalp.

Snap! Snap! Snap!

He reduces me to sniveling, snotty sobs.

My arms are on fire. My shins are aflame. My scalp is stinging and leaping up through my hair.

Not Halstead. He stands ominously before Brower and says: "We do something to deserve your wrath, Mr. Brower? Hmm? You trying to asphixiate us?"

The whole gang of us breaks up. Even badass Brower is looking just like a seventeen-year-old, just a kid riding that sawtooth edge between baby fat and whiskers.

Halstead, he's so nice.

"Maybe you could crack a window there for us, Mr. Brower," he says as he walks back to the front of the class.

Brower gets up and opens the window right next to me. He even smiles at me.

At the bell Halstead asks me to stop by his office later that day.

"I have a study hall seventh period." I say.

Fine, he says.

I grab my books and hustle on to my next class.

Now what have I done? Oh God. I'm always in trouble.

"I'm here to see Mr. Halstead," I tell Mr. Watson, the office administrator.

"Have a seat," he says. I take one of the three chairs set against the wall. I balance my books on my thighs. Watson's staring at me when I look up. He looks away as soon as I look up. He's one of the people Kuhns and those guys are all the time mocking in the locker room. They say Watson's an out-and-out queer. They say he's always trying to get the boys to come over to his apartment when they come in on passes on Saturdays. They say he's hot for Foster.

"You can go in now," Watson says.

Thanks.

I go in.

"Sit down, Fred," Mr. Halstead says.

I sit.

He is looking through some papers on his desk. He's searching for something. He looks a bit harried. The absentminded professor.

"Here it is," he says. He lifts out a two-page letter and waves it at me.

"I wanted to talk to you about this," he says, waving it again.

What have I done? It looks official. My stomach rolls.

"Here," he says. He hands the letter to me.

I take it.

"Read it," he says absentmindedly. He hasn't looked up from his shuffling and hunting. He's got a desk full of papers. He's assistant principal as well as physics teacher.

I look at the letter. It's from some lady in Louisville, Kentucky. She is with the Bellamy Flag Awards.

Halstead stops shuffling through his papers.

"Here's the scoop," he says.

I stop reading the letter and wait for the scoop.

He clears his throat and then launches into a little spiel about the Bellamy Flag Awards, which is this award given to a different high school each year to honor that school for exemplifying the great American spirit as represented in the Pledge of Allegiance. Bellamy's the guy who wrote the pledge back around the turn of the century. The Home won the award back in 1948, the year the Founder died. Each year we send a representative to congratulate the current year's winner.

"Got it?" he asks as he screeches to a stop. The man talks fast. I like that.

Got it, I say.

"We would like you to be the Home's representative this year."

Yeah?

"You've been on the dais before and seem to handle yourself okay. What do you say?"

I've been on the dais for the junior-senior banquet. I MC-ed, introduced everybody.

"Sure," I say. "I'd love to."

"Great!" Halstead says. He reaches across his desk. Huh?

"The letter," he says impatiently. "Gimme the letter."

Oh, sure, I say and hand it over.

"When is it?" I ask. He's about to send me on my way and I don't know jack squat about it.

"It's in the letter," he says. *"Watson!"* he calls and scares the shit out of me. "We'll give you a copy," he says to me and smiles when he sees I'm just now getting back inside my skin, thank you. "Sorry," he says, "didn't mean to startle you."

Watson appears in the office door.

"Copy this, please. For our friend here."

Watson steps forward and takes the letter. He starts to leave when Halstead stops him. "And Watson?"

Yes? Watson stops and turns at the door.

"Let Mr. Creighton know Gamble's our man, okay?"

Okay.

"Thank you," Halstead says. Watson disappears. Creighton's the principal.

We sit silently a moment. Waiting for my copy. I feel awkward. I like this guy, but I don't talk to these guys. I mean, what do you say?

Halstead breaks the silence for us.

"Glad you're not involved in all this football nonsense," he says.

"Huh?"

Is he talking about what I think he's talking about?

"All this trouble," he explains. He looks distressed. His forehead wrinkles together up over his eyes. He fiddles with the piles and piles of paper on his desk as he goes on.

"All this trouble the captains got themselves into," he says. "What was it? Drinking beer after the Moellar game?" He doesn't wait for me to answer. "That counselor who went up to the lake with you. The one who played tackle with OSU? What's his name. Big guy. He told me. He said it was up to the lake that he first suspected it. That the boys might be fooling with some beer."

I am flabbergasted. Dick?

Halstead is on a roll.

"He told me," he goes on, and he's shaking his head something awful here, "that he didn't want the boys to lose control."

Halstead looks at me the way Charles does sometimes when he's trying to be one of the boys. It's sorta neat and unnerving all in one.

"He told me he didn't want the boys to start the season off on the wrong foot." Halstead looks pretty disgusted. I'm afraid to ask. It's The Big Dick, isn't it? It's The Big Dick who's the rat. It's The Big Dick who turned their asses in.

Suddenly I remember The Big Dick coming onto the athletic bus after the game and how he just smiled as they flung all that fatass shit at him.

Halstead is shaking his head.

"I don't know," he says and looks up at me. Maybe it's the wide-eyed look I certainly have on my face. Maybe he just realizes I'm just a kid. I don't know. Whatever it is, he decides he's said enough. And says so.

"Well," he says, getting back to his piles and piles of paper " 'nough said."

Watson is back in the office doorway with my copy.

"Good," Halstead says, nodding to me. Watson hands

me my copy and scoots. Halstead looks at me in that funny, poor-poor-orphan way a lot of the visitors do. I squirm.

"I'm happy you have managed to sidestep this nonsense," he says. He looks so forlorn. It's probably tearing his ass apart that the starters are in such trouble. After all the stories he's told us over the years about his basketball days.

I fold my copy of the letter and clear my throat.

"That all?" I ask.

"Yes," he says. He's so sad. "That's all."

Thank you, I say and beat it out of there.

24

I TELL WINSTON ABOUT THE WATERLOO TRIP. HE IS ALL excited and happy for me.

''Way to go, Bull,'' he says.

Martinez comes in. Ignorant little shit Cruise is right on his heels like a fucking barnacle.

''Way to go what?'' Martinez wants to know.

Cruise, too.

''Way to go what?'' he squeaks. His fucking hair is standing to attention in six different places.

I show them the letter and tell them about this flag-award thing. Waterloo West High School is the 1962–63 winner, in Waterloo, Iowa.

''You're going to make a speech, Bull?'' Martinez asks.

Winston started this ''Bull'' business. Gam-bull, right? Mr. Frederick Joseph Gam-Bull, one of the tiniest seniors at one-twenty-seven. No Bull he. Har har.

Some of us humans just invite it.

Some of us like it.

Even the Bambi shit—not at first, though. The buck-toothed doe, right? But I do like it. Privately, alone at night I think, you know, that at least someone is noticing me. That counts for something. Take Cowen over there. He's sitting all by himself right now in the same place he sits every day, day in and day out, all by his lonesome. After school he's sitting there, after charges he's sitting there, after mass he's sitting there, after everything he's sitting there, in his corner of the study hall, doing nothing, smoking cigarettes.

Smoking cigarettes and doing nothing at all.

No one's nicknaming him.

The Cipher is what it should be.

"Yup," I answer Martinez, I am going to make a speech. "I have to write it first," I go on, "and then send a copy off to this lady." I point to the lady's name at the bottom of page two.

"Hands off," I say to ignorant little shit Cruise. He's got his grubby little hands all over my binoculars—Halstead's binoculars, I mean. I checked them out of the science lab to stargaze.

"Aw, come on, let me look," he begs. His tiny, squeaky voice is like fingernails on a blackboard.

"You can't see shit now anyway, jerk," Winston says. It ain't dark yet.

"Sure I can," he says and dashes to the window. He holds them to his face. They dwarf him. It's like holding up a tank to his tiny face. And his goddamned hair jutting up every which a way, it drives me mad.

"You be careful?" I ask, relenting. It ain't his fault he's such a jerk.

He nods.

"They ain't mine, you know? I got them out of the science lab."

He's looking out the window and doesn't seem to be paying attention. He's loving those glasses.

"Cruise!" I say.

"I heard you," he says. He looks at me now. The little fucker is just beaming away. He did hear me. He heard me relenting and just loves it.

"Thank you, Bull," he says and beams some more. He hoists those tank glasses back up to his mug.

It hardly takes anything to make the little fart happy. We ought to shove his ass in the john every day.

Winston catches my eye—he knows. This big brother thing. It's sorta gorpy but I do it, other kids, too, I've seen it. Acting loving and big brotherly to little ignorant shits like Cruise who need it. And need it bad.

Winston gives me one of his terrific Chicago smiles.

He's got this nifty button-down shirt on, it's open to his breastbone. There is not a hair in sight. His skin is satiny smooth.

My pores open up just to look at him.

I tear my eyes away.

"You okay?" he asks.

Huh? Oh, yeah. Sure.

I look at him again and remember what Charles warned him about. I can't believe adults sometimes. It really puzzled Winston. He couldn't believe it. He had to ask me, is this true? Can this be true?

Charles had warned him against wearing his favorite red cotton basketball shorts. Charles had told him he probably shouldn't do it so often. He'd said it could get some of the boys worked up what with Winston showing so much leg.

And fine leg at that.

"This shit can't be true," Winston says to me when he's asking me, can this be true? We're sitting on the top step, on the landing actually, of the stairs that lead upstairs to the bedrooms on the second floor. It's a Saturday morning. Everyone is doing their Saturday charges, which are like weekly spring cleanings. He is wearing his red cotton basketball shorts. We are sitting side by side on the top step. His legs run down in front of both of us.

You know, boys look like girls some before they start getting whiskers and deep voices and shit like that. Halstead had talked some about it in Biology when we were sophomores. He said you get sex hormones along about puberty, which he says hits you at 12, 13, 14, around in there, depending upon the kid. Me, along about thirty.

Anyway, here I am fielding this question. From Winston who has no idea, none whatsoever. He cannot believe a boy would be hot for another boy and he's asking me.

I don't know what to say.

I am sitting here drooling, right this fucking minute,

his beautiful legs running down before me and he's asking me.

And I know he needs to be reassured that *it just isn't so.*

When all the time I know it is so.

The Bull included.

The Bull especially.

I don't know what to say.

So that's what I tell him. We are there on the landing together. The house is filled with rock 'n' roll, there are sixteen radios going all at once. I look down through the banister and tell him: "I don't know," I say and realize it's a lie. So I change it: "I ain't sure why he'd be talking to you about that." Which is true.

Fucking Charles. What's he talking this trash for?

Winston looks only more puzzled. And pissed.

Here I am hotter'n a pistol wanting to latch onto his tight little ass myself, yes, right this very fucking minute. And Charles has gone and fucked it up. Putting this shit in his head. Damn.

Suddenly there's this very clear choice. A choice I realize I have managed to not notice before. Do I tell him the truth? Or do I pretend it just isn't so and continue to hope for the right situation? The right situation in which I can make my move?

Oh, shit.

I am sitting here aching with it. Full of it. I think it's love. Or like it. How I feel. I could just eat this kid.

I know I don't think I should.

I shouldn't try with a kid who is under me.

I've known that from the beginning, when Charles first picked me. I've known that.

And I have not let myself see it as clearly as I must see it right this minute. He is asking point-blank. He is trusting me to tell him true.

I've let myself sort of blur that idea in my mind: maybe it will just happen. Don't think about it too much.

It is time to choose.

I look at his lovely legs running down the stairs before us. I look at his face. He's all torn up here, wondering, not believing, disgusted.

He's a good kid. He doesn't know. He deserves to know.

I swallow my own desire.

I decide to tell him the truth.

''It's true, Winston,'' I start. ''That shit—''

I cannot bring myself to actually say it: a lot of us are queer. Most of us are queer.

''—that shit Charles is telling you about your red shorts and boys getting worked up. . . ?'' I say and then stop. I blow out a jet of air and then go on. ''Well, it's true.''

Winston pulls his legs in. He brings his knees up to his chest. It only makes him look sexier.

''C'mon, Bull . . .'' he protests. This shit can't be true. He doesn't want to hear this.

''I'm sorry,'' I say. I cannot look at him right now.

I get up. I am compelled to get up. I stand. I stretch on the top step here, my arms a way up over my head — I tell him again.

''I am sorry, but it is true.''

I look out over the first floor hallway spreading out below us. Then I look down at him. He's still sitting with his legs pulled up to his chest as sexy as ever.

''I wish he hadn't said anything to you,'' I say. He looks up at me. He's a beautiful kid. ''But it is true.''

25

AFTER NIGHT PRAYERS I GO INTO CHARLES'S OFFICE. There's something new in here. The fucker's got a brand-new stereo console.

I go right up to it. It's lid is open. It's on.

Why must I be a teenager in love?

Dion and the Belmonts do me in. Break my heart.

Sometimes I feel so happy.
Sometimes I feel so sad.
Sometimes I—

"Like it?"

I nearly shit my pants, *aye!*

It's Charles. He's just come in behind me.

"Yeah," I say, putting my hand to my breast. "You scared me."

He laughs and shuts the door behind him.

Sorry, he says.

It's okay, I say. I'm okay.

"This is *great,*" I say, turning back to his stereo. "When did you get this?"

He goes to his seat by the window. It's a bit crowded over there now. This stereo runs along most of the wall.

Each night I ask the stars up above
Why must I be-ee a teenager in love?
In love.

I sit in the loveseat.

''Just today,'' he says as he gets comfortable.

''It's beautiful,'' I say. ''Wood, too,'' I say, admiring it. It is beautiful, too. It really is.

''Walnut,'' Charles says. ''That isn't all, either,'' he says and nods to a box in the corner. It's a chess set. The board is out with a single pawn, the king, a knight, and a bishop on display. They're each about two inches tall and made out of sculpted wood.

''Holy shit,'' I say without thinking. I look at him in a panic, but he just smiles and tells me not to worry with a wave of his hand. Juan Carlos got us all into chess. He taught me and Whiteworm and Kuhns and Ezra and Maya and everybody. We played all summer, that first year Juan Carlos was here, out on the front porch of Building One. Lyman couldn't get at us. It damn near drove him wild. He would never play, neither. Not Lyman. He'd only play hard ball. It was fucking wonderful.

Tollens is at the office door.

''Everyone's in,'' he says. He's my assistant. Everyone's in bed.

''Thanks,'' Charles says. ''G'night.''

And then Tollens does the Building One chant.

''Good night, Charles,'' he says, surprising us both, ''God bless you.''

Charles is mildly shocked. Me, too. Tollens eats it up. He turns to me now.

''Good night, Bambi, God bless you.''

I'm on automatic pilot. Haven't done this in years—it's kind of nice: ''Good night, Tollens, God bless you, too.''

Tollens turns tail and skeddadles. Charles looks over at me.

''You *are* a good kid, aren't you?'' he says—asks.

I like that. I don't know what he's talking about, though. I look at him, hmm?

''This God-bless-you business. Your altar-boy work—what? six years now? Right?

Right, I say.

"And now this novena business?"

I can feel the heat rising from my neck. Careful, Charles.

"The boys respect you. Here in the house, you know?"

Yeah?

I am eating this up. As in *eating it up*.

"Like Tollens just now," he goes on, really warming to it. "I think he meant it. I think he really wanted God to bless you, you know?"

This God-bless-you business. It was a nice thing, a silly, funny thing sometimes, too. It was good. It was good. I remember when Lyman was on duty. He'd sing it out to us: "Good night, boys. God bless you."

And we'd roar it back at him, asking God to bless him and releasing our pent up terror at the same time.

With others, like Swift the Sneak—he's the one who got into the fight with Wyckoff, crazy fucking maniac Wyckoff with his two-and-a-half-inch wide, silver-star-studded, black leather cowboy belt. When Swift would sing it out—and it was like a song when he did it, he liked it so much—we'd blast that fucker right out of the dorm with it.

He'd have to turn on the lights and give us a talking-to, get us to settle down.

"You miss those days?" Charles asks.

"Not really," I answer truthfully. "We had some good times, though. We really did."

He gives me a big smile and tells me: "I am really proud of you."

Yeah? This is a nice little surprise.

"Yes. You've been doing a real fine job as commissioner here."

Thanks.

"And you've been doing real well with your novena, too, haven't you?"

He's just stepped over the line. He's stepped over and he's staying over.

"You haven't, have you?" he coaxes, trying to draw me out on this one. "Not with yourself or with others, hmmm?"

No. I haven't. It's been nine days now. But I ain't exactly too terribly keen on talking to anyone about it. But he's hot on it, ain't letting it go.

"I'm proud of you."

Yeah?

"You've been setting a good example for Whiteman," he says, shocking me.

That's Whiteworm. His real name's Whiteman. No one calls him that, though.

"We've been talking, Whiteman and I," Charles says.

I nod. I know. I know.

"He's a good boy, Whiteman," Charles adds.

I'm pretty lost here. I'm not sure what's going on. I don't like it much either, not knowing what's going on. It unnerves me. I wrestle for some control. I say: "You like helping boys, don't you?"

"Yes," he says immediately. He looks found out. Delighted and found out. "Yes, I do," he repeats.

I don't know what comes over me. Now I'm telling him: "You've helped me, y'know?"

I hear myself saying it. I amaze myself. It's true, though. He has helped me. I've thought it to myself. I've imagined saying it to him. And now I am actually saying it to him, and it is as if it is the most dangerous thing I have ever done. It is as if my very life is in danger. Weird, huh?

"Thank you," he says with a tenderness that just reels me in.

It's okay, I tell myself. There's no danger. Relax.

"I like you," he says and my fate is sealed. I am a complete and total goner now.

I like you, he says, and something breaks inside of me. Something soft and liquid and explosive. Suddenly I'm just yattering away here, take me, I'm yours: "I've never talked to any counselor before, y'know? I mean, I've really not talked to anyone, at all. You know? But with you, I have. I do. I don't understand it too well, but I like it. I like being able to tell you about Lyman and his nasty ways and how scary and awful it was. And Morton, too. It's meant a lot to me to be able to tell you about Lovely Lester and what he really wanted—and both of them, right, pushing me to open up, y'know? Open up. Trust. You gotta trust somebody, Lyman used to say, and I didn't even know then I wasn't. I know it now, that that's my problem. That I don't open up, that I don't trust none of these guys. And they're all doing the same shit, pushing me to open up, to trust them, to spill my guts while they're bopping me upside the head or trying to get into my pants or something screwy like that, the whole while telling me to open up, open up. And I haven't even told you about Daly, my freshman year. He was into the happy medium. He was always trying to get you to meet him at the happy medium. And I couldn't. I just couldn't.''

I catch my breath and notice the radio's still going. It's the Contours wanting to know do you love me now that I can dance. It catches me. It's a monster hit. Drives me mad. And Charles is totally unaware of it. He's fixed on me. All his attention on the Bambi Gambi here.

I can mashed potatoes. I can do the twist. Now, tell me, baby, do you like it like this?

I look at Charles. He really doesn't hear it at all. I think it's odd that he can be so oblivious but I am too preoccupied with myself to make anything of it. I press on.

''I thought there was something wrong with me,'' I say. I am right back into it. Right where I left off.

Do you looooove me?

I tap myself over my heart. ''Something's missing. Right here.'' Tap tap. ''That's what I think. Me not being able to open up, not being able to trust, don't you think? It's pretty clear, huh?''

He says nothing. He just watches me.

The Contours are gone.

"I know that's my problem. I really do. I've actually known it all along. I didn't need any Lyman Hall or Lester Morton ramming that shit down my throat—and then there's The Big Dick. Who could open up to him? Who could trust him? You know he's the one who ratted on the captains? Did you know that? Huh?"

Charles shakes his head. No. Of course not.

"I didn't think so. No one does. No one but me. And it's fucking me they say did it—Kuhns and all those guys, they say I'm the rat. *Me.* Me who wouldn't trust any adult around here as far as I could throw him. And they've been harassing me something fierce, no shit. It's been awful—"

Suddenly I well up with tears. I'm choking on them. I can't go on, can't see. God, I don't want to go and bawl here or some dumbshit stuff like that.

Charles sits, patiently waiting on me. He says nothing.

I like that. That's what it's all about. You wait on one. You attend one, wait on one, let one be.

I take a deep breath.

Holy shit.

I'm okay now. I ain't about to break down here. I got it under control now. I look up at Charles.

"And then there's you," I say to him, looking him right in the eye. I look right at him and fill with this power. I don't know what it is, exactly, but I like it.

He likes me. That's it.

He thinks I'm okay.

Jesus.

I am all awash again—thinking that he cares, that he really cares, oh, God.

What a fucking basket case I am.

The tears well up a second time. I choke them down. I can't go getting all woozie-floozie here. It's bad enough I go running off at the mouth like this.

It's like those times when I really feel for Mom. It happens in the movies usually. Something real sappy will be going on in the story. Someone will be honestly and truthfully caring for someone else. That first someone will be telling that second someone straight out that I love you, and it gets to me every time. Every time, I tell you. Every fucking time.

I need it. That's all. I know that.

I'll be leaning that way, leaning that way forever. I know that.

I swallow my grief and my sorrow at needing love. I swallow it whole.

Whoa.

I take another deep breath. And again. There.

Charles sits, silently watching me. He's soaking it up. Silently soaking me up.

He looks at me. He looks into my eyes. His love light's shining.

I look at him and realize it is true. He really does care for me. He really does.

Mother fuck.

"I'm all right," I say. I laugh nervously and swallow one more time. "Whew," I say.

"Whew is right," he says, smiling. A tiny, soft smile. He's looking right at me again.

I cannot hold his gaze. It's too rich for me. I look away. I remember my Waterloo trip.

"I've got some good news for you," I say. I'm gonna change the subject here.

"Wait a minute," he says. "Before that," he goes on and his eyes look all steamed up, "before that I just want to say, 'Thanks.' "

I look right at him when he says this. This looking right at people. It's amazing. There is something mysterious and powerful about it, something mysterious and powerful about looking people right in the eye. It is as if all that is in your soul is pouring right out and goes right on across that Great Divide and right into the soul of the other.

Whoa.

I am liking this. I'm telling you. I am liking this.

I drop my gaze to my lap. What a night.

I do tell him about my trip to Waterloo, Iowa. I do tell

him that I have been picked again. That I have been picked to represent the Home. That I have been picked to make a speech.

I am just full of this being wonderful and appreciated and cared for and attended to, and I hardly notice that he ain't paying two rats' asses worth of attention to my big speech.

What the hay.

26

WE SLAUGHTER THE BAPTISTS—THAT'S CEDARVILLE—35–zip. I ride the bench.

Everyone piles on the bus right after the game. There's no free time in Cedarville. Williams, the team manager, lets me sit with him.

The bus pulls out.

The Catholics superior once again. The Old Man always talks about that before the game, to get us up—let's show those fucking Baptists, he'll say.

Someone behind me is yelling out the open window.

"Shut the window, asshole," Huff yells. He's driving. He yells it into the windshield as he looks into the rearview mirror.

The funny thing is, though, the Home is supposed to be nondenominational. It says so right on the billboard that faces the highway. Father McFlaherty's Boys' Home, Home for homeless, neglected, and underprivileged boys regardless of race, color, or creed. It's just an accident that it was founded by a priest, that's all. The priest and his Jewish merchant friend.

But it's run by the Monsignor now, and most everyone is Catholic. If you're not Catholic, they work on you. They try to convert you. They got Pintner finally. He resisted for years. I remember. He was proud of it. Then, he's a sophomore, yeah. Then, as a sophomore he gave in and converted. It was sort of sad.

They never got the one Jewish kid to convert, though.

He'd get to go into Dayton every Friday night for shul. I thought it was school until Rasco straightened me out. Leibowitz was in his house over to the choir section.

I see the back of Rasco's head. He's sitting three rows up. His eye is coming back to normal. He started tonight, too, at center.

He ain't talking to me much, though.

I remember how irritated he got with me over the shul/school business.

"Not school, dipshit," he said to me then. Leibowitz was a freshman. Rasco and I were sophomores. Same year Pintner converted.

"It's shul," Rasco says. "They're Friday-evening services in the synagogue."

"Yeah?" I ask sarcastically. "So what makes you the genius?"

The asshole.

He's shaking his head and shaking his head and shaking his head.

"I'm no genius," he says. "I'm just curious, that's all. He's different, ya know?"

"No, he isn't," I say quickly—got your ass now. "Except for going to shul on Fridays, he's just like you and me," I conclude. Mr. Wisdom.

"That's what I mean, shitface," Rasco says disgustedly. "He ain't all the time praying to Jesus for salvation, ya know?"

I look at him. I think he's being sacrilegious. It scares me.

"My ma," he goes on, "she's all the time thumping her Bible, warning me about the wrath of God. Shit, who needs it?"

I am scared now.

"*Ras*-co," I protest.

"Jesus Christ, Bambi, God ain't gonna strike you dead in your tracks if you go and use your fucking brain, ya know?"

Well, no, I didn't know.

Bambi the boob.

"Catholics ain't the only ones who get into heaven, you know?" he says.

I am not a total basket case.

"I know *that,*" I say.

The thing is—I try to be honest—the thing is, I haven't really given it too much thought. Really. The Catholic church is the one, holy, apostolic Church. The one way. The only way.

There's a roar from the gang in the back of the bus.

The Jock-O heroes are full of their own wondrousness tonight. And rightly so, too. Kuhns threw for three TDs and ran for a fourth. Brower, his main target, caught two of them. Fogarty was ferocious. When he was protecting the quarterback, he's taking out two guys at once, no lie. Foster, too, our roving monster back, he was incredible tonight. The Mean Mother Monster Back is what they all call him. He's just like Fogarty—he loves to hit. Huff said he had fifteen tackles tonight.

The whole gang of them is back there really whooping it up.

They did play well, they really did.

Even Mac got a TD tonight. It was a little sideline pass. God, he's so graceful. He picks it out of the air, plink. Kuhns, he's hotshit, really, he just lays it out there so soft. Mac picks it off and springs into the end zone. I can't wait to see that one on the films.

You should have seen the size of the holes Fogarty was opening up tonight. Wide enough to drive a truck through.

I don't understand how they can get so savage out there. The killer instinct is what the Old Man calls it. His eyes shining. He just fucking loves it, that killer instinct. Damn near makes him drool, no lie.

I ain't got it.

I don't care either, honest.

Well, maybe just a little bit.

Anyway, they're all feeling terrific about themselves

tonight. That means they are leaving me alone, which I appreciate.

Meanwhile I ain't seen a minute of action, of course.

We get back to the Home in no time. It's all of about three miles away. Everyone goes his merry way, heading back to the cottages. I steer clear of everyone. I slip off the bus fast and boogie off into the night all by me lonesome.

I got Rasco on the brain. His eye.

It's Friday night. Most kids get to stay up late to watch *The Late Show* on TV. I circle out from the field house and go out across the varsity field. I'm taking the long way home. It brings me around to the back of our my house, the study hall side. I peer into the window. Cowen is in there smoking all by himself.

I sneak around to the front. There's a little slope to the lawn, so I have to go right up to the living room windows in order to see in.

Winston's sprawled out on the couch in front of the tube. Martinez is one cushion over. Both of them are prone with their feet jutting out onto footstools. Cruise is in a seat next to Martinez. There's a couple of other kids, too, all of them lit up in this Twilight Zone glow. Their faces and bodies are irraditated by the glow coming off the TV. Eerie.

I get a lump in my throat as I look at Winston. I really love this kid. I don't mean sex, either. I mean, he's really a neat kid. He's smart, he's interested in shit, he likes to do things. He does good work on his charge, he's a quick and precise waiter, and he walks with his spine straight. I really like that. He looks you right in the eye when he talks to you, too. He thinks that he is okay—you know, he isn't all the time moping around and moaning about how awful and wretched he is.

He likes me, too. That's a big part of my feeling for him.

He says something to Martinez. Martinez laughs. Cruise scoots forward, trying to get in on the act. Winston laughs now. Martinez backhands Cruise. It's a quick chop across the chest. A little love tap. It doesn't hurt him. Winston laughs again. It makes Cruise smile even as he's nursing his chest, poor baby.

This is my house.

These are my boys.

I am a god or something. Watching like this, sight unseen, it makes me feel like a god or something.

"You can't hear them, numbnuts," I say aloud. Some god.

I do feel good, though. Just being out here, being on the outside looking in. I like it. The great still of the Home settles all about me.

The Home is such a terribly peaceful place.

I check out Charles's window next. I scoot close to the house. Our little plot of stolen turf is three feet out from this wall. It is completely sunk in now. You could never tell it's a transplant.

The beginning of all my troubles, I think, with Kuhns and those guys.

I am thinking about it, about me working out in the yard last summer and Kuhns and Foster tooling by. "Off to play a little b-ball," Foster says. He's so cool. I'm remembering it all and ain't looking where I'm going. I stumble on one of the stumps me and Charles created. An old bush we cut down.

I catch my foot and fling myself chin first right into the brick wall under Charles's window.

"Fuck," I say aloud.

I catch myself before I really hurt myself or make a complete ass out of myself. I lean against the wall and rub my chin. I've just shaved an inch of epidermis off my face.

Cool, Gamble, very cool.

I peek over the sill. Charles's chair is empty. The door's closed, though. His lamp is on. So where is he? Is he in here?

Then I see him.

He's bent over his little chess table. It's this lovely, low table with a cute little pair of stools. He's standing over the boy he's playing with. I can't see who at first. This window's too high. The earth dips right here next to the house. A little erosion that runs right up against the house.

I move over to the next window. I chin myself up with my fingertips.

It's Whiteworm.

Charles is so close he's brushing up against him.

I drop to the ground. I lean against the wall and shake my hands.

These guys are really getting chummy.

Oh, well. They may as well. I'm not interested in becoming the great chess master.

Charles has been trying to get me excited about playing again. He's crazy about it. He wants to start a team or a tournament. He's as excited as a twelve-year-old, honest. He's acting silly. I tell him I am not interested.

"No, I'm just not that excited about it. Sorry," I say.

He drops to his knees. No lie, his hands are clasped in mock prayer.

"Please. Pleeeeezzz," he begs. Of course, he yuks it up good so we both know we are to pretend that he doesn't really care that much. Even as he is fucking dying to get me onto that stool.

I shiver as I remember him on his knees.

It embarrasses me when a grown-up goes and acts like that. They shouldn't be carrying on like that, really. It mixes me up if you want to know the truth. I mean, who is grown and who is not? Ya know?

I don't want to go in yet. I like being out here. I feel free. Even if it is just a few stolen minutes. I don't care. I like being out when everyone else is in.

I think about Rasco again.

It is the Jewish New Year now. He taught me that. It turns out he really got into it. He says he likes to study religions. Having a Jewish kid in the house, he said, was neat.

This time of year, early football season, it's the time of year for two of the most sacred Jewish holidays. Or holy days. Rush-a-wanna, I think. And Yum Keeper. Something like that. I don't know.

I decide to go see Rasco. Maybe I can find out about his eye.

I dash down the slope and race up the circle drive toward the choir section.

It is really a great night. It's cool, not cold. I smell the clean air. I am enjoying the hell out of myself, being out here all alone. Not a soul in sight. I haven't even seen the paddy wagon tonight. Just me and the stars.

Rasco's house is dark on the backside. I cut across the grass and come up on the street side, their study hall side.

Holy shit.

I cannot believe my eyes.

I skulk up close. Sure enough.

The whole gang is on punishment. They're in a huge circle that runs three-quarters of the way around the study hall. They're all squatting with their arms outstretched before them. Each boy has a pillow balanced on his outstretched arms. You have to hold the position, your arms stiff, that pillow balanced. It's murder.

Suddenly the window before me darkens.

Felix moves just before me. He's on the inside. I'm on the outside.

Everyone is looking pretty whipped, pretty grim. It is worse than having to hold up the wall. This pillow squat really kills your arms and your legs and your back and your neck and your butt.

I see Destern, a good friend of Rasco's. I like him, too. He's a good kid. He falls out. Lost his balance. Or is just fucking wasted, worn out. Can't hold it no more. He ain't no Amazon. Built more like me.

Felix springs forward. The man is agile. And I mean a-jile.

I hear it before I see it. It happens so fast. I am hearing it before it registers: flesh on flesh. An awful sound.

Destern lifts off. He's catapaulted off the floor by Felix's flying right. He sails into the wall, *splat*.

A right cross.
Felix.
I think I have diarrhea.
I beat it the fuck out of here.

27

I DO THE FOURTEENTH DAY OF MY NOVENA DURING SUNday morning mass. I did number thirteen last night by my bed. Charles has Whiteworm in again. They were holed up in Charles's office from nine-thirty on.

I don't dwell on it.

Today's pass day. Dad's coming. And I am doing well with my purity thing. Fourteen days. I am proud of myself. Bambi's being as pure as the wind-driven snow.

You should see Destern's eye, though. Now it is *his* eye I am worrying about. It is bulging from his face. It looks awful raw and tender out over his temple. I see him with Rasco coming out of mass. I pretend I don't. I let them motor past me as we trot back to the dining hall after mass.

Rasco's eye is looking normal again. You have to get up real close to notice the shadow of his bruising.

"You're going on pass today?" Charles asks me at chow.

"Yup," I say.

"Get me a jar of banana peppers, will ya?" Martinez asks.

"Sure thing," I say. I always do. "Cough up," I tell him as I stick my hand out. I don't pay. I deliver but I don't pay. And I get one pepper free for the service. They're not too hot. They're called sweet peppers, if you can believe that. They're yellow and do look a little like bananas. Martinez drinks the juice right out of the bottle when he's eaten them all. The sucker has a cast-iron stomach.

The only thing is, Dad doesn't show.

He is supposed to pick us up around 10 A.M.

Ten A.M. comes. Ten-thirty. Eleven.

I am fooling with my speech at my desk in the study hall. I am trying not to notice the time. We're going to a movie today, me and Franklin, at the Loew's Ames. Then we'll probably go downtown to Nixon's Smörgasbord for dinner. We always go to Nixon's. We head back to the Home from there and make it back just in time for the seven o'clock movie here.

"Where's your dad?" Winston asks.

I shrug. He doesn't usually miss. He did when Franklin and I lived at the Kenedy's farm, this foster home he had us in before he got us into the Home. He was in real rough shape then. I didn't understand it too well.

"Your dad is sick again," Ma Kenedy would tell us. Franklin and I would be waiting, raring to go and Dad's a no-show.

It's okay, boys, Ma Kenedy would lie. She wanted us to call her Ma. She told me and Franklin it would be best. That everyone else around here called her that. Our own mother ain't even cold in her grave, and Ma's all bent out of shape because we ain't calling her Ma. She cornered us.

"No more of this 'Hey, you,' stuff," she said. "You call me Ma."

I remember standing at the foot of the wooden stairs with my hand on the newel post. That post shook. I thought I was a sailor aboard an ancient sailing vessel with the sea coming up.

"You hear me, boys?" she asks sternly. "You call me Ma."

Charles comes out of his office. He comes right up to me.

"Sorry," he says. Asshole. He didn't have to actually say it. He lays his hand on my shoulder. "You okay?" he asks.

"I'm fine," I say quickly. Suddenly every molecule in my body is magnetized to his hand on my shoulder. He leaves it lay. An odd thing happens—I have this picture in my head, it ain't words or nothing, just this split-second moving picture. It is Charles leaping with joy, dancing about me, full of joy, reaching to hug me, the man in heaven.

I think I am crazy.

"It okay if I go over to see Franklin?" I ask.

"Sure," he says.

He leaves his hand in place. He makes no move to make way.

I slide off my seat. I slide away from his hand. I try not to be too obvious that that is what I am doing.

"Well," he says as his hand is momentarily left in midair. He steps back.

I feel weird here. I ain't sure what is going on.

"I'll get your jacket," Winston volunteers.

Thank you.

I follow him out of the study hall. I wait for him by the door.

He comes back carrying my red jacket, my James Dean jacket. I've had it for two years now. I've had it ever since we saw *Rebel Without a Cause.* It isn't warm enough. I don't care. It is *cool.*

"Here ya go," Winston says, handing it to me. He knows. He is being good to me. I need to feel cool now. I need something to feel okay about. And he brings me my sexy-self, cool-guy jacket. I appreciate it. I appreciate him.

I look him in the eye. We say nothing to each other. I am glad I have never tried anything with him. I really am.

Franklin's amazing, per usual.

"Lyman says he's fallen off the wagon again," he says.

"Yeah?"

"Yeah," he says.

"Maybe. I don't know," I say.

"What's fallen off the wagon?" he asks.

It makes me laugh. I punch him on the arm.

"I've never been too sure myself," I tell him.

We walk. I see the billboard out near the highway.

"Shall we?" I say, nodding.

"Yeah," he says.

So we cut across the Great Lawn and go out to the Home's billboard. It is framed by Franklin's two favorite trees.

"After you," I say with mock graciousness.

Franklin scurries right up. He takes the tree on the left. This one is his favorite. I watch him scramble up. He's halfway up in no time.

European beech. Ornamentals. That's what his *Trees of North America* book says. Margaret Mary gave it to him. She gave me a bird book.

These are amazing trees, no lie. We have them all over the Miami Valley. You see a lot of them in town—young ones not fifteen feet tall and older ones like these two that stand forty to fifty feet straight up and another forty to fifty feet wide, no lie. They're just gorgeous mothers with their silver-gray trunks. The older ones, like these two, often have multiple trunks.

Franklin's fifteen feet up now. He's going out on a limb.

"You okay?" I ask.

"Yeah, fine," he calls down to me.

The one he's in has six trunks springing simultaneously from the earth. And four of them, if you stand back and squinch your eyes, they look like a pair of dancers' legs—the bodies of the two dancers are shoved into the earth right up to the hips with just the very sexy legs jutting up in a pair of scissor kicks.

I know it sounds nuts. A sexy tree. But it is.

I stand back and squinch my eyes.

I just fucking love it.

They're solid, too.

I walk right up to Franklin's tree and lay my palm flat against the trunk. Against one of the trunks, I mean. They're like concrete, really.

Franklin's rustling overhead. I look up.

You should see these leaves. Stun your ass, no lie. From underneath you can see their reddish-purplish veins—they call them purple beech, too, and this is why. They start out in early spring being a bright silver-green. As the season wears on they sort of cook—they deepen to a July purple, get rusty in August, and turn black grape in the autumn. Too much. Simply too much.

Kids love them because they're so easy to climb. Great thigh-thick limbs every ten inches. With so many leaves that once you are up inside, no one can see you unless they come right in under like I am now. You can see out across the Home and no one can see you. It is just terrific.

"He's drinking again, isn't he?" Franklin calls down to me.

I really don't know. I thought he was sober. I thought he quit after he got us off the Kenedy farm.

"I don't know," I say. "I'm going up over here," I say and cross over to the other beech. A third of the billboard is buried in the millions of black-grape-colored leaves. Guys need a haircut.

I climb up.

We used to do this when we first got here. Jesus. It's been seven years. We'd come down here to the highway and climb up and talk to each other across the top of the billboard.

"I think that's what falling off the wagon means," I say as I get up and in. I scoot out on a limb leading out toward the highway. I can't see him for all the leaves.

A little breeze bumps us. I shut my eyes and listen to the leaves as they rustle against one another. If you try, you can imagine it is hundreds and hundreds of people going crazy with applause.

"Lyman can sure be an asshole," Franklin says suddenly.

I open my eyes. I do not believe my ears.

"What?" I say. I am shocked. "You and Lyman always got along."

Which is true. And totally and completely beyond me.

"Oh, we do," Franklin answers. "He likes me, Freddy."

I know. And it just slays me.

''I don't know how you do it, Franklin,'' I say.

''Oh, it's easy,'' he says back. Here he goes. My wise little brother. This I gotta hear.

''He just wants to be boss,'' he says. ''That's all. So I let him. It's no big deal.''

Suddenly he's singing out in a panic.

''Whoa-oh!''

I look over, I see the limb he is on dipping. The leaves are roaring—a million people delirious with applause.

''You all right?'' I shout. My throat's swollen. ''Franklin?''

''I'm okay,'' he laughs. ''About lost it there, though. I'm okay now.''

Suddenly I remember what Maya said about Franklin and his poison ivy that didn't come from taking a dump in the woods.

''You okay?'' I ask again. I ain't worried about him falling, neither. He understands.

''Yeah,'' he says slowly. ''I guess so.''

We listen to the wind in the leaves. We say nothing.

''I don't like it, though,'' he says after a minute.

''Naw. Me, neither,'' I answer. ''Fucks up my whole day.''

''Yeah,'' he agrees.

We are quiet again. The wind is soft, the leaves rustling. I can hear the crowds cheering.

''You get to play Friday night?'' he asks.

I laugh.

''Nope, I'll never get off the bench,'' I say.

''Too bad,'' he commiserates. He is being real sweet.

''It's all right,'' I tell him. It really is. ''I just went out because Kuhns talked me into it,'' I say. ''To make the trips together, ya know?''

''Yeeaaaah,'' he says. Everyone drools over the varsity football trips.

''You'll get your turn,'' I say. He plays midget ball. He's good, too.

''Yeah,'' he says excitedly, ''I can't wait to move over to the high school side.''

It ain't all it's cracked up to be, I do not say.

''You know the hard part?'' he asks.

About Dad not showing.

What? I ask. I don't really want to know. I can feel it—he's gonna talk about Mom. Don't—

''It makes me miss Mom,'' he says.

''Yeah, I know,'' I say. ''Odd, ain't it?''

''It's almost like he's dead, too,'' he says.

I damn near lose my balance on that one.

''It is, you know,'' he says with conviction.

I think about Dad. I remember the time he had Mom down on the kitchen floor. We still lived as a family in the house on Kenilworth. He'd go nuts, Dad would, when he got fucked up. He wouldn't let us go to bed at night. He'd sit on the top step and lunge at us with his huge farmer's paws. He'd snatch up my shirtfront and twist and jerk me around, lift me up, he's all slobbery and stupid, his fucking fly half zipped, his starched white shirttail hanging out, the asshole. He always wears his starched white shirts. A starched white shirt and tie every single day of the year, three hundred and sixty-five days a year.

''Fucking whore,'' I say.

''What?'' Franklin asks, startled.

''Huh?'' I didn't say anything, I say.

''Yes, you did,'' Franklin insists. ''You said 'Fucking whore.' ''

''Forget it,'' I say.

I feel woozy here. A little dizzy. I'm suddenly afraid I am unable to keep my balance.

''Let's get out of here,'' I say. I start climbing down. I am a bit woozy.

''Okay,'' Franklin agrees. ''Let's blow this Popsicle stand.''

Cracks me up. He talks like that. He really does. It just kills me. He'll say shit like ''Do you walk to work or carry your lunch?'' Or ''Is it colder in the winter or on the farm?'' I don't know where he gets this shit.

It is good, though. It makes me laugh. You make me laugh, that is good.

We both climb down.

It's chilly. Dumbass me, got to be cool and this fucking jacket wouldn't keep a titmouse warm.

''Dad said that, didn't he?'' Franklin says. ''Fucking whore,'' he repeats. ''Dad used to call Mom that, didn't he?''

We're heading back to his building.

''Franklin, c'mon,'' I protest. ''Don't let's, okay?''

We walk across the Great Lawn in silence. We come up in front of the main chapel.

''I remember that shit, too, you know,'' he says sort of whiny. Franklin never gets whiny, honest.

''I know, I know,'' I say hurriedly. As if saying it quick will make it go away. ''I'm sorry.''

''It's okay,'' he says, forgiving me immediately. ''We just got to keep on keeping on, eh?''

I look at him. I can't believe this kid.

He's looking at me now, too.

He's a stocky little shit. Everyone says he's cute. I don't know about that. He's just my little brother. My wise little brother.

''Yeah,'' I say finally. ''We just got to keep on keeping on.''

''I like you,'' he says and bumps me with his shoulder. Shit.

Homeless, neglected boys, that's us. A whole farmload out here.

''I like you, too,'' I say. I turn away quick. Got something in my eye.

''Let's go in,'' he says.

We're standing in front of the Arnold Lipnack Memorial Chapel. Ain't that something? Arnold Lipnack. He's the loving Jewish merchant who was the Founder's friend. He was the one who kept the place afloat when no one else would. A Jewish guy got a Catholic church named after him.

"In the chapel?" I ask.

"We can say a prayer for him," he says.

"God, Franklin," I complain. I am being whiny now. Mom said a zillion prayers for him. She'd do novenas for him, praying for him to give up the drink.

"Praying isn't going to help," I whine.

"C'mon," he insists. He takes me by the elbow. I am a sheep. You whine and you ain't got no power.

"It can't hurt," he says as he tugs on my arm.

So we do.

We go in.

There's not a soul in sight. We have the whole chapel to ourselves. Our Lady of Perpetual Help is gleaming away up front. Votive candles glow red at the baby Jesus' feet. My forty-year-old baby Jesus.

Clunk, unk.

The sound of boy body bumping wooden pew.

Dunk. Bunk.

The sound is hollow and comforting. It echoes throughout the abandoned chapel.

I guess Franklin's right.

We genuflect, slide bump clunk unk into a pew, and kneel.

It can't hurt.

We kneel side by side. We say a pair of silent prayers for Dad.

28

I AM ALL WHICKYWHACK INSIDE AFTER LUNCH. IT'S nothing major. I am just off my feed.

Oh, I know what it is.

"She ain't no whore," Franklin says to me as we come out of the Lipnack.

He is hurt.

Still I do not understand. Something is playing in the rear of my brain. I am on automatic pilot. It ain't as if I am saying the words myself. It's not even like they are words—except they are. They are just there, these words, as if my brain's a screen that is faded and distant.

This whickywhack feeling is the same sort of feeling I have when I awake from a dream and I can't quite get it to focus. It is just there, a sensation persisting: cuntbitch-whore.

I sit at my desk and work on my speech. I have to send it off tomorrow. The ceremonies are less than three weeks away. Three weeks from last Friday. We are supposed to tell about our school and then congratulate the winning school. I write about Father McFlaherty's Home for Boys.

Dad's got Mom on the kitchen floor. He has Mom's greasy butcher knife to her throat. He is raving fucking mad with drink. He's all slobbery. He's still wearing his navy blue topcoat and his stiff-starched white shirt. They've tipped over the kitchen table. He has her in a headlock up against the cupboards fucking cunt.

I write about the Founder in his first Home in downtown Dayton on the corner of Monument and Main. It is just kitty-corner from the fire station, which is still there today. I write how Lipnack the merchant was the Founder's friend and helped the Founder buy food, clothes, and presents for those first five boys on that first Christmas in Dayton. The Catholic priest and the loving Jewish merchant.

She ain't no whore.

She's fucking dead, ain't she?

Franklin and I lay in bed in the dark. We listen to the roving, raving bull bellowing down below. We hear him tromp, tromp, tromping up the stairs. He comes blustering into the room. He is here. He is in the room—he fills the doorway first. He's moving toward me. He still has his topcoat on.

"My favorite son," he says as he drops to my bed. His great weight sinks my bed to the floor. I roll toward him, I'm gonna fall out. He snatches my pj top and pulls me bodily up and out of my bed. He's stretching it. He's ripping it, my pj top.

"Da-aad," I protest.

The smell of tobacco and alcohol comes off him like a fog in off the bay. It is strong enough to knock over a horse.

"Jack," my mom calls wearily from the doorway. I cannot see her. I only hear her. Dad's girth, his great girth, blocks the way.

"Jack. Not with the boys. Jack . . ."

He tightens his grip. He's choking me now. He pulls me closer to him. He pulls me into his cloth coat. I can feel the chill of the out-of-doors in it. It chills me. He snarls at her over his shoulder.

"Unnnh? Unnh! My boys . . ." he says as he rolls his head in her direction. "My boys . . . don't tell me to stay away from my boys. . . ."

"Jack," Mom pleads, "Not now, Jack. Please . . ."

He explodes. He releases me and becomes a rocket going for her. He's so quick none of us can do a thing before he has her again with both hands around her throat—it is always her throat, he's gonna kill the fucking bitch cunt whore.

He crashes with her through the bedroom doorway out into the hallway, the all-wooden hallway with all the bedroom doors leading off it.

Fucking whore bitch cunt fuck you you fucking whore you fucking bitch you worthless cunt and down they tumble smash crash.

He pancakes her.

She's smashed beneath him.

"Jaaaack!"

"Jesus H. Christ! Will you look at you!"

"Huh?"

It's Winston. He's standing in front of me.

"You look like you just saw a ghost," he says. "Are you okay?"

Dad used to take us with him on Saturdays. Me and Franklin. He would tell us he had to stop for cigarettes. He would leave us in the car. He'd park it on a side street. He'd tell us, "I'll just be a minute."

Hours later Franklin and I screw up our courage and go in after him. He'd be on a stool at the bar, bellowing away, calling everyone Captain or Major, ordering drinks, a shot and a beer in front of him, his navy blue topcoat hanging down over the stool like a princess's cape.

"Dad? Dad? Come on, Dad. We got to go, Dad. Please, Dad."

Sometimes I would get to him first, sometimes it was Franklin. No matter.

"My favorite son," he says and lurches at you with great paw. And sing: "Doobee dooobee dooo, dooobee dooobee dooo . . ."

Winston sits at a study hall table in front of me. He's on the edge of his seat. He's staring right at me.

"Come on, Bambi," he says.

I look at him.

"It's no big deal," I lie.

I cannot get the asshole out of my head. It amazes me, honest. I ain't had this kind of stuff going on inside my head since I don't know when.

Yes, I do.

Since that first year on the Kenedy farm. That cold, barren, stupid farm way out past the airport.

Ma Kenedy is stalking us, stalking me and Franklin, wanting to see our stools. Can you believe that.

"Don't flush, boys," she says. "Let me check those stools."

She wouldn't let us take the polio vaccine neither. Every other fucking kid in the school lines up for a little swig. But not Ma's kids, no siree.

Blow me away, wanting to check our stools.

Fred the Mad Flusher, that's me.

That and her interest in our private parts. She was always wanting to know if we were yanking on ourselves. My little ying yang goes and stands stiff whenever and wherever it feels like it. In the most unlikely of places, too, no lie. Like the time I sat across from Susan at dinner, Susan with no eyelashes, and boing!

Poor Susan. She's a foster kid like me and Franklin. She plucks her eyelashes. All the time. Ma forbids it. She does it anyway, whenever she can. If she gets caught she gets whipped. And the Kenedy boys, Ma's kids, they're real sweethearts, they turn her ass in every fucking chance they can get: "Ma-aa! I saw Susan pulling out her eyelashes. Ma-aaa!" The little shithooks.

They turn her in and out comes the rubber hose. That's what Ma used on us, her old washing-machine hose, the one with the upside-down *J* hook in it. She'd wail on your ass with it, no lie. She broke her wooden spoon on me and Franklin. That's why she went to the rubber hose. This won't break, she says.

Spooky days, those.

"Bambi?" Winston tries again. He is trying, honestly, to do me good. I feel for him.

"It that bad?" he asks.

He is really surprised at how I am carrying on here.

Me, too, brother. Me fucking too.

I look at him. God. I guess it is that bad. I say so.

"I guess it is."

He nods. He is totally beautiful standing here. He is completely serious. He is being grown for me. He's like a forty-year-old, right this minute, *for me.*

"Your dad, huh?" he says softly, tentative and tender.

I nod, yep.

"I'm really sorry," he says. "He a real shit, huh?"

I look at him again, startled.

"Beat you?" he asks.

I shake my head.

"A womanizer?" he asks.

I don't know what that is: Huh?

"He run around on your mom a lot?"

I shake my head again.

"Aha!" he says, figuring something out. I stare at him. He says Aha! like the scientist in the lab who has just struck on the solution.

"Booze. That's it, ain't it?"

I'll be damned.

"You're something else," I say to him. I am amazed.

"Let's get out of here, okay?" he says. It feels like an order. I do what he says. I get up and follow him.

"You need your jacket," he directs.

I go get my jacket, my old letter jacket, the one I did not give to Beaudene.

"Okay?" he asks when I come out with my letter jacket.

I say nothing. I am mute.

"Okay," he says and out we go. He leads, I follow.

"Where are you taking me?" I ask when I realize I am being the goddamned sheep again.

"You are taking me," he says, "up to the cemetery. Massies Creek, okay?"

Okay.

So we go sit on the Tarboxes' tombstones. The creek shines below us. We smoke cigarettes and talk. I am glad I am wearing my letter jacket. It is warmer than my James Dean Cool Guy jacket.

He tells me about his dad, who died of a heart attack. He was a drinker, too. He beat his mom regular-like back in Chi-town. Shy-town he calls it. It's why he got sent to the Boys School, the reform school. He'd been running wild on the streets, he says, stealing, breaking streetlights, store windows, shit like that. Met a Jewish kid, he says—ain't many of them in places like that, he says. They take care of their own.

Yeah, I tell him. We only had one here in all my years at the Home, and he left after only one school year. He got placed, Rasco said, in a Jewish foster home.

"This Jewish kid, he got to me," Winston says. "He told me about this poet, an American guy name of Robert Bly, I think." He stops and looks at me real hard.

"Listen to this," he says. "This guys says you have to 'swallow your grief.' "

I gulp.

Winston nods to me: "You know? Swallow it whole."

I look out to Massies Creek. Six diamonds leap into the air escaping the blue-black sheen.

"Rasco told me once—you know Rasco, don't you?" I ask.

"Yeah. Big colored kid in the choir section, right? In Felix's house?"

"Right. He told me, he's all the time reading shit, studying the ways of other people, their religions, shit like that. He told me about this essay he read about being Negro and learning not to hate—how'd he say it?"

I try to remember where we were, the place we were in when he is telling me this. I can remember better what people say when I remember where we were when they said it—the weight room. That's it. In the field house.

"It was an essay about the guy's father. The guy is writing about his father, about how his father is crazy with hatred."

I stop for a minute. I want to get it right. Winston waits, no sweat.

"Okay," I say, starting again. "This guy's father is

crazy with hatred because he has been hated all his life for being colored, for being a Negro, and finally it just filled him so he's nothing but hatred himself—and then he was just a very sick man who couldn't do anything but hate and the hate ate him alive."

Rasco was so serious that day. There'd been a fight on the court, someone had called this kid a nigger and Rasco had helped cool things out. Me, too. Fights make me deathly ill. I always try to break them up. But afterwards I was a real basket case and Rasco is so very cool. Calm and collected, see? Water off a duck's back, see?

We went off to the weight room to talk. He told me you have to be able to hold two contradictory ideas in your head at the same time before you are really grown-up. That's how he got into telling me about this essay. He got that idea from the essay.

Winston's looking lost. Huh?

"Well, he told me," I say, "that he felt like he could kill the guy who had just called Wright nigger and he could care less, too. That he felt totally indifferent about it at the same time that he wanted to murder the fucker."

I look directly at Winston now.

"He told me," I go on, " 'That is my salvation.' "

Winston's nodding. He likes it a lot. Yeah, he says, yeah. I keep going.

"Let me see if I can get it clear," I say. I really want to get this idea into my brain. I think Rasco's got something here. I mash my cigarette out in the grass as I mull it over. I see our butts and decide to pick them up—there are four of them so far—I will pick them up and carry them away with me when we leave here. I make myself feel good as I decide this.

"Okay." I say, "the idea was, I think, that white people do hate people of color—that's what Rasco calls Negros," I say, "people of color—and if you are a Negro you have to accept this fact without being totally fucking insane about it. You have to simply accept it as a matter of fact, which it is—and now, here's the killer, you also have to be willing to fight it, be willing to fight this stupid hatred shit whenever and wherever you find it.''

I stop. We let that sit on the air between us.

''That make any sense?'' I ask.

''It's like accepting the fact that your dad's a boozer, huh? And not being totally fucked up over it—just know it, yeah?'' he says.

''I guess. Only—how do I fight it?'' I ask.

''I don't know,'' he says. ''Maybe you fight it in yourself, huh?''

I am feeling better. I am feeling awful, too. I get scared as I let myself think about how awful I do feel. I tell Winston.

''I'm scared,'' I say. I look at him and hope he doesn't—doesn't what? I don't know what, exactly . . .

Suddenly I am telling him all about the greasy fucking butcher knife and Dad's fucked-up crazy ways and I am flushing inside here. I am all liquid. I think I am actually coming apart physically when Winston leans into me with his shoulder. He gives me a little bump. It reminds me I ain't actually coming apart physically.

He tells me about his dad blasting him, about his dad blasting his mom. All over the house, he says. Really wailing the shit out of her.

''I hate him,'' he says. ''I do.''

Sparks fly from the surface of Massies Creek. The wind stirs a round of applause in the trees. I say nothing.

''Swallow it,'' Winston says. ''That's what Rosen told me: 'Swallow it, son, swallow it fucking whole,' he'd say.''

''What the fuck'd he mean, huh? You tell me. I don't get it.''

''I ain't entirely sure myself,'' Winston admits.

We sit silently. A minute passes. Two. Three. There is only the occasional moaning of the wind soughing through the trees. There is that soft and distant applause as the leaves rustle against one another. A bunch of leaves fall and drift down about us. It smells good. A truck comes over the hill behind us and comes down the hill. He looks like one of those plate-glass delivery trucks with the real high sides for strapping plate glass to.

"Rosen would get all fired up," Winston says as the truck disappears. He laughs remembering it.

"We'd be down on the handball courts—they only had two at the reform school. Not six like here. We're murdering the ball, yakking away when suddenly he's chanting this shit—"

Winston springs up, balls his hands into fists, and chants it, keeping time with his pounding fist:

Eee-tit, eee-tit
Swah-low-it
Whole
Eee-tit, eee-tit
Swah-low-it
Whole.

He stops, turns to look at me, his face lit up. He looks like Superman about to spring into flight.

"Eat it, huh?"

"Yeah," he says, "before it eats you."

I am what you call an obvious guy. I see Dad with Mom on the kitchen floor: Gulp. I swallow it. I see him roaring drunk at the top of the stairs, his hands flailing the air as he keeps us from going to bed: Gulp. I swallow that. I see him lying in the grass in front of the house, passed out: Gulp. Swallow that, too. I see me and Franklin helping Mom lug that dead weight into the house—a guy pass out on you, he weighs sixteen times his normal weight: Gulp. I swallow that one, too.

I see him not showing this morning.

Oh, holy shit. That, too?

"I gotta swallow his no-show, huh? Today? I gotta swallow that, too?" I say aloud. I'm asking. I'm begging. Not that, too, please.

Winston lays his fingers on my arm. It is totally without sex. He looks me directly in the eyes. I look back. There is power here, real fucking power here. We nod simultaneously.

Right.

Gulp.

Have you? I ask. He knows what I mean.

"Not much," he says, surprising me.

I tell him how he amazes me, how much I appreciate this, what he has just this very minute done, being so straight with me, not bullshitting around about how he's got his shit together.

He looks out toward Cedarville. It is only a mile or so down the road. Little Baptist town.

"The truth is," he says, still looking out toward Cedarville, "I ain't never done it too good. I haven't even thought about it much until right now, with you. Your dad and all. How awful you looked back to the house," he says, nodding back over his shoulder. The house is a million miles away. "I didn't even know your old man was a boozer until this afternoon," he says, blushing.

"You know the worst thing?" I say to him.

"No, what?" he asks, looking at me now. It's my turn to look out into the great and distant nothingness.

I can't say it.

"Go on," he encourages. "I ain't talking to nobody."

So I just say it, as crazy as it seems to me, I just say it: "I feel ashamed. Of my dad. Of my mom. Of myself for being their kid."

I say it and it washes over me, through me. I am shriveling up here inside. It is working on me now, right this very fucking minute.

"Yeah," he says softly. "I think I know what you mean."

A gang of birds—starlings—come chattering overhead. They're flipping around this way and that. They land, individually, one at a time, bing, bing, bing. There's about twenty of them in the treetop directly in front of us. They make a lovely sound, yodeling and gurgling away. I imagine they are all worked up about something. Everyone's talking at once, then they land, and it is perfect silence—they are all listening: you hear it?

My face works on me. I pay attention to it, to my face. I watch it from the inside out. I squinch my eyes, pucker my lips. It is as if I am eating something bitter, as if I am swallowing something bitter: the shame. The tons and tons of shame.

"Swallow it," Winston says. He's watching me watch myself.

"Go ahead," he says, "swallow it."

I relax. I let my eyes open to normal. I unwrinkle my face. I gulp.

I got Rasco on the brain:

"I am what I am, Bambi," he said to me when I wondered how he could be so cool when so much shit is coming down. "I can't change that, now, can I?" he says.

Gulp.

"You're all right," I say to Winston.

"You ain't so bad yourself," he answers me back.

"I guess we'll make it, huh?"

"I hope so," he says and I wish he hadn't.

I swallow that, too.

29

WE HEAD OUT. I REMEMBER MY BUTTS. I WAS GOING to pick them up.

"Just a sec," I say. I tap Winston on the forearm. "Okay?"

What? he says.

I dash back to the Tarbox clan.

"Our butts," I yell back at him as I bend over and scoop them up. I shove them into my jacket pocket. There.

"Okay," I say as I trot back to him.

We head up the road. We cross over and climb through the barbed wire. I hold the wire for him. He climbs through. We're on the grounds now.

When we reach the high school section, all the kids are pouring out of their cottages. Time for devotions. Our Lady of Perpetual Help devotions, every Sunday afternoon. Winston and I just keep on walking and go right on up to devotions.

Whiteworm's serving. Black Jack is leading the litany. That's Father John, our dean. Everyone calls him Black Jack on account of his boxing days when he was a boy here. He's a former boy, too, like Felix. When he was a boy here some fifteen thousand years ago and the Founder was still alive, they had boxing as a sport. The story is it was Black Jack who was in the ring the night the kid was killed. No one knows if that's true or not. We do know, though, that he boxed. You doubt it, just take a gander at his fucking nose. That ought to set you straight.

Black Jack lifts the monstrance.

Whiteworm is on the bells: tinkle. Tinkle tinkle.

Ring 'em, I say, *Blast those mothers.*

Black Jack blesses us with the monstrance. He crosses the air with that glorious, glittering, golden icon: tinkle. Tinkle. Tinkle tinkle.

Jesus, Whiteworm. You got no balls, boy, no balls.

I spy Rasco walking with Destern afterward. There's a third kid, Petersen, a sophomore, tagging along. I can cut in on a sophomore. I do.

"Hey," I say as I slice Petersen off the end. He whines as I take his place, skips behind me for a second before he catches up and comes in on my right shoulder.

"I see your eye's getting better," I say to Rasco. The flag circle is dead ahead. The grade school dining hall is directly beyond the flag circle.

It's been five days now, I think, since I noticed Rasco's eye. Yeah, last Tuesday. It's healing already. Quick, I think.

Rasco says nothing. Destern either. Petersen's crowding me. I shove him off and try to coax Rasco to say something.

"Huh?" I say to them as if I missed it.

I am walking on tiptoe.

We are at the end of the PRIVATE Dead End DRIVE that runs down to the Lipnack, our main chapel with the director's manse attached.

Neither Rasco nor Destern's acknowledged my existence.

I am walking on tiptoe.

I ain't giving up yet: "Not that it matters, of course," I say to the air, har har.

We are at the flag circle. We round the bend. We're cracking the whip here. Rasco's on the inside hugging the curb. Destern's next to him, in close. Me and Petersen swing out wide, doing double time. I am skipping to keep up, doing a little fast pedal to stay in step. Peterson's damn near into a full sprint.

It gets me off my tiptoes, though.

I try one more tack.

"Oh, really? You don't say? I would have never known," I say, playing the fool. That's me, talking to myself.

We're on the main drag now. I can see the high school dining hall's roof. It's dead ahead.

Rasco picks up the pace and leans forward, turning to me, glaring: "Why don't you just fuck off, faggot."

Ouch.

That stops me dead in my tracks.

I stand still, stung. I watch them go. Petersen slips back into the spot I have just vacated. The three of them motor.

Cowen cruises past, wordless and alone. He's got his head down. Studying the pavement.

I look about me. I am still stunned. I mean, what gives?

Just as I look about I see the Jock-O set bearing down on me, four pairs of eyes gleaming with joy; it's Mack truck and roadrunner time.

I leap away, jumping into the grassy berm and dance off, skipping, hopping, jogging away, making sure I get just out of danger's way, thank you.

30

I TRY AGAIN AFTER THE MOVIE. *Witness for the Prosecution.*

God, it's great.

Charles Laughton plays Sir Wilfred, this cranky old barrister who is recovering from a serious heart attack. Any excitement could kill him. Smoking his cigars could kill him. Drinking his brandy could kill him. And along comes this juicy murder case which, of course, excites him to no end. And gives him ample reason for needing a smoke and a sip of his brandy.

God, I just love the movies.

The truth, the whole truth, and nothing but the truth.

Bambi the Barrister. Sir Fred, that's me. I need my monocle like Sir Wilfred had. He'd whip it out whenever he's questioning someone and flash the sun into the eye of the person's he's grilling. His way of separating the liars from the truth tellers.

I beat it out quick and hoof it down the steps of the auditorium. I watch the crowd pouring out. I'm looking for Rasco. I've got one eye peeled for Rasco and one eye peeled for the Jock-O set—I am raw meat these days. They are after my ass. I have to keep on my toes.

There he is. Rasco. With Destern.

They go down the side steps heading for the choir section.

I zoom around and catch up to them.

"Great show, huh?" I say.

I may as well be a stone. Or invisible, one.

"Come on, you guys," I beg.

They just motor along. We reach the circle drive that runs through the high school section. They hang a left onto the circle drive.

"You guys gonna dump me, too?" I say. It's half question, half discovery. The discovery part stops me.

Fuck.

I am ready to give it up. And I am *not* going to cry.

I stand here and watch them walk away. That's the way it's going to be, eh? I'm an untouchable, that it?

I pretend I have a monocle. I get all arrogant and superior like Sir Wilfred did in the movie. Sir Will Fred. Sir Fred will. I adjust my imaginary monocle. There's no light. It's dark out. I have to pretend I have sunlight to beam onto their backs. I am going to burn a fucking hole in them.

I focus my pretend sunlight on Rasco's back. I imagine I have to fiddle with it a second to get the sunlight into this hot, pencil thin beam that burns. There.

Suddenly Rasco stops and turns around. He catches me in the act: Fred the four-year-old playing with himself again.

"You asshole." Rasco says when he sees me doing what I am doing. "What the fuck do you think you're doing?"

"Oh, nothing," I say shamefacedly. I drop my hand from my eye. I ain't got no monocle. I am grateful for the cover of darkness.

"Come on," he says.

I *am* a four-year-old.

I'm sorry but I am.

He says come on and suddenly I am so happy.

It sure doesn't take much to make me happy—me and little ignorant shit Cruise, right? Little ignorant shit Gamble. Little ignorant shit Cruise. We're a pair.

I dash up to them.

"I was over to your house Friday night," I say.

We walk in the dark. We three boys together walking in the dark. There are shadows, vapors, before us and behind us.

"What are you talking about?" Rasco asks with irritation.

"After the game," I say, flinching. I am always flinching, expecting to get hit. I'm always expecting someone's about to bat me one upside the head.

"I came over to your house after the game," I go on. He isn't going to hit me. "I saw all of you through the study-hall windows."

We are in front of their house now. I turn to Destern, touch his forearm.

"I saw what he did to you," I say. His temple bulges in the light coming off the streetlight. "Are you okay?" I ask.

"I'll live," he says.

"So what's going on?" I ask looking from one to the other.

They look at each other. They are a pair of silhouettes in the night. Something frightening passes between them. It is palpable. It is in the air.

"Tell him," Destern says to Rasco.

I look again from one to the other.

"What? Tell me what?"

"He was working Petersen over," Rasco begins.

"Petersen had gone to the Monsignor," Destern explains.

"It pissed Felix off something fierce," Rasco says.

"You *don't* go to the Monsignor," Destern says emphatically.

"He was plastering him all over the study hall," Rasco goes on. "He was chasing him, knocking him down, picking him up, knocking him down, picking him up, knocking him down—"

"So Rasco stepped in," Destern says.

I look at Rasco. He's shaking his head.

"I was just trying to cool him out," Rasco explains. He looks at me. Light leaps from his eye as he turns his head. "He was fucking off his nut."

Destern reaches with his fingers to Rasco's forearm and continues the story.

"So Rasco steps in and says, 'That's enough.' "

I get chills. He did that for me, too, in the shower when Brower was after my ass.

Destern gives a little hop and moves in real close to me, his nose right in my face. He's imitating how close Rasco got to Felix. I shiver.

"He's standing between Felix and Petersen. Petersen's on the floor holding himself."

Destern grips my arm. I can feel his breath in my face as he speaks.

"He was fucking out of his mind. You should have seen how he looked. His goddamned eyes. They were yellow and red, no shit. Ya know? His fucking yellow eyes all blood-shot?"

He shivers as he remembers it. I feel the trembling through his fingers on my arm. It makes me shiver, too.

Rasco picks it up now.

"So he says to me, 'You want some, too, nigger?' "

"That's when he blasted him," Destern says, nodding to Rasco's eye.

"A roundhouse right," Rasco remembers. "Put my fucking lights out, I tell you."

"It worked, though," Destern says excitedly. "He stopped beating the piss out of Petersen, didn't he?"

We both look at Rasco. We both admire him his courage.

Petersen comes out of the house onto the front porch.

"Rasco! Destern!" he screams. One beat short of total hysteria.

We three look. He is backlit. The front-porch light and the house lights pour through him, pour around him. He's a silhouette with a halo.

"Yo!" Destern calls back.

"Felix wants you guys inside *now!*"

The two of them bolt.

It happens so fast I think I missed something.

"Wait. Wait. Wait a minute," I call as I dash down the walk behind them.

"You *guysssss,*" Petersen calls again. He's desperate. He sounds like he is about to weep. The boy is coming apart at the seams. It gives me trouble.

I catch Rasco right at the porch. I grab him by the arm.

"I'm sorry," I say. "Really."

"I gotta git," he says all in a rush. He pulls his arm free. I grab him a second time. I want to do something. I want to touch him somehow. I want to give him something before he has to go back in that house. But I am lame.

"I really am sorry," I repeat. "I'm sorry you have to go through this."

He stops and looks right at me. Half his face is bathed in light. Sixteen things happen in it, in his face. I see colors there. I even see green. My heart is breaking.

"Yeah," he starts and the front door opens behind him. Felix steps out.

There is no air to breathe.

He reaches to me. His fingers fall short. He nods to me. It is tender. It is soft. There is something very fragile here, something about to break. Those fingers dangle just short of my forearm.

"I gotta go," he says and bites his bottom lip. "Tomorrow," he concludes.

"Okay," I say, steal a quick look up at the giant, and beat it the fuck out of there.

31

CHARLES ASKES ME IF I HAVE A MINUTE AFTER NIGHT prayers.

Sure.

He's all excited.

"I can drive you out," he says. "To Waterloo. You won't need to take the bus."

He's all smiles. Ain't this wonderful?

It turns out he has a conference in Rochester, Minnesota, at the Mayo Clinic. That's where the Monsignor goes every year to get his machinery checked. Nothing but the best for the Monsignor.

The only thing is, I have been sorta looking forward to the Greyhound out.

But Charles is not to be denied. He is terrifically excited.

"It's a natural," he says. "It's right on my way."

"Well, I—"

"And you can do some of the driving. Give me a break."

That does it.

"Really? You mean it? You'd let me drive your car?"

"Sure, why not?" he asks.

"Oh," I say suddenly feeling crushed, "I can't."

"What do you mean you can't?" he asks, crinkling his brow.

"I don't even have my permit yet," I say. I would have loved to drive his little red Falcon with the bucket seats.

"Oh, no sweat," he says, looking relieved. He really wants to drive out with me. "We can take care of that."

"We can?" I ask.

"Sure. We've got a couple of weeks, right?"

"Yeah," I say, "Two weeks from this coming Friday."

There's a knock on his office. I am closer to it. I reach for the knob.

"Wait," he says reaching to me, motioning for me not to open the door yet.

"Is it a deal, then?" he asks.

I have my hand on the brass doorknob.

"We go out together?" he concludes.

"Yeah," I agree and pop open the door. Whiteworm is standing there. He looks sheepish and very young.

"I'll be right with you," Charles says over my shoulder.

I look at my friend. He doesn't look at me. He looks about four. He looks about how I felt out there with my monocle when Rasco turned around and caught me.

"Hi," I say and feel silly.

"Why don't you wait for me in the living room?" Charles suggests. My friend who ain't said boo to me in days and days turns immediately, his head bowed, not even acknowledging my hi, and shuffles off to the living room. He looks so very young, so very very young.

I've done this to him. I have been so bad.

I feel so ashamed. I can't even look at Charles—I say a quick good night. I sort of toss it over my shoulder, "G'night," as I step out of Charles's office. I pull the door halfway shut behind me. I'm feeling all creepy-crawly. It's as if Charles's eyes are burning holes in my back. As if he's got a pair of monocles beamed right this instant upon my thinly pj-covered shoulder blades.

I follow Whiteworm to the living room.

I have been bad.

He looks so very young. It's really getting to me, how very young he is looking. It's as if he's about to stick his thumb in his mouth any minute now.

I have to say something. I have to make up somehow. I have to at least try.

I stop at the entryway to the living room.

I was a real prick. I was.

He is sitting in the chair he sat in when we first did it. He sits and stares at a blank TV screen.

I decide. Yes. Yes, I will apologize.

I start and two things stop me.

One is how he looks. He looks how I felt when Ezra finally talked me into getting on the roller coaster at Americana. Roller coasters frighten me. They frighten me so much, in fact, I feel ill, like I have the flu or something. No lie. But Ezra never gives up, never gives in. He thinks I absolutely must get on, that I will love it, once I try it, I'll just love it, just try it. Even when I beg him not to ask, he's asking.

Please don't ask me. Please.

And he does. He insists. He will not stop asking until I try it. At least once.

So I give in. Okay, I'll try it.

I went up there to the platform where the train comes in, its incredible wind whooshing up in your face as you watch it pull into the platform. Screaming, laughing, delighted passengers disembark, making room for the next load of idiots. I get on, I sit next to Ezra. I am sick to my stomach. I am full of dread and dreadful thoughts.

Whiteworm looks right now exactly how I felt that night I let Ezra talk me into riding the roller coaster.

The second thing is Charles.

He is right on my heels. I am about to open my mouth, my friend is in trouble here, I need to do something, and Charles is tapping me lightly on the shoulder.

"G'night," he says.

I get the message.

"G'night," I say.

I leave my apologies for another day.

32

I GET MY SPEECH OFF TO THE LADY IN LEXINGTON THE week of the Yellow Springs game. They ain't shit. They never are. We beat them 40–zip. The Old Man even puts in the Hamburger Squad. That's us. That's me.

He calls all the plays. He tells me not to pass to Brower, who is open on every fucking play. I do once. I can't not. I mean, he's just standing out there all alone, so I flipped it out to him, twenty yards, boom.

The Old Man calls me over to the sidelines and clips me upside the head a couple of times with his clipboard.

I don't do it again.

Saturday, the day after the Yellow Springs game, I go into the Old Man's office to ask permission to miss the Central Catholic game in East Lansing. So I can go to Waterloo to make my speech.

The Old Man is in there with Huff, our head line coach and athletic bus driver. They both try to act serious as I ask permission to miss a game. But it is clearly just an act. They aren't going to be needing a third-string quarterback against Central. Central is always tough. Besides, their coach used to coach under the Old Man when they were both at UD—that's the University of Dayton. The Old Man coached up there for a while and then came back down to high school ball. Everyone says he prefers high school ball. That's why he came back down.

Anyway, it is no sweat. It takes all of about three minutes for them to hear me out and make a decision.

Okay, Gamble, the Old Man says.

I thank him and split.

I go right back to the house and tell Charles.

Good, Charles says.

We'll be heading out next Thursday. My speech is next Friday, thirteen days away. Charles will drive me into Waterloo, drop me off at my host family, and go on up to Rochester for his conference. I'll take the Greyhound back—only it's Trailways. There isn't any Greyhound in Waterloo.

Whiteworm still looks rough. I try with him again after physics class.

I have to do something. I have to say something to him.

"Whiteworm," I call to him as we head out of Halstead's class. "Wait up."

He doesn't.

He gets away from me. He is ignoring me completely.

I chase after him. I catch up to him halfway to his locker.

"Are you okay?" I ask. I touch him on the forearm.

He says nothing. He doesn't zoom off, though.

Well?

Right.

I'm the one who's the asshole. I'm the one who punched him.

I just say it real fast, rapid-fire, just to get it out. It ain't easy.

"I-just-wanted-to-tell-you-how-sorry-I-am-about-the-other-day-when-I-you-know-. . ."

It's lame. I am lame.

He sure as fuck ain't helping none either. I try again.

"I'm-sorry-I-hit-you-I-shouldn't-have-and-I-am-sorry-I-was-wrong-okay ?"

"Hey, Bull!"

Winston zooms by. He jabs me one in the ribs, smiling beautifully. I whip my head around to him: he's flying off in the opposite direction. There's Ezra, coming at me, pimping along: he lifts that leg and sort of has to throw it so he looks like a colored kid being very cool: Hump, humpity hump, Hump.

He's upon me now. Whiteworm slips away without saying a word.

Ezra says hey. I say hey back.

We're in different worlds now, Ezra and I. He's in section three and I'm still in section one—he got moved right after I got picked to be a commissioner. We may as well be on different planets. We still like each other, though.

See ya, he says, hump, humpity humping away.

See ya, I say.

Now where's Whiteworm?

I look down the hall.

There he is.

OK: one more time.

I walk up to him at his locker. He is working his combination. I see him and feel it still. He turns my ass on. Oh, holy shit. He still turns my ass on.

"I just wanted to tell you I'm sorry," I say. "Honest. I don't know what my problem is, really . . ."

He works that combination. He says nothing. I do not watch the numbers as he spins his tumbler.

How come he ain't saying nothing? This isn't working out how I thought. I feel worse now than before. I touch him on the arm, gonna try one more time.

"Are you all right?" I ask. Come to think of it, he does look bad. Maybe he's sick or something.

He lifts his head, looks into my face. He squints his eyes a hair and says: "So who wants to know?"

Ouch.

"I know I've been a prick," I say as I back away. He is so pissed off. It surprises me.

"Maybe talking to Charles, huh?" I say, I'm so dumb, "that might help, huh?"

Wrong.

He damn near breaks his wrist when I mention Charles. He jams his lock into the handle, a violent reaction. It's as if I just poked him with one of those electric cattle prods, zoom.

His best friend, Hollingsworth, comes up. He's a tall kid, blonde and blue-eyed, real nice-looking, a good student, not a jock, and he's only been here two and a half years—not four centuries like me and Whiteworm.

"You do your trig?" Hollingsworth asks.

Time to take a powder.

"I'll see ya later," I say.

Whiteworm totally ignores me. He answers Hollingsworth. "No, I didn't."

"You didn't!" Hollingsworth is amazed.

Me, too. Whiteworm always does his work. I know. It's important to him.

I start to echo Hollingsworth, but I see that I am invisible. It is my own fault. I know. I deserve it, too, how bad I can be sometimes.

I just fade into the woodwork, bye-yeeee.

33

It's Thursday night. Wally Schirra's up there right this minute orbiting the planet. He's gonna do twice as many orbits as Glenn did last February. It's amazing. Men in space.

We play Lexington tomorrow night. Next week it's Central Catholic. Next week at this time I'll be with my host family in Waterloo. Tonight, though, my ass is dragging. I come hobbling into Charles's office. Everyone's just gone to bed.

"Charley horse?" Charles asks.

Yeah, I say. That's what Dawson says. He's our trainer. "Right in the old gluteus maximus," he said when he gave me the analgesic balm. You're supposed to rub it into your pain. You substitute the fire it causes for the pain of your charley horse. My right cheek, right now, aflame.

The reason I got it, this charley horse, is because Lexington is always a bitch. They are really tough. So we're beating our brains out this week in practice. Their offense is keyed on their quarterback. Lots of pass-options. So Fred here is all over the field, rolling out, running, passing, last-minute laterals, shit like that. It's been wild.

"Review with me?" Charles invites. He's doing progress reports.

"Sure," I say and ease myself down into my loveseat.

He runs through the names of the boys he is reviewing this quarter: Martinez, Tollens, my assistant whom Charles wants to fire—okay by me. No skin off my nose, I say.

Cowen's on the list.

Now, he's a mystery, I say.

He's the one who sits all day doing nothing. All day, every day, sitting, doing nothing. Really, I can't feature it. I say so to Charles. Charles smiles at me and says: "Not everyone likes to get beat up like you do."

Right.

See, this week the Old Man is out for blood. He wants gang tackles. He tells the defense not to worry about where those elbows go. He says it and grits his teeth as he lets fly with his own elbows. Just in case you didn't get it. Gang tackles, he says. Gimme gang tackles. I want to see *everyone* in on *every* tackle *all* week, understand? I want to see everyone on that ball carrier on every play. And he's saying this to the first-string defense as he's standing next to me, right? He's got his hand on my shoulder. I'm the opposing team's quarterback, a real threat, see? You get *this* man, understand? And you get him *before* he can release that ball, understand?

Well, they understand plenty. It's spooky. I get this picture of these maniacs in front of me, they're frothing at the mouth they're so anxious to get on my ass. And get on my ass they do. Which is why I have this incredible charley horse. In one of the four million gang tackles I am the target of, someone manages to jab me a good one right in the old kiester.

I do get a couple of passes off, though. Piss the Old Man off no end, a scrub like me showing up his hotshots. I get loose on a scramble a couple of times. Embarrass the defense some. So it's worth it, this charley horse. My badge.

"How do you get to someone like him?" I ask. Cowen. How do you get to someone who does nothing, huh?

"Oh, everyone has their button," Charles says. "It just takes time," he says. He mulls that over for a moment and then repeats himself: "It just takes time to find, that's all."

Winston's next.

"Wish they were all like Winston," Charles says.

"Yeah," I agree. "He's special," I say.

I think he is, too. He's like Franklin, my wise little brother who seems half the time to be my older brother.

''He helped me the day Dad didn't show,'' I say without thinking. I feel as if I shouldn't have said it as soon as it is out of my mouth. But there it is.

''Yes?'' Charles says, interested.

I think on the boy. There is something fine about Winston. Not just his beautiful billboard looks—which he has, in my book, anyway. It is something separate, how I feel about him is something separate from my just having the hots for him. Which I do. There is something fine about him. There is something fine about how I feel for him. It is a very good thing, this something fine I feel for him.

Is it love?

I wonder.

''D'you think it's odd,'' I start to ask. I am going to ask this. I screw up my courage. I've been wondering, really, about this feeling, this deep feeling that I think is fine. Me, Mr. Total Queer, right?

''What?'' Charles encourages. He wants to know. ''Is what odd?''

''Well,'' I say, still hesitating. Dare I? I look at Charles. He seems really interested. He's been my friend. Okay. I decide. Say it.

''Well,'' I start again, ''I like him so much, you know? It's just, oh, I dunno, it's just that sometimes I feel like I could just hug him, you know?''

There. I've said it.

It ain't sex either. It's how he was for me out to the cemetery. It's how he talked about his dad. How he understood about my dad. And all that stuff about swallowing your grief and how he's trying to be okay and how I thought he was really trying to be good to me, you know? I mean, I thought he was really trying to help me because he liked me and didn't want me to hurt, you know?

And I do, too, sometimes. I just want to hug him.

I wouldn't, of course. He'd just die.

''I think I understand,'' Charles says.

Yeah? I say gratefully. Yeah?

"Yes," Charles says. "I feel the same way toward you sometimes."

Oh.

Oh.

This ain't it. This ain't what I meant to be doing. I mean. Wait a sec. Oh, shit.

Charles is leaning forward in his chair. He has his hands clasped out over his knees. He's beaming away at me.

Naw.

This ain't it.

I'm all mixed up. My feeling for Winston is all of a sudden not so hot. God, what have I done now?

"I think it is perfectly natural," Charles says.

I feel angry at him. I didn't want to talk about him and me. That's different.

Damn.

"Listen," I say, my bum still on fire, my bones aching. It has been one whale of a week. "I'm pretty bushed," I say.

He's nodding. He understands.

I don't like it. I don't want him to understand all the time.

Well, fuck it. I'll never understand grown-ups.

I say good night and scoot.

34

"HOPE YOU SEE SOME ACTION TONIGHT," WINSton says. He's wiping off his half of the table. Martinez is down at the other end. They're cleaning up the breakfast dishes and wiping the table down.

"Fat chance," I say. I watch Winston stretching as he wipes his half dry. I remember my chat with Charles last night. This fine feeling.

Martinez finishes his end and comes up to ours. He has his number-ten can, his rag, and tray in hand. You wipe the crumbs from the table onto the tray.

"After his starring performance last week," Martinez teases. They've been razzing my ass all week about how the Old Man clobbered me upside the head with his clipboard.

I pretend-lunge and fake him out. He leaps back, shrieking.

"We did okay," I say.

"Your head don't think so," Martinez says.

"Well," Winston says, "I do hope you get into the game."

"I don't care," I say.

"C'mon," Martinez says. He ain't believing that shit.

It's true. I tell them.

"It's true. I don't care that much. I only went out in the first place so I could make the trips. Really."

They are both looking at me, trying to figure out if I'm serious or not.

"I ain't no superstar," I say. I turn to Martinez: "Though I am sure you ain't figured that out yet."

Martinez sets his tray down. He lifts his rag off it and snaps it at me.

"Well, have fun, asshole," Winston says.

"Yeah," I say grinning.

They have to go to school this morning and do the regular shit. We'll be on the bus this morning and be in Lexington this afternoon.

Lexington is tough. We win, but barely. 20–15, with Lexington inside the ten at the clock. No lie. Goal-line stand. Rasco is beautiful. Foster, too. Both of them in there fierce, a human wall of meat you ain't about to be penetrating.

The Old Man spit himself dry. He always does. Storming up and down the sideline, screaming, swearing, spitting, spitting, spitting, spitting. He spits all the time. Little nothing spits finally. He spits so much there ain't no juice left in 'em. He's got this little cleft in his chin, one of those miniature Kirk Douglas jobbies, right? And every practice and every game he fills that little cleft with that dry white powder he spits. The old fool spitting all over himself day in and day out. He'll spit all over you, too. He'll be telling you what play to carry in, whose head to bust on the next play, who to be watching for and spitting the whole time, spit, spit, spit.

On the bus back I sit next to Rasco. We're about halfway back. The heroes, the Jock-O set, they're pretty subdued in back. Lexington wore their asses out. Lexington kicked ass—you know how the first string has been doing my ass all week, right? That's how Lexington did the first string tonight. There's more than one charley horse tonight.

"Destern okay?" I ask softly. My voice matches the softness of the night-dark bus. There are only a pair of little bulbs that light the aisle. Another pair up front by the driver and that's it. The beauty of the millions and millions of horse ranches are lost in the midnight dark of the night.

"Say what?" Rasco asks dreamily. Poor fool is worn out. He worked his ass off tonight. They beat him to death down there at the goal line those last three, four minutes. Rasco's the rock holding up the center, no lie.

He rolls his head my way.

I tap myself on the temple. You know. Where Destern got it when Felix went off on him that Friday night?

''Oh, that,'' Rasco says. He's four million miles away. The boy is exhausted. Me, I'm fresh and frisky—when you're on the Hamburger Squad that's the way it is. You're as frisky after a game as you are before. Friskier, in fact. I mean, I ain't done shit but cheer.

Rasco rolls his head toward the window. He looks out into the night. I can see his face reflected back. It's ghostly. I can see right through his face. I can see the lights from the houses deep in the black night. Everyone's tucked up safe for the night.

He rolls his head my way again on that headrest.

''He's okay,'' he says.

''So what was going on?'' I ask. ''That night you all had to squat?''

He doesn't answer at first. He asks me a question instead. ''How did you get over there, anyway? It was pretty late, wasn't it?''

I tell him how I didn't go in that night after we got off the bus. How I just went tooling around in the night being the Peeping Tom. I tell him I was worried about him, his big black eye and all, so I decided, I say, to call on him.

''And then there you all are,'' I say in awe again. ''What was going on, huh?''

He looks straight ahead, his head still resting back on the headrest. He answers me without looking at me. ''Felix was making sure we all got the message.''

''Yeah?'' I say. ''And what's the message?''

Rasco turns to me now, looks me dead in the eye. He looks so fierce it scares me.

''You do not—repeat: do not—go to the Monsignor.''

He says it, holds us eyeball to eyeball a sec, and then looks straight ahead again.

I sit and say nothing. Rumor has it that Felix is crazy. Or so the story goes. Crazy fucking Felix.

Good God. In ain't just story. It is true.

"I'm sorry," I say to Rasco. He's still looking dead ahead. "It must be a bitch."

He doesn't look at me.

"Yeah," he agrees without moving his head. "The guy's nuts."

We talk no more of it tonight. We ride the bus north on 68 into the night.

35

SATURDAY MORNING CHARLES IS ALL EXCITED ABOUT going out to Rochester this coming weekend. He teases me about my driving.

He did take me to get my learner's permit. It was pretty simple. You just take the written test, you pass, and they give you the permit. Only *getting* there was an adventure. I mean Charles. He surprises me.

"Where you going?" I ask as he turns the wrong way onto Tarbox-Cemetery Road. He turns north. We want to go south, to Xenia. North takes you to Yellow Springs.

"Xenia," Charles answers.

"Xenia's the other way," I tell him.

"No, it's not," he says and proceeds to explain to me how he goes right on up the road here into Yellow Springs to catch 68 south into Xenia.

"Where're you from?" I ask incredulously. How could he be so dumb? I tell him to turn around. "You turn around, go half a mile to 42, and that'll take us right into Xenia in about a third of the time."

It doesn't faze him one bit.

"We're okay," he says. "Besides," he says, "I like Yellow Springs."

Right.

At chow I try to get next to Whiteworm, only he books. He's moving like a bug on a hotplate—I mean, the boy is motoring. He leaves me standing at the double doors with my mouth agape. Don't tell me he didn't know, either. He knew.

Winston comes up behind me. He bumps me. We go out together.

''He look okay to you?'' I ask.

''Who?''

''Whiteworm,'' I say.

''Never noticed,'' he says.

I want to talk to him about all of this. I want to run all of this past him. I don't, of course. I can't. Not without telling him what a queer I am.

''You ready for your speech?'' he asks. ''It's next Friday, right?''

''Yeah,'' I say as I lean into the outer door with both hands. I push and out we go right into the arms of the Fearsome Foursome.

Shit.

I try ignoring them. We'll just go around.

No way.

Kuhns is there, blocking my way.

''How ya doin', son?'' he asks. He puts his hand on my shoulder.

''Everything's just fine.'' I say hurriedly. I do a little half twist and try to slide between him and Brower.

''What's your rush?'' Brower asks. He snatches me by the arm, gotcha.

''Listen, you guys. I ain't looking for any trouble,'' I say.

Foster closes on Winston. I look. It grosses me out. Foster's being all lewd and leering. He pinches Winston's chin.

''Goot-chee gootchee goo,'' Foster goes.

''What's with you, asshole?'' Winston says. Winston shoves Foster's hand away.

Brower grabs Winston by the arm. He's still got a hold of me, too.

''We thought you might like to take a little hike out to the sheep farm, hmmm?'' When Brower says this they all laugh. You should hear the fucking stories about the sheep farm. You wouldn't believe the stories about the sheep farm.

They are really being assholes here.

Foster spreads his legs and rubs himself on his nuts. He's still standing right in Winston's face.

Fogarty gets in on the act now. He steps up to Winston, the both of them now, Fogarty and Foster right in Winston's face. Fogarty licks his lips. It's whore time, boys, whore time.

"C'mon, you guys," I complain. I try to yank myself free of Brower. His grip only tightens; his fingers are like a vice.

"What?" Kuhns asks in disbelief. "You too good for us?"

Now Kuhns is right in my face.

"Leave us alone, will ya?" I protest.

I hear Winston next to me: "What's with you? I ain't no girl."

Foster yanks him now, yanks him hard: "Maybe you are," Foster says ominously.

This is really getting out of hand. I am about to cry or pass out, one.

Suddenly Atlas, the head of the high school dining hall and former head of the grade school dining hall, steps out. All four thousand pounds of him. He's known us for years. Me and Kuhns anyway.

"Vat's opp, boys-a?" he wants to know. He's a huge guy. Built like a barrel. And he always wears the same outfit: gray baker's pants with his starched white kitchen shirt and that godawful silly ass chef's hat that reminds me of toothpicks from fancy luncheons the Monsignor takes his altar boys to. Atlas, he comes from another world. Atlas, he brings another world with him.

"My goot boys-a, vat choo opp to, chyes?" he asks.

It gives us the chance we need.

Winston jerks free of Brower and kicks Foster by accident—he jerked so hard he's kicking up his toes, a reflex action which startles everyone, especially Foster and

Brower. I lurch backward while everyone's still surprised at Atlas's appearance and Winston's sudden moves. I slam full blast into Atlas and ricochet off his great barrel body, boing! Winston dashes back inside. Brower loosens his grip on me as I bounce off Atlas. I leap back into the dining hall right behind Winston. The four of them spring forward, only Atlas ropes them in, his huge, thick arms extended in a great fat cross. He's alarmed. You don't go back into his dining hall after chow. That is not right. He stops the Jock-O boys and yells over his shoulder to me and Winston: "Choo come out! Vat choo vwant? Trouble, chyes?"

Winston beats it straight back through the kitchen. He's heading for the back door.

"No!" I call to him. I catch up to him right at the screen door. "No," I say again. I see Brower just coming around the corner. "This way," I say and aim him back inside, past the walk-in coolers to the back stairs.

"What's this?" Winston asks.

I dash down the steps. They take us right into the priests' quarters. I stop at the entrance to the priests' quarters, peek inside, and take a quick look about. No one's in here, it's all clear.

"Okay, go!" I say.

We scoot in and across the front room and go directly to the priests' quarters front door, which is under the main dining hall on the opposite side of the building from the kitchen's back door.

There's not a soul in sight. We beat it the fuck out of there.

"What the fuck's going on?" Winston wants to know.

I tell him how they have me pegged for a rat.

Rat for what?

That stops me.

I ain't sure. They got into trouble after the first game, I tell him. Halstead told me about the beer. I guess that's it. For drinking beer.

I am a little bit amazed. It has just dawned on me that

I don't really know what I am supposed to have ratted on them about.

"You didn't rat on them, did you?" Winston asks.

I can only moan.

"Sorry," he says. "Why don't you just tell them that?" he wonders.

"I did at first," I tell him. "I told them I didn't do it. I told them I didn't do anything, that I didn't even know anything about it. But they didn't give a shit about that. They didn't give a shit about anything I had to say. They'd already made up their minds. In fact," I say, discovering it right now as I say it to him, "it just pissed them off all the more if I said anything at all."

"God," Winston says, "It sounds awful."

"Yeah," I say and I'm surprised by this sudden rush of feeling. It rolls over me like a two ton wave all full of needles and broken glass. I stand here stunned by it, shivering through it, Jesus.

"They just needed someone to blame," I say when the wave has passed. "That's what I think."

"And you got picked, huh?"

"Boy, did I ever," I say. I don't tell him that my becoming friends with Charles has a lot to do with it, how they've been hating their counselors while I'm over here getting all chummy with mine—opening up and planting gardens and shit like that. I don't understand it too well, but they really hate me for this, too.

We're in front of the cottage now. It's time for charges. I want to talk.

He scoots past me and takes the steps two at a time.

I really would like to talk. I yearn for it and notice his legs as I yearn. It dawns on me: I am looking down. My eyes are downcast. I am all the time looking down. I ain't looking anyone in the eye.

I want to talk.

I don't.

* * *

Charges save me. They always do. Me and my Aunt Margaret Mary. She cleans all day, every day. She does one awful job, though. Her place, I'd say, it's pretty dirty, but she's at it, see? She's busy, see? She can't be thinking about no communists if she's busy.

Me, too.

Keep busy.

Martinez has the front hall as his charge. He's washing and waxing his floor. Cruise has the downstairs can. I am going to teach this child something yet. Winston's not waxing this study hall this morning. He waxed last Saturday so he's just buffing it all this morning. Which is job enough.

The whole house is roaring. Rock 'n' roll pours from every crevice. The place is raucous. It makes me happy. It is chaos that ain't.

"Hey, you asshole," Martinez shrieks.

Tollens is coming down the stairs with a bucket. He's banging away and slopping it, spilling it—and slopping and spilling it all over Martinez's just washed and waxed floor.

I jump in and help Tollens with the bucket and wringer. These suckers weigh a ton, no lie.

"I got it," I say to Tollens. I turn to Martinez. "We'll clean it up," I say, nodding to the slop and water on his newly waxed, now drying floor.

"Okay, Bambi," Martinez says to me. He takes a swing at Tollens and pulls it short, faking both me and Tollens out something bad. The two of them snarl and glare at each other. Poor Tollens. He's got a bad case of the Superheros without having any superhero talent. He's strutting about all the time, strut strut, looking like he's got the corncob up his butt, yakking away the whole time, all the time, yak yak yak. And the whole time he's yakking away, yak yak yak, it's about himself, about I, me, and mine: Ain't I this? Ain't I that? Yak yak. Don't you agree? I'm this? I'm that, yak yak yak, Ain't I? Huh? Ain't I? Huh?

We dump the water in the big sink by the back door. I ring out the mop and take out real quick like to Martinez's floor. I quickly mop up our spills.

"There ya go," I say to Martinez. We got 'em before they fucked up his wax. Martinez is standing in the entryway to the study hall, watching Winston buff away and guarding his own floor as he waits for it to dry. As soon's it's dry he'll be buffing away himself.

He nods his appreciation to me but says nothing.

"Inspection, Bambi," Cruise pipes. He loves to call me Bambi. Makes him feel so cool to use my nickname: you are Bambi and I am grown, too.

It's fine by me.

I follow him back down the hall to the can. He pushes the door open for me and stands aside: it's all yours.

"Jesus, Cruise," I say. It's awful. The toilets are for shit. The floor's half-ass swept and doesn't look like it's been mopped at all.

"Come on," I say. He's got to be kidding.

"What?" he asks with total innocence.

I look at him. He really thinks he has done one bang-up job here.

"Get the toilet bowl cleaner, the brush. Get the broom, mop, and bucket," I say.

He moans and trots down the hall to the equipment room. Then I see the mirror, which is streaked, spotted—filthy. I yell after him: "Bring it all, Cruise. Bring it all."

We do the whole can over, me and Cruise. I show him how, let him try, then do it with him, criticize him, praise him some—he does do the bowl okay. He holds the broom, the mop, too, for that matter, as if they are irradiated, as if they are going to infect him.

"Grab a hold of it," I say. God, I wanna wring his little ignorant fucking neck. And he's eating it up.

We finish up, mopping. I show him how to wet-mop.

"You get it good and wet, full of suds, lots of water, and slop it around. You're scrubbing when you're wet-mopping, see?"

I bear down on the mop. See? I give him the mop.

"Oh, sure," he says and proceeds to flip that mop

about just above the surface of the floor. He hardly grazes the tile itself.

"No," I say. "Pressure. You gotta put some pressure on it. You're scrubbing now, rub-a-dub-dub, right?"

Yeah, he says.

"And really slop it up in the corners," I say. "Under here especially," I say as I jam the mop head up under the stools. Two per can. "Everyone pisses all over the goddamned place, right?

"Not me, not me," he proclaims proudly. He doesn't, either. I've seen him, his little peanut pecker in his fingers, he's directing his stream ever so carefully. Little shit is so proud. He can pee a straight line.

"Now the dry mop, see?" I say and wring that mother out. I do it by hand. Lyman taught me this move, I'm sorry. Up to Building One. You don't use the wringer. You use your hands. You straddle the handle, pin it down with one foot hooked over the long handle, and then just twist and twist and squeeze those long gray strings. You do it right and you can get it so clean and so dry that those gray strands will be looking white. And that is dry. And I mean dry.

I do it for him. We have to go to the big sink by the back door. You have to have a big sink to prop your mop on.

"You try," I say. I hand him the mop and step aside.

He tries. Poor little pussy. He weighs all of about eighty-eight pounds. Boy ain't got muscle one, really. He's as soft as butter set out in the summertime.

I can't take it. I grab the mop out of his hands.

"I'll do it. You need to dry-mop, you call me, okay?"

The little fucker beams. "Okay," he says.

"Inspection," Johnson calls.

I go upstairs to the second-floor can. Johnson does good work. I say so.

"Nice work."

"Thanks, boss," he says.

I eat it up. He likes me and calls me that. Shit. It makes me feel important.

I come back downstairs and go right into the study hall.

"You gotta stay," Martinez says to me. He's just put his wax down. I have to wait for it to dry.

"Okay," I agree. I sit at my desk and watch Winston buffing away over in the far corner. It's a big room. Twenty-five by forty foot. All the study halls in all the high school cottages are the same humongous size.

I figure it out. I take a pencil out of my desk and multiply on the cover of my physics notebook. A thousand square feet.

It takes some time to do the study hall.

Winston is good. I watch him work his buffer. It isn't easy.

Each buffer—or shiner, we call them shiners, too—has a twenty-five-pound metal weight at the bottom. The weight sits atop a five-by-seven horsehair brush. You stand at the end of the five-foot-long hollow metal pole that is attached to the weighted horsehair brush. You push and pull that weighted brush up and back. That's what brings up the shine.

There's a pin at the bottom where the hollow metal pole attaches to the brush and weight. If you do it right, get a rhythm going, get that pin popping against that pole, you can make a little music.

Winston works it like a pro. He's never been taught, either.

I watch and take some comfort here.

I enjoy how well he handles that buffer. There's an art to it, there really is. You have to use your whole body. Most of the kids just use their arms. They try to muscle it. That will kill you—and fuck up the floor, too. Every time someone tries muscling it they are flipping that baby right over on its back and that twenty-five-pound weight, with its sharp metallic corners, is digging crevices and gouges into your newly waxed tile. It takes forever to get those scratches, crevices, and gouges out, too. Dannon, the kid with the wretched zits, the cratered face? He is always trying to muscle it. He won't let me show him any different, either. The poor fucker, he tears his floors up something awful, and then he has to work four times as long to get that shine.

Winston is working away. I enjoy myself watching him pump that shiner up and back, up and back. His entire body rocks with the movement. I am lost in it, lost in his movement, his rocking. It is lovely. You see someone do it right, no shit, it is simply lovely.

I notice his breathing. It is heavy work, whether you do it right or no, it is heavy work.

He attacks his work. I watch and listen.

He's got it, that rhythm. He's making music.

Click. Click.

Clickety click.

Click.

He has his back to me. He is bent at the waist. His legs are spread-eagled. His entire body is rocking back and forth.

His buttocks flex with each forward thrust and that pin sings: Click.

He catches the buffer at the top of his thrust and that pin sings again: Click.

He yanks her back over the same line of tiles: Clickety click.

He's back to go, catches the buffer right at the bottom of his swing: Click.

He starts it all over again, his buttocks flexing, he's thrusting her forward once again, and that pin sings anew: *click.*

Click. Click.

Clickety click.

Click.

"Inspection!" Cowen calls.

I look. He's come from the bedrooms on the first floor. He's stepped out onto Martinez's newly waxed floor.

"You value your life, asshole!" Martinez shrieks.

Martinez lunges. Cowen leaps back.

"It's dry," I call to Martinez. I walk quickly to the edge of the study hall. I stop short of Martinez's turf. I ask permission to cross.

"It okay for me to cross?"

Martinez abandons his assault upon Cowen. He turns to check out my request. He looks at my feet and notices that my toes are right at the edge—right at the edge but not over the edge. I am respecting his turf. He allows me to cross.

Cowen bolts.

"Next time, asshole," Martinez threatens.

"Thank you," I say as I follow Cowen down the corridor to bedroom one. This is his charge, bedroom one. It is easy work. You dust-mop the floor, clean the two sinks, clean the mirror, dust the blinds, and that's it. You never need to buff back here—or maybe once a year. That's why I gave the job to Cowen, it's so easy.

He's no great shakes but he does okay.

I check the venetian blinds. Cowen watches me inspect. As I run my hand over the venetian blind louvers I see Whiteworm out back. He is heading off across the ball diamond all by himself. I wonder. Is he okay? Will he ever let me be his friend again? Or have I screwed it up for life?

"It's okay," I say to Cowen.

Cowen says nothing.

We head back out to the study hall together.

I probably have fucked it up for life. Forever and ever. God.

36

I KEEP MY NOSE CLEAN ALL WEEK. CHARLES AND I PLAN our trip to Waterloo. We'll be heading out Thursday morning right after first-period physics, hitting the road by nine forty-five. Charles asks me to navigate.

"This is all I've got," he says, showing me his Vacation and Travel Guide. It is not an atlas. All it has is this two-page map of the entire United States which is a mileage-and-driving map. It just shows gross distances. Not how to get there.

Charles looks a little lost.

"I'll get us a road atlas," I say.

Charles looks relieved.

"I'll be our navigator," I say.

He loves the idea.

"Pilot to navigator," he says. He's just beaming away.

Sometimes the guy can really embarrass me.

"Pilot to navigator," he repeats.

Like right now, the simple shit.

The Fearsome Foursome are too busy to bother with me this week, thank you. The Old Man is working them to death. Central is going to be tough. The Old Man always wants to kill Central.

Kuhns even forgets to pick me as his tackling-practice partner on both Tuesday and Wednesday.

I think it is finally blowing over. It has been almost four weeks—it will be four weeks next Monday since they lost their jobs and got into all this trouble.

Rasco is being my friend. That is good.

Gamble's on the comeback trail.

All in all—except for Whiteworm—things are shaping up quite nicely once again. I've got a nice route laid out for me and Charles. I've got my permit. I will be driving, ya hear? Bambi behind the wheel. On the road in the real world. I can dig it. I can really dig it.

On Thursday morning I am up—as in *up*. I go to mass in the high school chapel and say my thirty-second day of my novena. I've got thirteen more days to go. I have been pure for thirty-two days. Thirty-two. I am strong.

At breakfast I wolf down my Frosted Flakes and eat my elephant ear—which was made right here in the Home's trade school, the boys learning a trade. I eat my one piece of cold toast buttered and smeared with strawberry jelly. I snarf up my grapefruit half, Winston's grapefruit half, and Cruise's grapefruit half. I wash it all down with two glasses of frothing, frosty fresh milk trucked in direct from the Home's dairy farm.

I am raring to go.

Physics class takes an eternity.

The bell rings.

Halstead wishes me good luck.

"What?" I ask in surprise. I am at the door.

"With your speech," he says. "You go to the Bellamy Flag Awards this weekend, don't you?"

"Yeah," I say, still surprised. I didn't expect him to remember.

"You just be yourself," he says, "and you'll do terrific."

Thanks.

Charles is just about ready when I get back to the cottage. His car's out back. He's driven her down the back lawn right up onto the back slab of concrete patio. I can see his tire tracks in the grass. The trunk is open.

"Here," I offer, "I'll take that." I grab his suitcase. It's sitting by the office door.

"Thanks," he says.

I grab it. It weighs a ton. Takes two hands to lift.

"What've you got in here, an anvil?" I ask.

He laughs as I duck waddle it out to his car. I toss his anvil in the open trunk and then hoof it back inside.

"I get mine," I say, meaning my suitcase, "and I'm ready," I call to him.

"Fine," he says.

I hoof it down the short corridor to my bedroom and skip across the bedroom to my locker.

Say! What's this?

There's an envelope taped to my locker. "BAMBI THE BULL" is scrawled on it. Above my name it says, "25¢ DEPOSIT REQUIRED."

I take it down and open it. It's from Winston and Martinez. There's a folded note and one of those Antioch bookplate bookmarks in the envelope. The bookmark has a rainbow on it, a brightly colored tassle tail, and a picture of a tiny cupid angel. The bookmark says: "ANGELS FLY BECAUSE THEY DON'T TAKE THEMSELVES SERIOUSLY."

I open the note. A tiny card falls out. I pick it up. It reads:

YOU WERE JUST FUCKED OUT OF
25 CENTS
AND ARE NOW OFFICIALLY A MEMBER
OF THE
DUMB FUCKERS CLUB.

I laugh out loud. Then I open the note and read it.

Bambi: We know you will knock them dead.
Good luck, you dumb fucker.

They both signed it.

I stick my Dumb Fuckers Club membership card in my billfold. I fold the note back up, turn around to my suitcase on my bed, open it, and shove their note in under my novena booklet. I shut my suitcase back up and hoof it out to Charles's car.

Charles is ready to go. I toss my suitcase in the trunk—it's half the size of Charles' anvil case—slam the trunk, and dash around to the passenger's side.

"Let's do it," Charles says. He climbs in the driver's side. I jump in on the passenger's side—your navigator rides shotgun.

He takes us up the grassy lawn. I hold my breath. The tires will tear this lawn to shreds. We roll off the curb onto the road, bumpity bump, and I relax. I look back real quick. The grass looks okay. You can see our tire marks, but we didn't dig it up none.

Charles takes us out to Tarbox-Cemetery Road. He starts to turn left.

"Wait," I say quickly.

"I'm going to Xenia first, right?" he asks.

"Nope," I say as I realize he was about to turn the correct way to get to Xenia via 42. I like that. He does listen to me.

"No," I say, "you go ahead on up into Yellow Springs."

He shrugs and hangs a right.

"You like Yellow Springs, right?" I say and make him laugh.

We take Grinnell Road to Corry. This is Yellow Springs. He's about to turn left, the wrong way.

"No, wait," I say, but this time he waves me off.

"I do like Yellow Springs," he repeats, laughing as he takes us the long way out Corry so we end up at the south end of the village when we want to be at the north end. It's no big deal. We just drive down through the village. We're on 68 anyway, which is what we want. This will take us to 40.

"Stay on this until 40," I tell him as we cruise through downtown Yellow Springs.

"Fine," he says.

We both gape at the story-book town. There's a "BAN THE BOMB" sign in a store window.

I don't relax until I get us onto Highway 40, which is all the way into Springfield. It's a mess but we do it.

"Okay," I tell Charles. We're on 40 now, heading west. "It's about twenty, twenty-five miles to 48," I tell him. "That's our next turn, okay?"

"You're the navigator," he says warmly, gratefully.

I'm pretty happy. I'm excited about this trip. And I have a job. I like having a job. You get me excited and happy, and I just start jabbering away. Which I do now. I just start chattering away and ask Charles a million questions.

You got brothers?

Two, he says.

What do they do? Where do they live?

Bobby's a pipe fitter, he says. Out West.

Out West? Where?

Somewhere.

Oh.

Two. You said two?

Yeah. Billy's dead.

Oh. Sorry. What happened to him?

He ain't saying. Mum's the word.

You okay? I ask.

He's pursing his lips. He looks like someone who's trying to swallow something real bitter.

Charles? Charles?

He looks over at me, snapping his head sharply. There is something hateful in his eyes.

Ex-scoooooozzzzzz me.

Sisters?

He says nothing.

Englewood, the sign says. 48 coming up.

"That's us," I say, nodding at the mileage sign as it whizzes past.

Huh?

"We go north," I say, "on 48. At Englewood."

48? he asks as if it's something in Chinese.

You drive, I say. I'll watch for the signs. I'm navigator, remember.

Okay, he says. He sounds sour.

Poor babe. Wonder what his problem is?

Before we reach Englewood the terrain starts to roll. More trees, too. Coming up on a river. You always get this roll, all these extra trees, whenever you approach a river.

"I would have liked having a sister," I say, thinking about it. I bet it would be interesting.

"No, you wouldn't," he says malevolently.

I leave that one alone.

Where you from originally?

Richmond, he says. Richmond, Indiana.

The Rose City.

Yep, he says. The last city we lived in.

The Englewood dam's dead ahead. 48 just off it.

The last city? I ask.

"My old man," he volunteers, "career Air Force." There is something mean in how he says it: my old man.

"We've been all over," he goes on. "Omaha. Panama City, Dayton."

The Panama Canal? I ask.

"No," he says, laughing at me.

Don't laugh at me.

"Panama City, Florida," he says. "There's a big base down there. We've been overseas. too. Germany. The Philippines."

It sounds great. I say so.

"Sounds great."

"Yeah," he says unconvincingly. He's bullshitting both of us. I don't know why. He ain't such a happy guy this morning. I can't figure it out. I'm delirious with joy. So what's with him? Back at the Home, when he's around all the boys, he's pretty happy. I wonder about that, how he got involved with the Home, boys, shit like that.

"How'd you get hooked up with the Home, anyway?" I ask.

We come out onto the Englewood dam. Route 40 goes right out across her. We emerge from our rolling, tree lined route out into the great open spaces, two hundred, two hundred fifty feet above the river. It's just fucking breathtaking.

"Route 48's right off the dam, here," I tell him. He ain't paying me no attention. We come off the dam. There's a light.

"This is it. Forty-eight. Turn here. Route 48 north. Okay?"

He turns right onto 48. He doesn't say anything, he just turns right. A weird guy.

"Fifty-five, sixty miles on this," I tell him. "Up to Grand Lake."

He doesn't seem to be in.

"Yooo-hooo," I call out. Being playful.

Wrong: he looks over at me as if I'm a mosquito carrying malaria just for him. He lifts one eyebrow.

It's me. Bambi. You remember me, huh? Don't ya, huh?

"We stay on this to Grand Lake," I repeat.

Fine, he says, short, a bit snooty even.

Who knows what his problem is. I sure don't. Now, where were we? Oh, yeah: "How'd you get interested in us? In working with boys?"

We are sailing along. I lean over to check our speed. Sixty, sixty five. Traffic's light. He starts to warm up. Talking about boys does it.

He says he doesn't know exactly. How he got interested. He's just had this feeling for boys, he says. Ever since he was in the Air Force himself.

You were in the Air Force?

Yeah, he says. Didn't I tell you?

No, I tell him. Only that your dad was. Not that you were.

His face shrivels up when I mention his dad. Something awry here. I remember Winston's tenderness with me about my dad.

"Your dad, huh? Pretty rough on ya, huh?"

I'm doing my best Winston. He did me good. I'll do Charles good.

"No, no, no," he says quickly, too quickly. He ain't about to be talking about his dad, that much is clear. He does want to talk about boys, though. Young boys, he says. He's always wanted to work with young boys. Says he's always felt more comfortable, you know, with young boys. Felt more like himself, he says. Like when I was in scouting.

"You were in scouting?" I ask.

Yeah, he says. Down in Florida.

It makes him smile, at first, remembering. He's getting terrifically relaxed here. Which is good. Which is how it should be. We're on a trip. On a little vacation, a little adventure. Right?

"I feel like a boy myself," he says in a great rush of intimacy.

I look at him. It's odd. He does look young. Right this very minute. Awfully young, in fact. Sort of gorpy, dumbshitty.

It makes me squirm a bit, seeing his young gorpy dumbshitty look. Let's not get carried away here, Charles. We have to remember who we are.

We enter Minster. There's a lake here. You can tell. The town has that resorty look to it. Little white cottages. And a breeze that suggests water close by.

Loramie Lake's here, I tell Charles, flashing the map at him.

He takes a quick look.

Grand Lake's next, I tell him. We switch highways there.

Fine. Fine.

We leave Minster in no time. Suddenly he's terribly animated and is telling me this tale about this boy named Donald. Donald down in Florida. In scouts. A boy from a broken home. Donald.

That's like us, see?

Kids at the Home, we're mostly all from broken homes.

Which means your parents are fucked up or lame or something and can't handle being grown up and all. So they check out, either dying or drinking or going crazy and leaving you to your own devices.

Broken homes do not mean broken boys. They don't. I don't care what you say. Father Flat used to say it. He was our dean in Building One. He was an orphan himself, he told us often enough. He taught us religion in eighth grade. He'd go on and on about himself. As an example, right? Trying to help us, see? Adults do that. They will talk about themselves and act as if they are only interested in helping you, the poor, neglected child—pretending so hard that they believe it themselves. Pretending what they are doing is helping you, the homeless kid, by giving you an example about real life and real people when all they are really doing is talking about themselves. You know? We all love to talk about ourselves. That's what I think.

So Father Flat's telling us about being an orphan himself, weep, weep. He's telling us how he was the only jarhead to drop to his knees every night next to his bunk to say his night prayers and that we should be so brave. In the barracks. On his knees. Saying his night prayers.

Rah rah.

He scared me when he was talking this broken-home, broken-boy shit. He says to us, it's in religion class, so it's gospel. He says:

"We are all broken some."

He looked so sad. He's been broken some. He is saying so. He is telling us about himself. How sad, how lonely, how hard to understand: we are all broken some.

Father's asking us to understand, to care, to pity and here's his head counselor, Lyman fucking Hall dead set on breaking us. I've heard him say it. That that is his job. To break these young colts.

Well, fuck him.

I ain't broke.

I look over to Charles. He's yakking away about his boy Donald. He's in love with this kid. He's in love with this kid and something wretched is coming. Charles is being so broken up here, he's telling his tale so haltingly. Something fishy is going on here. I'm sorry. I ain't liking this too terribly much.

Charles is talking about how this boy was broken, how life can do that to you. It can break you. Life can do that, he says.

We're coming into St. Mary's. This is where Grand Lake is. Lake St. Marys. Route 48 ends here. We have to pick up 66 here, take it north to 30. I try to tell Charles.

I think he's going to cry. Really. I think the guy's about to cry. It is too gross.

"Route 48 ends. We take 66 north," I say.

I'm sorry. Business is business. We got to take the right road.

He could care. He's having trouble just like Father Flat had trouble, the kind of trouble a man makes and likes, all happy to be broke and weepy.

He looks at me. He is teary-eyed, I shit you not.

"Here. This is it," I say, nodding to the sign for 66 North.

He looks so hurt. I'm paying attention to the road, not to him and his sad tale of the poor broken boyfriend of his, Donald. He wants to go on some more.

To tell you the truth, I ain't too terribly interested.

Charles catches my eye and the strangest thing happens. I am suddenly lightheaded. I am looking into his eyes and I get dizzy. It's just for a split second, but my brain, my eyes, and my ears they go *bwaaaa.*

My brain goes *bwaaaa* and Charles is suddenly younger than me.

This cannot be.

He is younger than me now. His eyes are glued to me. I try to look away. I am compelled. Something is being sucked out of me. I can feel it pouring out of me, right out through my eyes and into him and he is younger than me, right this minute he is younger than me and I feel as if I am but six.

The light changes. We take 66 north.

I take a deep breath, mystified. Charles takes his eyes off me. He stares out the windshield at the road ahead and says it very softly. He says it so softly, in fact, that I have to lean into him to hear it. I nearly miss it. I wish I had.

"He hanged himself."

Jesus fucking Christ.

37

YOU THINK THAT DOESN'T PUT A CRIMP IN YOUR STYLE and you got another think coming.

I look at him. He is younger than me now. I am seventeen again. Going on a thousand.

We drive in silence. We head north along the St. Marys River. I am terribly grateful for the earth itself and the seemingly sudden forest that runs thick everywhere about the river. The earth itself is beneath us in deep swells, in lifts, in drops, in short runs across the rich farmlands at river's edge. Soybeans run in rows from the highway right back into the trees, the fields wending and winding into, around and about the thick stands of trees huddled there along the river.

I let the land soothe me.

At Delphos we catch 30. The land has opened up again with flat fields of wheat, soybean, and corn running out and away in every direction. Route 30 takes us northwest into Indiana, where there's a terrible openness, a tremendous expanse interrupted only occasionally by the neat, well-kept farms set hundreds of yards back from the highway.

Charles remains uncommunicative.

The silence oppresses me. It's got me counting again. I'm counting the miles, counting the rivers. We hit the Maumee just before Fort Wayne. St. Josephs River runs right through Fort Wayne. Twenty-two miles out and we cross the Eel—this is the first one with a name, anyway. Twenty-three more miles and it's Tippecanoe.

"Tippecanoe and Tyler, too," I say.

He ain't talking. And I'm still counting. I am all the time counting. Back at the Home it's steps. I don't know why, I just do. I count steps. I can tell you how many steps there are in front of the main chapel: seven. I can tell you how many steps there are in front of the auditorium: six. I can tell you how many steps there are in Building One, from the first floor to the landing: eight; and then again from the landing to the second floor: seven.

"I knew a kid who hung himself," I say. I am stuck on Donald. Charles has clammed up completely. Maybe I can get him to talk.

"You did?" he says.

"Yeah," I say. "A kid here. At the Home."

I remember him. His name was Aquinas. Like the saint. He was a big kid. He stuttered something awful. He was a total basket case. He really was.

He didn't do well in school. Had no friends. Failed in sports. And couldn't talk.

He grew up here. Spent six, seven years as a kid here, graduated, couldn't cut it on the Outside, and came back to work on the lawn crew.

Awful humiliation, that. Everyone knows they hire only the idiots and retards to work on the lawn crew. And a lot of kids do it. They come back after graduation to ask for a job, no lie. I cannot feature it.

Yes, I can. Only I don't want to do it myself.

God, I hope I can make it. I hope I don't need to come running back here with my tail between my legs. It's pathetic. And it can happen, too. The kid who was mayor my freshman year, he did it. He's this terrific kid, real sweet, wonderfully tender and caring, a good athlete—Latham's his name. He won a scholarship and everything, and he came back and got a job on the lawn crew. He was terrified, humiliated, but back.

"He hung himself," I say, remembering Aquinas. "With the venetian-blind cords over to the Founder's quarters. They found him strung up one morning."

I remember the morning. I was only a seventh-grader.

I was out in front of the grade school gym. One of the guys who worked in the gym told us, me and Ezra.

It was pretty awful. I think about it. It's my turn to clam up.

We drive a long way in silence. We drive until lunchtime.

We pull into a truck stop in Schererville. Charles offers to pay for mine. I tell him I have my own money. I get a cheeseburger with onions and pickles and nothing else, an order of fries, a large milk, and a piece of apple pie à la mode.

We finish. Neither of us says much. The food helps, though. When we get back into Charles's car I show him the map. Chicago's coming up.

Charles is still in some never-never land. He ain't tuned in here.

"You just drive." I say. "I'll navigate."

We get past Chicago without too much trouble. We have to ride a tollway, a first for me. It's a road you have to pay to ride on—you have to pay a toll, so it's a tollway. Charles says it's a way to pay for the road. I think it's neat.

You have to drive past these little tollhouses. Each one has a plastic basket-mouth jutting out from its hip. You toss your money into these basket-mouths. Bing! THANK YOU, it says in green and off you go. The real nifty part is that there are ten or eleven of these little tollhouses with a great apron of concrete leading away from them that quickly narrows into two lanes of highway. You gotta haul ass in a mad rush from the line of tollhouses to get one of those two lanes, *va-rooooom.*

I try to crack Charles open again. I blab away about Aquinas. I just go on and on about how we all pushed him to it, all of us at the Home. If you just think about it a moment, you'll see.

We all made fun of him. All the time, too. You couldn't see Aquinas coming without someone going off on a terrible imitation stutter. And he really stuttered bad. He would shower you and himself whenever he spoke. He had to work and work and work to get a syllable out. It would take forever, too. He's leaning hard into you, leaning forward hard, a great and powerful constipation jamming him up—he's pushing it, whatever it is that is imprisoning each and every word—the boy really trying to communicate. And here is every boy, every counselor, every priest, every teacher, every dining-hall worker, every laundry worker, even every goddamed lawn crew worker, all of us, acting superior, laughing right in his face, finding hilarity in this poor idiot's struggle to simply speak.

It's true. Honest to God.

We were all so bad.

Oh, some of us would try to be good, try to be patient, try to listen and wait without laughing. Some of us would try to take the time needed to let him get an entire sentence out, but he was so pathetic, so wretchedly lost and confused and angry and stupid that you would finally lose it. There would always be one in any crowd of three or more who simply could not resist.

Poor Aquinas. He had such a short fuse—of course.

Shit. Just think of it.

He would go into a rage which only made him that much more ridiculous. He'd get totally pissed off and then spit and sputter and shower you twice as much as usual. His face would go purple, red, splotchy and he'd lunge after you—the fucker would murder you if he could ever get his hands on you. Except that he's also a terribly uncoordinated person, so the least athletic boob in the place can and did dodge him, slip and slide away, zoom zoom, bye-yeeeee.

They had a closed-casket funeral for him up to the Lipnack. Father Al Budowski celebrated the mass. Father Al Budowski who can't speak American none too well. Father Al Budowski who gets so all fired up whenever he gives a sermon that he will start banging away on the pulpit with his fist and start ranting and raving at us in Polish, so none of us had the foggiest idea of what he is saying. He gets to say the funeral mass. He gets to give the eulogy. Father Al

Budowski, who can't speak the language. Father Al Budowski, who never even knew the boy—or man, rather. Aquinas was twenty-two when he hung himself.

I run all this past Charles. I want to talk.

You want to talk? About Donald?

Charles isn't interested.

I look at him. I think he's feeling sorry for himself. Now isn't that all bass-ackwards? I mean, it's Donald who did himself in, right?

I cannot believe this. I cannot believe it is Charles we're supposed to be feeling sorry for. I must be wrong. Charles is a counselor. He helps boys. He wouldn't get it all backwards. But then, ninety minutes west of Chicago, after I've gone on and on about Aquinas, he goes and makes this comment that convinces me I am right and that he does have it backwards.

I can't believe what he says. It sounds so truly wretched I just know he doesn't even know he's saying it out loud. He's staring hard at the road before him with both hands gripping the top half of the steering wheel.

''The little snit,'' he says softly, ''he was just trying to get even.''

This makes absolutely no sense to me.

I look out the window. We're in Illinois now. There is nothing but corn as far as the eye can see. The rows flash past like a deck of cards being flipped rapid-fire under someone's thumb. I stare at the flash of flying corn and let my mind go blank.

Near Rockford the highway splits. Highway 20. It becomes four lanes, two going each way with a boulevard in the middle. What do they call it? A medium?

Charles says I can drive now. We pull over. We both get out of the bucket seats. I walk around front. He goes around back. We switch places.

I am shitting my pants—happy shitting my pants, but shitting my pants all the same—behind the wheel. It is four lanes, which helps. I stay in the far right-hand lane, hugging the berm.

A fucking mother semi *wails* past.

"Whoa!" I shout.

Its wind alone throws me. Right after she passes I am wobbling and blow off onto the shoulder. Charles is laughing.

Asshole. We both die. He think that funny?

It pisses me off, his laughing at me. I hate it when someone laughs at me. It gives me added willpower. I can do better sometimes if you piss me off.

I only drive about thirty-five miles. I pull over at the Highest Point in Illinois. Highways 20 and 84 meet here. State Route 84, Highway 20.

I am glad to pull over. I am proud of what I have done, but I am ready to give the wheel back to Charles. We switch places again. I check out the terrain. Get this: the highest point in Illinois is 1,234 feet above sea level. One, two, three, four.

We push onto Dubuque, Iowa. It is right on the Mississippi. It is just ninety miles short of Waterloo.

It is already dark when we reach Dubuque. There are great cliffs lining the river. Houses with their windows lit look like angel's eyes, yellows and whites winking out of the darkness, running up the cliffs.

We eat at a little roadside restaurant. It is all wood inside and out. It's like eating in a cedar chest. It is very neat and orderly inside.

Charles orders prime rib. I have never heard of such a thing. It pleases him immensely to introduce me to the world. He beams away as I start to order another cheeseburger. He stops me. He insists that I let him pay. And that I order something other than a cheeseburger.

OK.

I order a T-bone.

He likes that.

We are almost the only people in here. There is a family and one couple out in the main dining room. Charles and I have this little alcove room off the main dining room all to ourselves. It has three walls of windows. There are trees black against the windows on all three sides.

He offers me a taste of his prime rib when the waitress serves us. It looks pretty interesting. It's awful pink, though.

"Here," he offers. He spears a piece on the end of his fork. He holds it out to me the way a lover holds it out to his girl, the way a mom holds food for her babe.

Charles.

It embarrasses me.

Go on, he says. No one's paying any attention, he says. He cranes his neck to be sure.

Great, asshole. They may not have been looking before, but you go craning your neck that way. . . .

"Just take it," he says. He has that fork with its piece of pink meat attached right at my lips.

I take it. It is good.

We arrive at the Hansackers' around nine-thirty. Mr. and Mrs. greet us at the door. They are terribly sweet. We stand in the doorway and shake hands all around. They have a daughter, she's a fifth-grader, her name is Melanie. She shakes my hand. She nods to Charles.

I have to explain to everyone who he is. He's my counselor. Oh, they say. People in the real world don't go carting counselors around with them, I guess.

Bob, their son, will be my school host. He's a junior. He will take me to school tomorrow. I will go to classes with him in the morning before we all go to the assembly for the awards ceremony and our speeches.

We stand in the doorway forever. Their house is too clean. There is carpet everywhere. The whole place is spotless. It seems to gleam in the soft lamplight.

Everyone has shoes on. Even little Melanie has her shoes on. I feel this overpowering urge to take mine off. I think I must. I feel like a farmer with shit on his boots as I stand here in all this perfect, gleaming cleanliness.

I wish Charles would just say good-bye and hit the road.

Charles is explaining that he is on his way up to the Mayo Clinic.

I stare at the lime-colored carpet. It is beautiful. It is very thick, so thick that Melanie's feet are half swallowed up in it.

"Just part of my training as a professional counselor," Charles is saying.

I look at him: gimme a break. He's serious. I can't believe it.

"Guess I better be getting along," he says. Finally. "I got a couple more hours of driving ahead of me."

He says all of this and stands there stationary like a hundred-year-old oak tree.

Mrs. Hansacker says she just can't have any of that. We can't have that, now, can we, Bob, she says to Mr. Hansacker.

Oh shit.

"Oh, no," Mr. Hansacker agrees.

I study this beautiful carpet some more.

"You can stay here," Mrs. H. is saying. It's so late. And we have a queen-sized bed. She turns to me now. You wouldn't mind, would you, Fred? she asks. You wouldn't have any problem sharing a bed with Charles, would you, Fred?

No.

I look at Mrs. H. I look at Charles. His eyes are a kitten's eyes full of the question: it's up to you, boy.

Oh, God. I don't sleep with anyone, ever. No. No. No.

"No," I say finally. No problem. No.

"Fine. That's settled, then," says Mrs. H. "Help them with their suitcases, Bob," she says. Bob Jr. hops to.

How'd he know which one she meant?

I take my suitcase from the trunk. I let Bob Jr. carry the anvil. I follow him back into the house and tiptoe down the lushly carpeted hallway. I tiptoe into the room they have prepared for us. It's got golden-lemon carpet. Jesus. They got carpet every fucking where. It's just like the Monsignor's residence. I should have on my cassock and surplice. I feel horribly out of place. I am a whitehead about to burst. I am puss about to spill on this lovely luscious carpet. Jesus. This house. This perfectly immaculate totally carpeted house.

With but one fucking bed.

38

We go to bed. Charles and I turn in the same time as Bob Jr. We have a big day tomorrow.

I am happy to get into bed, too. I feel so alien in this house with these people. The house is so different. The Hansackers are so different.

They're nice. They smile at each other. They are real sweet to each other. They are so neat, though, so clean. Their clothes seem all brand-new. Maybe they dressed up in new clothes to meet us? But when their kids get ready for bed, they have new bathrobes and new pj's on underneath.

My pjs are four thousand years old and have been worn by six thousand boys before me—we send our clothes out to the laundry each week, but you don't get the same clothes back. They just pile all the clothes in one great stack. Each boy gets one of everything, pjs included. It doesn't matter to the laundry people which shirt, which pair of socks, which pair of underwear, just so each kid gets one of everything he is supposed to get.

I put on my four-thousand-year-old pajamas. When Charles gets into his pajamas I am totally grossed out. He *is* just a boy. He steps into the can. We have our own little bathroom right off the bedroom here. He emerges from the can a moment later wearing the kind of pjs you see little boys wear, the kind with the elastic band at the waist, at the neck, and at the wrists and ankles. And the elastic band part is a different color than the rest of the pajama. Charles is deep chocolate with buff at all his edges. His pear shape is wildly exaggerated by his elastic-fast outfit.

I climb into bed on the far side of the room.

Charles gets in from the bathroom side. He's acting funny. He's being real sweet. Shy even.

I squish up against the edge of the bed. I am full of horror at the prospect of my body rolling accidentally into his. I don't like to be touched. I don't like people to get too close. People get too close sometimes and I have trouble breathing. I get all whickywhack and nervous Nellie and hurting-antsy inside if someone gets too close to me with their body. Unless, of course, I'm hot, ya know. Like for Janson in the shower and then I want to do the navigating there.

I pull the covers to my chin, flick off the lamp next to my bed.

"Good night," Charles says. He's sitting up in bed. He's going to read or something.

"Good night," I say and roll onto my side with my back to him.

In a minute he turns off his light and I fall asleep.

I am startled awake. I don't know where I am.

My body is electrified the same way it was electrified when the Old Man clapped me upside the head with his clipboard.

Where am I?

Charles rocks next to me. His body brushes mine in a half a dozen places. His arm is thrown across my hip.

I fill with heat and terror. A hundred thousand knots the size of miniature butterflies fill my stomach.

Charles rocks a second time. His body cups mine.

I force myself to awaken fully. I try to get my wits about me. I need to take my bearings.

I am still on my side. My back is to Charles. My knees are pulled up toward my chest, but only slightly. I can feel all of Charles up and down my back. I feel the skin on my back crawl. All up and down my back my skin crawls.

His arm is like an anchor across my hip.

A dead weight.

I am pinned.

I think I am pinned and I flush with panic and nausea.

I don't want his arm there.

I notice how my whole body is scrunched up so the edge of the bed is right at my nose. He is jammed in behind me, crowding me something awful.

The room is dark except for this soft, pink glow that comes from the streetlight as it pours through the thick red curtains that have been pulled shut for the night. There is not a sound in the house. I lay perfectly still. I listen. I can hear a soft, distant whirring. The refrigerator?

Charles makes sleep sounds and adjusts his weight. I think he has just inched closer into me.

I can see his forearm plainly now. My eyes have adjusted to the soft pink light. I can see his fingers dangling right in front of my pecker. His body is flush to mine. We are a pair of spoons. He is cupping me. I am about to go down the drain.

I don't feel well at all.

It is just an accident of sleep. When we were still a family and I slept with Franklin he'd roll into me sometimes. We'd bump into each other sometimes in the night. Bump and roll into each other. It is just an accident of sleep, that's all.

It's moving.

I am out of my mind.

His forearm. It is moving. It is sliding on my hip.

Time stops.

His forearm skids forward. His dangling fingers come to life. His dangling fingers grab onto me. Right onto my pecker.

I bolt from the bed.

I am out of my mind.

I find myself in the can. I am leaning on the sink. I am leaning on the sink with both arms extended before me. I lift my head and see myself in the mirror.

Now what, asshole?

I have to sleep. I can't stay in here all night. I have a speech to make in the morning. I need to sleep.

The sonuvabitch.

The asshole motherfucking sonuvabitch.

The cock-sucking motherfucking sonuvabitch.

I have to go back in there. I have a speech in the morning. I have to sleep.

Okay.

I flip off the can lights. I am momentarily blinded. I stand at the closed can door absolutely fucking blind. I wait. The flashing stops in my head. I open the door and step back into the bedroom. I can't see shit. I step toward the red-curtained windows. I navigate out around where I think the end of the double bed is. I stand at the foot of the bed. I can see it now. I can make out the shape of Charles's body. He's way over on my side of the bed.

Shit.

I won't get in on his side. Then he'd come rushing back over full of the idea that I want it—why else would I be over there on his side.

I can't get in on my side. He's on my side.

The fucking scumbag.

The motherfucking scumbag.

I climb onto the foot of the bed. I lay sideways across the bottom.

I am afraid.

My body makes a *T* with his body. I hold myself tight. I am tight. I still don't feel all that well.

I am on top of the covers.

I am tired.

I sleep.

39

IN THE MORNING WE DO NOT SPEAK.

I am terribly confused.

It is a very odd thing being in this room with him this morning. I want him to disappear. To not be. To be gone. He won't, of course.

And then there's the Hansackers. We have to deal with the Hansackers.

We dress in silence.

I wonder who he is.

Mrs. Hansacker has a beautiful breakfast prepared for us all. I come out and can't believe what I'm seeing.

''Good morning, Fred,'' she says from the stunningly sunny breakfast nook. She smiles at me with great warmth.

I think I am going to freak out.

''Sit anywhere you like,'' she says.

Bob Jr., and Melissa come out. They go directly to the table and sit.

The table is covered in white linen. Each place is elegantly laid out with silverware that sparkles in the sun and a white cloth napkin. The table is jam-packed with food. A plate of scrambled eggs sits in the middle. Steam rises from the eggs. There's a plate of toast, another plate of hot-buttered cinnamon rolls, and a silver platter full of fried bacon. There's a pitcher of milk, a pot of steaming hot coffee, and at each place a tiny juice glass filled with freshly squeezed orange juice.

It's a fucking feast.

Mr. Hansacker comes out. He's dressed in a suit and

tie. Mrs. Hansacker is all dressed up, too, like they're going to church or something.

I feel like a booger.

''Sit,'' Mr. Hansacker says invitingly. Bob Jr. and Melissa look up at me: Yeah, sit down.

I sit. I put some eggs on my plate. I take two strips of bacon.

''Pass the salt please, Melissa,'' I say.

''My name isn't Melissa,'' she says to me. She is indignant.

God. I'm sorry.

Now, now, Mrs. Hansacker says. ''My name is Melanie,'' she says. The little kid is miffed.

''I'm sorry,'' I say. I really am. What a dumb cluck I am. The original member of the Dumb Fuckers Club, that's me.

Charles comes out and joins us. I do not look at him.

''Coffee?'' Mrs. Hansacker asks.

I look up: Me?

No. She's offering it to Charles.

I poke at my eggs. I steal a look at Bob Jr. He's eating his bacon with his fingers. Okay. I pick up a strip of bacon and eat it.

I ain't actually all that hungry.

Charles finishes fairly quickly and excuses himself. I study my eggs. They are uncommonly white for scrambled eggs.

''It was a pleasure having you,'' Mrs. Hansacker is saying.

''Thank you,'' Charles answers. They are at the door.

Mr. Hansacker is there, too. He takes Charles's hand. They shake and are polite one to the other.

Go. Please go.

I just want him gone.

I am shrinking here, getting small, folding in and down upon myself. What's he hanging around for? Oh, go. Please, please go.

I have my head down. I stir my uncommonly white scrambled eggs, fiddle, fiddle.

"Your man's leaving," Melanie says.

I snap my head up at this. I look at her. She sits across from me. She's a girl. She doesn't know. She repeats herself. She doesn't know what she's doing. It's a rusty nail into an open wound. I am an open wound.

"Your man's leaving. Aren't you going to say good-bye?" She's incredulous: of course, you most certainly will want to say good-bye. I look at her with a great wet pleading in my soul. I can just see her lifting her face to her mother when they say good-bye: it is love, there's a kiss, a smile, bye.

"Huh?" she says, innocent, mildly exasperated with my idiotic silence.

"See ya, Charles," I say. I turn my head toward the door, a quarter turn of my head and then I'm back into my eggs, my uncommonly white scrambled eggs.

Charles exits. I hear the door shut. I hear the Hansackers move from the door.

"Aren't you going to eat your eggs?" Melanie asks.

I do something we do at the Home and it really grosses her out.

"No," I say, "you want mine?" And I offer to scrape me eggs off my plate onto hers.

She screams and calls for her mom.

"Mom!"

Sorry, I mumble. Really, Melissa, I'm sorry.

What a jerk I can be. I didn't know.

"My *name* is Melanie," she says with great irritation.

I excuse myself as quickly as I can. Being normal is going to be a lot more difficult than I imagined.

There are a couple of thousand people packed into West High School's auditorium. It's a big school with over a thousand kids. The governor is here. He's a nifty-looking guy. He looks and smells good. He comes around and shakes hands with all of us high school kids who are going to make speeches. I wonder if he is for real. This morning that is absolutely critical.

They sit us on stage. There are eleven of us who could make it from previous winner schools. The governor talks. The West High principal talks. A person from their school board talks. Then the lady who we sent our speeches to in Lexington, Kentucky, she talks and makes the award presentation. This brings the governor, the principal, and the lady from the school board back up to the podium. There are cheers and claps on the back all around. Then they let us do our bit.

I'm the third one up. I follow this girl from Virginia. She tells us she is from a nautical school. I wonder about that, what is it? Do they have classes in ships? Do they learn to be sailors?

She finishes. She returns to her seat. She sits next to me again and looks straight out into the audience.

They call my name.

I smell the girl from the nautical school. She smells nice. She crosses her legs. Her dress makes an interesting sound when she does that.

"It's your turn," she says to me.

Oh.

I give my speech. I tell them about the Home. I tell them about this book I have brought which is a book about the Home and that they should probably read it if they really want to know about the Home because I cannot begin to tell them the fifty-year history of the Home in the few minutes I have this morning. I wave the book over my head. I am donating this book to your library, I say. Read it, I say. Really, I say. Check it out, you'll like it.

I am surprised at my own fervor.

There are some interesting stories in here, I say, waving that book still.

I congratulate them and suggest to them that they go ahead and read this book. I hoist it on high one more time. As I do I suddenly notice this glass eye dead ahead.

It shakes me.

Straight out in front of me, right at the balcony level, there is this glass eye. A single glass eye staring right at me.

I lose my place. I look at my notes.

The entire house is still. We all wait. I am stuck. That thing out there, that glass eye. What is it?

I cannot look up.

The house remains still, so very still.

I hear someone behind me.

"Son? Son? You okay, son?"

I lift my head, stare right into that glass eye and congratulate them all one last time, wave the book at them, and get the hell off.

They tell me about the glass eye afterward. Actually they do not tell me. I fade into the woodwork and listen to other people talking to one another. I cannot converse. I cannot speak.

Like at the West High football game that night. I am alone. I am speechless. And half the kids here are girls. The West High cheerleaders stun and baffle me. Their outfits are so colorful, they have such energy—and they are so happy. I cannot keep up with such happiness. All around me there is such terrible happiness. Cheering, screaming, laughing, poking, joking kids brim full of Friday-night-football-game happiness.

And I am Dannon.

I am Dannon who picks at this face every single night. Dannon who plasters Clearasil, pHisoHex and that chalky-brown shit from the clinic all over his poor cratered face every fucking night of the fucking year.

I am Dannon.

I sit alone at the end of the bleachers, watching the cheerleaders having a gloriously happy time. I consciously try not to look at their underwear, it is red, when they leap and frolic and do splits in midair.

I am ashamed to be so ashamed.

I am ashamed to be Dannon.

I am happy—relieved, anyway—when it is over, when the game is over and I must go back to the Hansacker house. To sleep. To forget. To get the fuck out of here.

40

THE GLASS EYE IS THE LENS OF WEST HIGH'S CLOSED-circuit camera. Bob Jr. tells me. He says they filmed the whole thing. He says they film a lot of stuff from their Friday morning assemblies.

I ride the Trailways Silver Express out of Waterloo and think about that, about me on film. I think I would like that. I do. I think I would like to see myself making a speech.

I get to be feeling okay again. I am happy to be heading home. I am happy to be on my own. I like riding the Silver Express all by my lonesome. I think I am going to be free of this wretchedness I've been full of since yesterday morning. And then I do one more stupid thing. Bambi the boob.

I go to a movie.

We lay over in Marshalltown, Iowa. We have a couple of hours. So I go to see *The Chapman Report.* I go alone. It is the middle of the afternoon. The theater is practically empty. I sit in the balcony by myself.

I am alone in the balcony and it frightens me. The movie frightens me.

There is this woman who cannot say no. This woman who does not say no. This woman who drinks and drinks and drinks and gets had and gets had and gets had until finally she can take it no longer and then she kills herself. She takes a bottle full of sleeping pills. The camera takes us across her apartment, her disheveled apartment, the apartment as disheveled as her poor blighted lonely fucked-up now dead self.

I sit in the balcony all alone and tremble. I cannot

leave. I cannot. I paid my way. I will stay. I will stick it out. I do.

It is wretched and horrible and frightening.

I get back on the Silver Express. I yearn to be back to the Home. I cannot trust myself. I am such a boob. I do the dumbest things.

I am a miserable wreck all the way back to Ohio.

That poor fucked-up woman. She never had a chance.

I call the Home from the depot. Wombat's on Security. He answers.

"McFlaherty's Home for Boys," he says.

His real name is Bobby. Bobby Carriere.

"Bobby? This Bobby?" I ask.

"Who's this, skirt?" he asks.

He calls everyone skirt. He thinks he's a real scream.

"Gamble," I tell him. "I'm downtown. At the bus depot. Can you come get me?"

"Downtown?" he asks. "Downtown Dayton?"

No, Honolulu. Jesus.

"Yes, downtown Dayton," I say. "At the depot. You know where? On Fifth Street, right?"

He's offended.

"I know where it is, skirt."

Then he pulls his mouth away from the phone. I feel like I'm on a submarine or in a bunker in a war zone. I am losing my connection. Crank it up, Sarge.

I hear papers shuffling. I hear Bobby's muffled voice. Then I hear him very clearly: "I can't do *everything!*"

"Bobby? Bobby! You there?" I call into the phone.

He comes back to me.

"Hang on, skirt," he says into the receiver. I am secondary. Something's going on back there.

I wait. I lean on the little lip ledge they have here under the phone. I survey the depot. A lot of people for a Saturday night. There's a guy talking to himself. The Wombat's back.

"Okay, Bambi," he says, "I'll be there in, oh . . . say, twenty, thirty minutes."

And then he just hangs up on me. Click.

Right.

Nice talking to ya, Bobby.

I hang up the phone and smile. I'm back home now. Fucking Carriere. You wouldn't believe this guy. You really wouldn't. He is really and truly strange.

First off, he's deformed. From birth. His right side, his eye and arm especially, but his leg some, too. His eye and arm, though, they are really fucked up. His eye is out of control. It goes all whickywhack off into space—I don't know if he's blind in the eye or not. He does wear real thick glasses. But he may as well be blind in that eye because when you talk to him it is going all over kingdom come, flipping this way and that. Spooky. Then his arm, his right arm, it's odd. It is pinned to his body with this 180-degree twist at his elbow which flips his forearm, wrist, and fingers right into his crotch. No lie. So you look at this guy and it looks like he is frozen in this half shrug—his right shoulder is lifted just a hair—while he's also permanently digging his underwear out from under his nuts.

It is gross.

He is gross.

And there's more.

He sort of drools all the time. Not real strings of spit that hang down. No. Wombat's problem is that his lips are just permanently slicked. Whenever you see him his lips are just a bit too wet, as if he is constantly licking his lips when, in fact, he isn't.

And to top it all off he is the most obvious fairy in the whole place.

Honest.

The poor bastard just can't contain himself. He will spy a kid who really turns his bizarre ass on—which is about half the kids here—and he is frothing at the mouth.

Really.

I know this sounds fantastic. Exaggerated. Too much.

But it isn't.

Ezra and I caught him grab-assing with Jimmy Baker once, this real pretty girl-boy. Baker was one of those kids—this was five years ago when we were seventh-graders—who was too simple to hide his true feelings. Let me give you an example.

That same year, we had our annual physicals in the building. I don't know why. We usually go on over to the clinic. But not this one time. They had the intern come to us.

We are lined up. There are twenty-four of us standing in line. We are naked save for our towels wrapped Polynesian-style around our waists. Baker's up.

''Cough,'' the intern directs.

''Ooooh, that tickles,'' Baker squeals, giggling.

No, Baker, no.

We are dying. All of us standing in that line, we are simply dying.

It is the same obvious simple shit when Ezra and I spy them, Baker and Wombat, rolling around in the grass. It is up to the Home's summer camp. They are out in front of the main building. The two of them wrestling in the grass. The two of them squealing with joy and abandon. The two of them touching on each other in the most obvious ways.

It is just too gross.

Too obvious.

It is an hour later when the Wombat pulls up to the curb in front of the bus depot. He honks. I grab my suitcase and hoof it out to the curb.

''No, you stay put,'' I say sarcastically.

He's staring straight ahead. It isn't about to be getting out to help.

''I can do it myself,'' I say.

I pop open the rear door of this old, old station wagon. It has seen its better days. You can hear it coming a half mile off—''Rods going,'' Winston says—and the inside smells like a metal armpit.

''You just stay put,'' I say nastily. The asshole's apparently oblivious to me. I toss my suitcase in and hop in behind it. He tears ass away from the curb before my fanny even hits the seat.

"Look out!" I scream.

He's bolted right out in front of this big Buick.

The Buick slams on his brakes and screeches to a halt inches from my rear door. Wombat flips him the bird, jumps on the accelerator, and we are off 'n' running.

We zoom around the corner, zoom up Jefferson to Fourth Street, zoom across Fourth to Ludlow, lay rubber at the corner of Ludlow and Fourth, zoom up Ludlow to the entrance ramp to 35 East, zoom up onto 35 East, and *zoom* away.

Bambi at 4G's. Plastered to his seat in back.

We get up onto 35 and I can catch my breath.

"You think we could speed it up some?" I yell.

"So the rat thinks he's a real comedian tonight, eh?"

"I ain't no rat!" I shout.

He's blasting across two, three, four lanes, heading for the outside. He is oblivious to other cars. I am hanging onto the door latch in back, my knuckles white.

"Oh, yes you are," Bobby shouts. "Kuhns told me," he says proudly.

We are safely in the far left lane, the express lane. And we are flying.

"What did ya say?" I yell again.

I can't hear him. He's got his window down an inch at the top. The wind roars through this wagon.

"You say something about Kuhns?" I shout.

"That's right," he says with this huge smile. "He told me about the Moellar game," he says, leering now. He looks at me in the rearview mirror: "Bobby knows."

There's a slow one in front of us now. He's only doing sixty in the express lane. It is pissing Bobby off.

Bobby tosses his head back sharply. I think he's going to bite me at first. Then I realize what he's doing—he's changing lanes, looking for an opening. He spies one and jerks the car over, jerking me along with it. We pull up alongside the slowpoke.

Bobby lifts his lips up to the crack at the top of his window and snarls at the driver of the other car: ''Cocksucker.''

He really gives his upper lips a tremendous curling-back. It is almost funny.

He floors it and we zoom ahead.

He rips us back into the far left lane in front of the cocksucker, who is now eating our dust. I go flying off to the right as he jerks us left.

''I know what you did,'' he says. We're in the open, clear sailing ahead.

''What did I do?'' I say furiously. I get my balance, setting both hands down on the seat on either side of me. I lean forward.

''Tell me,'' I demand.

''You don't rat on your friends, skirt,'' he says smugly.

''Yeah?'' I challenge. I try to put as much viciousness into it as I can muster. It hooks him. He whirls his head around—I think of Howdy Doody. What a fucking blockhead.

''Tell me about it, Bobby,'' I say as I try to ridicule him, a grown man with a little boy's name. ''Bob-beeee.''

He is happy to oblige. He is looking right at me—who's watching the fucking road?

''You fink on your friends and you have to *pay,*'' he says with great pleasure. He tosses his chin in triumph. He focuses his good eye right on me—he still ain't watching the road—and pronounces sentence: ''Somebody's gonna get his little lily-white ass kicked.'' He says it with absolute glee.

I don't know what comes over me. I think I am losing my mind.

I go for him. Right here in the fucking car. I try to grab a hold of him. I try to grab him by the throat. I can't believe it: he's driving this car. We are sailing along at seventy miles per hour, and I am lunging for him with both hands because I am going to kill him.

I smash my hands into the caging instead. I damn near break three fingers in the process and he just cracks up. He thinks it is positively hilarious. And he wants more. He takes a quick gander at the road in front and whips his head back around. His one good eye is shining bright. The asshole. He is simply delighted.

''You fink on your friends, skirt, and you have to pay-ay-ay!''he squeals, just cracking up something awful.

''Look out!'' I scream.

He whirls around. We are off the road. We're on the shoulder, the ditch is about to gobble us up. He catches her, whips her back onto the road. I am bouncing around in back. I bang my head on the roof of the car.

He throws his head back and laughs hard.

This guy is fucking delighted, honest to God.

I sit back and shut my mouth.

He calms down and is sort of laughing to himself.

''You kids think you know it all,'' he says. ''You think you're so hot. You think you know everything,'' he says, nodding agreement with himself. ''Well, you got another think coming,'' he concludes. I watch him nodding to himself. He is terrifically satisfied with himself. Professor Wombat.

I grab onto my suitcase. I lift it into my lap and hug it to me.

We barrel along at seventy miles per hour.

''Let me tell you,'' he says, repeating himself. ''You got another think coming.''

I keep my mouth shut and say a little prayer we make it home alive.

41

THE WOMBAT DROPS ME OFF IN FRONT OF THE HOUSE. I am relieved to get free of him. I go in, throw my suitcase on my bed, and Winston comes to the bedroom door.

I am happy to see him. We go out to the study hall.

''You know we lost to Central,'' he says as we sit down.

Martinez comes in: ''Yeah.''

I could care.

They stare at me, waiting—for what?

''So we lost?'' I say finally. ''Who cares?''

''You should,'' Martinez says.

Right. Football's the last thing I'm worrying about now.

''He's right,'' Winston says. ''You should care.''

I look at them. They are acting as if this is some very important item. I don't get it.

''They say it is your fault,'' Winston says.

What?

''The captains,'' he says.

''We heard them talking about it. In the dining hall,'' Martinez says. ''They say you cost them the game.''

''This is nuts,'' I say. I'm the third-string quarterback. The Old Man would have never put me in. Not against Central.

''The problem is, they didn't have a quarterback after you left,'' Winston says.

''Yeah,'' Martinez says. ''Kuhns got hurt Friday morning. And the second-string quarterback, the choir-section kid, what's his name—?''

"Smith," I say.

"Yeah, him," Martinez says. "He broke his thumb. He couldn't play, either."

I can't believe this. "When did all this happen?" I ask.

"I don't know," Winston says. "What I do know," he says, going on, "is that the Old Man had to call up the reserve quarterback. The sophomore. Leeder."

"And he really fucked up," Martinez says.

They look at each other. They look frightened.

"You know what that means, don't you?" Winston asks.

No, I say. Tell me.

"It means you lost the game," he says.

"And that you're in deep shit," Martinez adds.

C'mon. Tell me another one.

"Really," Winston says. He can tell I'm not taking this shit seriously. "We heard them talking, Bambi. About you."

"They're after your ass now," Martinez says. He's really worried, too.

"C'mon, you guys. You can't be serious."

They look at each other. Winston makes a face, lifting his eyebrows, sorry.

"We are," he says. "We are serious."

Martinez takes a half step toward me. "It's true. We mean it."

"C'mon," I say. "I can't believe this. This is a crock."

I look at them. I halfway expect them to suddenly crack up and punch me one in the arm. They don't. They both look terrifically worried.

"You are serious, aren't you?" I say.

They both nod.

"Just be careful, okay?" Winston asks.

He says this to me and then looks over at Martinez. They nod to each other. They have discussed this. They have prepared for this little chat. They are dead serious.

"We mean it," Martinez says. Just in case I haven't gotten the drift.

"Tell us, okay?" Winston urges. "Tell us you'll be careful, okay?"

Jesus. They are so earnest.

Okay, I say. I will. I'll be careful. Honest.

They nod, satisfied that they have done their job.

I still think, though, it's foolishness. I mean, how am I supposed to be careful? How are they going to get me?

I find out soon enough.

42

MY FIRST WARNING COMES IN PHYSICS CLASS. Brower grabs me. I am right at the door. He grabs a hold of my ass, a full five-fingered handful, my left cheek. I leap away frantic. I smash myself into the door frame, a classic Three Stooges move.

Brower laughs. He comes at me.

"Gonna get me some of that," he leers.

Halstead marches in. I beat it across the room to my seat.

My second warning comes on the practice field. We're running plays. Each quarterback takes a turn. Kuhns limps in. His knee is taped and braced. He's wearing shorts. His knee is as big as my head. He hobbles through a play. He is being *very brave.*

Smith is next. His thumb is in a splint. It is wrapped and bandaged. He manages a play, bobbles the ball, but manages to get through okay. He is being *very brave.*

I am next. I step in. I get in over Rasco, who's over the ball. The Old Man says: "Why don't you go make a speech somewheres?"

What?

I look at him. He refuses to look at me. He says to Huff, the line coach: "Tell our little deer to get his dainty fucking self out of my sight."

Huff says to me: "Okay, Gamble, out of there."

I step out and fade into the background. I spend the entire afternoon on the periphery doing nothing, being invisible. All afternoon people are looking right through me as if I ain't here. As if I am a pane of glass.

C'mon, you guys.

No one speaks to me again. No one looks at me, only through me.

I am invisible.

When practice is over, no one will even let me walk with them to the showers. I get near anyone and they move away. It is as if I am contaminated. It is how we use to treat Kormac, the kid who had all the trouble controlling his bowels. The kid we hounded and pounded. The kid who always smelled like shit.

Today that is me. I am Kormac. What you might call a Class A turd.

Well, fuck it.

I give it up. I build this imaginary bubble around me. Fuck it. I walk in my bubble.

At my locker, Kuhns is on one side, Fogarty on the other, they continue to ignore me.

Fine.

They look at me but say nothing.

I sit on the bench and take my time. I'll just let them all get out ahead of me. It's not so bad being invisible. Maybe they are finished fucking with me. Maybe I'll get some peace now. Just in time, too. I tell you, I am just about out of gas.

Kuhns comes back from his shower, ignores me, dresses, and leaves.

The shower is empty. I go on in. I am the last one. Fine. I'll be the last one in the locker room, too. Which also suits me fine. I would rather be alone right now than have to put up with this hateful shit. It hurts. I don't know why I am so surprised to know that, that it actually hurts in a physical way to be hated, but I am. And it does. It actually hurts in a physical way.

I stand under the hot, hot water for a long time. I let the hot, steaming water massage me and wash me free of this oddness, this culled-from-the-pack sensation. I stand under the hot water until everyone is gone.

I listen. I hear no one. I look out into the locker room. I see no one.

I am free.

I shut the water off and get my towel off the rack by the door. I dry my face and double-check the locker room.

No one.

Good.

I finish drying off in the warmth and steam of the empty shower.

I hear something.

What's that?

"Who's there? Someone there?" I call out.

Nothing.

I peer out again. Nothing.

It is eerie. If you stand alone in a locker room after it has just emptied out, the sounds still ricochet in your head.

I am okay. No one's here.

Just relax, I tell myself and finish drying off. As I step out of the shower I hear it again. A whirring? A swishing? My bowels heat up. Be careful. The Dumb Fuckers Club dictum. Be careful.

Then I think I hear it again. Is it coming from the training room? I look. The door is shut. Isn't it usually open? Yes, it is usually open.

I wrap my towel around my waist. I step up to the training-room door. You can't see shit through the frosted glass. There's a rubbing table in there, a tub whirlpool, an athlete's-foot powder bath set right into the floor—it's this huge two-foot-by-four-foot area set off by two-by-fours. It is brim full of Desenex. A thousand white-powder footprints lead off in every direction.

This door. It is usually open, yes?

Yes.

I start to push it open. Wait a minute, bub. Maybe they are waiting for me in there.

I back away quickly.

Be careful, Winston says.

I said I would. I stay away from that door.

I dress quickly. I have my back to the training-room door. I can't stand it. I am too scared. I turn to face it. That closed door becomes the attic door from my house when I was just a kid in a normal family in town. I was terrified of that attic door. It was directly across from the top of the steps leading downstairs. Every time I came up or went down, especially after dark, I felt it, felt the monster behind that door, felt the monster all up and down my back, a monster that engulfs me like a blanket—my fear is liquid and I am racing a million miles an hour, trying to outrun my own panic.

I can't get my zipper to work. It's stuck.

Shit.

I yank hard and lose my grip. I drag my fingers the full length of the zipper without the pull tab. I leave an inch of epidermis on the zipper.

Nice work, Bambi. Swift, very swift.

The door. I remember the door.

Move it, kiddo. Move it.

I do.

Fuck the zipper. I jump into my shoes and tuck in my shirt.

Go.

I grab my books. My fly is still stuck open.

Jesus, I'm scared.

I slide past the closed-up training door. I can feel the monster there. I keep my eyes glued on it as I slide past. I hit the varsity locker room door, blast it open with my shoulder and forearm, and beat it the fuck out of there.

I'm late for chow. Too late to eat, in fact. Everyone's pouring out as I'm going in. Stupid me, I ain't thinking too well these days, I push straight in, right into the teeth of the crowd of boys mashing out. I don't know what I am thinking—that Winston saved me some chow? I ain't even hungry and here I am barreling in, mash, mash, mash.

I get through the entryway foyer when it happens.

I don't even know what hits me. Or who. I think afterward it is Brower. I don't know what hits me but it does. I'm packed in tight, the serving line is right in front of me, the entire hallway is jam-packed with exiting kids and I hear him, Fucking rat, and there's this blinding pain, right in my ribs. Once. Twice. Three times. Boom, boom, boom.

I go down.

You go down in this mob and you're dead.

One, two, three, drop.

I can't breathe.

He's knocked the wind out of me. My rib is on fire.

Is it broken? I wonder as I sort of black out. I don't know if I really do or for how long—a minute, two?—but I remember coming to and it is the same way it was when we were just grade school kids and we would knock ourselves out on purpose. You take ten deep breaths and then clamp your hands to your throat. Fingers to the back, heels of your hands up against either side of your Adam's apple, and then you squeeze.

We'd do it at formation before the movies. We're sitting hip to hip on the front porch. Everyone's talking, yakking, hooting, and carrying on, and we'd take turns.

Coming to, just like right now, it's eerie. It's why we did it, I think. You're not out and you're not in. Voices all about are wabbling loud, soft, in and out, up and back, sounds only, no discernible words, *bwaaaa, bwaaaa, waaa, aaaah.*

"C'mahn," I hear, only the ahn is long and drawn out: *ahnnnnnnnnnnnnn.*

My skin is buzzing. The light is funny. Nice.

"C'mahnnnnnnnnnnnnnnnnnn . . ."

Huh?

"It's okay. C'mon," he says. He is miles and miles away, high above me. I feel something far away. An armpit touched far away. A giant, faraway armpit touched, tugged.

"You're all right," he says.

It's Rasco.

He's got the fattest lip.

''What happened your lip?'' I ask.

''Shut up, asshole,'' he says.

''Your lip,'' I insist stupidly. ''Sohn-un's punched your lip?'' I say again. I am tremendously concerned about his lip, the fattest fucking lip—

''You don't shut up, asshole,'' he says, ''and I'll be giving you a fat lip.''

Okay, I say. I shut up. Okay.

''Get up,'' he directs. I feel his touch. It is my armpit.

''Hey, what happened?'' I ask.

''Just get up, will ya, asshole?'' he says quietly.

It hits me. He's been talking as if we are in church. Being private. I am laying on the cold quarry tiles.

Oh.

I help him get me up.

The mob's gone. Atlas is standing here, too. He says: ''Here. Chou come here.''

Rasco says: ''No. No thanks. We're okay.''

He leads me, faces me, I am a dummy, Jesus, did I faint? I ask him, he's leading me to the doors, leading me out. Did I, huh? Did I faint?

Ow.

At the door he turns me sideways to make room. He touches my ribcage.

Don't!

My legs feel faraway from me. My feet feel like giant flapper clown's feet. I am coming to.

Did I faint?

Rasco hobbles me out across the flagstone porch. He sits me on the low brick railing. My legs are near now. They are here with me. My feet shrink, too.

''You okay?'' Rasco says.

I touch my ribs. I am tender.

''Yeah.''

We sit a few moments silently. Everyone's gone. I see in through the windows the dining hall workers, boys and Atlas's paid crew all in starched white uniforms, bustling about. The yellow light pouring out onto the porch, and the familiar sounds of banging, clanging pans and mops and wringers calms me.

"Where are my books?" I remember my books.

"I gave them to one of your waiters."

"Winston?"

"He a Mex?"

"No, that's Martinez."

"Martinez, then."

Okay.

"Somebody clobbered me."

I just say this. I am discovering it. I am not making conversation.

Rasco says nothing. I look at him. I see his lip.

"Jesus. What happened to your lip?" I ask as if this is the first I know of it.

"Forget it," he says. His voice is hard.

I forget it.

In fact, if I'd just use my noggin I wouldn't have to ask stupid questions.

"Sorry," I say.

"They saved you a plate," he says.

I think about it. Who saved me a plate? I don't ask.

I ain't all that hungry.

I tell him.

"I ain't all that hungry."

I wait a second. I don't want to go back to the house.

"You want to go somewhere and talk?" I ask.

Sure, he says.

We walk on up to the varsity football field. We climb into the bleachers. It is very dark. It's all of six, maybe six fifteen, and it's pitch-black out.

"Smoke?" I offer. Winstons.

He takes one.

We light up. It is amazing to light up in the dark. Your face is illuminated for an instant. There is this circle of light that glows red and pink that switches to yellow and white—from the match. Facial fireworks.

Simultaneously we say:

"You okay?"

It cracks us up. Then we do it again. Only now we are simultaneously answering each other:

"Yeah."

It makes us laugh a little more. That's all. We sit quietly. He leans into me with his shoulder, bumping softly, tenderly, my shoulder. We both realize that we both meant it. We both really wanted to know if the other one is okay. It is an important thing to ask. Hardly anyone ever really does.

Franklin pops into my head.

"You wanna blow this Popsicle stand?" I ask.

He looks at me in the dark. I can't see his fat lip in the dark.

"You serious?" he asks.

Your ass is grass you go AWOL. Neither of us has ever done it before. He takes a big hit off his Winston. I see his swollen lip now. It is a whopper.

"Yeah," I answer him. "I am serious."

Charles returns from his trip to the Mayo Clinic tonight. I ain't up to that yet. My stomach thinks I'm on the Tilt-a-Whirl when I remember that he's coming back. I just ain't up to it.

"Yeah. I am serious," I repeat.

"Okay," he says.

So we do.

We go AWOL.

43

WE WALK ALL THE WAY INTO WILBURFORCE. IT'S not too bad. Six, maybe seven miles all told. A Wilburforce student picks us up. He takes us as far as Xenia.

We have to walk partway out of town before we can catch another ride. A trucker picks us on 35 West.

"Hop in," the guy says as he flips open his cab to us.

Rasco shoves me in first.

"How far you going?" I ask.

"Dayton," he says.

Terrific.

He drops us at First Street in downtown Dayton. We hoof it over to Main Street and catch a number 12 bus to Dad's house.

The front door's open. It's locked but the door isn't completely shut. It is as if someone pushed it shut behind him, but it didn't catch.

I push it open.

There are thirteen steps leading up to Dad's apartment. He has the top half of this house. I call out his name as I shove the door open: "Dad?"

I step in. I smell it right away. I do not believe I smell what I smell.

I take two steps up, freeze: "Dad?" I call out again.

Nothing.

The smell is unmistakable.

I take the remaining steps two at a time. When I get to

the top step I see it. There is this little trail of shit. Little dollops of human shit. It's a Hansel and Gretel trail leading from the one bedroom down the wooden hallway into the can.

Rasco is right on my heels. He's sniffing. He ain't seen it yet.

"That what I think it is?" he asks matter-of-factly. I don't answer.

"Dad?" I call again.

There's no answer.

"Just a sec," I say to Rasco. I follow the trail back to the bedroom. The door is shut. I push it open, reach in, and flick on the lights.

"Dad?"

He ain't in here. His bed's a mess. It is full of shit. It looks like he had diarrhea. It's in the sheets. It's on the blanket, too. The blanket is all wadded up and knotted. It looks as if someone had one helluva go here.

I back out. I'll check the can next. I avoid looking at Rasco. I get to the can and push the door open.

"Dad?"

There he is. On the commode. He's got his starched white shirt on. His tie is hanging down between his legs. His pants and underwear are at his ankles. His thigh is naked, as white as alabaster and totally hairless.

It ain't human.

It's a beast.

"Dad?"

The beast slowly swivels its head toward the sound of my voice: uuuuunnnh.

His eyes are glazed over. There's a thick, nearly opaque mucous sheath over his pale powder-blue eyes. He cannot focus. He aims his face in the direction of my voice.

"Unnnnh," he sounds.

"Dad? Dad?"

"Unnnnh," he goes, louder this time. Those sticky eyes are aimed right at me and see me not. The beast is blind.

''Uuunnnh,'' he goes again and slowly swivels his head back from whence it came.

Jesus.

I back out. I shut the door behind me.

The kitchen is a total wreck. The table is tipped over. It has one leg missing. There is shit all over the floor—a broken drinking glass, an empty Miller's can, a green glass ashtray that's spilled its ashes and butts. The phone is on the floor, too, the receiver three feet from the cradle.

I pick my way through and go into the living room. I walk over to the davenport from the old house from when we were still a family and Mom was alive. I sit on the edge of the davenport. The TV set's right in front of me.

Jesus.

That ain't Dad. He ain't inside that beast.

Rasco comes in. He stands at the doorway between the kitchen and the living room. He says nothing.

I look up and am a little surprised that he is here.

''Oh,'' I say. Then I feel responsible. ''I'm sorry,'' I say.

''Don't sweat it,'' he says sincerely.. ''He . . . ?''

''Yeah,'' I say. ''Totaled.'' I look at Rasco. I am amazed. ''I ain't never seen him like this. God.''

Rasco says nothing. He just stands silently.

I hear him, the beast. He's moving, coming out of the can. He's humming, unnnh, unn, ummm. We freeze as he lumbers down the hallway. I start to jump up—I think I should hide or something. He shouldn't know I have seen him like this.

Rasco stops me with a wave of his hand. He lifts his index finger to his lips: Shhhhh.

The beast hums and moans as he shuffles down the wooden hallway. He goes into the bedroom and drops himself into his own mess. We hear the bed creak, crack, and moan under his weight.

Rasco mouths it silently, exaggerating with his mouth so I'm sure to read it: "He does not know we are here."

The beast moans one more time, rolls in his own mess, and is silent.

"I'm sorry," I say to Rasco.

"Fuck it," he says. "You've met my ma," he adds. Then he sticks both of his index fingers into his mouth and pulls his lips back over his teeth. It makes him look toothless like his ma. It makes me laugh.

"She's no prize either," he says as he takes his fingers from his mouth.

"I'm sorry," I say, "I shouldn't laugh."

"Sure, you should," he says. "What else is there?"

He turns around and steps back into the kitchen. He reaches for the refrigerator.

"May I?" he asks.

"Sure," I say.

"There's beer in here," he exclaims. "You want one?"

I get up and go to the refrigerator. I stand next to him. There's eleven Millers in there. Eleven Millers, an empty ice water jug, and nothing else.

"Sure," I say.

I notice Dad's suit coat laying on the floor. It's up against the wall. There's a tipped-over chair on top of it. I go to it and rifle the pockets.

Dad used to shove all his change into these side pockets.

It is no different now.

I pull out a handful of bills. The pocket is heavy with coin as well.

"Well, well, well," Rasco says approvingly. We are always happy to see cash. He hands me a beer. I count the money. There are three ones wadded up, some quarters, a half dollar, some dimes and nickles, no pennies, a five and a ten.

"Two-seventy in change, eighteen in bills," I announce. "Fifty-fifty?" I ask.

"You don't have to do that," Rasco says.

"I know," I say as I divvy it up fifty-fifty. It makes me feel good to do it.

We then proceed to get mildly blitzed.

44

I FALL ASLEEP ON THE DAVENPORT AND THE MOST WONderful thing happens.

I get laid.

In my dream.

I cannot believe it.

I dream I am fucking this woman who looks a little like my mom and a little like the woman I saw in the movie in Marshalltown and a little like the girl Foster says he is fucking. The only thing is she doesn't have a pussy.

We get naked and rub on each other. I am on top. We take her pants off, her underwear, and her crotch is smooth—exactly like the doll my mom had in the house when she was alive.

Mom took care of other kids when Franklin was real tiny. She had this doll. It was about two feet long with soft cotton arms and legs. Its body was plastic. It had this hard smooth rounded plastic crotch. The woman I fuck in my dream has the same smooth rounded plastic crotch.

It is a *dream.* I am delirious with happiness. I am warm in my spine. Heat that is light, a happy liquid Technicolor warmth shooting through me.

I come and as I do I know that this is a dream, that I am asleep—and I know that this is okay, that this is not a sin.

I awaken in orgasm, my entire body thrilling and chilling to this wondrous thing that is happening to me.

I am happy.

It is not a sin. It is as wonderful as ever has it been.

And it is not a sin.

Oh, God. How nice.

My entire body smiles in it. I fall asleep and dream no more.

I wake up very early Tuesday morning. There's a note from Rasco. He's gone to his mom's. He's put her number on the back.

I check the time on dad's Little Big Ben. It's six-fifteen.

Dad's curled into a fetal position. His face is to the wall. His ass is aimed at me. He's still dressed with those shitty sheets tangled in his legs. His trousers are loose. I can see the crack of his ass. He's still got his wingtips on.

I want to call Rasco. It's too early.

I go into the can, go to the sink, and see myself in the mirror.

I look like little ignorant shit Cruise. My fucking hair is standing up every which a way.

I wash up. I wash the sleep out of my eyes. I wet my hair down and try to comb it. It's a waste.

I need a towel. None in here.

I walk all over the apartment looking for a towel. I hold my hands up like a surgeon before surgery. I can't find a towel anywhere.

Jesus, Dad,

I dry my hands on the davenport.

I remember my dream as I dry my hands. It thrills me anew. I shiver with the memory of it. I am suddenly bursting with energy—now what?

I can't call Rasco yet. It's too early.

I know—I'll clean house.

So I do.

It's a good thing, too. It gets me going, gets my motor running, my brain in gear. And it gives me something to do with this incredible energy.

I find an ancient old broom. There's no dustpan. There's this old sponge mop and no bucket. It's okay. I'll use the sink. There's no trash cans, either, so I use an IGA grocery bag.

Okay. All set.

I do a job. I straighten everything. I pick up all the shit that's strewn all over the kitchen floor. I prop the table against the wall. I brace that fourth leg, the one's that broken off, up under her—it works. The table stands.

I sweep everything—the can, the kitchen, the living room, and the two living room rugs. They're from the old house like the davenport. Makes me think some of Mom.

I gotta open a window. I've raised a whale of a storm in here, the air's thick with dust. I can't breathe.

I pry open a window in the kitchen and then open another one straight across the apartment from it. The wind blows through. Good.

Now, the dollops.

It's a big job. Most of it has dried, so I need a scraper. There's no scraper, of course. I use an old butter knife, which works fine. There are thirty-seven dollops. Thirty-three of them are completely dried. The other four are only half dried. It gags me at first. Then I get used to it and it's not too gross, actually.

I get them all up. I look at the floor. Shit stains. I can see 'em, it's like giant raindrops running all the way down the hallway here. I need some kind of wax or something.

Dad rolls over in bed. I hear it creaking and moaning under his weight.

I think I am done. I look around and give myself inspection.

The phone is still on the floor. It's up against the stove. I pick it up, set the receiver in its cradle.

Nothing.

Huh?

I follow the cord. It's been yanked from the wall.

Where's the jack?

I look, find it. I hook it back up—it isn't the best hook. It's wobbly but it's holding. I pick up the receiver and hear the tone. Good.

I collect my tools—my broom, my three-quarters-full IGA-grocery-bag trash can, and my sponge mop—I set them against the inside wall of the sunporch. The sink could use a scouring. But there's no Bab-O. Too bad.

Okay, I say to myself.

It is seven o'clock now. I can call Rasco now.

I dial his mom's. The phone rings three, four, five times. His sister answers.

Rasco home? I ask.

He's not here, she says.

You seen him, I ask.

Nope, she says.

She ain't volunteering anything. She's twelve, could care less.

Your mom home?

Nope.

She at work?

Guess so.

At the Marriot?

Uh.

Maybe I could call her there, ya know?

Uh.

This is great, just fucking great.

He was there, I say. How come you didn't see him?

I dunno, she says. I gotta go, she says and hangs up.

Just fucking terrific.

I am sitting here stewing when Dad appears.

"What are you doing here?" he asks.

He startles me. I give a little jump and almost tip the fucking table over. I grab it, right it, there. I look at him.

He's looking rough. His hair is just like little ignorant shit Cruise, too. He's clutching his trousers with his left hand. If he let go there they'd drop, boom!

"Senior skip day," I lie.

The moment I say it I realize what a preposterous lie it is: it's seven o'clock in the morning. But he's no mental threat this morning. He just stares at me a moment and then pushes into the can. I sit and listen. I can hear him taking one of his sink baths. Matthew told me about it. He never takes a regular bath. He only washes up in the sink, splashing water all over himself.

I listen to the sounds of him splashing water. I bet he's dropped trow: I can just picture it, he's let loose of his trousers as he reaches the sink and boom! down they go, straight to his ankles.

In a moment he comes out and lumbers down the wooden hallway in his wingtips. Those shoes, they weigh a ton, they really do. They're leather on the bottom, too. It makes for a great noise, the weight, the hollow wooden hallway, the leather heels and soles, and his great lumbering self.

He hangs a right at the end of the hall. He doesn't go back into his bedroom as I expected. Instead he comes into the living room and enters the kitchen from there. He goes directly to the refrigerator. His pants are buttoned now, buttoned and zipped—I remember my broken zipper from last night: I look at myself. Jesus. My fucking fly's still open. I been like this all night? Into Wilburforce? Hitching a ride with that student, that trucker, my fucking fly open? What an ass.

I yank on my zipper. I yank hard, expecting it to stick. It doesn't. I end up bopping myself in the lower lip I am pulling so hard—the zipper comes up right away and my hand just keeps on flying.

I'm a hopeless case.

Dad's got the refrigerator open. He's surveying the damage.

"You drink my beer?" he asks.

"Me and Rasco," I say and immediately regret it.

He jumps back from the refrigerator and looks around in a panic.

"He's not here now," I say. "It was last night."

He collects himself, but not before he throws me a little dirty look: my fault, see, that he had to panic like that. Sorry, Dad.

He reaches for a beer. He has a helluva go getting one

loose. He is shaking pretty bad here, the poor fuck. He finally gets one free, whips out a church key—where'd that come from? He carry one on him at all times?

He sets the beer on the table across from me and pops her open. The table wobbles precariously. He lifts it to his mouth. His eyes are wide open. Too wide, if you ask me. The refrigerator door bumps him softly from behind as he holds that can tilted up over his nose.

He looks like a babe at the bottle. I swear.

I look away.

He finishes it off and walks back into the bedroom. His wingtips drum the wood floor: *clu-dumb, clu-dump; clu-dump, clu-dump.*

It'd be funny if he wasn't so pathetic.

Dad and the Wombat.

Jesus.

I can clean his bedroom now, I think. I get up and go in right behind him. I immediately regret it.

He is standing at his walk-in closet with a pint up to his lips. He panics when he hears me enter: he's a kid caught beating his meat.

He tries frantically to hide his pint. He's a total wreck. He is shaking and quivering something awful. The sucker has the Saint Vitus' dance.

"You drink all you like," I hear myself say.

He looks at me with those huge cow eyes, those baby doe eyes.

Jesus, don't look at me that way.

"Really," I say. "It's your life."

He says nothing. He sets the pint down on the top shelf there in his closet. He pulls a clean white shirt from the next shelf down. It is still in its wrapper from the laundry. He sends all of his clothes out. He never washes anything, never has, neither. Not in all his born days.

"I'll just straighten up in here, okay?" I ask.

He doesn't answer.

He's in trouble over there. He can't get the paper wrapper off his clean white shirt. Those ancient, quivering hands will not do what he wants them to do. Suddenly he goes into a minor rage. He tears that mother open and then drops it to the floor. He stands immobile over it. Paralyzed.

"Here," I say as I scurry over to him. I reach around him—he is filling the doorway to his closet—I pick it up, open it for him, and hold it out, one sleeve at a time. There. Not bad, huh? I spin him. I am on automatic pilot here, I am watching myself, marveling at myself, wondering: what am I doing? I spin him around. He faces me. I button his shirt for him. He stands still for it. I am amazed. It is good. I fill with it. I am good.

"Tuck it in," I direct when I finish with the buttons.

He does as he is told.

I pick out a tie. It's a club tie. Matthew told me. I hand Dad the tie. I get out his blue blazer as he puts a Windsor in it—Matthew taught me that, too; I can tie a Windsor, too.

I wait as he finishes his Windsor. His trembling hands do it on their own. It is like that, you learn something, your body remembers for you. I hold the blue blazer open for him. I am the perfect valet, patient, composed, at the ready.

He finishes his Windsor and looks at me. I nod at his blazer here.

Right arm. Left arm.

There.

I look at his Little Big Ben: seven-fifteen.

His topcoat's next. It is chilly this morning—oh! the windows. I have to shut up the windows before I skedaddle.

I offer him his topcoat. I am enjoying this perfect-valet business.

He slips into his topcoat.

"Here," I say. I take his half-empty pint of Old Grand Dad from the shelf. I stick it into his topcoat pocket for him. It fits perfectly. It is totally invisible.

He gives me this wild-eyed, crazed animal look, as if I am about to murder him. Except for all the terror he's got the most beautiful eyes, these clear, powder-blue eyes. Both my aunt, Margaret Mary, and my little brother, Franklin, have them, too. Pools of pastel light pouring over you. Lovely to behold.

He sticks his hand in his pocket, the pocket with that pint. His eyes are wild with terror.

I slip around him.

"I have to shut the windows I opened," I say by way of exit. I will let him be, let him have his hit. Just at the bedroom door I steal a look: his head is tilted back, he has that pint up to his face like a trumpet. He is trembling away as he sucks.

I go into the living room and shut the window there. I cross to the kitchen window. He comes out of the bedroom, comes down the hallway.

"I have to go," he says apologetically. There is something else in his voice, too. I can't place it.

He lingers at the top of the stairs.

"Well," he says still lingering. Still waiting. For what? Permission?

"It's okay," I say, giving him permission. I am sorry to do it but I do. "See you later, okay?" I say.

He starts down the steps as soon as I tell him it is okay. He moves very carefully as if he is a man in great pain.

I bet.

I bet he is.

He is at the door.

"You come see us next month, okay?" I say to his back. He nods his head and pulls on the door. He says nothing. There isn't room down there for him and that opening door. He has to step back to make room. As he does, the pint in his pocket flares his topcoat open and bangs against the opening door.

Don't break it, Dad.

He steps out, pulls the door shut behind him, and he's gone.

45

I HAD NO IDEA DAD WAS SUCH A MESS.

I walk down the shit-stained hallway to his bedroom. I peek in. It's a total disaster. I decide: no.

No. I will not.

I back out and pull the bedroom door shut behind me.

He can clean up his own mess.

The phone rings and nearly gives me a heart attack. I peel myself off the wall and answer it. It's Rasco.

"Where are you?" I ask.

"Downtown," he says. "I rode to work with my ma. You okay?"

"Yep."

"Hungry?" he asks.

"Yeah, I am," I say. I didn't realize it until this very instant.

"White Castle's open," he says. "You handle that?"

I say that's fine.

Okay, he says.

"Cheeseburger, onions only," I say.

"I know," he says.

I like that. He knows what I like. It makes me feel just fine.

"See ya," he says.

Yeah, I say and we hang up.

I set the phone back into its cradle. I am doing it very carefully, very tenderly. I notice myself doing it. I exaggerate it some. I play act. The phone's alive. I'm the doctor.

My patient's neck has been cracked. Careful, nurse, careful. Right. That's it. Careful.

I like it. I am smiling.

How come I ain't all fucked up?

I wonder at myself.

I should be all fucked up. Look at Dad. I had no idea. Really. Oh, I've known for a long time now that he wasn't gonna come out to get us. I used to wish for it. I got all surprised at myself once when he mistakenly put his own address on a letter to me. I was in Building One. I remember sitting in the Tin Room. I am looking hungrily at his mistake: Frederick J. Gamble, 600 Kenilworth.

He's drawn a line through it and put my correct address in under it.

I was surprised then at how I felt. I didn't really know that I had still been yearning to go home. It only lasted a minute. I sat in my Tin Room locker until the feeling went away. I knew better. Even then when I didn't know how really fucked up he was. I mean, kids would go AWOL. Kids who lived in another state, they'd run away, and I live right here in town, not twenty miles away and I'm not doing it. If I thought of it I'd just ask myself, where will I go? To Dad's. And what will he do? Just feel bad and bring me back. I mean, he brought us out here in the first place. And he's left us here. So.

And what me and Rasco have done. It ain't like we were trying to get away. We both knew we'd be going back. Today, in fact.

We just needed a break, that's all.

I bet I scared Dad. "What are you doing here?" he had asked. They guy would probably die if he had to take responsibility for us.

The phone rings.

I jump in my seat, aye!

I let it ring. And ring and ring. After twelve rings it quits.

"Thank you," I say aloud.

I get up from the wobbly, three-legged kitchen table.

God, I'm so stupid. Stupid and blind. Stupid about Dad. Blind about Charles.

I really had no idea Dad was drinking, let alone being this fucked up. Shit, I didn't know anyone got this fucked up. I mean, he shit his pants. Literally.

And what is going on with me now? I'm sort of excited by it. It's as if it is someone else's life.

I walk into the living room. I walk up to the window. I look out.

It's like it was when I was a little kid. I had this tremendous feeling for Mom and none at all for Dad. Honest. I remember climbing up into her chair to kiss her good night and not wanting to even look at him—he's sitting across from her reading his newspaper. I puzzled over that, too. I really did. I must have been five or something like that. How come I feel so strongly toward her and nothing toward him? Even then I thought there was something wrong with me.

I want to feel sad. I want to cry. I stand looking out the window and sense myself withdrawing. I think about Dad with this soft push—you know how you push a boat off from the dock? In my mind, at this window, I'm the boat and Dad's the dock.

I look at the davenport. Where I had my dream.

Charles, too.

I push off from Charles.

I mean, I don't want to be queer.

Push.

I play act some more.

"Push," I say to myself. I say it aloud. "Push."

I say it and this murderous fucking rage lifts inside of me.

The cocksucker.

I have really been had.

I am so fucking stupid.

Rasco's out front. I see him coming up the sidewalk with two White Castle bags in his right hand.

I bare my teeth.

I look at Rasco clipping along, swinging those two bags at his side. I've got maybe two minutes before he's knocking on the door.

I bare my teeth and snarl.

I picture Charles and snarl.

I am a wolf. I will snap his fucking jugular.

I snarl.

I go for his fucking throat.

''Knock, knock!'' Rasco calls. He's at the door. He raps it twice as he calls out. Bang bang. ''Time to eat,'' he says.

''Come on up, shit for brains,'' I yell and walk to the hallway to greet him.

We chow down. White Castle makes great burgers. Really.

''Ready,?'' I ask.

Yup, he says.

I call the Home. Get the Wombat. I tell him where we are and ask him if he could come pick us up. He squeals with delight.

''Gone AWOL, eh skirt?'' he says. Poor fuck. Makes him delirious.

''Can you come get us?'' I ask again.

''Sure thing, skirt,'' he says. The man is upbeat. ''Be happy to.''

I hang the phone up. I tell Rasco how delighted the Wombat is.

''Yeah, he loves to see you get into trouble.''

Yeah, I agree.

We look at each other. We in trouble?

Yep, I guess so.

Rasco shrugs his shoulders and looks away.

''Let's wait outside,'' I suggest.

We wait for the Wombat.

46

THE WOMBAT IS QUICK THIS MORNING. HE COMES within twenty-five minutes. He is very serious. The man has a mission.

He drives us directly to the high school. He tells us that Mr. Halstead is expecting us.

Halstead?

"That's right," he says. "You are to report to Mr. Halstead immediately," he says with the same seriousness that I'm seen Cruise adopt: you're in trouble, son, serious trouble.

Halstead turns us right around and sends us to our deans. Me, I have to go see Father Jack—Black Jack. Rasco has to go see Monsignor Witt.

"Good luck," I say to Rasco as we leave the high school to head over to their offices.

"We're beyond luck now," Rasco says.

I fill with doom when he says that.

"Don't," I plead.

"Sorry, Bambi," he says, meaning it.

I look at him. His lip is still puffed up some. He'll probably tell Witt, if he asks, that he got it in the game against Central Catholic. I tuck my elbow into my rib cage and give myself a little ouch. I do it a second time, oww, I don't know why. I do this sometimes. I'll press on a bruise or sore to make it hurt a little. And enjoy it. The little hurt.

"You'll be okay," Rasco says. He's trying to take care of me. I try to give him some back.

"You, too. You'll be all right."

He raises his eyebrows. We'll see. We'll see.

* * *

I knock on Black Jack's office door. It's on the second floor of Cottage Fifteen. I'm not feeling too well. He'll probably knock me around some. That's what he does. I know. I saw him do it to five seniors who'd gone AWOL. I was just a freshman. Black Jack ran the bank and I had gone over for an interview. I wanted to be a teller. And he had these five seniors in his office just ahead of me.

I sat right outside his office door. Only the door over at the bank was half glass. I could look right in. I saw the whole thing.

Wham *bam* bam bam *bam.*

Five times. Five boys.

Wham *bam* bam bam *bam.* Wham *bam* bam bam *bam.* Wham *bam* bam bam *bam.*

It was amazing. It made me a little sick.

Five of them standing in a quarter moon before his huge desk. Five of them getting it: Wham *bam* bam bam *bam.* Wham *bam* bam bam *bam.*

I am shitting my pants when he lets me in. And he's real nice.

No shit.

He is real concerned about me. He's real concerned about me going AWOL. This isn't like me, he says. Is it your dad not showing for pass day? Is that it? Is he drinking again?

Jesus.

Does everyone know?

I relax, though, once I realize he is not going back to knock me around.

He thinks I need to talk.

I say nothing.

''Talk to Charles,'' he suggests.

Right.

''Charles tells me you have blossomed wonderfully this fall,'' he says.

He is trying to be real nice. I wish he wouldn't. I'd rather he just knock me around some. I'd rather that than this talk of Charles.

I say nothing.

"You can't talk to me, talk to Charles," he says sweetly.

I swallow iron.

I ain't about to be talking to no Charles.

He goes on. He thinks talking is the best solution. He says so.

I'm pretty confused. He's being so nice. Why don't you just hit me and get it over with?

That's why we have counselors, he says.

He is being so nice.

I can't tell him that it's talking that got me into this mess in the first place. I can't tell him that I cannot talk to anyone anymore. I can't tell him what happened, not what really happened.

It's my fault, see, that Charles did what he did. I should have known and cut it off at the pass. I didn't. It's my fault.

"Charles is a good man," Father goes on. "You can trust him."

It's a hot poker in my belly.

I look at him. I look at his nose-traversing scar, his broken nose boxing scar. He is all man. He'd never believe a word of it. No one would.

He's waiting for me to say something and I can't even look at him.

I drop my head. I stare at my hands in my lap.

"I'm sorry, Father," I say. "I'm sorry."

I see Charles at lunch. He comes out of the counselor's dining hall just as I come in the front door. He doesn't see me. I look at him. I study him. It was my fault. I should have known. Lovely Lester. The Wombat. Fruits everywhere. I really should have known.

I go directly to my seat.

After grace Winston asks about Black Jack.

"How'd it go?" he asks.

"Okay," I say.

"Yeah?"

''Yeah, really,'' I say. ''He was actually pretty nice.''

I stop to think about that for a moment. It still surprises me.

''He took away a month's passes,'' I add. I think about what I had expected. I feel this tremendous physical relief.

''He didn't hit me,'' I say.

Charles walks past me and moves down the aisle between our table and Cottage Eleven's table.

''That's what I expected,'' I go on as I watch Charles move down to the other end of our table. I think it is pretty amazing that Black Jack didn't knock me around some. I say so.

''I thought he'd knock me around some.''

''Me, too,'' Winston says right away. His eyes are wide. ''I'm glad he didn't,'' he says.

''Thanks,'' I say and reach out to touch his wrist with my fingertips. ''That means a lot to me.''

Charles is saying something to little ignorant shit Cruise. Cruise steals a quick look my way.

I smile at him and nod yes. It's OK. He's got his hair greased down. Holy shit. He's trying to control his wild flyaway who-gives-a-shit hair.

''Look at Cruise,'' I say to Winston with a tap on his forearm.

''Hmmm?''

''Cruise. Look. His hair. Lookit Cruise's hair.'' I am amazed.

''Oh, yeah,'' Winston says, looking from me to Cruise and back to me again. ''He did it for you.''

This stops me.

''What?''

Winston looks me right in the eye. I think I am going to melt or cry or pee my pants or something. I really like this kid.

''Yeah,'' he says, holding my eyes with his, ''we've all been pretty worried about you.''

It's too much. It gets me where I live. I look away. I look down the table at the other kids here. Cowen nods his head in agreement. Nothing Cowen, he's been listening to this, too. Jesus.

"C'mon," I say in protest. I really can't believe this.

"God," Winston says in exasperation. "Sometimes you can be such a numbnuts."

"Fuck you very much," I say.

It gives me chills. I shiver a bit. God. They like me. What a waste I am, it means so much to me.

Charles comes back to our end of the table. He smiles down on me. I smile back, surprising myself. What am I doing, smiling at this guy—and then I see them all watching me, the whole table of boys, their eyes on me, on us. They're worried for me. Rooting for me. Counting on me.

"You see Father John this morning?" Charles asks warmly.

I nod.

"I hope he wasn't too rough," he says. He is being so very warm. It gives me a little chill. I turn my face up to him and surprise myself some more:

"He was pretty nice," I say. I look him directly in the eye. "I think I've been pretty lucky all around."

He gives a faint, barely discernible flinch. I turn back to the boys.

"Pass the soup," I say, nodding down the table toward the soup tureen.

There's this moment where nothing happens. It's as if everyone's brain is on hold.

"The soup," I repeat. "Please."

Winston passes me the soup.

As I ladle it out I realize how calm I am. Charles is right here at my shoulder and I am not all fucked up with terror and rage.

"After you," Cowen says as he gives the soup tureen a nod.

I finish filling my bowl and pass the tureen to Cowen.

"I'm glad Father wasn't too rough on you," Charles says. He is speaking softly, tenderly.

I give him a quick look. He really means it. It's a little embarrassing. And a bit pathetic, too.

I drop my gaze and sip my soup. It is good soup, homemade vegetable. I sip my soup and it settles down upon me: this guy Charles is hot for me. He wants me. He's probably in love with me.

I look up at him with my spoon halfway to my face. He's waiting on me, waiting for me to speak.

I put the spoon back into the soup. I realize that he really isn't any great threat to me. He really isn't. He's just another poor fuck. Like the Wombat. Like Dad. Like so many of the assholes around here.

I look at him now.

"Me, too," I say. "I'm glad he wasn't too rough on me, too."

A shiver of relief runs the full length of the table as I speak these words. I look down at my boys and look at them anew. Tollens, he's still assistant commissioner, he sits at the other end of this long table. He faces me directly. Martinez sits at his left hand just as Winston sits at mine. One waiter at each end. Little ignorant shit Cruise sits two places up from Martinez. His eyes are glued to me. Even goddamned Cowen, old do-nothing, say-nothing Cowen is in on this, the boy sitting four places down from me, alert and tuned in.

"Good," Charles says.

The bell rings.

We stack our dirty dishes. Winston carries away the leftovers from our end of the table. Martinez carries them away from his end.

The second bell rings.

We stand to grace.

Charles steps away and turns to face the crucifix.

I steal a look over at Whiteworm as we pray.

We give thee thanks for these thy gifts which we have received from thy bounty through christ our lord amen.

The dining hall explodes into total cacophonous bedlam as we rush the door.

* * *

Winston catches up to me on the flagstone porch.

"Are you okay?" he asks with genuine concern.

"I'm fine," I tell him. I think I am, too.

We skip off the porch and head back to the cottage.

"I think I'm gonna quit the team," I tell him, surprising us both.

"What? And miss the best trips?"

He's right. We have Beria at home this Friday and then the rest of our games are on the road. We'll go to Chicago and play on Soldier's Field. Then we'll go to Hamtramck, which is outside of Detroit, this Polish school, and finish the season in Pittsburgh against South Catholic, on South Catholic's total dirt field.

It's why I went out in the first place.

"Yeah," I say, "I know but I don't care. I can live without 'em."

We get back to the house, go in, kick our shoes off, and hoof it into the study hall to have a smoke. Cowen's in his corner. Martinez and Cruise are already at a table next to my desk. Tollens comes in the front door just as I sit at my desk.

"It's the AWOL Kid," he cries out, the asshole.

"Give me a break, will ya, Tollens?" I half plead. I don't mind too much, actually.

"They took Rasco's passes away for a month," he announces to everyone when he has his shoes put up and joins us for a smoke. Except he has no cigarettes. He never does, but he smokes like a fiend.

"Me, too," I say.

"Really?" Cruise asks. "That mean they aren't going to fire you?"

"I guess not," I say.

Little ignorant shit Cruise jumps in his seat and gives a little cheer. Martinez reaches over and bops him one upside the head. Cruise cools his jets.

"Can I bum a smoke?" Tollens asks.

"Sure," I say and shake a Winston out for him. I'm feeling okay. Being with these guys. Cruise is beaming at me.

"Light?" Tollens ask.

Jesus Christ, Tollens. Everyone hoots him down.

''Want me to kick you in the chest to get it started for you?'' little ignorant shit Cruise asks proudly.

''Want me to hold it for you between drags?'' Martinez asks. He and little ignorant shit Cruise smile at each other.

Tollens goes for Cruise: ''I'll kick you,'' he says half menacingly.

''Don't,'' I say.

''Whatever you say, boss,'' he says to me warmly. He's being nicer to me than he's ever been before. Then Martinez does something that sort of stops us all.

''Hey, Cowen,'' he calls.

''Hmm?'' Cowen murmurs from his nothing corner.

''Why don't you move your ass over here?''

I look at Martinez. We all do. Then we look over to Cowen. He's inviting the nothing kid in. How about that?

Cowen hesitates. This is a joke? his face asks.

''Join us,'' I add, nodding yes to him.

He does.

Charles comes in the back door. He sees us gathered about my desk. He starts to say something, looks at me and I at him, and then decides not. He motors across the hallway, goes into his office, and leaves us alone.

I turn to little ignorant shit Cruise.

''Nice hair,'' I tell him.

He blushes and touches the top of his head.

''Really,'' I say, ''I'm proud of you.''

He goes completely scarlet. It is too much to resist. Martinez screeches: ''Look at Cruise—he's blushing!''

We all focus on little ignorant shit Cruise. Who is eating it up, of course. He looks at me. We smile at each other.

''Fuck him,'' I say to Cruise. ''Fuck him if he can't take a joke.''

''Yeahhhh!'' Cruise says, turning to Martinez: ''Fuck you if you can't take a joke.''

We all howl with joy and abandon, happy to be together.

47

I DO QUIT. RIGHT AFTER SCHOOL.

I stall around so I get to the locker room after everyone's gone out to practice. Then I empty out my locker and take all my equipment down to the equipment room.

"What's this?" Carson, our trainer, asks.

No one quits varsity football. Not after making the team.

"Early retirement," I say.

It's terrific. It's nothing like I expect. The guy's aghast. He's staring at me as if I am out of my mind. You saying no to the Old Man? No one says no to the Old Man.

He is gaping at my pads, shoes, helmet, and practice togs. They are all piled up in front of him. It's as if he's paralyzed.

What a lovely surprise. I didn't think anyone would give two shits. He is actually stunned. I am liking this.

"This should be everything," I say as I nod down at my pile.

"You sure about this?" he asks incredulously.

I look right at him. I do have some power.

"Yeah, I'm sure."

"Okay," he says, "it's your funeral."

But it's no funeral at all. It's a short vacation, in fact. Three weeks before wrestling starts. Three weeks I get to spend with Winston and the new not-so-ignorant little shit Cruise. He's slicking his hair back every day now, caking on the butch wax. He's really trying to look okay and only looks worse, if you want to know the truth. But he's trying.

Cowen is back in his corner, only now he notices us and we notice him. He isn't looking dead or terrified any time one of us says something to him.

Charles has got himself a new project. He and Putnam, the counselor next door in Cottage Thirteen, they're going to put on a play. A senior-class play. They're real busy getting things ready for tryouts the week after football season ends.

Winston says he thinks I should try out.

I tell him I think I just might.

He says he thinks I'd look good on stage.

I tell him I think he would, too.

Sure thing, boss, he says, tossing it off.

Calling me boss, how Tollens did that time. I like it. I really do.

I look at him. We're alone in the study hall.

''I really like you,'' I say.

His face flushes pale pink. He recovers quickly.

''Sure you do, Bambi,'' he says smiling that great Chicago smile of his. ''Who could not?''

Right, I agree, laughing, who could not?

48

IT'S THURSDAY MORNING, TWO DAYS AFTER I'VE RETIRED from the varsity football team.

"Where you off to so early?" Winston asks.

"I'm serving this morning," I say.

"Okay," he says. "Just checking."

"No need," I lie.

I walk up to the main chapel in the early morning chill. The air is rich with the scent of decaying, rotting leaves. The sunlight is amazing. It seems to be skidding off the surface of things. It is as if it is peeling the color off of everything it touches. Everything is so brilliant, iridescent.

I jam my hands into the pockets of my letter jacket. The tip of my nose is icy cold.

I tuck my chin into my chest. I am serving with Whiteworm this morning. I am looking forward to it.

No one's in the sacristy when I arrive. In fact, the whole chapel is deserted. I don't even know where Sister is.

Which is fine by me. I like having the place to myself.

I dress in front of the full-length mirror.

Well, I *look* the same.

This makes me smile. I realize I am surprised to see myself looking the same. I expected that I would look different.

"You think you're different, eh?" I say aloud to myself.

I don't answer myself.

I do think I am different. I am not exactly sure how, but I definitely think I am.

I look at myself again.

"Well, you sure don't look any different," I say.

I finish dressing and go around to the priest's side. I will put out the cruets. I will leave the candles for Whiteworm. I feel good when I decide this. The candles are best. I will leave the best for Whiteworm.

I get busy with the cruets. Sister's here because the wine cruet's filled. That's her job. I get the empty water cruet, take it to the priest's can, and fill it at the sink. I get the damn thing all wet. I always do. I look around for something to dry it off with. Toilet paper.

Good.

I take the water and wine cruets, the little finger-bowl dish we wash the priest's fingers in before he touches the host, and the little accordian-folded finger towel, and haul them out onto the altar.

I set them into their little recessed slot in the wall next to the two patens that are stashed in here, too. When I was real little I thought the patens were real gold. They aren't. They aren't even gold plate. They're just gold colored.

I turn to face the still empty church. It's amazing. It will fill up in a matter of minutes once the boys start rolling in. But for now it remains empty and it's all mine.

I drink it in. I just love being in church. It's such a beautiful place. I especially love being on the altar. I love serving mass. Standing on this marble, it's too much. No lie. The altar, including the two steps leading up to it, are marble. The real thing. Shiny, slick, ice fucking cold and the hardest goddamn thing ever have you knelt upon. They have little pads for the altar boys. It's that bad.

I stand next to the altar near the cruet station. I fold my hands, pressing my palms together, pointing my fingers heavenward, my left thumb crossing over my right. I lift my hands to my lower lip and touch myself, and think for a long moment.

I lift my chin away from my hands and let my eyes

travel up to the high-raftered ceiling. The sanctuary lamp burns, its soft red glow marking the presence of the Eucharist in the tabernacle. I am in the presence.

I think about seeing Whiteworm. I take a deep breath.

Please, I pray. Oh, please.

The side door opens. A low, fast shaft of sunlight shoots straight out across the sanctuary. It is a beam of light. It fires right down in front of the communion rail. The side door squeaks softly shut. The beam is drawn up. The door shuts. The light is gone.

It is him.

He doesn't see me at first. He crosses to the middle of the sanctuary, turns to face the tabernacle, and spies me just as he drops into his genuflection. It startles him. I startle him. He gives a little jump. He's a mini-spastic with a little curlicue there in his genuflection.

I make a face: sorry.

He makes a face back: no big deal.

I come in off the altar. I kneel at one of the two altar-boy kneelers set right by the door leading out onto the altar. It's where we wait once we're ready.

It's really warm in here. Sister's got the furnace on already and it's only mid-October. The last day of the World Series today. The Yankees and the Giants.

It's warm and I shiver.

Whiteworm dresses quickly, silently.

"I left the candles for you," I say. I think I sound very young. Frightened even.

If you kill something you should be frightened.

He closes the cassock locker door and comes to the surplice rack behind me. He gets a surplice, sticks his arms in—I'm watching him from the corner of my eye in the mirror—and now his head. He comes around and picks up the candle lighter. He get matches from Sister's kneeler. He lights the wick and as he passes me to walk out onto the altar he says: "Thanks for saving the candles for me."

My heart leaps.

He does the candles. I watch him on the altar. He's taller than me.

Sister appears in the doorway as Whiteworm comes in off the altar.

''Time, boys,'' she says.

We both scoot on around to the priest's sacristy.

Black Jack's saying mass this morning. As he dresses the chapel is filling fast. Two minutes. Seven twenty-eight.

Whiteworm reaches the door leading onto the altar. He stands back a foot or so from the doorway. He is making way for me to go first. He is going to let me ring the entrance chimes. It's his turn, too.

How nice.

I step to the door. I take the long, yellow, braided rope cord into my hand. I wrap my fingers around it. I turn my head toward Black Jack. Gotta keep your eye on the priest. When he says Go! we Go!

I hear the click, click-clack of the wall clock overhead as the minute hand jumps first backward one minute, click, and then forward two minutes, click-clack.

Seven twenty-nine.

I am about to burst with it. I must. I am terrified: he will hate me. He does hate me. But I must. I must.

I look fast to Black Jack.

He's not looking. Good.

''I *am* sorry,'' I whisper and metal leaps to my throat. I look furtively to Black Jack. He's still in prayer.

Whiteworm is being big. He's waving it off.

''Really,'' I press, whispering, my face down. I think I'll die if Black Jack sees, hears, knows.

I need to atone. I need.

''I know,'' Whiteworm says very softly.

I want. I need more.

Black Jack's all dressed. He's ready. We three wait for the final seconds to tick away.

It's too late. There's no time.

I need more.

I despair.

Take what you get. He's spoken to you. Huh? Accept that.

Black Jack looks up just as Whiteworm touches my arm. I panic. Not in front of Black Jack.

"I'm okay," Whiteworm says softly. Black Jack drops his gaze to the floor.

"Really?" I whisper. My eyebrows lift nearly off my face. I so want this. I so need this.

"Really," he whispers.

The clock goes off: click, click-clack.

Seven-thirty.

Time.

Black Jack turns, lifts his covered chalice off the dressing table, turns back around to Whiteworm and me. He nods to me, coming my way: "Okay."

I steal one final look at my friend. There's no time for anything else. I want more. More.

I turn to face the altar.

I yank on the long, yellow, braided rope cord. And I yank hard.

The jangling, jingling bells fill the entire chapel. The whole high school side, boys and counselors, lift themselves in one great and wondrous roar.

We are off and running.

The mass has begun.

And my friend has forgiven me.

Thanks be to God.

Forever and ever.

Amen.

About the Author

JIMMY CHESIRE was born in Omaha, Nebraska, in 1945. He was the sixth of seven children in a very Irish Catholic family. The family broke up when his mother died in 1954. Jimmy and his younger brother, Dan, spent a year in a foster home before joining their two older brothers, Tom and John, at Father Flanagan's Home for Boys, Boys Town, Nebraska. He was a resident of Boys Town for the next eight years, until his graduation from high school in 1963.

Chesire earned his bachelor's degree from Cornell University in Ithaca, New York, and his master's degree in counseling and guidance from the University of Nebraska at Omaha. He is married, has one daughter, and lives and writes in Yellow Springs, Ohio. HOME BOY is his first novel.

ACKNOWLEDGMENTS

It has taken me a decade to write this story. Many people have helped me along the way. I am grateful to: Dan McCall, my Cornell writer friend and teacher who stuck by me for over twenty years; Bob Aldenhoff and John Deitering, my friends from Boys Town days whose honesty about their own experiences steeled my resolve to complete this tale; Dan Chesire, John Chesire, and Tom Chesire, my brothers, who lived it themselves and who mothered and fathered me through all our years of growing up; Kevin Mulroy and Chris Schelling, my editors at NAL who loved the book and whose vision made it possible for me to have my own; Barney Karpfinger, my agent, who's a terrific guy, an astute literary critic, and one whale of a salesman; and finally, Adrienne Suits Chesire, my daughter, whose love and friendship have given me renewed hope and sped my healing.